© 2012 Rosemary Cosserat

ISBN 978-1-909473-11-9

Text prepared by www.willowebooks.org.uk

Turn Left at the Sunflowers

by

Rosemary Cosserat

Published by Willow Books

To
Nick McCarty with many thanks for your
encouragement

CHAPTER 1

The pub on her right was lit up in a dull, wintery way, but the rest of Stockleigh gave the impression of a community in hibernation. One street light was casting a gloomy, yellowish glow onto the front of the church and the other was flickering wanly in front of the village shop; the tired pools of light serving only to emphasise the opaque blackness which surrounded them.

Caroline pulled up at the edge of the green and sat for a few minutes gazing across at Edward's and Vicky's house, reluctant to face the waiting pandemonium and strangely soothed by the sonorous purr of her car engine.

The first thing that her sister and her husband had done, when they'd bought the house, was clip the two straggling bay trees which had flanked the front gate and now they stood, a couple of perfect toffee apples, twinkling under their halo of fairy lights. The house beyond the bay trees shimmered in the surrounding darkness like a river cruiser and, even at this distance with her car windows closed, Caroline could detect the faint beat of music together with snatches of cheerful conversation as people parked their cars and headed for the house. She was too far away to see them but she could envisage the bows, the bottles of champagne, the crisp wrapping paper.

Tonight was St. Valentine's Day and their parents' thirty sixth wedding anniversary. The family had always celebrated the occasion after a fashion, even when the three children had been small, just because it was a good day to have a party, but for the last fourteen years, since Harriet and Mike had moved permanently to France, they had made it a regular excuse for a proper party and a family get-together. Vicky, the eldest of the three, had the largest house so Hampshire was the most popular venue, but Mark, the youngest, had given a memorable thrash in his flat in Docklands for their thirty second anniversary and nine years ago, when they were quite newly married, Caroline and Phillip had crammed a marquee into their garden in Petts Wood.

That had been tremendous fun despite the filthy weather. The marquee had been ridiculously large and they'd had to erect it around the cherry trees and a huge japonica which had been in magnificent full flower on the night. Mark's girlfriend at the time –

1

Caroline couldn't even remember her name now – had helped her to make elaborate paper hearts to decorate the bare cherry branches. She smiled as she recalled how Phillip had charmed their next door neighbours into having lines of tent pegs hammered into their herbaceous borders. He had been quite different then. She was probably being unfair – perhaps she was the one who had changed; perhaps she was looking for something more in life.

Paradoxically, the annual anniversary celebration charted the emotional vagaries of their children's lives, while Harriet and Mike's own marriage sailed on with a sublime and enviable stability. She'd always assumed her parents' marriage was normal and that she and Phillip would be equally happy, so it had left her with a terrible feeling of failure when it had all fallen apart after less than ten years. Of course, Vicky and Edward were happy as a couple, she was certain of that, but their inability to have a second child after more than seven years of trying was causing noticeable tensions between them. Perhaps Mark would be the one, out of the three of them, to emulate their parents' charmed marriage. Caroline smiled as she cast her mind back over Mark's rackety track record with girls. Maybe he'd settle down with Julia – unlikely if he'd got any sense.

Her thoughts were disturbed by the horn of a passing car and she recognised her brother as he drove past looking for a parking space. Julia waggled her arm cheerfully out of the window and Caroline felt her face form into an automatic smile in return, although they wouldn't have been able to see it in the darkness.

She had actually been feeling moderately cheerful when she'd left home. Phillip had been in good form when she'd visited him after lunch and they'd sat in the grounds of the hospice for half an hour before the cool wind had driven them back inside. She'd had an easy journey out of London as well and been looking forward to seeing her parents for the first time since Christmas.

Her downward emotional spiral had been triggered by the sudden realisation that this would be the last anniversary celebration during Phillip's lifetime and once she'd allowed the word "last" to surface in her mind it had multiplied uncontrollably into a series of "lasts" of increasing painfulness. The Christmas, fourteen months previously, had been their last one before their separation, and Phillip's last one before the onset of his terrible illness. Now all the special occasions were closing in on her – birthdays, anniversaries, New Year's Eve, Christmas, especially

Christmas – with a bruising finality.

The car engine began to make a discordant, whining noise and Caroline realised that she'd been sitting for ten minutes or more with it running. Reluctantly she put the car into gear and continued her circuit of the green in search of a space to park. The brilliant rectangle of the open door seemed more threatening than welcoming as she walked up the path and she was relieved to see that the hallway was empty. Unnoticed, she slipped up the stairs past the noise of the drawing room, and sank onto the bed in the second floor room which she always occupied. Vicky had put a mixed bunch of forsythia and small wild daffodils in a blue Provençal vase on the dressing table and Caroline felt an extra surge of warmth towards her sister.

"Auntie Caroline." Emily's voice sounded hesitant as she pushed the door open just wide enough to poke her head through the gap. "Mummy says I'm not to pester, but this is the first time ever, EVER, that they've let me stay up for Granny and Grandpa's party. Do you want to see my dress?"

"Hello darling. Yes of course I want to see your dress. Come on in and give me a twirl." The sight of this excited little confection in chocolate brown layered chiffon made Caroline smile. Seven years old and allowed to stay up for the anniversary party for the first time; Emily had provided the most positive antidote to Caroline's catalogue of "lasts".

Caroline held the sticky little hand aloft and rotated her small niece so that the soft tiers of material flew straight out from the sash around her waist.

"It's lovely, really lovely. You look quite grown up."

"Mummy and I chose it in Winchester. She said it was more sophisticated than pink. Do you think it is?" Her forehead wrinkled with the effort of weighing up this concept.

Caroline nodded solemnly. "Your mother's absolutely right. It's much more sophisticated. I'm afraid that mine is rather ordinary. I think it's the same dress I wore last time."

Emily shook the layers of kingfisher blue taffeta until they hung smoothly from the black velvet bodice and held the dress against herself, careful not to trip over the hem. "Well I think it's really beautiful. You and granny and mummy are the prettiest ladies here tonight. Julia looks nice too," she added as an uncertain afterthought. "She made her dress herself and I heard Grandpa say it was a pity she didn't buy quite enough material."

3

Caroline hid a smile as she struggled inside the folds of her dress. Julia had been living with Mark for nearly two years but no one in the family had been able to fathom what he saw in her. Pretty, in an insipid sort of way, curvaceous with a tendency to plumpness, and not over bright. She really seemed a poor match for Mark. He often seemed irritated by her clinginess, but yet she'd lasted longer than any of his previous girlfriends. Harriet said that he was bone idle and he wouldn't get rid of her while she took such marvellous care of him. So much for his projected "new man" image! Anyway, Julia was harmless enough, Caroline decided, as she tweaked her hair into a better shape and squirted some scent behind her ears.

Emily held her face up, her eyes screwed tightly shut, and Caroline sprayed scent over the child as well. "There we are. Since we're both looking so glamorous let's go and join the party."

There was no question now of creeping unnoticed past the long first floor drawing room. The double doors were wide open and people were flowing in all directions like multi-coloured lava.

"Darling, you look as stunning as ever. Have a drink." Edward gave his sister-in-law an affectionate hug and pressed a glass of cold buck's fizz into her hand. "Vicky's really gone over the top this time. We're expecting more than fifty people I think." He rolled his eyes at Caroline in mock despair as they stood side by side watching the mingling guests, the men's monochrome making a perfect foil to the women's more exotic colours.

Emily wriggled her hand free and zigzagged away from them through the crowd, allowing herself to be kissed and petted on all sides. In the distance Vicky looked gorgeous in red velvet and Edward and Caroline smiled at the occasional glimpses of red velvet and brown chiffon as the crowd parted and shifted before them.

"She's going to be as bloody sociable as her mother."

"I don't believe you mind really. Anyway, I'm stopping you from mingling. I'd better pluck up courage and start talking to people." Caroline took a large gulp from her drink and stepped tentatively into the crowd. She saw her mother waving to her from beneath a bunch of heart shaped balloons and her father's head was just visible a yard or so beyond her. Even in February, Harriet and Mike Hamilton looked bronzed and fit compared with everyone around them.

"You look pretty," her mother whispered, as she kissed her,

"but you're pale; much too pale and thin. Phillip's asking too much of you – expecting you to go back to him at this stage."

"Don't nag and happy anniversary. It's not Phillip's fault that I look pale. You mustn't be unfair about him. We've been very busy at school the last few weeks and I've been extra busy tidying up loose ends since I'm leaving at half term. I've only got three days left and I really must make the transition as easy as possible for my replacement, and for poor Cliff. He's been so kind you know and it wasn't easy persuading the education authority to give me a term and a half's sabbatical." Caroline patted her mother's hand, but Harriet was not reassured.

"I just hope you know how much you're taking on. I still don't understand why his new woman isn't sacrificing her career to look after him. After all they were living together for nearly a year."

"It was nine months, and I know you're only trying to protect me, but I wish you'd listen and be less biased. Phillip and I have agreed that we are going to do this. We are still friends and, after ten years, he just feels more comfortable with the idea of my looking after him than of her looking after him. And, after all, I lived in that house for more than nine years so moving back doesn't seem so strange." She sighed at her mother's intransigent expression. "You're not going to make me change my mind. It's all organised now and I can be just as stubborn as you can."

"I'll second that," Mike laughed, coming up behind Caroline and putting his arms around her in a great bear hug. "How's my baby daughter then? Do you want me to protect you from your bossy mother? What are you both being stubborn about?"

"Hello Dad and happy anniversary." Caroline hugged her father and shook her head helplessly in the direction of Harriet. "Mum won't accept that Phillip has asked me to move back in with him when he comes out of the hospice. I can't persuade her that it's what we both want."

Her father looked from one face to the other, but didn't voice his alarm at seeing his daughter looking so washed out, especially in comparison with her mother. Harriet really did look good; just as attractive as she had thirty six years ago. "Of course we're worried that it's going to be too much for you," Mike said calmly. "But you've made the decision now and we'll support you in any way we can. Don't you agree darling?"

Harriet looked as if she longed to disagree but she nodded dumbly. "Of course we will. Did you visit him before you left today? Can they do anything more for him at the hospice?"

Caroline felt suddenly close to tears and she squeezed her parents' hands gratefully. "Thank you. Phillip was worried that you'd be unsympathetic, so he'll be relieved that you're on our side." Tears threatened but she managed to continue. "The hospice can't do anything more for him now, but it's a very reassuring place and he's quite comfortable there. He was cheerful today when I went in, but he's longing to come out next Friday. I think that the hospice's main priority is to regulate his drugs so that we'll be able to cope once he's home. They've given him three months…"

"Mummy says you're all to go down into the kitchen because we're ready to eat," Emily suddenly announced, bounding up to them and swinging from her grandfather's hand. "She says I can take some of your cake into school on Monday if I can get everyone downstairs by the time she's counted to a hundred." Having delivered her announcement at top speed she raced off again to the next group.

"I can't actually envisage my sister standing still in the middle of the kitchen counting to one hundred, but she's certainly managed to galvanise Ems into action," Mark laughed as he suddenly materialised next to them. "You look terrific Caroline. How's Phil doing? Did he tell you that I popped in to see him the day before yesterday?"

Before Caroline had a chance to answer, Julia sidled up and insinuated herself between them, leaning against Mark in a proprietorial fashion. Caroline's eyes were drawn to the straining stitches down the side of Julia's dress which seemed to be fighting a brave, but doomed, rear guard action.

"Mark and I think about you all the time, don't we darling?" She managed to combine a look of tragic concern for Caroline with a lingering simper in Mark's direction. "Phone us at any time, day or night, if we can do anything at all to help."

A look of such intense irritation crossed Mark's face that Caroline actually felt rather sorry for the unfortunate Julia and gave her hand a quick squeeze. "That's sweet of you Julia. As soon as Phillip's settled at home you must both come over to see him. I know he'll be grateful for some company."

"Come on Uncle Mark," Emily reappeared looking crosser than she had on her previous attempt and dragged at his hand. "Mummy's going to get in a state soon if you don't all come

6

downstairs."

"I'll follow you down in a moment," Caroline murmured and turned back to the nearly empty drawing room. She had always loved this room and now she derived a strange comfort from seeing it in this unaccustomed state of chaos. The sofas and chairs were pushed back against the walls to create extra space and some of the cushions had been knocked onto the floor, making glowing pools of colour against the soft tone of the carpet. The bunches of heart-shaped balloons were rotating and swaying gently in the rising heat from the open fire. As she stood there one of the balloons burst and the unexpected noise made her jump. She laughed out loud at her nervous reaction and then felt inexplicably cheerful. The tape was still playing and, picking up a large tray, she started clearing away some of the debris, humming in tune to the music as she retrieved empty glasses, picked up strewn peanuts and replaced cushions. She knew that Vicky would be relieved to see the room restored to some order when the guests drifted back upstairs after dinner, and she'd been such a lame duck recently that it was a nice feeling to do something useful, however insignificant.

"Caroline, my love!" Heather's voice broke into Caroline's thoughts. "We wondered wherever you'd got to. How are you?"

"I bet you haven't eaten anything yet." Cliff sounded accusing. "Heather and I thought we'd eat up here in peace. Give me that tray and I'll fetch you a plate of food. Vicky's put on a terrific spread."

Caroline laughed as she struggled to hang on to her burden and then surrendered it with a helpless shrug. "I suppose I have to obey my boss," she smiled at Heather. Cliff and Heather were her parents' oldest friends – Cliff and her mother went back to earliest schooldays – and Cliff had offered Caroline a teaching post as soon as she had married Phillip. It was meant to be temporary until she found a job which would justify her French degree, but the convenience and the pleasant atmosphere had carried more weight than her ambition and she was still there ten years later.

"Vicky says she's very cross with us for lurking up here," Cliff announced as he returned with a loaded plate of food for Caroline. "I've promised we'll go down in ten minutes for the toasts and champagne. You look better anyway than you did this afternoon – not so washed out," he observed. "What do you think Heather?"

"I think you're much too interfering and you have the tact of a

7

warthog," his wife replied firmly. "Caroline looks lovely and she always looks lovely."

"I felt a bit overcome when I arrived in Stockleigh this evening, I must admit, and I nearly turned round and drove home. But it's been so heartening, just seeing everyone, that I feel surprisingly positive again."

"You're a survivor and we'll all make sure you survive," Cliff declared, patting her hand. "Oh help! We're all in awful trouble with Vicky." He leapt to his feet in alarm as Vicky materialised in the doorway.

"Come on! We're waiting to drink a toast and don't forget you're making the speech, Cliff." Vicky scolded. "Do you think the party's going well?" she whispered to Caroline as she ushered her gently towards the stairs.

"Of course it is. You're a real star. I don't know how you manage to do it all. The parents are in great form too. Every year they seem to look happier. I wish that Phil and I had done even half as well."

"Never look back," Heather announced, gathering up their dirty plates and following them to the stairs. "There's absolutely nothing to be gained from looking back. You're much too young to feel so negative about life." She sounded more emphatic than she felt. Caroline was their great favourite and she and Cliff longed to protect her from all her present problems. Personally, she wondered why Phillip didn't just stay in the hospice, but Caroline had made up her mind to have him home and nobody could dissuade her. She shrugged to herself as she followed the others into the kitchen.

Emily was hopping up and down between her grandparents and she shrieked out as soon as she saw the rest of her family appear with Cliff and Heather. "Come on, come on. We've been waiting for you lot for ages. I'm going to cut the cake and Granny and Grandpa are going to make a wish."

Mike and Harriet rested their hands on Emily's as she forced the knife through the pale green icing, her face screwed up with concentrated determination and then they kissed to noisy applause. Harriet blushed with embarrassment which caused even more tumultuous cheering and Mark proposed a toast to the next thirty six years. Julia gazed up at him with limpid blue eyes, obviously hoping that marriage might be a contagious condition, but he managed to avoid her gaze.

Vicky whispered to Caroline. "Can you see the solitaire

diamond twinkling through Julia's mascara?"

Caroline snorted. "I feel sorry for her actually, but she's only got herself to blame. If she stopped looking like an unwanted Christmas present from Battersea Dog's Home he might take her more seriously."

It was late by the time the last guests had gone and Harriet stretched back on the sofa and closed her eyes. She had put up some feeble resistance but finally agreed to leave the clearing up to the rest of the family. Mike had been in London for three days already, but she had only flown in this morning and the tiredness was just beginning to wash over her. She could hear snatches of conversation and bursts of laughter, but they were floating in and out of her consciousness in disjointed flurries. She'd been aware of Emily coming to kiss her goodnight and she could still feel the softness of the child's chiffon dress as she'd given her a cuddle.

"And granny, did you know that mummy painted my toenails the same colour as hers?" Emily had confided. "I'll show you in the morning."

Harriet smiled at the memory as she relaxed further into the sofa. A few minutes later she realised that she was still smiling and this realisation made her smile even more. It had been a marvellous party. Every year seemed better than the previous year, but in fact she could remember some magical high spots going right back to the first years, when Mike used to take her out for romantic evenings – just the two of them.

There was the muffled crunch of stockinged feet treading on dropped potato crisps and Vicky muttered, somewhere close at hand, "damn I've trodden a piece of green icing into the carpet." The deeper murmur of Edward's and Mike's voices came from the far corner of the room, accompanied by the clink of glasses being gathered up.

Mark and Julia were the only members of the family who hadn't been able to stay the night – not that Julia was family, of course, nor likely to be if tonight's performance was anything to go by. Mark really did have appalling taste in women, she thought and he wasn't getting any younger. At thirty he was already six years older than Mike had been when they'd got married. Everyone had said that they were too young – she'd only been twenty two – but they'd proved them all wrong and it worried her that her own children weren't as settled. Vicky and Edward were happy, of course, but Vicky was desperate to have another child and she would like more grandchildren before she was too old to cope with them.

The house in France was made for children and she thought longingly of it suddenly. She loved to see her family and friends but she missed the light of south west France when she was back in the oppressive English greyness. Her beloved Lasserre was really home now after fourteen years. The daffodils had just been dying back when she'd left, but the mimosa had still been glorious. Within a couple of weeks the banks of bluebells would be in flower, mixed with the vivid pink of the campions. The camellias in the courtyard were at their best at the moment and she was already anticipating the day when she'd be able to stand in the hall and see the big pink tree peony through the front door and the banks of camellias through the courtyard French windows – both at the same time. That would be about another fortnight, she calculated, if the weather stayed as warm as it had been for the last week or two. They'd be uncovering the pool next month too – ready for the family at Easter. Her stomach churned suddenly at the thought of Easter. No one was going to be in a mood for celebrating this year – particularly not Caroline.

"Ready, steady, push!" she heard Edward's voice in her ear and she laughed as she felt the sofa careering across the room to its normal position in front of the fire.

"Well that's woken me up. What can I do to help?"

"Absolutely nothing! I've made some coffee and then we'll go to bed. Do you know that it's half past two?" Vicky collapsed in a chair opposite her mother and rolled her eyes. "I never know which I prefer: if people leave early I'm mortified; and if they stay half the night I'm exhausted. Anyway, my problems seem very small at the moment." She leaned across to her sister and squeezed her hand. "Tell me how you are coping Caro? How are you really? We just haven't had time to talk tonight. "

"I must admit I was dreading coming, but in the end I enjoyed it and it was such a break from, you know, from everything that's happening at the moment. But you must be worn out after all that effort."

"I shall be tomorrow, I expect, but at the moment my adrenalin is still keeping me going. I'm glad that you decided to come. Please don't cut yourself off from me. I'm always here to support you in any way I can. I don't think I could do what you are doing, but I admire you for your loyalty and for your generosity. He had better appreciate you."

Vicky swivelled back towards her parents, who were now sharing the sofa. Well what's new in France then?"

"We've had fantastic weather since Christmas, so everything's out early in the garden and your father's grumbling that the lawn needs cutting already," her mother laughed.

"We've got a new arty farty neighbour so your mother feels the need to gee up everyone's social life to keep her constantly amused."

"Don't be such an old misery," Harriet teased. "She's rented the Lartigue's holiday house in the village for six months to do some painting and to get over a messy divorce. She's called Honor Kershaw and I think she might be vaguely well-known in artistic circles. She paints landscapes."

"Is she young and nubile?" Edward asked, looking suddenly interested.

"No. Don't get over excited," Harriet laughed. "She's another wrinkly – our sort of age. She's very well preserved though," she added charitably. "Actually, she said something the other day which made me think she'd been married several times, so perhaps it's the variety that keeps her looking so young."

"You're not looking too bad yourself, considering your monogamous state," Vicky pointed out. "But you'll have to keep your eye on Dad if there's a sex-starved divorcee rattling around Peyrusse Haute."

"She's not my type at all– she's big boned and dark."

"With a moustache and a nice personality?" Edward enquired, laughing.

"She's a very attractive lady and she'll be a great asset to the neighbourhood. I don't know why men are so uncharitable." Harriet gave them a severe look. "Anyway there's no other news and I'd quite like to go to bed now if nobody minds. Thank you very much, all of you, for a wonderful party and a super present. That patchwork quilt will look gorgeous in our bedroom, won't it darling?"

Ten minutes later Harriet leaned her head against Mike's in the big, comfortable guest room bed, her fair curls contrasting with his dark, now greying, hair. "We're very lucky aren't we? It's been a marvellous thirty six years." She waited for a reply and then smiled softly and turned the light out. He was already fast asleep.

CHAPTER 2

Clifford hesitated, his hand resting on the brass finger plate of the old door and peered into the classroom beyond. Through the lopsided crack between two pictures which had been stuck to the other side of the glass panel he could see Caroline sitting at her desk, laughing, and he could hear children's voices vying with the clatter of chairs being stacked. A narrow shaft of sunlight, speckled with chalk dust, occasionally touched the top of her head as she moved and he smiled nostalgically. Another Botticelli angel, just like her mother. Probably not plump enough for Botticelli's taste, he pondered irrelevantly, although she certainly looked less strained now than she had at Mike's and Harriet's party.

Clifford had been at school with her mother. He chuckled as he remembered Harriet – a china-pretty blonde – with her pink, wire-framed, National Health Service glasses, one lens permanently covered with sticky tape.

"Those specs blighted my life for six years. I still thought that bicycle sheds were for storing bicycles when I was fourteen," she would grumble whenever he teased her about it.

It had been one of those friendships that had endured and enveloped both families. Heather was Caroline's godmother and he had made a speech at her wedding when she'd married Phillip. What a day that had been. Bugger, bugger, bugger! Why couldn't it just have lasted for her? He adored Vicky, of course and Mark was a smashing chap but little Caroline had always been his favourite. "Little Caroline" indeed; and he laughed quietly at his maudlin foolishness. Here she was, a woman of thirty two, not only separated from her husband, but about to be widowed as well.

She and Phillip had been such an attractive, golden couple when they'd first met. Now he wondered whether something had always been missing from their relationship, or whether they had simply changed during the course of ten or more years. Perhaps they'd never possessed that indefinable sparkle which made his and Heather's marriage, and Mike's and Harriet's so unassailably solid. Caroline's parents had looked just as happy at their anniversary party on Friday as they had on their wedding day. But life hadn't always been easy for them, he reflected, not financially at least.

Perhaps the difference was that their generation had expected to work at their relationships. Modern couples gave up too easily.

Suddenly he heard running footsteps behind him. "Don't run in the corridor Blake!"

"Sorry Sir!"

He glanced down at the cheery, contrite little face and felt a wave of guilt. He'd only pounced on the child because he had caught him looking rather ridiculous, spying on Caroline through her classroom window.

"And have a nice half term," he called after him in a kindlier tone.

"Thanks Mr Jackson. You too, Sir.."

He heard the boy's footsteps accelerate again as soon as he was out of sight and he gave a resigned sigh as he finally pushed the door open.

"Well, I hope that Mrs Grant is paying you well for working the nightshift," Clifford boomed.

There were just two children piling up books and heaping chairs upside down on desks. Darren, a sharp-witted Londoner, the son of Heather's and his cleaning lady, and Muriel, a hard-working, clever West Indian child whose solemn little face was set in a perfectly formed halo of tiny, intricate plaits.

"It's a pleasure, innit Mue?" Darren replied cheerily. Muriel nodded but maintained her solemn expression.

"Do you think that I'd get all this help if I'd got blonde curls?" Clifford asked wistfully.

"Course ye would Sir, I'd just as soon do fings for a bald 'eaded old git."

Muriel looked scandalised and Caroline tried to stop her mouth twitching as Clifford advanced threateningly on young Darren.

"Not you sir! Not you, I didn't mean. 'Sides you've got a bit of hair round the edge. And capital punishment's not 'lowed no more!"

"Corporal punishment, stupid," hissed Muriel.

"I think Darren was closer to the mark," Clifford chuckled.

Muriel pursed her lips disapprovingly, ready to argue the toss with the headmaster, but Mrs Grant gave her a little conspiratorial smile and she subsided grudgingly.

"Shall I come wiv me Mum in the mornin' sir an' clean yer car?"

"Report for duty at ten o'clock sharp and we'll discuss terms and conditions," Clifford agreed.

"D'yer fink the boss'll be making any o' them chocolate fingies tomorrer?" Darren gazed up at Clifford with a hopeful little grin on his face.

"I'll put in a word for you at the highest level," Clifford promised solemnly. "Now I think that you had both better run along before two irate mothers come searching for you."

"Thank you very much for staying so long. I'd have been here all night otherwise." Caroline smiled at them both. "Have a lovely half term and I'll see you in September."

"Cheerio Miss. Cor. I wish I wasn't coming back till September. Cheerio Sir."

Muriel glared after the jaunty, disappearing, back view of the boy and sighed heavily. "My Mum said to tell you that she's very sorry, Mrs Grant." Muriel's voice came out in a stiff little staccato and then she tailed off at a bit of a loss. She gazed down at the floor and proceeded to spread a bit of crushed chalk into a complicated pattern with the toe of her shoe.

Caroline gave her a little squeeze. "That's kind of her. Now, shall I give you a ring if Emily comes to stay?" Caroline's voice was cheerful and Muriel perked up at once. She liked Mrs Grant's niece Emily, and last time she'd gone to play they'd been allowed to make pancakes.

The classroom felt strange once Muriel had gone and Caroline was gripped with an awful feeling of panic. Until now she had been able to think in terms of "after I stop working," but now she had stopped and there was no buffer between her and a terrifying, lonely abyss. By the time she returned to this cosy, secure little world Phillip would be dead.

"You've gone white as a sheet, love and your hands are frozen." Clifford's voice seemed far away. "Are you all right?"

Caroline shrugged. "I'm fine most of the time, honestly. It's just that sometimes I feel overwhelmed by everything. Please stop looking glum and help me gather up all this treasure. I must say, I felt a bit of a fraud accepting all these gifts since I'm not really leaving at all."

"Any more bootees and mittens among this little lot?"

Caroline laughed. "No. Thank goodness. They downed the knitting needles once they knew."

It had been difficult to explain to the children. Flushing deceased goldfish down the loo was all very well, and probably their closest encounter with death. They had obviously relayed the news home, however, because Caroline had noticed that the parents she met outside school now fell into three camps: those who scuttled off with their eyes averted; those who couldn't wait to regale her with blow-by-blow accounts of the grizzly ends their own loved ones had suffered; and a very small group who sympathised quietly and offered genuine help.

Anyway, she thought defiantly, as she stuffed parcels and packets into Clifford's waiting carrier bags, she shouldn't be expecting sympathy or support from anyone. The problem was entirely hers and Phillip's and plenty of people had made it very plain that it was really just Phillip's and that she was a fool to go back to him just because he was dying. Well, perhaps she was a fool, but she'd agreed to do it and that was that! And at least she'd finally persuaded her family, albeit with some difficulty, that she was doing the right thing.

"Thanks, Uncle Cliff," she said, seizing her carrier bags from him.

Clifford turned away abruptly and gazed hard at a wildlife poster on the wall. She hadn't called him "Uncle" for a long time, definitely not since she'd married Phillip and perhaps not since she'd left to go to University. She'd probably said it without thinking, but subconsciously she might see him as an oasis of security. Being needed was rather an alien concept for Clifford, sandwiched as he was between Prue Howard, the school secretary, and Heather, both of whom organised his life with draconian efficiency, but if she needed him then, by God, he would do his best.

He thought affectionately of Heather. She would tell him that he was being emotional and foolish. In thirty seven years of marriage those were two faults that she had certainly never entertained. Even when their local general practitioner, a long-standing family friend, had quietly advised, after ten years of futile and time-consuming tests, that they should put all thoughts of having a baby out of their minds, she had remained calm and decisive.

"I won't adopt a child. I can help more children if I don't have one of my own." So she had thrown her remorseless energies into doing just that.

He loved her for her sheer splendidness. A tall, attractive woman, always perfectly turned out and with the sort of presence that made captains of industry go weak at the knees while parting with indecently large sums of money. He sometimes worried that she would meet someone glamorous on one of her fundraising committees and abandon him, and Chislehurst, for ever. She always pointed out, reasonably, that she hadn't met anyone she fancied more than him in the twenty seven years she'd devoted to relieving the rich and famous of their worldly goods, so she probably never would. But did she actually need him? Doubtful, very doubtful, he thought mournfully.

"I didn't know you were so fascinated by hedgerow flowers," Caroline prompted gently. "But I really must dash now. Why don't you take the poster home with you?"

"Sorry, love. Here give me those things to carry and let's just go and say goodbye to Prue. She'll be hopping up and down by now because it's her Sainsbury's night."

The empty corridors added to Caroline's feeling of desolation, but the office lifted her spirits. Prue was racing frenetically between the desk and the photocopier, a small lady in her mid fifties, in high heels and a bright red sweater which accentuated her enviably magnificent bosom.

"The poor girl looks absolutely shattered," Prue announced briskly. "She needs a drink – something stronger than sherry really, but I think that's all we've got."

"Oh no," Caroline protested, "I won't even have a sherry thanks. Oh well, just an enormous one then." She pulled a face as Clifford pushed a tumbler of rather dark sherry in front of her.

"No expense spared at St Mary's Junior," Clifford laughed wryly. "Best British sherry and crystal glasses courtesy of Prue's petrol coupons."

"Now look Caroline," Prue announced, clearing a little space on Clifford's desk. "Nobody wanted any gloomy farewells, especially as we'll be seeing you constantly, but here's something for you and something for Phil. I know that you've got a state-of-the-art stereo system, but we thought he might like this little portable radio and tape deck because it's nice and light. Apparently you can get a fantastic selection of taped books nowadays." She finished rather lamely, but then felt obliged to continue. "He may find reading gets too tiring."

"He'll be pleased with that," Caroline said simply.

"Now this is a chef d'oeuvre, devised and executed by Shelley – a single-handed effort," Prue announced proudly.

"The first time anything useful has come out of a student's teaching practice," Clifford grumbled.

Prue tut-tutted at Clifford and carried on demonstrating the masterpiece which appeared to be a large and complex graph, in several colours and mounted very professionally on a board with a wipe-clean finish. In the corner was a little yellow sticky note from the deputy head. "If you haven't phoned one of us within the week we'll all phone you simultaneously. THAT'S A THREAT! Love Frances."

"Whatever is it?" Caroline looked mystified and held it at arm's length.

Clifford squared his shoulders and cleared his throat. This was his well-tried and occasionally successful technique for silencing Prue for a split second and he seized his opportunity.

"It's a graph," he beamed amiably, "and it's very simple. The left-hand column gives you the names of people – the staff at St Mary's and their husbands and wives, in fact – and the strip across the top gives you the days of the week, divided into morning, afternoon and evening." He paused for effect and immediately lost his advantage to Prue.

"Yes it's really a doddle," she said, looking at Caroline whose face was screwed up with lack of comprehension. "Supposing you want to go shopping on Wednesday afternoon, you look down the Wednesday afternoon column for a blue square. Blue means that it's very convenient. And there's Stan and me because it's Stan's afternoon off. So every time you want to go out and you need someone to sit with Phillip you look at your graph and first you ring the person with a blue square. If you can't get through for some reason try someone with a pink square. That means that it's slightly less convenient and a yellow square means that it's not very convenient but always possible in an emergency." Prue drew breath for a moment and searched Caroline's face for a glimmer of comprehension.

"For God's sake tell her that you've grasped the concept," Clifford groaned, "or she'll rattle on for ever."

Caroline laughed weakly. "Of course I understand and it's a brilliant idea. I remember Vicky running a baby-sitting circle on exactly the same lines when Ems was tiny. But will people really not mind if I ring them?"

"You saw the note that Frances wrote. Ignore us at your peril. Anyway, I must whizz round Sainsbury's and Stan and I'll be round later to exorcise the mother-in-law. Bye Cliff, love to Heather, and we'll see you both for dinner on Saturday."

Clifford and Caroline sat back in their chairs and laughed as the brisk staccato of her heels receded down the corridor.

"So," Clifford nodded sagely. "What's this about black magic rearing its ugly head in Petts Wood?"

Caroline was confused for a moment and then she smiled. "Prue and Stan are coming over tonight to shift all that ghastly dining room furniture that Phillip always refused to get rid of because it had been his mother's." Clifford's words had amused her but now she had to struggle with her mounting feeling of panic. He didn't appear to notice anything as Caroline fought to make her voice sound normal. "Mrs James, the Macmillan nurse who has been allocated to Phillip, wants him to use the dining room as his bedroom. It's really convenient because there's a shower in the downstairs loo, and apparently the doorways are wide enough for a wheelchair." Caroline continued to talk calmly. She could hear her voice sounding solid and clear. It seemed to be coming from some corner of the room entirely unrelated to her. Inside her chest she was gasping for breath and struggling to continue. Clifford was looking at her with a kind, sympathetic expression on his face. Such a dear face and registering absolutely no recognition of the turmoil that was overcoming her. "I'll ring you as soon as he's settled and you can come and thrash him at Scrabble," she continued brightly.

"You know you could have asked me to help move the furniture." He sounded rather wounded at this omission.

"Don't forget that I've been asking you to do things all my life," she reminded him gently, "and Prue and Stan actually live opposite us."

"Sorry. I'm being stupid. It's just that you're very precious to Heather and me and we feel helpless. Phil shouldn't have asked you to do this. Not after the way that he's behaved this last year. Still, I know that I'll never dissuade you. You've always been headstrong. Do you remember sitting on the pavement next to the removal van when you moved from Croydon to Chislehurst and screaming and screaming because your favourite doll had been packed right in the front of the lorry?"

"I was only five."

"Yes, but they had to unpack half the lorry."

Caroline gathered her bags and leaned over the desk to kiss Clifford. "You're a wicked tease and I still haven't forgiven you for telling that story in your speech at our wedding. I'll ring you soon and thank you for cheering me up."

The traffic was congested along the main road from Croydon to Petts Wood and she soon turned off down a maze of smaller roads. The light began to fade rather earlier than normal as a huge storm cloud, which had been threatening in the distance since mid afternoon, flung itself across the sky like a dark pewter shroud. Huge spots began to hit the windscreen and by the time she turned right into The Avenue the futile slapping of the wiper blades was deafening. She looked at her watch and panicked. Definitely no time to sit the storm out. The hospice was open to visitors twenty four hours a day but she liked to get there before supper; otherwise Phillip tended to be asleep.

She parked on the drive and dashed for the front door. The carrier bags seemed more unwieldy in this torrential rain and Caroline ended up dropping her keys inside one of them. "Sodden weather, sodding keys," she muttered as she grovelled around under a dripping gutter. "Sodding gutter, sodding life."

She pushed angrily through the front door and as she kicked it closed behind her the bottoms of both soaking carrier bags gave way, disgorging presents all over the floor. The colour-coded graph was balanced on top of the pile for a moment and then slid slowly onto the carpet.

Caroline sat down on the stairs and cried. The sound of the rain thundering onto the landing skylight above her head seemed to be encouraging her to join in its wet downpour. She could feel tears dripping between her fingers and falling onto her knees as she crouched on the bottom step with her face in her hands. She couldn't recall crying like this since she was a child. Her whole body was convulsed now with great spasms of grief and, as the flow of tears gradually abated, she took her hands from her eyes and wrapped her arms tightly around her chest, frightened by the intensity of her own despair. Slowly she overcame the wracking sobs and sat quietly, rocking to and fro, aware suddenly that she was in almost total darkness and that the torrent on the landing skylight had changed to a gentle patter.

She reached up and turned the light on, still crouching on the bottom step, and looked down at the chaos which had triggered her misery. She sniffed, wiping her wet face on the end of her scarf, and smiled weakly. She was behaving like a child and now she was going to be late at the hospice. She dragged herself to her feet and had another scrub at her face with the scarf. The silence was oppressive and she plugged a random tape into the machine. Tears and self-pity wouldn't solve anything and she marched briskly into the kitchen in search of a large container. The sound of a voice on the tape recorder and a sudden sense of purpose restored her spirits, despite the odd sob which occasionally erupted like an errant hiccough.

The laundry basket came to hand and she swept the gaily wrapped packages into it, extracting one, which she was sure contained Belgian truffles, and putting it on the hall table ready to take to Phillip. Then she picked up the graph and looked at it with dislike. Despite Shelley's obvious skills with her teachers' training college's shrink-wrapping machine and her colleagues' desire to offer positive support, the result was depressing. Oh dear. Self-pity threatened to drench her again. It was the cosy togetherness of all the names in the left hand column which was so crushing. She felt extra desolate as she looked at the secure list of people with 'other halves'. Somebody and somebody... Even young Shelley had put down a 'somebody', although the thought of phoning an unknown student called Darren and asking him to sick-sit on a Monday morning (his only blue square), though rather touching, struck Caroline as slightly ridiculous.

There was no more time for feeling sorry for herself, if she was ever going to get to the hospice, and she liked to make an effort to look nice for Phillip. There were pamphlets lying around at reception giving advice to visitors, and one of them advised a cheery manner and a bright appearance. Well tonight was going to be the tear-stained, half-drowned look and that was that. She rubbed her hair briskly with the kitchen towel, pushed the rather snotty scarf into the washing machine, grabbed a glamorous silk one that Cliff and Heather had brought back from Italy and applied some fresh lipstick. Not exactly Cindy Crawford – more a case of 'half-drowned of Petts Wood', she grimaced into the hall mirror.

Outside it was already dark, but the air felt crisp and fresh after the unexpected downpour. The car headlamps picked out the fragments of dead twigs smashed to the ground by the storm, and now they crunched under the wheels like popcorn. The early spring flowers would have taken a battering – she'd have to try to salvage them in the morning. She wasn't a keen gardener, not like Phillip, but she was determined to make an effort for his sake. It was all too easy, however, to concentrate on the organisational aspects of his homecoming: kitting out a sickroom; tending his beloved garden; finding tapes and books to entertain him. If only it were as easy to contemplate actually caring for a fast deteriorating body.

The gravel splattered as Caroline drove up the drive. The hospice was, in estate agency parlance, 'a sympathetic conversion of a Georgian mansion' and the original driveway passed between stately entrance pillars into the beech plantation which sheltered the mellow old house from the outside world. The wards were modern and extended behind the main building, but they'd been well landscaped to enclose an attractive courtyard garden. It would have been set in hundreds of acres of rolling parkland when it was built, but over the years this land had been sold off for development and now its boundary walls were nudged by neo-Georgian, young-executive estates with ridiculously inappropriate bucolic names. Phillip claimed to have seen a Gamekeeper's Bottom, but Caroline remained sceptical.

"Good evening Mrs Grant," the sister at the reception desk called out cheerfully as Caroline stepped into the hall.

This was a place where people came to die and yet she was always struck by the incredible feeling of warmth and happiness that all the nurses projected. She wondered humbly if they ever lost their tempers or woke up in the morning feeling thoroughly crabby. Her shoes sank soundlessly into the thick carpeting and she felt a tiny pang of irrational nostalgia for the squeak of green lino and the smell of Dettol as she inhaled the combined scents of beeswax and pot pourri.

Phillip was fast asleep when she arrived and she sank down into the bedside armchair with a small sigh of relief. She felt guilty for being later than normal and guiltier still for being relieved to find him asleep. She still felt wobbly after her weeping fit and they were both affected by the strain of these visits. She suddenly realised that she was actually looking forward to his coming home the day after tomorrow and to seeing him in normal surroundings.

The ward sister interrupted her thoughts. "He's exhausted, poor man. He's had several visitors today and he insisted on helping to wheel the tea trolley around the rooms as well. Anyway, you look tired too." She gave Caroline a reproving look. "I'll get you a cup of coffee and then I'm sending you home. Put your feet up and collapse in front of the telly." She turned back and laughed at Caroline from the doorway. "It's not easy being as bossy as me. It's taken years of practice."

Phillip's hand was cold and papery dry. She put her cup down and leaned across to smooth his hair, but she smiled ruefully as the fluffy scraps manifested a will of their own. Before the chemotherapy sessions his blonde hair had been thick and had flopped heavily to one side. She sighed as she remembered how he used to push the unruly mane impatiently to one side. The loss of his hair had been a bitter blow for him and the first indication to the outside world that anything was wrong. In fact, for several months, it had been the only clue to his worsening condition. Now his condition was more painfully apparent. He had lost weight and his skin was unnaturally yellow.

Caroline squeezed his hand gently and wasn't sure whether she'd imagined a slight response from him. She knew that she could never have gone back to him – it had been a mutual desire to end their marriage – but she felt overwhelmed now by a different sort of love. During their year's separation they had, surprisingly, sought each other out quite often and, gradually, a failed marriage had blossomed into a firm friendship. Perhaps, if the friendship had come first, the marriage would have survived but it was too late now to speculate – too late and too painful.

Not long after Caroline had moved out of the house in The Avenue – first of all into Cliff's and Heather's spare room, and then into a small rented flat over the butcher's in the High Street – Phillip had met a redhead called Jane. She had not been slow to move in with him and Prue had been a very indignant, partisan neighbour.

"I can't stand flaming redheads myself. Fred says that she's not a patch on you." Prue succeeded in giving the word "flaming" an extra dose of vitriol and managed to bring it into every conversation relating either to Phillip or the much-maligned Jane. "She's even driving his flaming car," Prue spat out crossly.

It had been fairly early during this year that Phillip had first mentioned that he'd had trouble recently with indigestion. He had called in at the flat for a quick drink and a chat, but he seemed abnormally preoccupied. Caroline hadn't taken it particularly seriously and had teased him about Jane's flaming cooking. In the end even the doctor had not taken it sufficiently seriously and, six months later, the first operation had been too late. Once the prognosis had been established his first reaction had been to reject Jane and turn more and more to Caroline.

Her family and friends had been furious at first, but pity won them round in the end. Her father's support at the St Valentine's Day party had been a relief and even Prue had climbed off her high horse in the end. "I know it's a flaming nerve," Caroline had teased her gently, "but you'd do exactly the same thing."

Now she smoothed the sheet gently across him, kissed him on his forehead and propped the truffles on his bedside cabinet. The soft carpeting cushioned her departure as effectively as it had cushioned her arrival, but Phillip had sensed her presence and now he knew that she had left. Perhaps death would be like that – he'd be floating around, aware of everyone around him, but unable to communicate with them. Perhaps he was dead at this very moment.

"Good evening, Mr Grant." Matron was beaming down at him. That was the end of that theory, Phillip smiled wryly. It would have been a nice, simple way to go.

Matron drifted away regally and two nurses gently and expertly made him comfortable for the night. They were pretty girls and, not so long ago, he would have indulged in a bit of mild flirtation with them and they'd have reciprocated appreciatively. Now he was about as attractive to them as an octogenarian maiden aunt. He drifted back into unconsciousness. He could still feel the warmth where Caroline's hand had rested on his and it seemed to be spreading over his entire body, like summer sunshine.

CHAPTER 3

The sun was shining in Phillip's eyes and he had to lean back slightly, into the protective shade of the copper beech, before he could focus on the slim blonde figure. She was crouching by the side of the pond, solemnly handing bits of bread to two small boys, who, in turn, were poking them in the general direction of a couple of ducks and leaping back crossly when they felt that the ducks were taking liberties.

He could hear occasional snatches of laughter and scraps of conversation as the children made their offerings and then snatched their hands away, admonishing the offending ducks.

"Naughty boy! Go away! That was for your friend!"

"Don't snap at him. You've had two pieces now. You're a greedy old duck."

"Look, try throwing it to the other side of him like this," the girl demonstrated the art of duck management.

Phillip walked closer. He was almost one hundred per cent certain that it was the pretty curly-haired blonde from the French Department. He wasn't quite sure enough to make a fool of himself, however, and he sat on a bench as close to the water as possible pretending to read his book.

He was staying at his aunt's flat in Hammersmith for a few days, but there was no garden and he found it insufferably claustrophobic in good weather. Even his student flat in Durham had a roof terrace and he already regretted his decision to leave it for this short holiday. It was the place where he had felt most at home since his parents had been killed. He'd kept the house in Petts Wood, where they'd lived for as long as he could remember, but the family solicitor had suggested it would be sensible to let it while he was at university, so Phillip had left it for him to organise with a reputable agent. Sometimes he went and looked at it, between lets, but he still found it upsetting, even after more than three years.

"It's going to chase me," wailed the smaller boy." It's going to eat me."

"You're just a stupid cry-baby," his brother mocked. "I'm not scared. I'm a big boy."

Right on cue both of the ducks began to wade decisively out of the water, intent on cutting out the middle man and helping themselves directly from the bag, which was now in the possession of the older brother.

"Baby! Baby! Baby!" the little one shrieked in delight, as he watched his erstwhile tormentor hurtling towards a clearing in the rhododendrons, howling for his mother. "You're a silly sausage. You're a cowardly custard," he sang cheerfully, and toddled after him, intent on pouring more scorn before he lost his advantage.

The girl picked up the bits of paper and shook the last scraps out for the ducks. She turned and started to walk in his direction and their eyes met briefly. Then she looked at him directly and smiled with obvious recognition.

"Hello!" he said. "I've been watching you for a few minutes, but I wasn't sure it was you until you turned around. Are you here with your family?"

"No." She looked confused for a moment and then she laughed. "No. Those two little chaps were just sharing my bread. I've come here to escape from Central London and to get some exercise. I just seemed to sit around last term, eating and reading Molière. Richmond Park's a bit daunting for walking on your own, so I thought Kew Gardens would be friendlier." She smiled triumphantly at him. "And you see; I was right."

"Dead right. Do you mind if I join you?"

"What about your book?"

He felt like throwing the book into the middle of the pond, but instead he thrust it into his pocket. "It was very boring and I only brought it so that I wouldn't look as if I was lonely. Sorry! That wasn't meant to sound pathetic," he added awkwardly.

"Right, well I'm Caroline Hamilton."

"How do you do; Phillip Grant," he announced, solemnly bowing over her hand, which was soft and warm in his.

"Aren't you English?" she asked, looking up at him.

"Oh, yes. Frightfully," he acknowledged. "There've been Grants in Petts Wood since Magna Carta."

She laughed shyly and he thought it was the most marvellous sound he'd ever heard. "Aren't you in the English Department? That's what I meant."

"I was, but I've just done my finals." Perhaps he was mistaken, but he thought that he detected a hint of disappointment on her face. "If my results are good enough I'm going back for a year to do my Master's."

"Lucky you. I've got another year to struggle through.

French," she added as an afterthought.

"I know. I've noticed you."

She blushed, and glanced down. "What degree are you hoping to get?"

"I've been told that I should get a First and, after I've done my Master's, I'm going into Banking. I've been offered an opening in The City," he added, trying to look modest but failing. "Sorry if I sound a bit pompous."

"I'd be hopping up and down if I'd done that well," Caroline enthused. "Your parents must be thrilled too."

"They were killed in a car accident, just over three years ago," he said simply. "But they would have been delighted, of course."

"I'm so sorry. How awful. I just didn't realise." She put her hand on his.

"How could you have realised?" He squeezed her hand and she left it willingly in his. "Do you fancy a stroll? I'm a bit of a gardening freak, so we could exercise you and get some gardening ideas for me. Though looking for ideas in Kew Gardens must be a bit like looking in Buckingham Palace for soft furnishing tips."

They walked in silence for a few minutes admiring the last of the rhododendrons. Some of the gigantic bushes were already bereft of blooms, but there were still enough wonderful displays of colour, from glacial white to deep purple, to draw gasps of amazement. Little groups of mothers with small children made even more splashes of colour against the magnificent backdrop, their bright summer clothes glowing in the late June sunshine.

"Oh look." Phillip pointed at two small boys. They were playing football with an enormous pale pink blossom, the brown edging to the petals being their sole alibi that it had already passed its sell-by date before they'd added to its demise. "There are your fearless duck trainers, reunited in brotherly love. Oh whoops!"

"I can't bear to look," Caroline laughed weakly, as both small boys missed the rhododendron bloom and landed fairly hefty kicks on each other's grass-stained bare knees.

They strolled away from the scene, to the now familiar refrain.

"Cry Baby. Cry Baby."

"We were just the same when we were that age. It used to drive my parents up the wall. Vicky and I were the worst. She's two years older than me and we used to fight really violently. I remember a friend of my mother's saying that we'd taught her the meaning of the word spit cats. We get on marvellously now and I feel really ashamed when I think about it," Caroline confided. "Mark is two years younger than me and he and I never fought, but he and Vicky used to row quite violently. Poor girl, she got it from everyone. Anyway that's my family. Do you have brothers and sisters?"

"No," he said shortly. "There's only me."

"Do you mind?" she asked gently.

"Sometimes I think it would be nice to share things a bit. You know, after the accident..." He hesitated. "I minded being on my own then. It would have been nice to have a big brother, or even a little sister like you." He smiled and put his arm around Caroline for a moment.

Her eyes were troubled as she looked up at him. "You must have some family somewhere. You can't be totally alone."

"Auntie Doris, my mother's sister, is very kind and I'm staying with her at the moment, in Hammersmith. She's got two daughters, both unmarried, in their late thirties. My father used to describe them as having marvellous personalities and I remember my mother telling him off and giggling. I haven't seen them for a while," Phillip laughed, "but I seem to remember their being terminally plain."

"Is that it?"

"I have very elderly maternal grandparents living on Anglesey, who I visit once a year, and a distant cousin of my father's who turned up for the funeral, cross-questioned our solicitor about the will, then vanished back into the woodwork. So there you have it. My entire family tree in a nutshell. I'm very lonely and I need round-the-clock loving care to compensate. It's an excellent job with good long-term career prospects," he continued, "and if you're interested I can put your name on the list."

"Are there many names on the list already?" she asked casually. "Not that I'm really interested, of course."

"Hundreds, but for the right applicant I could whittle it down to one." He gave her hand another squeeze and started pulling her along. "Come on! Let's get away from the baby buggy brigade. Shall we walk along the Thames, or would you prefer to go towards the Pagoda?"

"I always think the Pagoda's disappointing. The river's nicer." She glanced at her watch. "Oh good! It's only twelve o'clock."

"Is there some problem with the time?" He'd stopped walking and was looking at her quizzically. "I know, you're getting married this afternoon."

"Would you mind?" She laughed at him mischievously. "No don't answer that." She put her finger on his lips and he bit it gently. "Actually I'm not getting married today at all, but I am going away, you'll probably be relieved to hear."

"Don't fish. Who are you going with?"

"A tall, dark, handsome young man. Come on don't keep stopping." She dropped his hand and began to run across the grass, laughing back at him.

Phillip stood still and watched her for a moment. She seemed to sparkle in the sunlight. People were strolling all around them, but they were grey and two-dimensional in comparison with her. She had stopped now, a few yards from him, her head on one side, smiling at him. His throat went dry, and he couldn't tear his eyes away from her. The cornflower blue of her dress accentuated the golden glow of her skin. He had a sudden vision of his grandmother, her lips pursed, reprimanding his mother, when he was a child, for wearing a 'very skimpy little frock.' He grinned at her. "You look fantastic in that dress. You mustn't ever wear anything else."

They wound their arms around each other and drifted across the well-trampled grass. Their destination had lost its previous importance. She tilted her head back lightly against his shoulder.

"My parents moved to France two years ago," she explained simply. "My brother and I are catching the midnight ferry from Portsmouth tonight."

"Will you stay long?"

"Three months. We come back at the end of September."

He didn't speak; they kept walking.

"I was really excited about it this morning."

"I'd got my life mapped out an hour ago," he agreed solemnly. "I blame it all on those bloody ducks."

She drew his head down and kissed him. They stood, oblivious to the world, thick, straight, blonde hair falling heavily onto fair curls.

"When must you leave?"

"Mark's bringing his gear round to the flat at six o'clock and we're planning on going at eight."

"That's a quarter of a year. I shan't see you for a quarter of a year."

"Come down to France."

"I don't want to share you with your family." He rested his nose on hers and gazed into her serious grey eyes. "I want to take you to a desert island and rip your clothes off."

"That's really sexist," she interrupted, prodding him accusingly with her finger. "Why do men always get the best action parts? I might decide to rip your clothes off first."

He kissed her again. "I'm all in favour of female equality in that case. But do I still have to open doors for you?"

"Yes please, but not necessarily simultaneously." She grinned up at him and he ran his finger across the small dimple which appeared in the middle of her chin when she smiled.

They were suddenly aware that picnics of various complexities were beginning to blossom in the shade of the ancient trees. The glorious June sunshine had, apparently, tempted half of London from its normal lunchtime hibernation. Office workers were snatching the cling film from granary buns with exotic, health-enhancing fillings. Sloane Rangers were creating a Glyndebourne-on-Thames with travelling rugs and Laura Ashley tablecloths, their piercing vowels shattering the tranquillity as they summoned various small Octavia's and Theo's to eat up the pitta bread and guacamole.

"I'm hungry," Phillip announced. "Shall we go and have a celebratory lunch?"

"Are we celebrating my departure?"

"No. We're celebrating your arrival. In my life," he added in response to her quizzical look.

"We'll be very poor if we celebrate every two hours. In fact I'm very poor now. Are you sure that you can afford this at the end of term?"

Phillip hesitated imperceptibly. "My parents had several insurance policies. They were very ordinary, but cautious. My father always worried about providing for my mother. I don't make a habit of telling people."

Caroline kicked at a blade of grass. "I can quite see," she said, her eyes round and earnest, "that someone as grossly repulsive as you might be pursued for his money."

"It's been a problem and if you persist in teasing me I shall make you pay for lunch."

"Baked beans for two then."

She raised an eyebrow when they emerged from the gates and she saw his car, crouching on the floor several feet lower than any of its more sober neighbours.

"It's the love of my life, or at least it was." He gave her a little apologetic shrug.

Getting in was an art, which involved rather a lot of interaction between driver and passenger. Lowering the soft-top was an even more tactile experience.

"That dress is inadequate, Miss Hamilton," he said with mock severity, gazing at her slim thighs.

"It was quite adequate before you helped me to do up my seat belt."

The wind whipped through her hair and the noise of engine and traffic was deafening, but she felt gloriously and unreservedly happy. She lay back against the old leather upholstery, slipped her hand lightly under his leg and closed her eyes.

She nearly asked him whether he would write to her, but she couldn't bear to break the spell by mentioning her imminent departure, so instead she murmured, "This is nice. Thank you."

The restaurant was quite small, but there was an attractive courtyard at the back, with tables set under a creeper-clad pergola. It was gone half past one by the time they arrived so some of the tables had already been vacated and it was almost like eating in a private dining room. Three men, in apparently identical grey suits, were having an earnest discussion in the opposite corner, but the snatches of conversation that drifted across the courtyard were more concerned with cash flows and forward projections than young love.

"How did you know about this place? It's lovely. It's just perfect."

"Good. So are you." He pressed her foot gently between his.

The food was delicious – Italian – heavily laced with garlic.

"People will be taking to the lifeboats when they smell me coming on board," and she put her fork down reluctantly. "Wonderful, but I really have ground to a halt. I can't even manage a zabaglione."

"Do you realise that we have less than four hours left to do our complete life histories?" Phillip called the waiter and ordered cappuccino coffees. "You start. Are you sure that there isn't a man already in your life? I want to know everything," he said leaning over and placing his hand over hers.

Caroline's heart turned over in a turmoil of foreboding. She drained her coffee and popped the final piece of bitter chocolate in her mouth. "The waiters are hovering," she said brightly. "They're probably worried that we're going to take up squatters' rights. Let's go somewhere quiet to tip out our skeletons."

Phillip paid the bill and ushered her out to the car. He had felt the sudden wariness in her voice. He kissed her lips as he helped her with the seat belt and she responded warmly, but he knew that he had touched a nerve somewhere and that she had drawn away from him.

He headed for Richmond Gate. "Have you organised your accommodation for next year yet?" That was safe ground, but it sounded ridiculously impersonal. What he really wanted to say was, "Please come and live with me." It was so simple, but he couldn't quite say it.

Again Phillip sensed the edge of laboured enthusiasm in her reply. "Yes; I was really lucky. Another girl in my department was offered a super flat and she asked me to share it. The owner's only asked for a small deposit to reserve it through the summer so, between us, we just managed to scrape the funds together. What about you?"

Phillip felt profoundly depressed. He didn't know whether to ask her point-blank what had upset her, or just to continue the conversational charade. "I bought a flat last year. It seemed like a good investment. Another post-graduate is going to share it with me. It's the top two floors of a Victorian terraced house and it's got a lovely roof garden." He laughed as he suddenly remembered the present shambolic state of the flat roof and added, "Potentially."

"It sounds nice – a bit like my parents' flat in Pimlico. I've been staying there for the last two nights."

"What made them move to France?" Phillip felt that she was beginning to relax again.

"They'd wanted to go for the last five years I suppose, but they waited until Mark got into University. He's at University College, London," she added. "He's the only one who's followed in our father's footsteps to study science."

"Did you mind? That they went to France I mean."

"I was half excited at the thought of holidays in the sun with a swimming pool. It seemed rather glamorous after Bromley, but I did feel a bit rootless at first I suppose. We've actually made some friends down there now and it's easier for me than it is for Mark and Vicky, because my French is reasonably good."

"So we were almost neighbours."

"What do you mean? Oh of course, I'd forgotten – Petts Wood and Bromley. Yes, we might even have some mutual friends."

"That would be odd." He turned off the road and stopped the car. Roehampton was visible in the distance. A herd of deer was grazing a couple of hundred yards away, but otherwise they were alone. He put his arm casually across the back of the seat and let his fingers rest gently on her arm. "If you don't want to tell me about it that's fine, but if you do, I'm ready to listen."

She put her hand on top of his, where it rested on her shoulder and he saw that her eyes were glistening, but she kept the tears in check. "I've never told anyone before – only my parents – and I'm not sure that I can tell you either, but I think that I'd like to try." She sat staring ahead while he stroked the back of her neck with a slow, comforting pressure.

"That's nice," she whispered, arching her head against his fingers. "I think I might be brave enough in a minute."

Phillip carried on caressing her neck and shoulders without speaking, until finally she half turned towards him. "I went to a friend's house for a party when I was sixteen. Her parents were away and she'd invited some boys – various friends' brothers home from boarding school. Apparently very nice and respectable – and it was all great fun. I'd been getting on really well with one of them and after a while we played that silly game where the boys put their keys on the table and then everybody pairs off for a snog until the music stops. It was all quite innocent at first, but one of the boys must have put something in the drinks." She bit her lip and sat silently for a moment, drawing courage from Phillip's hand on her neck. "I woke up in a bedroom in an awful state – bleeding and with my clothes torn – and the other three girls were hysterical downstairs. The boys had vanished. Our parents were as distraught as we were but they didn't blame us and the police were marvellously kind."

Phillip couldn't find the words to comfort her, but he knew he had to make her pour everything out now that she'd started. "Were the boys prosecuted?" As he spoke he placed his hand on top of hers and squeezed her fingers protectively.

"We were advised not to pursue them. It's difficult enough to bring a charge of rape anyway in those circumstances and we were advised that they might claim we'd egged them on." Caroline shrugged. "It was horrible being examined by the police doctor, although she was very sympathetic, and we just decided that we'd had enough, so we dropped charges. Only our parents knew. We didn't tell anyone else. So that was my first and last experience with boys."

"My poor girl." He took her face between his hands and kissed her closed eyes and then her lips. "My poor precious girl. So that must have been four years ago."

"Yes, nearly four years ago. After that I couldn't bear the thought of being touched. Every time I've met someone I've panicked and run away... until today."

Phillip tried to draw her closer towards him but she sat rigidly, only moving her hand to touch his as it continued to caress her shoulders. She began to shiver slightly, despite the stifling June heat, and he reached into the back of the car for a sweater. He sniffed it. "It's a bit pongy I'm afraid." He slipped it over her and this time she allowed him to put his arms around her. "This is the last time I buy a car with bucket seats," he whispered, breathing in the fresh scent of her hair. "I'll get a really sensible one next time, so that you won't feel inhibited by the gear lever when you feel like ripping my clothes off."

Caroline gave a couple of hiccoughing sobs and then she turned towards him with a watery smile. "Thank you for listening – I'm glad I told you."

He wiped the tears away with his finger and then kissed her damp face. "I'm glad too."

"I was so happy today," she gave a great shuddering sigh, "and I thought that you'd hate me when you knew. I felt so dirty and ashamed after it happened" She slipped her hand inside his shirt for comfort. "I would have told you, of course, in the end, but everything just began to happen too fast and I'm going soon." She glanced at her watch, her eyes round with horror.

"Nearly two hours to take-off. So if we allow three quarters of an hour for getting back to Pimlico in the rush-hour." He caught her look of alarm. "All right, an hour," he conceded "Then we can sit in the sun under those trees for the other hour."

They climbed out of the car and Caroline struggled out of the sweater. As she pulled it over her head her dress shot up with it, revealing very brief white knickers.

33

"Gorgeous," he sighed.

Caroline emerged blushing from the depths of the sweater and tugged at her dress.

"It's a losing battle sweetheart. I should just take it off."

"What, in Richmond Park?"

Phillip started laughing helplessly. "I'm glad it's only the location and not the general principle that bothers you."

"You're impossible," she scolded. "What shall I do without you for three months?"

"You'll have a wonderful time sunbathing, swimming and captivating dozens of Frenchmen, while I languish in my hovel in Durham."

They spread the grotty sweater out on the warm ground under a huge beech tree. "We won't both fit on that," Caroline said dubiously.

"We'll squeeze up very close." He sat down and drew her towards him and they lay under the tree, kissing and talking, locked in one another's arms as if their lives depended on it; quite oblivious to the sounds of distant traffic crossing the park.

Phillip sat up suddenly and peered at his watch. Then he pushed his hair back distractedly. "Ten more minutes," he said looking down reassuringly at Caroline's face. "No honestly," as she gave him a sceptical look. Then he shifted his weight with an exaggerated groan. His leg had gone to sleep and now he'd got pins and needles. As he moved the intensity of the sunlight seemed to increase. He was confused and passed his hand before his eyes to shield them. The trees had cast a slightly dappled shadow a moment ago, but now he was in the full glare of the sun.

Caroline was shaking him and she sounded strange.

"Are you all right Mr Grant? You were talking in your sleep and so restless that I wondered if you were uncomfortable." The night sister looked concerned.

"Do you believe in love at first sight Sister?"

"I think it probably works for some people, but not for others," her voice was practical. "Now, do you want me to remake your bed?"

If only she'd go away so that he could try to recapture those glorious moments with Caroline. The most perfect dream he'd ever experienced had just been rudely shattered by someone who didn't realise that his physical needs were less important than his emotional needs. "I'm fine as I am thanks. I must have had a little dream." His voice sounded slightly cracked. It was an effort to talk, especially at night when he was tired.

Sister turned his light off and vanished into the adjoining ward.

He closed his eyes and sank back into the pillows, trying to recall the lost warmth of his dream, but he couldn't bring it back. The glory of that youthful exuberance had gone forever. He tried to bring back the memory of that soft compliant skin that he'd caressed so tenderly and then he looked with distaste at his hands as they rested on the bedspread. The thought of being touched by those parchment-covered claws would make any woman recoil. He lay still, overwhelmed by feelings of bitterness and helpless rage. A wet line fringed his lids as his eyes closed and he fell into a dreamless sleep.

CHAPTER 4

Mark twiddled the thick piece of card thoughtfully in his fingers and swivelled round to face the window. He never tired of looking out from St Katherine's Dock, across the river to Bermondsey and Rotherhithe. The lights from the buildings on the south bank were echoed in the dark waters and criss-crossed constantly by river traffic, which never stopped, day or night.

He still remembered the enormous sense of pride and achievement he'd felt when the estate agent handed him the keys six years ago. She was an absolute stunner and they'd had a bit of a thing going for a few months. "Samantha – that was it." He trawled the name up from the depths of his memory. Then there'd been Isabelle. "Clever, he seemed to remember and something to do with commodity broking. Ultimately, not all that nice." He sighed. Emily and Sarah had both floated in and out of his life without really rippling the waters. In fact, they'd become so hopelessly intermingled in his mind, that he wasn't sure he'd be able to tell them apart after nearly three years. He grinned – at least not with their clothes on. Julia had been the only serious one and, finally, after two years he'd been forced to accept that things weren't working with her either. Was there ever going to be a right one?

"I'm nearly thirty one and I'm going to be a crusty old bachelor. All the best birds will be married and I'll end up picking up tarty trollops for one night stands." He looked mournfully round his huge living room with the wall of windows opening onto the terrace and the Thames beyond. The storm had passed, but the sky was still streaked with leaden remnants against a dirty yellow-ochre.

He swivelled back to have another look at the room. "Minimalist," he thought with satisfaction as he surveyed the leather and chrome, the couple of good modern originals and the Hockney prints.

"Yuk!" Julia had said." It's so bare and…" She'd searched for words. "soulless. Do you really like living in all this emptiness?"

"The trouble with you is that you don't understand the concept of minimalism. All you want is English Cosy, just like your mother and your grandmother and," he had sighed. "I'm surprised you haven't got chintz knickers."

They'd been forever bickering lately and deep down he was glad he'd pulled the plug before he'd been plunged into a miserable marriage. The last straw had been his parents' thirty sixth anniversary party; she'd worn that awful dress and behaved as if they were umbilically joined.

He had to admit though that the solitary state was just that. He was bloody lonely. It was making him less than his usual sunny self.

"I haven't seen much of Miss Davenport lately sir," the porter had given one of his laddish insinuating leers.

"Perhaps you need new glasses," Mark had snapped back. He had felt instantly ashamed and, on a more practical level, feared for the timely delivery of his mail. "That's another bottle of Very Special Old Malt," he thought gloomily, "or the old bugger'll hide anything that looks as if it might have a cheque in it behind the weeping fig."

He had another look at the invitation that he'd been mangling restlessly for the last half hour. It was pretty impressive. Frederick Mallow – the name looked good in print – and a one-man show in a prestigious gallery just yards from Cork Street. Old Marshmallow was obviously becoming recognised and the least he could do was go and support his chum. Yes, he'd boost his culture quotient and take his mind off women.

The phone rang. It might be Julia. He left the answering machine on and listened.

"Mark. It's me. Are you really out or are you just hiding?"

He pressed the switch. "Just hiding. Hello Mum. How are you both?" He asked cheerily. "Yes, we're fine," he replied without thinking. "Actually I'm fine and there's only one of me," he corrected firmly. "Uh hum… Yes. The day after the party to be exact and it's too boring to go into now, and too expensive. I'll weep on your shoulder when I see you."

He regretted saying that immediately. "No, honestly Mum. I was just being flippant. I'm really fine. Yes of course I'm eating."

He closed one eye, and training Marshmallow's card against the horizon, he systematically gunned down the unresisting office lights of Bermondsey. "Yes, I did. Yes I tried to phone her when I got home from work, but she wasn't in. I don't suppose she'd got back from the hospice." He nodded automatically as his mother rattled on. "I'm sure she's eating, and I expect Vicky's eating too. In fact we are all getting grossly fat in order to keep you cheerful."

He watched as the last drips from the terrace roof dripped onto the geraniums – Julia's geraniums – and waited for his mother to wind down. "I'm going round in the week, as soon as she's got Phil settled. Yes, of course she's coping. Are you coming over the week after next? Oh good. I'd like a few more cases of the Madiran wine, please, if you've got room in the car. Yes please, the 1985." He looked down at his dark suit. Too sombre for an evening with the chattering classes. "What's the weather like?" He leaned back with his eyes closed. He'd need a cleaning lady. He and Julia had shared chores but she'd been the commanding officer. "Well, I promise you that I have not been having lunch by the swimming pool, with or without a cardigan," he laughed. "It's pissed down here every day this week." The thought of a couple of weeks at Lasserre was suddenly very appealing, but he'd have to wait a few months. "Okay. Yes of course I will. Yes, as soon as she'll let me. I'm going to see Vicky and Edward at the weekend too. Right. Thanks for ringing. Yes of course. I'll speak to you soon. Bye."

He made a quick call to Vicky to organise the weekend trip. She assumed that Julia would be coming, but sounded fairly distracted by her own life and didn't press for explanations.

"Look I must go because I'm helping Emily with her homework and I've got eight people coming to dinner in half an hour. See you for lunch on Saturday. Oh my sauce is curdling," she wailed and slammed the phone down.

Still no reply from Caroline. He'd change and then try again. He rummaged along the rail and wrenched out a flimsy little silver number of Julia's which had been lurking between a dark pinstriped suit and a trench coat. Hmm, accident or intent he wondered and stuffed it into a carrier bag with assorted knickers and ends of make-up, which had already surfaced. Perhaps she'd left a few more doodle bugs, ready primed, about the place. He'd turn the flat over thoroughly on Saturday morning.

He flung his Armani jacket and a pair of grey mohair trousers onto the bed and surveyed the combination critically. Not bad for an impulse buy in the January sales. The soft green shirt was clean – a major consideration in the wake of Julia – but his ties were uniformly boring. He delved to the back of his tie rack. Eureka!

He looked fondly at the vibrant silk tie. He hadn't worn it for years. Was it late Emily, he ruminated, or early Sarah? Alternatively perhaps it was late Sarah or early Emily.

"You handsome devil." He surveyed himself cheerfully in the

full length bedroom mirror, ten minutes later, when he'd finally stopped pondering the pedigree of his tie. He felt altogether less maudlin now that he was showered and dressed. "A good choice," he thought smugly. He'd pass for a "luvvie" with no trouble.

He tried Caroline's number again and puzzled as he heard a sharp voice say, "Anorexics Anonymous." Then he roared with laughter.

"I hope that you're eating properly, Mrs Grant," he said solemnly. "Well you can't do that because you can't reach," he taunted her. "I know about Mum, because she's just phoned me."

He smiled as she reeled off the list of people who were worried about her calorific intake.

"Well I'll ring you at the weekend and I'll be over later in the week. Give my regards to the old bugger," he said cheerily. "How was he tonight?" He caught his own reflection in the hall mirror through the half-open door. A tall, robust, attractive – apparently, he smirked, then remembered his solitary state and stopped smirking – young man, with his life ahead of him. Ditto Phil a year ago, eight months ago even. "Keep cheerful darling." He suddenly felt fiercely protective towards his sister. "Don't let the bastards get you down!"

The lift went right down into the underground car park, so he was able to bypass Mr Parry's insidious grubbing. The car park was low and dark and always gave him the feeling that he was in an old Humphrey Bogart film. The baddy was going to emerge from behind a pillar at any moment and say "Stick 'em up Buster!"

He strode towards his car, whistling jauntily, pressed his remote control and tried to exude an air of insouciance as he scrambled hastily to close the door behind him and locate the central locking button. Julia had never understood this phobia and had always insisted on lingering in the subterranean gloom, admiring the more exotic motors and chiding him for being a pathetic wimp.

The more he thought about her shortcomings, the more amazing it seemed that he'd stuck her as long as he had. "I'm very fortunate not to have any shortcomings," he mused and then laughed excessively at his own blatant immodesty. "Well, only really imperceptible ones," he snorted half an hour later as he squeezed the car into a ridiculously tight space round the corner from the gallery.

The exhibition was already quite busy and Fred was in the

centre of a group of gushing admirers. Mark took a glass of champagne from a passing waiter. Hmm, obviously no expense had been spared.

It was an up-market champagne – premier cru – and there were trays of elaborate, albeit inadequate looking, canapés being dispensed graciously by a bevy of moonlighting chalet girls. An impressive number of the pictures had already got little red stickers discreetly attached. Mark wondered cynically if this was just an exercise in sales hype.

One caught his eye. He moved back slightly to get a different perspective. It would look perfect on the double-height wall at the back of his living room. He could envisage it between the doors to the terrace and the spiral staircase which lead to the galleried study. He felt a surge of enthusiasm and tried to get a bit closer, but he'd lost his opportunity.

Four people had planted themselves firmly in front of the picture and were discussing it animatedly. Two of them were definitely a couple. They were fairly short and he had a feeling that he'd seen them somewhere before, quite recently. Their fingers were entwined and they turned towards each other, smiling with a private rapture, every time they spoke. The girl put a hand to the man's lapel to remove a small hair and Mark whistled to himself in admiration. That was some engagement ring. The other man in the group was very tall and distinguished looking, with handsome silver hair. He had a very discreet name badge on his lapel and was treating them with suave deference. Probably an art dealer, Mark guessed.

Of course, the couple had been on the front of that vilely garish magazine that the girls had been poring over in the office earlier in the week. Mark remembered now. He'd been less than enthusiastic, in the wake of Julia's departure, and Emma, his secretary, had accused him of being an old misery guts and having an unromantic soul.

The tall man was slightly obstructing Mark's view of the fourth person – a woman – but he could see that she was tall, with shoulder-length dark hair. His main preoccupation at the moment, however, was to get closer to the picture. Obviously the couple knew the tall woman quite well, because the three of them were discussing something very intently, but suddenly the smaller girl gave a quick shrug and towed her fiancé off behind the deferential dealer.

Only the woman remained and, as she turned in his direction, Mark realised that he was staring at her quite openly. Luckily she was engrossed; writing notes in an elegant, leather-bound pad and she moved slowly past him, totally absorbed, without noticing his open-mouthed admiration. She was tall, perhaps five feet ten inches. He glanced down to see whether she was wearing high heels. Yes, so she was really about four inches shorter than him. Married? Engaged? He tried to see her hand, but it was concealed under the notebook. Dammit.

She had slightly olive-coloured skin and big, rather serious brown eyes. Suddenly she saw somebody she knew and her eyes took on an unexpected radiance as she waved and smiled across the room. He followed her glance and then saw that Fred was also ogling her cheerfully from the opposite corner of the room.

Mark pushed his way towards him. "Well done Mallow!" he beamed. "You'll be able to retire on the strength of all those little red stickers."

Fred Mallow grinned with pleasure when he saw Mark." How are things on the Stock Market then? Don't be deceived by all this, old man." He wagged his head towards the seething mass. "The overheads are crippling. You'll have your Porsche long before I have mine."

"I've seen something I'd like to buy as a matter of fact," Mark confided. "But there's a very knowledgeable looking young woman over there, in a yellow suit, with whom I'd like to discuss it first. Can you introduce me?" he asked, trying to sound casual.

Fred nodded solemnly. "Look Mark, if you want some serious advice, let me introduce you to that chap in the corner with the ginger moustache. He's an art critic for one of the big nationals and he'll give you first rate advice." He watched Mark's crestfallen look, without a flicker of a smile. "A bit tickly in bed though," he guffawed loudly and slapped Mark on the back. "She's a bit preoccupied tonight, you know," he confided in a loud whisper. "She's brought some important clients – minor royals – quite a coup for her company."

The girl span round at the sound of Fred's voice and gave him a peck on the cheek.

"Tessa, I want you to meet an old school friend of mine, Mark Hamilton. Tessa Simmons. Mark wants to ask your advice," he added mischievously. "I must get back to my fans. Meet me for a drink in the week old man. Bye sweetheart." He kissed Tessa's hand with mock gallantry and vanished into the crowd.

Tessa looked confused and waited, her pen poised. He could see her left hand now and she didn't have a ring. His heart was beating hard and he couldn't think of a word to say. Suddenly she stopped looking so business-like and gave him an encouraging smile. "I can't think what advice I could give you. I really don't know the first thing about art."

"I saw you looking at the very large picture on that wall, number thirty one," he stammered, "and I just wondered if you were going to buy it. I quite like it myself."

"I'm not here to buy." She had a very soft, low voice. "I run a company that organises wedding lists and I've brought some clients. They haven't made their final choice yet."

"Whatever happened to the mandatory electric toaster and the flight of china ducks?" Mark made an attempt at flippancy.

Tessa gave a fetching little shrug and Mark's heart turned over several times. "Some of my clients have friends and relatives," she paused discreetly, "who like to feel that their gift is a good investment, as well as being attractive. I discuss their requirements with them and then my staff and I draw up a list of possible choices for them to consider. Most of the clients are charming and it's great fun to work with them." she added with a sweet smile. "Actually I can see them coming my way now. It was very nice to meet you."

"No, don't go." Mark's voice registered panic, despite his efforts to sound casual. "Can I see you again? Will you have dinner with me?"

"I'll be working anti-social hours for the next few days," she sounded apologetic, but he wasn't certain whether she was just giving him the brush-off.

He saw the young couple waving from somewhere near the doorway. "I really must go." Her voice had become very firm and business-like. Mark's heart turned over miserably. "If you give me your card, I'll ring you when things have calmed down. This is my evening bag," she apologised, rummaging, "or I'd give you one of mine." She took his card, squeezed his hand and then, slightly moved by his forlorn expression, she gave him a quick kiss on the cheek and left.

She wouldn't ring him, of course. He was a fool. He should have insisted on having her number. He could have just written it down on something – the back of his hand. He'd have to try to get her phone number from Fred, but he had vanished. In fact the crowd had thinned out noticeably in the last few minutes.

He went back to have another look at his picture, but it didn't do anything for him this time. Wherever he turned, large dark eyes were smiling at him and everything else looked flat and lifeless in comparison. He asked for Fred, but he had left for a gala dinner party. Of course she'd guess that he'd ask Fred for her number and make him promise not to give it. He cursed his own stupidity.

The flat seemed gloomy when he got back and his head was aching. He'd had too much to drink and nothing to eat since Emma had fetched him a bacon and lettuce bun from the coffee shop at lunchtime. He looked in the fridge. There was quarter of a bottle of milk, with a peculiarly watery substance floating on top. He sniffed it and yelped. The bottom layer was so solid that he had to prod it down the plughole with a washing-up brush. A small triangle of Brie with desiccated orange rind and mysterious white spots was sharing the salad drawer with a grey, furry tomato and three inches of deflated, brown cucumber. Mark slid the drawer out carefully and tipped the contents into the bin. The tomato surrendered with good grace, leaving just a circle of green fluff, but the cucumber hung on stoically to the plastic. He straightened up and the cucumber relaxed its grip, splattering itself with a foul smell onto the kitchen floor.

He cleaned up the mess and wiped the fridge out, beginning to feel that he was getting on top of his domestic problems. The cupboard revealed a tin of baked beans and two tins of anchovy fillets. Life was looking rosier. He turned the stereo on and hummed as he rummaged around the kitchen. Bread next. He opened the bread bin with a flourish and then slammed it closed again. He wasn't up to coping with that tonight. "The Curse of the Green Fluff," would make a good horror movie.

He slumped down on the sofa and weighed up his options. He could go to a restaurant, but he couldn't bear the thought of eating alone. He could ring for a Pizza, but old Parry would see it arriving and make obsequiously concerned remarks about living alone. There was a Chinese takeaway in Wapping High Street, but he'd still have to creep past the porter. He could go to bed early and hope to stave off terminal malnutrition until he got to the coffee shop in the morning. He made a cup of black coffee, found a single square of dark chocolate behind the coffee pot and started to feel more positive.

He closed his eyes and re-conjured his image of Tessa. The

picture was strangely incomplete. She was tall and she was slim. He could see her shape in that extremely chic little yellow suit and he sighed appreciatively. He couldn't remember her legs, although he had certainly glanced down to check whether she was wearing high heels. Fred Mallow was a legs man and he'd obviously been taken with her, so they were probably terrific. Her face had a slightly Mediterranean look about it. Of course, the olive coloured skin added to the Southern European appearance, but it was also the large dark eyes and the wide, full mouth.

His crass stupidity, in not insisting on her phone number, was mind-numbing. She just might phone. Pigs might fly. Fred would be bound to let him have the number. What if he didn't have it? Her company couldn't be that difficult to track down. He glanced across the room and noticed that the light was flashing on the answering machine. His heart leapt irrationally as he turned the tape on.

"Hello Mark," Julia's breathless little voice seemed to belong to another existence. "I'm staying at a friend's flat near Putney." She read out the telephone number slowly and clearly and then repeated it even more slowly and clearly. "Why don't you come and have dinner with me tomorrow to talk things over?" Her voice sounded wistful. "I really do miss you. Try to make it if you can. Ring me at work. Bye darling."

A couple of hours ago he might have been tempted to phone her, flattered by the unhappiness in her voice and moved by his own loneliness. Now he just felt irrationally cross and disappointed that it wasn't Tessa. There were no other messages.

He made another cup of black coffee and trailed off to bed with the Times. He'd seen the main news already at the office, so he folded the paper over, and frowned over the crossword. He got a clue immediately, and wrote "armed to the teeth," in wobbly, indistinct letters down the central column. What perverse law required that any pen or pencil used for crossword puzzles must immediately either run out of ink or break its lead he wondered, stabbing with frustration at the paper. He read through the clues again, but it was quite hopeless. He realised suddenly that he was just sitting there smiling inanely at a charming vision in a yellow suit. He threw the paper onto the floor and turned the light off. He would give her until Monday to telephone him and if she hadn't, then he'd start to track her down.

CHAPTER 5

It was mid-morning, three days later, when Mark threw his brief case and overnight bag onto the backseat of the car. He had stuck to his resolution of Wednesday night and was quite pleased with himself. He had nearly phoned Marshmallow on several occasions, and he'd had a cursory glance through Yellow Pages but, in the end, he had held out. He was certain that she wouldn't phone, but Monday was only the day after tomorrow and he was confident that she wouldn't be difficult to find. Vicky was bound to know someone, among the whinnying classes of Hampshire, who'd used her company.

He liked driving through the City on Saturday mornings. The people out walking looked as if they were there to enjoy themselves. Despite the typical greyness of the sky, the streets were full of colour and activity. The weekday pinstripes had retreated to Weybridge and Tunbridge Wells. The void had been filled with cheerful families in iridescent shell suits, and young backpackers in their uniform of torn jeans and Doc Martins. In between these jolly invaders was the indigenous population – elderly widows of the British Empire, in their sensible tweed suits, shopping for their cream crackers and cat food and desperately struggling to maintain standards on a fixed income.

He drove past the Tower. However often he saw pictures of it the reality of its imposing – rather menacing – massiveness never failed to catch him unawares.

St Paul's Cathedral suddenly loomed between two tall office blocks, looking unexpectedly clean, and then he lost sight of it again. He was fairly certain that he never went out of London by the most direct route, but he felt cheated if he didn't see his old favourites. He knew Central London well and, having taken in The Houses of Parliament, he nipped around St James's Park, past the Palace and out of Constitution Hill into Knightsbridge.

Harrods' windows, as usual, were a testament to conspicuous consumption and he sat stationary in traffic alongside a window that glowed with canary yellow clothes. A simple, wide-brimmed hat, trailing a navy silk ribbon, caught his eye and he longed to rush in and buy it for Tessa. The thought of her sent him into a temporary trance and he jumped and accelerated as the driver behind him gave

45

an impatient hoot.

He crossed Chiswick Bridge and headed out, through Sheen, towards the M3. He was making good time and, as the sky lightened slightly, he realised that he was looking forward to his weekend in Hampshire. Vicky had sounded a bit preoccupied when he'd phoned on Wednesday, but she was always pleased to see him. He suspected that she sometimes got bored with life in the country, especially now that she had stopped working, and she loved to hear a bit of London gossip. He left the motorway, just after Winchester, and turned slightly north.

When Vicky and Edward had first bought the house the directions had seemed impossibly complicated. He'd driven down with Caroline and Phil years ago and they'd all ended up having a very heated argument on a garage forecourt on the outskirts of Winchester. He smiled as he remembered. Phil had been driving and Caroline had got inordinately furious with him, after he'd taken the wrong turning, because he'd reversed down a winding lane, very fast, and made her feel sick.

Now the tiny turning to Stockleigh Village looked perfectly familiar and he felt quite relaxed as he drove slowly towards the green, avoiding meandering locals, who would have been surprised to learn that the car reigned supreme in most other parts of the country. The village exuded an air of permanence which contrasted with Mark's present mood. It was only eight days since he and Julia had driven around the green in total darkness for his parents' anniversary and now their two year relationship was over. Not only was that relationship over, but he had met Tessa or more or less met Tessa. In his more rational moments he knew he was deluding himself by pinning too many hopes on that possibility, but it wasn't always easy to be rational.

Vicky and Edward had spent every weekend for nearly two years searching for what Vicky called an 'Enid Blyton' village and they'd moved into Court House nearly eight years ago, when Vicky had been eight and a half months pregnant. It appeared, at first glance, to be the centrepiece of a higgledy-piggledy Georgian terrace, but closer inspection revealed that each house was actually detached.

Court House was built symmetrically around a central, pedimented front door. It was on three floors, with a pair of small casements on each side of the front door and a larger, more ornamental pair of windows either side of the arched landing light

46

on the first floor. The top floor had a pretty row of slate hung dormers and the whole house was painted a comfortable shade of cream.

To one side was an equally tall, but much narrower house, painted a soft Suffolk pink and called, rather confusingly, The Green. Court Cottage, a smaller version of Court House and decorated in cream to match, was on the other side. North Court and West Court sat like a pair of stout, white bookends – one of them now turned into a small retirement home.

Opposite the line of houses was a triangular green, flanked on the remaining two sides by the church and the pub. In front of the pub was a south-facing covered terrace. A row of council houses stretched neatly down the hill behind the pub and two rows of cottages fanned out on either side of the church. Beyond these the roof of the ridiculously large Victorian vicarage vied for space with two old oak trees, which had stood there long before either the church or the vicarage had been conceived. Various small developments of modern houses had sprung up on the outskirts of Stockleigh in the last five years; welcomed by the village because the subsequently enlarged population guaranteed the survival of the pub, and the post office with its adjacent small shop.

There were outbuildings behind Court House – garaging, a couple of stables, and the stable yard – and beyond these was a small paddock for Emily's pony, Pickwick. Mark left his car in front of the house and looked around with pleasure.

"Uncle Mark!" Emily shrieked and raced across the green towards him, followed by a couple more children, who stopped hesitantly a few yards away. "Go and get your bikes." Emily dismissed them with an imperious wave. "I'm coming out on mine in ten minutes." She turned her full attention back to Mark and seized him proprietorially by the arm. "Come on," she urged, tugging urgently. "Mummy's waiting in the garden. Did you remember my birthday's next Tuesday?"

Mark screwed up his face with feigned confusion. "Oh dear! I forgot all about it. Does that mean you're going to be seven on Tuesday?" He gazed at her, his eyes roundly innocent.

"You're being mean! Really, really mean!" She shook his arm violently. "You know I'm going to be eight. You hadn't really forgotten had you?" Her anxious little face stared up so appealingly, that he couldn't keep a straight face any longer. "I knew you hadn't." She gave him a demure little smile. "Can I have a piggyback? PLEASE?"

Vicky was upended, in a corner of the front garden, yanking great lengths of convolvulus out of her precious pampas grass. She stood up when she heard the commotion.

"Poor Uncle Mark," she murmured as she walked, smiling, towards them.

"He doesn't mind," Emily insisted, as Mark struggled through the gate, with his niece entwined around his neck and a bag in each hand. "Anyway," she wriggled to the floor, "he's just been terribly, terribly naughty. He said I was going to be SEVEN next week."

"But I knew really," Mark gave Vicky a kiss. "As soon as I saw you I realised how very, very grown-up you were looking today."

Emily looked at him dubiously and then turned to her mother. "Can I take my bike on the green with Hannah and Oliver?" She gave her mother a beseeching little smile.

Vicky looked at her watch. "Do you fancy a drink before lunch? That's a silly question," she laughed at Mark. "I mean in the pub, so that we can keep an eye on Ems?"

Emily fled to fetch the bike before her mother could change her mind and Mark threw his things down in the hall.

"Where's Edward?" He enquired, after they'd installed themselves at the last free table on the pub terrace.

Vicky twirled her glass in her fingers and squinted through the pale amber liquid, to where Emily was playing with her friends, on the green. "He had a meeting today and he may not be back until the small hours. You'll see him in the morning. He's very busy. I suppose that's a good thing in this awful recession." She smiled brightly at Mark and helped herself to a crisp.

"But you're miserable and lonely."

She nodded dumbly. "The trouble is," she hesitated, "we want another child. I have to go every fortnight to my gynaecologist and then he tells me," she looked round furtively, before continuing in a stage whisper. "when we should have sex." She giggled. "It's not very romantic having sex on demand, but it's even more difficult on your own. He's only been home one night since the party."

"I can see that this could be a problem."

"I sometimes wish I was an earthworm." She rolled her eyes heavenwards.

"Why? Does Edward fancy earthworms? That explains things. I've often seen him pottering around the garden in his

48

pyjamas. I'd better get you another sherry."

"You are an idiot, honestly." She took a gulp of her second sherry, feeling pleasantly squiffy. "Earthworms have a male end and a female end and they can do it all on their own." She had a feeling that she'd spoken more loudly than she'd intended when she noticed the vicar smiling at her from two tables away.

"That sounds a dead ringer for my sex life too at the moment," Mark said grimly.

"Oh poor you! I haven't even asked about Julia. I never really liked her you know."

For some reason this confession made them both laugh and they set off towards home feeling more cheerful.

Emily pedalled up behind them, puffing from her exertions. "You've been drinking too much. I heard you giggling from the other side of the green." Her disapproving frown and pursed lips made them laugh even more.

"Sorry Ems," her mother looked penitent. "Now please stop looking like the vicar's wife and I'll tell you a secret." She bent down and whispered in Emily's ear.

"All right. See you in a minute," and she zoomed off, pedalling furiously across the wet wintry ground.

"What was that about then?"

"I said that we'd take her somewhere really exciting for the afternoon if she set the table for lunch. Do you mind? The Isle of Wight might be fun," Vicky said rather dubiously, looking at him for approval.

"Great idea. We'll have fish and chips out of newspaper for supper. It'll take our minds off sex."

It was one of those magical days when everything just went right. There was a ferry waiting at Southampton and, although it was cold, the sun shone weakly for most of the afternoon and Emily thought it was all wonderful. The main hotel was serving cream teas and they persuaded the waiter to wipe a table and chairs on the balcony so that they could sit outside to watch the sun beginning to set over the Solent. Then they got a taxi to a small rocky cove and looked for crabs in the last of the light.

Back on the mainland they discovered that fish and chips no longer came in newspaper. "Sorry," Mark announced. "This isn't the real thing. They wrap them in white paper nowadays, but the chips look quite nice and crisp."

"Delicious. Really, really scrumptious," Emily sighed, and

49

then slept all the way back to Stockleigh.

Now Mark was carefully measuring coffee into a cafetière in the kitchen while Vicky tucked Emily up. She'd been so fast asleep when Mark had carried her upstairs that she hadn't woken up even when he'd tripped over the end of the valance and dropped her rather heavily onto the bed.

"I don't know why we're creeping around," Vicky whispered, as she followed him upstairs to the drawing room. "She's absolutely out like a light." She organised the coffee tray, and drew the curtains. "I'm exhausted too, aren't you? But it was a super day and I'm really grateful to you for taking us."

"I haven't enjoyed myself as much for years. Do you remember going to The Isle of Wight for a week when we were small?"

"That's too long," she protested, "but it's a perfect place for a day-trip." She padded across the thick carpet and rummaged in the drinks cupboard.

Mark sank into the soft feather cushions on the sofa and looked round appreciatively at the drawing room. "You've got fantastic taste you know Vick. You should do this for a living."

"It has crossed my mind," she said loftily, "Now do you want a drink with your coffee? We've still got some of that vintage Armagnac that Edward and I bought from a marvellous old boy in France last summer. He looked about a hundred – he was probably pickled in the stuff."

"Christ, that's strong." He put his glass down, and took a deep breath. "Emily's a fantastic advertisement for having children, you know. Can men get broody?"

"I'm certain that Julia was very eager to oblige." She looked at him quizzically. "Perhaps you should have hung onto her."

"Well, I must say, that's rich. You said at lunch time that you couldn't stand her."

She shrugged. "I didn't like her for you, but that's different. Anyway you must have been quite keen on her – you lived with her for two years, after all."

"She was pretty, and reasonably good company," he admitted, "and she was a brilliant housewife, except that she wasn't my wife and I couldn't string her along indefinitely. She kept diving off to look in jewellers' windows and muttering about Docklands being unsuitable for families. Apparently there's a marvellous school in Strawberry Hill – Montessori or something – where all her friends send their children." He swilled his Armagnac thoughtfully around the bottom of his glass for a few moments... "I've met someone else," he volunteered cautiously. "I met her at old Frank Mallow's art exhibition on Wednesday."

"You poor lamb," Vicky mocked him. "So you were all on your own for four days, or was it only three? "

"I'm still on my own actually," he corrected her. "I met her briefly at the exhibition – all of three minutes – and I haven't even got her phone number. She runs a very up-market wedding list company, so if I can't trace her via the art gallery, I'm relying on you to find me the number. It must be the sort of outfit your smart friends use."

"And what happens when this one – what's her name by the way? – starts hovering around jewellers' windows?"

"Her name is Tessa and she can whisk me along to Bond Street as soon as she likes. But first I've got to find her," he ended on a plaintive note.

Vicky started to gather together the coffee cups. "I'm sure you'll find her if you're that keen. An even bigger priority is Caroline. We mustn't forget to phone her in the morning. I spoke to her last night and she sounded surprisingly cheerful. Have you rung her?"

"Not since Wednesday, but I thought I'd go over to see them in the week." He looked thoughtful. "She looks fragile but she's tougher than any of us."

"She's driven by guilt," Vicky announced.

"Well she's no reason to feel guilty," he rallied to Caroline's defence.

"Silly," she laid her hand on his arm, smiling. "I'm not criticising her, but I've thought about it over and over again and if you consider it from her point of view she has a lot to feel guilty about. She stopped loving him. No, don't interrupt. I know that he stopped loving her too." She carried on despite Mark's protests. "He's dying and she isn't. I know it's irrational, but apparently survivors always feel guilty. Thirdly, he's going to leave her extremely well provided for."

Mark still looked unconvinced.

"I'm going to bed," she said briskly, herding him out of the room as she spoke. "Sleep well and we'll talk about it again in the morning."

It had been a long, rather strange day and he didn't wake up the next morning until Emily came bouncing into his room, wearing jodhpurs and clutching a vicious looking riding crop.

"I don't know what you want," he grumbled, "but since you're armed and I'm not, I give in."

"Oh good," she giggled. "Daddy's put some enormous jumps up in the paddock and I want you to come and watch me and Pickwick. You can have breakfast first though – Mummy said." She added.

Vicky was looking more relaxed this morning and Edward was standing at the stove, presiding over bacon and eggs. "Morning Mark." He was always pleased to see his brother-in-law. "I hear you entertained my womenfolk yesterday. Sorry I couldn't get back sooner."

The morning passed happily, despite Pickwick being less amenable than Emily had foreseen, and the jumping exhibition finished with the pony winning by an impressive margin. Vicky mopped up the mud and the wounded pride and Mark put a large parcel on the hall table. "No looking until Tuesday," he warned and a little watery smile swept over her face.

Caroline sounded reassuringly normal when Vicky phoned her and they all spoke to her in turn, until she said that she had to go because the Macmillan Nurse was on her way.

"Do you fancy a stroll over the green to fetch the papers?" Edward asked Mark innocently.

"I wasn't born yesterday you know. Don't you be late back for lunch." Vicky admonished. "Or else…"

"She misses you, you know, when you're away so much," Mark tried to sound casual.

"I know. I'll make it up to her one of these days, but if I don't struggle now, I'll never make it to the top. I've seen plenty of barristers start well and then just stick on a plateau. I'm determined to be a Queen's Counsel by the time I'm forty and that's only three years away." He frowned as he considered the dilemma. "She wants another child, you know," he confided. "Well, of course we both do, but it means more to her."

They walked on in silence for a while.

"It would make all the difference if she could get pregnant again," Edward sucked at his lip thoughtfully.

"Immaculate conceptions aren't much in fashion nowadays," Mark ventured.

Edward stared at his brother-in-law. Then he gave a great

guffaw and slapped him on the back. "Right – six times a night from now on."

"Don't overdo things and give yourself a heart attack," Mark advised drily.

They picked up the papers and then wandered over to the pub. It was popular at Sunday lunchtime and by the time they'd been served they began to fear the wrath of Vicky.

Lunch smelt delicious as they wandered back into the house and the kitchen felt warm after the damp chilliness outside. Vicky was standing near the window, looking pretty in a clean dress, and a couple of neighbours were having a drink and helping Emily to lay the table. Mark found himself envying this secure domesticity, for all its problems, and felt vaguely dissatisfied and depressed as he drove away from the warm, busy, Maude household to his own empty, austere flat.

At least it would be clean, he consoled himself. He'd made his peace with Mr Parry. A very expensive bottle of old malt whisky, and a few moments of male bonding on the subject of female capriciousness had ensured, not only the continued reliable delivery of his mail, but also the on-going services of Mrs Parry in the cleaning and ironing department.

London seemed bleak and unfriendly at six o'clock on a Sunday evening – suicide hour – and the underground car park stank of tomcats. A woman was waiting at the reception floor and she hesitated visibly before deciding to share the lift with him. He tried to catch a glimpse of himself in the mirrored door. No, he wasn't looking more like a homicidal psychopath than normal. He bade her goodnight when she got out and she scuttled off like a frightened rabbit. He sighed heavily and went on up to the top floor.

"Fantastic," he breathed, when he opened the door of the flat. It smelt clean and all the surfaces were sparkling. He went into the kitchen and saw a note leaning against the kettle. "Have put sundry small items in bag of same in bathroom. Hope all is to your satisfaction, Cynthia Parry."

He poked his head around the bathroom door and glanced at the aforementioned "bag" – definitely fuller. He prodded tentatively at the new items. Then his eye caught the shower rail. "Bliss," a dozen or more pristine, perfectly-ironed shirts were dangling in military precision. Life was looking up.

He walked into the sitting room and gazed critically at the

wall where he'd thought he could put Fred's painting. He'd discuss it with him tomorrow, when he asked him for Tessa's number. He'd be able to save face by making the picture seem the more important consideration. He glanced at the telephone and noticed that the light was flashing and he turned the tape on. His mother wanted to know whether he wanted her to bring some cases of 1985 Plaimont next week, as well as the Madiran. Julia wondered whether he'd received her previous message and repeated it, painstakingly, in a tremulous little voice. Tessa apologised for the short notice, but wondered whether he'd like to have dinner with her tonight.

CHAPTER 6

Caroline leaned on the end of the high metal bed and gave a small sigh of satisfaction. "That's such a relief." She turned and smiled at Angela James, the Macmillan nurse, who was negotiating the hall doorway with a wheelchair. "Thank you very much for organising all this equipment."

"It's easier to cope if you've got the right appliances." Angela's voice was matter-of-fact and comfortable.

"My neighbour's going to make a ramp for the French windows." Caroline sounded slightly dubious. "Do you think Phillip will be able to get into the garden? It's his great passion."

"Coming home will be a tremendous morale booster for him. Let him try to do as much as he possibly can." She gave Caroline an encouraging smile.

"What are you doing this evening?" Angela asked abruptly, as they sat in the kitchen ten minutes later drinking coffee.

"Visiting Phillip; I hope it will be my last trip to the hospice."

"It's my wedding anniversary tonight." Angela's voice was casual. "Why don't you join me for a curry at The Golden Horn, after visiting hours?"

"What about your husband?"

"He died of cancer five years ago." She smiled reassuringly as she saw the younger woman's stricken face. "That's why I opted for Macmillan nursing. I received so much support, you know, often from unexpected sources, and I suppose that I wanted to make some sort of repayment."

"Do you have children?" Caroline asked quietly.

"Yes, twin boys. They were sixteen when Alan died and they've been absolutely marvellous, but in the end I knew that I had to get on with it in my own way. So here I am! And do you fancy dinner tonight?"

"That would be nice." Caroline gave her a grateful smile. She remained, sitting at the table staring out of the kitchen window, with a faraway smile on her face, long after Angela had left. A distant fire engine suddenly roused her from her reverie and she realised that she'd been sitting there, motionless, for more than an hour. She remembered the storm of the previous evening and walked into the garden to inspect Phillip's battered plants. There were decapitated yellow flower heads scattered on the wet grass and the long stems of the forsythia and the japonica were splayed out like broken bicycle spokes – victims of the high wind and torrential rain. She stooped to repair some of the damage. Then she thought of Angela's advice and straightened up again. Phillip would like to be involved, even if he could only give advice through the French windows.

"Mrs Grant!" her next door neighbour's voice floated over the fence.

Caroline could see that she was limping ostentatiously, while grasping the dog's lead firmly in one hand and a walking stick in the other.

"We popped in to see him yesterday." She indicated that the "we" referred to the dog and herself. "I hear that he'll be out tomorrow. You must be pleased."

Caroline nodded assent.

"I've done my ankle in." Mrs Heath gave a dramatic wince. "I don't suppose you fancy a turn round the block with Dora?"

Caroline looked down into the rheumy old eyes of the elderly red setter and couldn't resist. "Of course. I don't mind at all." She grasped the lead and lurched off at a brisk trot. Prue was in the front garden and waved an encouraging hand as they bounded past.

The air was fresh after the previous evening's storm and Caroline was pleased to have the unexpected exercise. As she turned back into The Avenue half an hour later she could see Mrs Heath standing outside Prue's house, deep in conversation. Then she saw her nip across the road and disappear through her garden gate.

Caroline was amused, when she got back, to see that the stick and the limp had re-materialised.

"That was super," Caroline laughed, letting Dora off the lead. "I really needed a bit of fresh air. I'll do it any time you're stuck. Just let me know."

She went back into her own house and climbed the stairs thoughtfully. She threw herself down on the bed, smiling with relief. It wasn't going to be easy, of course, but she knew suddenly that she was going to cope, because her friends simply wouldn't let her fail. An hour to go to visiting time and she found that she was quite looking forward to it. She took some fresh clothes out of the wardrobe and held them up to herself in the mirror. Phillip had always liked her in blue and she wanted to make an effort for his sake.

She sat in the bath soaking herself and struggled to formulate some positive thoughts. She couldn't do anything to save Phillip now, but she could certainly make him as cheerful and comfortable as possible in the remaining time. What was more she was surrounded by people who were gunning for them both. She climbed out of the bath and made a fierce face into the mirror. "Stop feeling sorry for yourself!" she snapped, "and just keep walking that dog."

Phillip was sitting up when she arrived and he whistled when he saw her. "You look smashing, love!" and he leaned over for her to kiss him. "That reminds me of that blue dress you wore when I first met you. Except there's too much of it," he added with a croaky laugh.

"There was plenty of the other one until you started to interfere with it."

"I don't remember your putting up a lot of resistance." His voice sank to a whisper.

She blushed and he thought how pretty she was when she looked happy. He couldn't remember when he had last seen her smiling. His fault, mostly, and now it was too late to start again, even if either of them had been willing.

"Anyway," she said mischievously, "I'm not tarted up just for you. I'm going out to dinner with Angela James this evening."

He looked surprised.

"It's her wedding anniversary. Her husband died five years ago and…."

"I know, and he just wasn't feeling up to joining her." Phillip interrupted. "I'll be a stick in the mud like that in five years' time. He has my sympathy."

"We're going to the new Indian Restaurant in the shopping precinct," she continued, trying to remain unruffled, "and I don't like your black humour. Do you just do it to upset me, or does it really amuse you?"

"Sorry love." He looked contrite, and squeezed her knee. "The thought of dying's a bit grim you know, so I have to be cynical, or I'd die of boredom." He gave her an incorrigible grin. "I'll try hard to behave myself once I'm home. Cross my heart and hope to... Ouch!"

"Sister's on her way with coffee, so just stop winding me up." Caroline hissed and busied herself with his new crop of greetings cards, while sister tidied Phillip up and organised the coffee.

"He looks brighter tonight doesn't he Mrs Grant? He's dying to go home I think." She gave an artless little smile and drifted away.

Caroline looked suspiciously back and fore, between the ward sister's retreating figure and Phillip's bland expression.

"This is the second time today that the world's ganged up on me," she grumbled and she told Phillip about her enforced dog-walking. "I know there wasn't anything wrong with Mrs Elliott's leg, but she and Prue were worried that I'd get depressed if I didn't have enough to do."

"They've probably organised some street cleaning to keep me occupied, as soon as I get home," Phillip added.

"Well actually, that reminds me. I've left the forsythia and the japonica for you to sort out. They're doing the splits all over the place after last night's storm and I think they need some new stakes. I was worried I wouldn't do it properly so, if it's warm enough tomorrow afternoon, we could go out and try to straighten them up." Her voice sounded unnatural, even to her and she shrugged. "I'm afraid we're all doing it aren't we? I'm ashamed to say that I even wondered, for a second, whether Angela James had invented her dead husband, because she thought it would do me good to go out tonight."

"Idiot." Phillip stroked the back of her hand as it lay on his bedspread. His face suddenly looked very tired and drawn. "You've exhausted me," he whispered. "I don't remember feeling this exhausted since we spent that week at Lasserre when your parents were away."

Caroline leaned over and kissed him gently on the mouth. "I can remember plenty of other occasions. Sleep well and I'll see you in the morning." She smoothed the cover gently over him. His wasted body hardly changed the contours of the bedclothes. She gave a silent wave to the night nurse and walked steadily out of the building. Tonight marked the end of the penultimate stage of Phillip's life. Tomorrow would be the beginning of the ultimate stage.

Angela was already waiting outside the restaurant when Caroline pulled up and parked. "Come and sit down in the warm. You look shattered." She ushered the younger woman inside and chose a quiet corner table. "Well, how was he tonight? Looking forward to coming home tomorrow?"

"I think he's really pleased to be coming home but he looks terrible, of course. Every time I see him I get a shock, even though I know what to expect. Perhaps I'll get used to it when I see him all the time," she mused. "But mentally he's in fine form. He keeps making awful black jokes about dying and I'm sure the sister was encouraging him." She shrugged. "It upset me at first, but perhaps it's normal. I've never had anything to do with anyone dying before. At least, not slowly like this."

Angela ordered two brandies while they were looking at the menu and reflected a moment. "Alan kept his sense of humour right to the end. I used to think that he was the strong one, not me and he could never resist joking about death. It used to embarrass his visitors sometimes, especially the women," she laughed, "My mother used to get furious with him, but I think that it was a way of coping and he certainly had his moments of terrible despair."

They ate in silence for a while, juggling dexterously with the bowls of exotic, spiced food on the two little hotplates.

"You know that we separated last year and that Phillip had been living with someone else until his illness was diagnosed?" Caroline snapped a corner off her popadam and waited for Angela to respond.

"Phillip said that you had separated, but I didn't realise that he'd met someone else. How has she reacted to his having terminal cancer?"

"As far as I know he hasn't told her. He made her move out of the house – our house, because I'd already moved out into a rented flat – and he refused to see her again once he knew that there was no hope of a cure."

"What made you go back now that he's dying?"

"He asked me." Caroline crushed the last crumbs of her popadam into the white damask cloth. "I'd have done the same for a close friend and that's what he'd become. Then there's the guilt, of course. Did you feel guilty?"

"Oh yes!" Angela pulled a wry face. "I felt guilty constantly. I'm afraid that it's the lot of the survivor to feel guilty – just for surviving. It's illogical, but there you are." Angela reorganised the little bowls and they fiddled abstractedly with the remaining spoonfuls.

"I suppose that I feel extra guilty because I'd stopped loving him and he'll leave me fairly well off financially. If this hadn't happened he'd probably have divorced me and remarried." She made a little pattern with her fork in the remains of the onion bhaji, and scrutinised the yellowish design critically. "I'm thinking of contacting her. Do you think that I should?"

"You know her then?" Angela was surprised.

"I found a letter from her. It was stuck in the back of the hall drawer. She must have written it just after he'd insisted on her moving out of the house, because she'd put a contact address and telephone number on it. What do you think I should do?"

"Have you discussed it with Phil?"

"Yes. He says that it's all over, but I think that he just can't bear the thought of her seeing him looking so terrible. Perhaps he's right," she smiled thoughtfully. "He really was extremely good-looking you know. Irresistibly attractive and that was very important to him, poor lamb."

"Just don't let yourself fall in love with him all over again," Angela warned. "Oh dear! I'm sorry! It's really none of my business is it? Here, let's finish this wine." She poured the last of the wine and they sat back quietly, while the waiter cleared the table and discreetly slipped the dessert menu in front of them.

"Don't worry. I've seen that danger looming already. It's quite a narrow line don't you think? I mean, between loving someone and being "in love" with someone." She paused for a moment. "On the other hand, I find myself planning my life ahead, you know, after he's died and then I feel really heartless and even guiltier. Did you do that?"

"It's natural to do that. Of course I did. I had children to plan for, as well as myself. What will you do?"

"I'll go down to spend some time with my parents in France. They've been living there now for about fourteen years and we all try to spend part of the summer with them. It really depends on Phillip." She trailed off and shrugged. "How long do you really think he's got? The consultant said that he might only have weeks left. Sometimes he seems so lively, mentally, that I can scarcely believe it."

"The problem isn't in his brain," Angela reminded her gently, "and he is very weak physically now. Don't be misled." She waggled the menu in front of Caroline. "Come on, choose something really fattening and indulgent. You need building up."

"Oh no! Not you as well! My mother phones me every night to check on my calorie intake." Caroline laughed and picked up the menu. "Number eighty two sounds fairly gooey. I'll have that please."

Angela ordered puddings and coffee and then sat back, contemplating Caroline, with a little smile. "You'll meet someone else you know. I did. It only lasted six months, as it happened," she gave a noncommittal shrug, "but we had fun together and it made me realise that the possibility was there."

"I can't imagine ever meeting someone else. I don't think I'd ever have the necessary self-esteem to embark on a new relationship. I felt such a failure when our marriage collapsed and now I feel partly to blame for Phillip's illness. I know it's irrational but I can't help thinking that his depressed state of mind made him more vulnerable in some way. Also, if I'd been living with him, we might have noticed the symptoms sooner."

Angela looked across the table, and pursed her lips. Even the obvious strain of her present situation couldn't detract from Caroline's natural loveliness. "I think you're blaming yourself for far too much and there'll be plenty of men longing to bolster your self-esteem," she pointed out. "And it's no good blushing. You know it's true. Now." she looked suddenly brisk. "What's top of your list of worries? You know that Liz Walsh, the district nurse, will come in every day to check on mundane problems – bed sores, tummy problems, anything like that – and I'll be in fairly often to give moral support. Your own general practitioner will come whenever you need him and he'll probably call routinely a couple of times a week. So that's the nursing sorted out. What else?"

"Well, when you put it like that," Caroline smiled, "I'm absolutely surplus to requirements."

Angela snorted. "You've got the other twenty three and a half hours a day to organise and whatever you do don't mollycoddle him! Alan used to get very frustrated when people tiptoed and whispered in front of him. He'd be downright rude to people who discussed his health with me, in front of him, as if he wasn't there – the 'does he take sugar?' brigade. So if he makes you cross, go ahead and yell at him and let him do as much for himself as he possibly can. Over the weeks his periods of wakefulness will get shorter and shorter, but help him to make the most of them. Alan sorted out all our family photographs, going back to the year dot, and we filled thirty seven albums." Angela leaned over and patted Caroline's hand. "There. End of lecture. You'll do fine, I promise. Let's have one more coffee before we go. Have you got anything left to do before he comes home?"

"No." Caroline said dubiously. "Can you think of anything?"

"He might like a telephone by the bed, if there's a convenient socket. Perhaps that could be the first thing he sorts out for himself."

"Caroline laughed. "The poor chap. I've already told him he's got to go and tidy up the garden."

"Excellent," Angela nodded in agreement. "Then he can start on mine."

The women gathered their belongings and strolled outside.

"Thank you very much. I don't think that I was very cheerful company for your wedding anniversary," Caroline apologised, "but you've really helped me. Will you be calling tomorrow?"

Angela looked at her anxious face, and smiled encouragingly. "Yes, I'll stop by at about six. Thank you very much for coming. I really appreciate it because I get very maudlin on birthdays and anniversaries if I'm on my own."

The two women embraced and Caroline watched for a moment as Angela walked briskly towards her car. Groups of people jostled around her on the pavement. She wondered where they had been, or where they were going. She remembered being in similar carefree, laughing groups herself, in the past, holding hands with Phillip many years ago. She was struck now by their normality. They didn't know that she was going back to a dying husband. Why would they, and why would they care anyway?

She wondered, as she drove home, whether she would ever have a normal life again. Not at this rate, she thought grimly, as she let herself in through the front door. She'd never really liked the house, but it seemed quite friendly tonight. She marched across the hideous hall carpet, with its peculiar yellow and red pattern. Mark said that it reminded him of American breakfasts – bacon and eggs, 'sunny side up'- and she smiled as she found herself subconsciously avoiding stepping on the eggs.

The bedroom had always been her special domain and she closed the door now with some relief. She mused over Phillip's reluctance to change anything in the house. He seemed to regard it as a kind of shrine to his mother and her inestimable good taste. It was strange really because they'd had such fun decorating and furnishing the flat in Durham. She had persuaded him, finally that their bedroom was rather important and even he had admitted that the result was attractive. They had bought some lovely old doors on one of their many trips down to Lasserre and Phillip had recreated a magnificent French armoire. The curtains were a pretty Provencal design, with matching tiles in the tiny bathroom, and, most important of all, he had reluctantly allowed her to have thick white carpet in place of the ubiquitous bacon and eggs.

She'd intended using the guest bedroom when she'd first agreed to move back with Phillip. "I'm not sleeping in the same flaming bed as his floozy," she'd announced to Prue and then felt ashamed of her uncharitable outburst because the room appeared totally unchanged and actually rather welcoming. The wedding photographs were in their usual place and she began to feel, not just guilty for ever disliking the girl, but actually sympathetic and she sighed as she thought of the sad little letter. She buried herself under the bedclothes to shut out the world, just as she had when she was a small child, and fell straight into a deep, dreamless sleep.

CHAPTER 7

Mark drove slowly out of central London, weighed down with an awful feeling of dread and apprehension. He hadn't seen Phillip for three weeks, but Caroline had warned him that his appearance had deteriorated rapidly. He smiled to himself as he remembered introducing a new girlfriend to Phil, probably ten years ago, or even more. All the way home afterwards she'd drooled, "Ooh, isn't he lovely, just like Robert Redford."

He was surprised to find himself turning suddenly into The Avenue. He'd been so preoccupied that he hadn't noticed the journey at all and his mind had switched from Phillip to Tessa. He had met her exactly one week ago, but she was still keeping him at a distance. She'd been pleased to see him on Sunday evening and, after all he reminded himself at low moments, it was she who had invited him to supper. She had a large studio flat in a very impressive Victorian block, just north of The Kings Road. "

I tidied it up before you came," she'd smiled disarmingly, seeing his approving gaze. "It's not easy keeping one room looking nice, especially when I'm working in it, as well as living in it."

"It's stunning, absolutely stunning." What he'd really wanted to say was that she was stunning, but the words had stuck in his throat. She'd been standing in the doorway waiting for him when he'd got out of the lift and, if he'd had any worries about being disappointed second time round, they were immediately dispelled.

She was wearing a short, black skirt, with a simple white silk blouse. There was a plain gold chain around her neck and her bare feet were encased in flat black and gold sandals.

"Here's a bottle of wine," he'd said casually as he'd kissed her lightly on both cheeks. The material of the blouse felt soft and warm as his hand rested fleetingly on her arm. "I hope it'll be all right. Shall I open it, to give it time to breathe?"

The meal was excellent. She'd gone to a lot of trouble and he couldn't remember when he'd last had such a relaxing and enjoyable evening. He could still feel the softness of her lips as she'd kissed him goodnight but the briefcase, with a toothbrush and spare shirt, which he'd thrown into the boot of his car had definitely been over-optimistic.

He jumped suddenly, as he heard Caroline's voice. "Are you

going to stand outside the kitchen window for ever?" She was waving cheerfully, flour all over her hands and a liberal dusting down the side of her face. "You've been there for ages, just staring into space." she laughed. "Come on in."

Mark took a tea towel, and carefully cleaned her face. "There!" he said, "That's better!" and gave her a hug. "You look blooming."

"Blooming what?"

"Blooming lovely, as always. Where's my undeserving brother-in-law?"

"He's in the garden pruning the roses. Go on out while I put something in the oven and then we'll have a drink."

There was a gardening magazine on a white cast-iron table under a large cherry tree, newly in bud, but no immediate sign of Phillip. Then Mark saw him behind a tall forsythia bush, his weight supported on a walking frame and a pair of secateurs grasped in both hands.

He had walked nearly up to him before Phillip heard him coming, so he didn't see the shadow of shock pass over Mark's face. No amount of forewarning could have prepared him for the dry croaking voice and the physical deterioration. Phillip readjusted his frail body against the frame and held out his hand.

"Hi. Great to see you. Sorry, I'm a bit dirty. I've been gardening."

"I don't know how you do it." Mark looked round with genuine admiration. "I can't persuade two geraniums to stay alive."

"Over-watering's the great killer." Then he roared with laughter. "Someone must have given me a good soaking."

"Well there's no point in drying out now," Mark replied evenly. "Caroline says we're to go in for a drink."

Phillip walked into the house, manoeuvring the frame in short, laboured jerks. "I'm just going to wash my hands," he muttered, breathing painfully.

"Should he be doing so much?" Mark asked when he was out of earshot.

"Why not?" Caroline shrugged. "He's not going to get better if he stays in bed all day, so he might as well do something that he enjoys doing. It's a virtuous circle, you see, because if he has a busy day he sleeps better and he doesn't wake up in the night with terrible fits of depression. The depression is very frightening sometimes." She stared hard into her glass as she spoke.

"Why don't you two come up to town and have lunch with me one day?" Mark suddenly asked while they were sitting round the table after lunch. "I've got an ulterior motive actually," he added. "I'm trying to impress the new woman in my life and I want to convert that concrete slab of mine into a proper roof garden. I think that it would make the flat into a much more des. res. if it were really well done." He raised his eyebrow at Phillip. "What do you think Phil? You're the only gardening guru I know."

"I'll have to discuss it with my social secretary," Phillip laughed. "Would you put one of those little brass plaques on the garden seat?" He asked innocently. "You know – In loving memory of…"

"…a dear brother-in-law, gone to hoe his herbs in Heaven," Mark added helpfully.

"Mm, yes. Or what about, to cultivate the celestial cabbages? What do you think sweetheart?"

"Don't you "sweetheart" me!" Caroline snapped crossly. "I think the pair of you should get that dog and yourselves out from under my feet before I get really furious."

Phillip made a conspiratorial face at Mark and limped out of the room.

"You haven't got a dog," Mark gave Caroline a suspicious look.

"No, but there's one next door and she's got a very well-developed internal clock." Caroline laughed, as a large red setter plodded through the French windows, trailing a lead.

"I'm not allowed to die in peace," Phillip grumbled, trundling back into the room in a wheel chair. "Every time I think that I'll sit down quietly and pop my clogs, someone finds me a little job to do."

Caroline watched the two men going very slowly down The Avenue. She could see from the way their heads were nodding that they were talking animatedly. Phil would probably be exhausted tonight, although in the week that he'd been home she hadn't noticed any worsening of his condition. Angela said that sometimes people remained on a plateau for weeks, or even months and then declined very quickly. She gave an involuntary little shiver of fear.

"What were you and Mark talking about?" Caroline asked later, as she poured Phillip's tea.

"He's in love."

"He's always in love," she laughed.

"I think that he's usually in lust. This time he's actually in love."

"How does he know?"

Phillip laughed. "You do say some daft things sometimes."

"Well it's very difficult to define love and, anyway, he was still living with Julia two weeks ago, so he hasn't had time to fall in love."

"Don't be so boring and practical. And I seem to remember falling in love with you between the duck pond and the pagoda."

"I don't think it took quite that long," Caroline smiled. "We didn't actually get as far as the pagoda."

"Well," Phillip persevered, "she's got a flat in trendy Chelsea and a high-powered job and he hasn't managed to get her knickers off yet."

"Honestly! That's all you men think of. It's disgusting."

"She's going to dinner at Yuppie Towers tonight, so he was rushing home to slip into something comfortable and make a delicious, seductive dinner for two." He sat looking smug. "Seriously though she sounds wonderful and I told him to bring her down one weekend – soon," he added. He was going to say something more, but decided against it.

When Angela popped in at six o'clock he was asleep on the sofa.

"Phil looks as terrible as I feel," Angela said, sinking into a chair.

"Here you are," Caroline handed her a glass of red wine and then noticed that she'd been crying. "What's wrong?" she asked anxiously. "Not a problem with one of your boys?"

Angela took the glass gratefully and leaned back in her chair, shaking her head, her eyes pressed closed. "No, it was a patient. He was only twenty eight and he died last night, leaving a widow of twenty seven and three children under the age of five. I stayed with her until her family could get down from Scotland and then I went and cried in my car for an hour." She blew her nose loudly and then took a large gulp of her wine. "Not very professional. Oh dear! But I knew I'd get a welcome and a drink here."

Phillip stirred slightly on the sofa. "He's doing too much I expect. We'd better wake him or he won't sleep tonight." She grinned at Caroline. "It makes him sound like a baby, doesn't it? Oh that was a stupid thing to say. You haven't had one."

"No, and Phillip always thought it was my fault."

"You're talking about me," he croaked.

"You sound like a foghorn. I'll get you some water." Angela bustled out to the kitchen. "I think you're overdoing things," she announced when she was sitting opposite him again. "Can't you take up a more sedentary hobby than gardening? What about stamp collecting, or knitting? Actually you should go to bed and watch television. There are two good series starting tonight: a four-part costume drama on BBC2; and a twelve-part bodice-ripping blockbuster on ITV."

"Good idea," Phillip said disarmingly. "Perhaps we'll plump for BBC, shall we darling? Otherwise I might miss the end."

"Well you never know," Angela retorted sharply. "If you're enjoying it enough, you might decide to hang on for the dénouement." She stood up and smoothed her skirt down. "Ring if you need me and I'll pop in again in a few days' time. How are you getting on with the district nurse, Liz Walsh?" She asked as Caroline walked to the front door with her.

"She's really great. I don't think Phil would have the willpower to get out of bed without her, and he does what she tells him too, which makes a change."

Phillip was sprawled limply across his bed when she returned. His eyes were closed and illness and exhaustion had made the lids almost transparent. Today had been just too much for him – she really would have to limit visits in future. He partly opened one eye and gave her an apologetic lop-sided grin.

"Bed," Caroline announced briskly. "I'll bring you some supper in ten minutes. Make sure you're tucked up."

"Oh don't worry I'm well and truly fucked up. That was what you said wasn't it darling?"

He was asleep by eight o'clock. Caroline turned off the phone by his bed, switched on the baby alarm – kindly lent by Prue – and wandered into the living room. It was a peculiar existence, but more manageable than she had dared to hope. Phillip was leading an almost normal life between lunchtime and early evening. He was weak, but he was capable of some limited activities. Angela was right, of course, it was his brain that needed occupying more than his body. The phone rang, and she answered it quickly before it woke him up.

"Hello Heather. I was just feeling lonely, so you've called at a good time." She flicked idly through the Television Times while she was listening. "Oh not at all! I don't mind your asking him to help. It's just that Mark came today and on top of that he did some gardening and then he took the dog out – ," she smiled as Heather debated the wisdom of getting a dog. "No, it's next door's dog, and we all thought it would be good for Phil to get out, but trundling to the end of the road and back in a manual wheelchair is an awful grind." The room suddenly felt cool and she twiddled the thermostat on the radiator with her toe. "Oh! I see!" She grinned. "It's a conspiracy! I didn't even realise that you and Angela knew each other." She nodded cheerfully into the phone. "Yes of course. Well I'd forgotten about the Friends of the Hospice. It's exactly what he needs. Great! Yes – . Oh yes! He's got his laptop and there's a printer and a copier here."

Heather fired a few more brisk technical questions.

"I've no idea," Caroline said dubiously. "You'll have to ask him yourself. He's very slow in the morning. That's his worst time. The District Nurse comes at about ten, so you can call him any time after twelve." Heather really was rather bossy, in a loveable sort of way. "Call just before lunch," Caroline said firmly, "and we'll have everything ready by the time you arrive at three." That seemed to do the trick. She was audibly winding down. "Give my love to Cliff and we'll see you tomorrow. And thank you very much for thinking of it."

* * *

"What's this then? Silicon Valley?" Prue raised an impressed eyebrow. "I wish that we could afford equipment like this at school. Cliff thinks it's low priority." She gave a resigned little shrug.

Phillip winked at Caroline. "I'm not planning on taking it with me. You can have it. That's all right isn't it love?"

"Absolutely. I'll make some sticky labels to put on the equipment you want to donate. Now we'll leave you in peace for a bit. Come on Prue. Come and have a cup of tea in the kitchen." She pursed her lips firmly, and ushered a very confused and embarrassed Prue out of the room and closed the door.

"Heather only left half an hour ago, so he hasn't had a chance to get started properly yet," Caroline explained.

"I feel terrible about the computer," Prue began.

"Don't be an idiot. Who else is going to have all that stuff?" Caroline pushed Prue gently into a chair and turned the kettle on. "Phil says that I'm computer illiterate," she laughed cheerily, "and everyone else in the family's got state-of-the-art machinery coming out of their ears."

"What's he doing with all that stuff, anyway?"

"He's helping The Friends of The Hospice with a fund-raising appeal. Heather's involved, of course, although it's very small beer by Heather's standards and she wanted someone to sort out some of the administration. Angela was worried that he was trying to do too much, physically that is, and she happened to mention it to Heather." She prodded her toe at Dora, who was stretched out under the table. "I think that even Dora's a bit relieved. Walking to the end of the road and back, attached to a wheelchair wasn't particularly scintillating. So he's organising mail shots and entering data," she finished. "And I think he may have to take a few phone calls. Although he's not so keen on that because he's self-conscious about his voice sounding so laboured."

The work, for Heather, was fairly menial but it gave a shape to Phillip's day and a sense of purpose. He was often up and dressed by eleven, and sometimes after supper he wanted to watch television, listen to music, or just talk until nine or ten at night.

"I know that I'm not ever going to get better," he said thoughtfully. They were having tea in his room, looking out at the garden which, in early March, was just beginning to take on some colour. It had rained in the morning, but now a weak sun was shining patchily through the clouds and the drops of water on the daffodils in front of the open doors were luminous against the soft shades of yellow. "But I feel that I can cope with it better after three weeks at home." He ran his finger gently across her wrist.

"I think that we both can." Her smile was calm. She thought fleetingly of Angela's warning. It would be very easy to fall in love with him all over again. She reminded herself of Jane and lifted his hand gently from her wrist.

He watched her as she cleared the tea things away and then listened as she moved about in the kitchen, just the other side of the hall. He'd been a fool to let their marriage fall apart. If none of that had happened he'd be sleeping in the big double bed, not relegated to a hospital surplus, in the dining room. He'd have warm arms round him at night. Selfish bastard, he thought, and turned back to the computer.

"I'm going to Sainsbury's for a few things." Caroline's voice came from the depths of the under stairs cupboard. "You remember my parents are coming to lunch on Sunday? Is there anything that you want?" She reappeared wearing a belted raincoat. "Shall I ask Stan to come over while I'm out?" She looked slightly anxious.

"Yes, I'd remembered. I couldn't really forget since your mother phones for a bulletin every night." He looked at her with his head on one side. "Most of what I fancy isn't available, but I'll settle for some jumbo prawns and I do not want a baby sitter. I won't speak to you again if you call Stan." He stabbed his finger emphatically on his keyboard and then groaned. "Jesus Christ! Now I've buggered the whole thing up."

Caroline was still smiling as she drove out of the garage. She found it hard to believe that he'd been home so long. In three weeks he'd been almost unfailingly positive and she felt ashamed of her own early misgivings. She sat in the car park, her hand still resting on the handbrake and wondered how she would have reacted in his place. She shivered slightly, certain that she wouldn't have had his stoicism or courage. And she certainly wouldn't have had his sense of humour, she thought, as she seized the nearest trolley.

CHAPTER 8

The Hamiltons had already made several trips to England since Phillip had been home, so they didn't register any shock at his appearance. "If anything you look better," Harriet announced giving him a battery of kisses and an appraising stare.

"Sorry," Phillip said meekly. "You should blame Caroline."

"Actually it's the nice weather and his fund-raising project which have perked him up," Caroline said modestly, "so you should blame God and Heather."

"Ah." Mike looked thoughtful. "I always assumed they were one and the same."

"Darling!" Harriet gave him a scandalised look

Caroline laughed and went.off to make coffee. As she crossed the hall again she could hear Phillip explaining what he was organising for the Hospice. His voice sounded less strained but his appearance caught her off guard for a moment; it contrasted so starkly with her parents' sunburnt healthiness.

"Are you all right love?" Her mother grabbed the tray anxiously.

"I didn't have breakfast," Caroline lied. "I'll feel better after I've had the coffee."

Her mother gave her a suspicious look and she sat down meekly.

"How was the wedding?" Phil asked, suddenly remembering the prime reason for his parents-in-law's trip.

"Harriet drank too much and can't remember a thing about it."

"Don't believe a word he says. It was a marvellous wedding and I behaved impeccably."

"Lunch!" Caroline announced. "Sorry it's in the kitchen," and she gave Phillip a quick scowl before he could elaborate on the reason.

He opened his mouth to speak, but thought better of it, and they all sat down.

"Not as many courses as in France, I'm afraid."

Her father shook his head at Phillip. "Why do women find it necessary to apologise constantly?"

"We don't, and don't make sexist generalisations," Harriet

reproved him. "This is delicious darling", she smiled at Carrie. "Men are too fond of making sexist generalisations!"

She joined in the laughter and then returned to the subject of the wedding. "The bride's mother turned out to be the travel writer, Francesca Penn." She looked at their blank faces. "Well I've read several of her books, because they've been relevant to my articles for the expats' magazines, and she'd read some of my articles," she finished smugly.

"It was a real mutual admiration society," Mike grinned, "but you'll be relieved to hear that the father of the bride and I had never heard of each other, had absolutely nothing in common and wouldn't recognise each other again in a month of Sundays."

"You are an awful old philistine," Caroline glared at her father. "You should be proud of Mum. That article in the Times Travel Supplement last week was really good."

"Well, the really exciting bit," Harriet rattled on, ignoring her family, "is that she has asked me to collaborate on a new style of travel book. I'm meeting her at a book launch on Wednesday. The crime writer, Alexander Buck, is bringing out a new book. Why don't you come along? It'll be quite fun and a good lunch." She looked enquiringly at Caroline.

"Oh, I don't think..." she looked dubiously at Phillip.

"I like his books but I can't possibly spare her!" Phillip said firmly, not a flicker of expression on his face.

"Rubbish! You'll cope perfectly well," Caroline blurted out.

Phillip shrugged and looked hurt. "It'll look bad on the front of the papers; 'Good-time girl abandons dying husband.' Don't you think?" he appealed to Mike.

"He's right you know," he nodded solemnly at the two confused women.

They're winding us up," Harriet said, looking suspiciously from one glum face to the other.

"Sorry darling," Phillip cringed. "Of course you must go out and have fun. I expect I'll be all right," he couldn't resist adding, winking at his father-in-law.

"Somebody from my baby-sitting list can come in for the day," Caroline pointed out.

"Over my dead body! Oh Whoops! Sorry love."

"At this rate it will be," she said crossly.

"Cliff's on his own this afternoon," Mike mentioned casually, once lunch was over. "Heather's gone to see her mother in

Leatherhead. Do you fancy a ride over to Chislehurst to keep him company?" He raised his eyebrow at Phillip.

"I just don't understand him. What keeps him so cheerful?" Harriet asked when they were back in the living room, after the men had gone. "Does he get depressed ever? He does accept, does he, that he's dying?"

Caroline shrugged and smiled ruefully at her mother. "Oh yes, he certainly accepts that. And his body is very weak, of course. You haven't seen him trying to move around much. He can't go down the garden without a walking frame and they've taken the wheelchair to Cliff's this afternoon. I don't really understand how he can be so brave." A tear trickled down her face. "He's much braver than I am." She wiped the tear away, and gave her mother a bleak smile.

"I hope you're not falling in love with him again."

Caroline gave a short laugh. "I'm eating properly and I'm not falling in love with Phillip again. Those are the only two things required of me at the moment, so I should be able to manage."

"You may scorn, but it's easily done. I know Phillip's lost his looks now, but he was a very attractive man once, and he still has great charm."

Caroline squeezed her mother's hand. "Stop worrying."

"You're young and very pretty. You'll meet someone else you know."

"At the moment I don't feel as if I ever want to be involved with anyone again."

"You'll change your mind. Everyone says that at first," Harriet observed and then changed the subject. "I'm going over to Vicky's tomorrow. I haven't seen Emily since her birthday."

"They popped in to see us a couple of weeks ago, on the way back from the dentist. Poor old Ems looked like a chipmunk, but she was being very brave." Caroline smiled as she thought of the lop-sided little face. "She accepts the change in Phillip, you know, without any comment. She knows that he's dying, but she doesn't stare at him, or treat him any differently from usual."

"How did you think that Vicky was looking?"

"She looked very glamorous but I think that she's a bit depressed – the same worry as ever."

Harriet nodded in agreement. "She sounded quite down when I spoke to her in the week. She's so desperate to get pregnant and, now that they think they've diagnosed the problem, Edward is hardly ever home to dispense the treatment." Harriet stuck her lip out thoughtfully. "They need to get away together for a bit. Perhaps they'll come down to Lasserre for a few weeks in the summer. It's not exactly romantic, with everyone there, but it's better than nothing."

"It's lovely and it's very romantic," Caroline said defensively. "By the way, have you met Tessa yet?"

"No," her mother shook her head. "Vicky said that they met them for lunch while they were in town last week. She thought that Tessa was really super, but apparently she works slightly anti-social hours so she hasn't been able to fit in a weekend in Hampshire yet."

Caroline laughed softly. "I think your handsome little boy has met his match at last. I gather that this time he's the one gazing longingly into jewellers' windows and she's more interested in pursuing her career."

"He's supposed to be coming down to France in August, for a few weeks and I think he's hoping to bring her down. That'll be interesting, won't it?"

"I may not be there to observe," Caroline reminded her mother gently and they sat in silence for a few minutes, unsure what their reaction should be to that possibility.

Practicalities, however, were always fairly close to the surface of Harriet's mind. Mike had once accused her of having no soul. "Yes I have and I remember where I've put it," she'd retorted quickly and he hadn't tried that tack again.

"Madame Lartigue's daughter is expecting a baby in May," she sounded glum.

"How lovely," Caroline replied rather absently.

"Inconvenient is the word I'd have chosen," her mother snapped.

Caroline looked questioningly at her mother. She knew that she was very fond of her cleaning lady, so this should have been an occasion for mutual joy.

"Her daughter lives in Australia and her son-in-law is paying for her to go out for two months. She leaves on May the first," she added.

"Selfish."

"Exactly."

Caroline laughed. "You, I mean. Surely you can manage for two months. It's so exciting for Madame Lartigue, but she'll have to improve her English in the next six weeks."

"Six weeks? Oh sod it, I thought it was seven. I'm going to advertise for a temporary replacement in The Lady, and in that English monthly, The Recorder."

"Mum, you're looking quite manic. Why is it such a crisis? She'll be back again by the time everyone descends on you for the summer."

"What's that my love?" Mike walked through the door, followed by Phillip leaning heavily on two sticks.

Caroline helped Phil onto the sofa and carefully lifted his legs onto the cushions, before settling down next to him.

Harriet sighed to herself, as she saw them look at each other. "I was just telling Caroline about Madame Lartigue going to Australia in May and June. It's not the cleaning as much as the house and animal-sitting. If we have to be away for any reason during that time…" She trailed off awkwardly, and gave Phil a little apologetic smile.

"How was Cliff?" Caroline asked in an attempt to rescue her mother.

"In good form," her father said, "and Heather arrived home just as we were leaving, so we've had a social afternoon."

"We must go now, or we'll never find a parking space again near the flat. I'll ring you about lunch on Wednesday," her mother said hesitantly.

"Your mother thinks I'm serious about Wednesday. I know I've been a selfish sod, persuading you to come back and so on, but even I'm not such a selfish sod as that," Phillip said quietly after they'd left.

"I know." She got up from the sofa while she could still trust herself and smiled down at him. "Shall we watch television for a while? We could have supper on a tray."

The unseasonably mild weather continued into the first week of April and Phillip was in good spirits on the day she was due to meet her mother for lunch. He refused point blank to have any company while she was out.

"Honestly, I don't think you need worry," the district nurse said as Caroline came into his room to say goodbye. "I've sorted his medicine and you've left him food. He's perfectly mobile and if he has a problem he can telephone someone."

"Stop shilly-shallying woman and go." He gave her a kiss. "You look fantastic. Don't pick up any strange men."

CHAPTER 9

Caroline went into central London by train and had the same weird sensation that she'd had outside the Indian Restaurant. The whole world was just carrying on as normal. She didn't stand out as being different. Nobody knew that she had left a dying husband at home. She felt as though she had a flashing light on her head but, obviously, it was invisible to the rest of the world..

Her mother was already waiting outside the hotel. It was not one of the more famous London hotels, but the interior was opulent. "Nice isn't it?" Her mother wasn't easily overawed, but Caroline sensed that she was steeling herself to rise to the occasion. "This is the second time I've been to a launch here," she confided. "It must have been a private house once. Can you imagine it?"

They were shown through tall, carved double doors, under an elaborately gilded pediment, into a spacious drawing room. There seemed to be beautiful people mingling with beautiful furniture in roughly equal proportions. Caroline suddenly realised that she was clutching a glass of cold champagne, although she hadn't noticed anyone giving it to her. She felt very suburban and out of place in this seething mass of glamour and she stuck close to her mother. Caroline was surprised by the number of people who seemed to know Harriet quite well. Her articles were obviously highly regarded – she was a bit of a dark horse really.

Her mother introduced her to a tall, rather foppishly dressed young man, who spoke in an affected drawl, his eyes flitting round the room as he spoke. Obviously looking for someone less boring than me, Caroline assumed crossly. Behind her she could hear her mother speaking and then a man's voice answering. It was a deep, warm voice, which suddenly broke into a soft laugh. She had the impression that they knew each other quite well and, excusing herself from her bored companion, she turned to join them.

"My daughter, Caroline," her mother drew her towards them. "Alex Forbes-Buckingham. Alex is house-hunting near us so he knows Lasserre quite well. He's actually stayed with us a couple of times. Oh! There's Francesca." She waved gaily across the room. "Will you be all right for a while?" she asked Caroline and vanished.

Caroline realised suddenly that she had been staring at him

fixedly while her mother was talking. She lowered her eyes now and felt herself blushing slightly. He was still holding her hand and she felt no urge to remove it.

"I'd have recognised you anywhere. You look just like Harriet."

Caroline raised her eyes to his face again and smiled. "It's the blonde curls – we both hate them."

"Well you shouldn't." His eyes passed calmly over her slightly upturned face. "I think they're *adorable*."

He pronounced it with a French accent, which broke the tension and made her laugh. "So, you're another francophile," she looked at him questioningly. He gave a little sigh. "The trouble is that I've fallen in love with your parents' house and so far I haven't found anything that matches up."

The emphasis which he gave the words made her shiver imperceptibly. His eyes seemed to be burning into her. "Are you intending to live in France permanently?" She struggled to keep her voice casual.

"I shall keep a base in London, but I'm planning on making France my real home. It'll give me a perfect environment for working and it'll give my son a proper home. He finds it claustrophobic being holed up in a Central London flat in the summer and I hate the constant noise and disturbance."

She was a fool not to have realised that he would be married.

"What about you? Do you spend much time down there?"

"When my parents first moved down I was a student and I spent nearly all my vacations at Lasserre. Mother was very tolerant and we'd all bring a constant stream of college friends. But I still try to go down a few times a year."

"Will you be there this summer?" He willed the answer to be yes.

She hesitated. "That depends on my husband." She wanted to elaborate suddenly and explain the whole situation to him, but at that moment a tall, rather severe-looking woman walked up and rested her hand on his shoulder in a proprietorial fashion.

"Angelo's arrived and he can only stop for ten minutes. You really should speak to him." She turned to Caroline with an apologetic smile, "I'm sorry to interrupt."

Alex introduced the woman, Mavis, and then turned back to Caroline. "I'll be back in a moment. Will you join us for lunch – quite a big group, I'm afraid?" He was still holding her hand.

His face looked boyishly anxious and Caroline smiled. "That would be nice but I'm afraid that I don't know what my mother has planned."

He raised her hand to his lips and then weaved through the noisy groups in Mavis's wake.

"Darling, come and meet Francesca," her mother's voice came from just behind her. They were nearly shouting now to make themselves heard. "My daughter, Caroline." Harriet screwed her face up in dismay at the increasing volume.

Since it was such an effort to make herself heard and since the two older women were engrossed in their forthcoming literary enterprise, Caroline scanned the room for a glimpse of Alex.

He was standing, with his back slightly turned, talking to a distinguished-looking man, probably in his sixties, with that slightly flashy, over-gilded appearance that rich Italian men seem to perfect.

For some reason she found herself comparing him with Phillip. He was older, early forties at a guess, and he was darker and shorter – but quite a lot taller than her, five foot ten perhaps – and his face looked lived in. He didn't have the film star looks that Phil had once had, but his face had an animation which she found compelling. At that moment he turned slightly and caught her eye. She felt a perverse pleasure in being caught looking at him and returned his smile. He mouthed something to her, but she shook her head in incomprehension. He tried again and they both laughed, as she shook her head again. His foreign companion turned and gave her an openly approving look, then spoke a few more words to Alex. Caroline felt that she was being discussed in complimentary terms and was relieved to be drawn back into her mother's conversation.

"Listen," Harriet hissed. "Francesca and I can't hear ourselves think. Let's go and have lunch in Mount Street and get away from this awful smoke." Harriet didn't notice the disappointment on Caroline's face as they pushed their way out of the heaving vestibule and set off across Mayfair in search of a suitable restaurant.

"That's better," Francesca breathed a great sigh as they sank into their seats around a quiet table. "I'm amazed at the number of people who still smoke. I don't think I could have survived another moment."

Caroline thought that she could have survived for a lifetime, but it obviously wasn't meant to be. The food was excellent and she picked at it, while they discussed the various means of producing a travel book that would be entertaining as well as informative, with plenty of local interest. She must have been very far away, because she suddenly heard them discussing Alex.

"He's got bedroom eyes," her mother giggled. "That's why he's so attractive to women."

"Who's that?" Caroline asked innocently. "I hope you're talking about my father."

They all laughed. "I introduced him to you just before we left," her mother explained. "Perhaps you don't remember. He's got brown hair, medium height." she considered a moment, "and the sort of smile that makes you believe you're the only woman in the world."

"Not exactly heavily built, but sort of – " Francesca paused, "How would you describe him Harriet?"

"Protective and solid," Harriet announced firmly.

"He was telling me about his son," Caroline fished casually. "Was his wife there today?"

"They were divorced last year. He took it badly," Francesca added. "She went off with an Argentinean polo player."

"It's those tight jodhpurs," Harriet sniggered. "She'd been reading too much Jilly Cooper."

"Honestly mother!" Caroline looked scandalised, then she added wistfully, "I should think he'd look rather good in tight jodhpurs himself."

Francesca left them outside the restaurant and they waved as she headed for Bond Street at a brisk pace.

"Come back and have tea," Harriet insisted, hailing a taxi and Caroline was quite relieved to postpone her return to Petts Wood.

The flat in Pimlico was small and very convenient, but it had a slightly unlived in feel about it. One or other of her parents was often there, but never for more than a day or two at the time. Her father operated his business from France and was reluctant to spend more time than was absolutely necessary in London. Her mother came over slightly more frequently, but equally reluctantly.

"I liked Francesca," Caroline said, leaning against the door of the tiny kitchen. There was only space for one person at a time. "What's the next move on this book?"

"She's coming down to Laserre for a few days to have a look around. She doesn't know Gascony at all. It'll be fun, because I never do any sightseeing nowadays – not now that I'm practically a native." She wrinkled her nose at the dust on the table, as she put the tea tray down. "The last time I did any sightseeing," she continued, "was when Alex popped in, last February, to have a look round. He wanted to see some of the more beautiful bastide villages, so we had lunch at that unusual round one."

"Is he serious about buying a house in France?" Caroline passed the biscuits to her mother.

"Oh yes. He's taken a long let on a house at Montegut; you know, it belongs to those Americans, whom we didn't particularly like, and he's going to use it as a base for house-hunting. Of course, he's going to be very busy this summer, what with the launch of the new book, and everything that that entails, so I don't know how often he'll be down."

Caroline sat quietly, absorbing this new information. Of course; how stupid of her. She should have realised why everyone wanted to talk to him at the launch. It was *his* launch – Alex Forbes-Buckingham, alias Alexander Buck. Well, she had been an idiot if she thought that the famous Alexander Buck had shown some interest in *her* – a little hausfrau from Petts Wood. Nevertheless, she found herself hoping that more information would be forthcoming, but her mother didn't return to the subject.

"Stop and have a drink," Harriet pressed her, as Caroline looked anxiously at her watch. "It's only quarter past six."

"I'd better go, honestly. I don't like leaving Phil for too long."

"Your father's gone over, to mow the lawn, so he's not on his own."

"He'll be furious, you know. He'll think that I organised it."

"No he won't." Harriet looked triumphant. "They organised it themselves, on the way back from Cliff's on Sunday."

Caroline laughed. "But I'm still going," she said firmly, standing up, and looking round for her bag. "Thank you very much for asking me."

As Caroline was leaving the telephone rang. "Bye," she said, kissing her mother hastily. "I'll see you soon. You go and answer the phone."

Harriet was surprised to hear Alex's voice. He'd never phoned her in London before. "It was an excellent do," she said, thinking of the terrible noise and the smoke, but trying to sound enthusiastic. "Oh yes, Caroline enjoyed herself," she laughed. "You're a shameless flatterer, Alex." She began to guess at the reason for the call, and smiled. "Yes she will be down at some time but not with her husband." He continued to fish casually for information and finally she decided it was simpler to explain than to evade.

"So now you know," she said, "and that's why she won't be down with Phil." She sank down onto the nearest chair, suddenly overwhelmed by waves of depression and exhaustion and allowing his sympathetic voice to wash over her. She had been clutching the phone so tightly that her fingers were cramped. "Yes, I promise. Yes, of course I will. I'm sure she'd be pleased, but not until… Well, you know, when it's all over." Her voice sounded firmer than she felt. "I'll phone you, I really will. Bye, and have a good trip."

Harriet didn't move from the hall chair for several minutes. She sat brooding over this new development. Alex was an attractive man, with plenty of admirable qualities, but he had a lot of very glamorous women throwing themselves at him. Caroline had suffered enough already in her thirty two years and Harriet didn't want to be instrumental in pointing her down another disastrous path. Harriet sighed heavily. Her children had been a source of great pride and pleasure to her over the years, but just now she was worried about all three of them.

* * *

Caroline was amused when she walked into her living room, later that evening. Phil and her father were having an animated political discussion with Prue and Stan, surrounded by the remains of a Chinese takeaway and at least a dozen beer bottles.

"Hello darling. Have you had a good day?" Phillip's skin looked healthier tonight and he didn't even look particularly tired.

"I'm exhausted, but it was fun." Caroline poked hopefully among the debris. "Have you managed all right without me? Is there any food left?"

"Yes and yes," Phillip nodded complacently. "I'm thriving, your father's mown the lawn, he's strimmed around the edges, and Prue and Stan have provided the food. Yours is in the microwave."

"And we've tried to wean him away from his misguided right-wing theories," Stan added with a helpless shrug. "We'll continue the discussion another night," he threatened, as Prue prepared to leave.

"I must go too. Your mother will be wondering what's happened to me."

"Do you realise that you've been up for twelve hours today?" Caroline said later when he was finally in bed and she was about to switch on the late evening news. She looked at him with her head on one side. "Your hair's nearly grown back and you've looked better this week than you have for months. How do you feel?"

"Under no delusions," he answered quietly.

He fell asleep during the news and she turned it off and sat watching him thoughtfully. Another face kept floating in front of her eyes and she tried to shake the memory away, but it persisted. When she finally went to bed and turned the light off she could still feel the warmth of those smiling brown eyes and hear the distinctive, mellow tones of his voice.

"He's been looking better for more than a week," Liz Walsh announced next morning, as Caroline helped her to remake the bed, while Phillip was in the shower. "I expect the sun has helped, and being home with you, of course, has done wonders for his morale."

"Why don't my corners look like your corners?" Caroline gave a frustrated shake to the sheet and started again. When it was reasonably tidy she leaned her hands on the bed and looked across at the nurse. "You don't think…?" She began.

Liz shook her head before Caroline could finish. "Put it out of your mind, my dear." Her voice was gentle, but she didn't flinch. "Sometimes people can have a remission at this late stage, but it is only a remission and not a reprieve." She walked quickly around the bed and rested a hand on Caroline's. "It's often followed by a very sudden decline. You must be prepared for that."

Caroline nodded, tracing the pattern on the counterpane with her finger and watching the doodled indent in the material as if it were miles away from her.

"Be positive with Phillip, but it would be unkind to allow him to feel optimistic." She sorted out his medication and prepared to leave. "There you are," she announced as he returned from the shower. "One remade bed. You're very lucky to have staff in this day and age."

"Not that lucky," Caroline gave a rueful laugh. "I've made a pig's ear of my side."

Phillip spent the afternoon working at the computer. It was progressing well and he was gaining disproportionate satisfaction from the exercise. He'd written a very simple program and now he was entering all the names of potential and existing Hospice benefactors in order of munificence and chronology. Heather was coming over tomorrow and he was hoping to have finished the whole exercise by then, unless she brought any more data to be entered. When Caroline came in with a cup of tea he'd turned everything off and was rummaging in the dark recesses of the writing desk.

"Can I help you to find something?" she enquired as she placed the tray gingerly on top of his printer.

"I'm looking for those tapes you gave me a couple of years ago." He looked at her quizzical expression. "You know, French for Those of Low Linguistic Ability."

"I don't think that was the title."

"Here we are, French for the Moronic Monoglot." He stood up suddenly and caught her unguarded expression. His face clouded with comprehension and he sat down heavily on the sofa. "Caroline." He spoke slowly and gently as if she were a small child. "Is any of Heather's fundraising for the Hospice ever going to benefit me?"

Caroline shook her head, a tear beginning to roll slowly down her pale cheek.

"But it didn't stop my wanting to help and it's been an interesting occupation for me this past week."

She nodded in dumb agreement.

"Now, I don't see the sense in sitting here twiddling my thumbs for the next unspecified number of weeks so I might as well do something that you've been nagging me to do for ages. It doesn't mean that I suddenly think I'm immortal."

"Sorry," she shivered suddenly and then attempted a smile. "I didn't mean to be negative."

"Why don't you take this disgusting cold tea away and fetch one of those bottles of red wine that your parents brought over? Then you can test me on the first lesson."

When Angela arrived at about seven they were arguing amicably over the language tapes.

"It's really grossly unfair," Phil grumbled, as he limped into the kitchen to find a third glass. "All that we're doing is brushing up Caroline's French and I'm still looking for the plume of my bloody tante. Are there any nibbles?" he called cheerfully.

"I'm sorry I haven't been to see you for a few days." Angela helped herself to a couple of black olives and swirled the red wine gently round her glass. "This is very nice," she commented appreciatively. "I wouldn't mind a few bottles of this. Is it from your parents' area?"

"It's her parents' local wine and I'm sure that Caroline could bring you a case or two, next time she goes down by car. Couldn't you darling?"

"Oh yes. The same producers do a very good white wine too. It's lovely as an aperitif before lunch on a sunny day." She gave Phillip an even smile.

While they were discussing the merits of Gascony wine the telephone rang and Phillip went slowly into the bedroom to answer it, supporting himself carefully on the furniture as he went.

"You know this is just a remission," Angela insisted gently, when he'd closed the door.

Caroline nodded. "Yes; Liz was very careful to point it out to me this morning and I don't think that Phil is harbouring any false hopes."

"You're both coping well." Angela's voice was matter of fact.

"He's stronger than I am."

"I don't think that you're giving yourself enough credit," Angela said softly.

"It's going to get much worse."

"He'll seem much sicker," Angela agreed. "But in some ways it'll be easier. He'll sleep for longer and longer and then he'll drift into unconsciousness. He'll be less aware," she added simply, "of the life he'll be leaving behind."

They sat quietly for a few minutes, waiting for him to return.

"Well love," he gave Caroline a broad grin, "I hope you're not going to be cross. Emily's coming to stay for a couple of days next week. She won't be much trouble and Vicky says it'll save her marriage." He raised his eyebrow anxiously waiting for her approval.

"Are you sure you won't mind the noise?" Caroline was a bit dubious.

"It'll be fun and Edward's booked a week in Venice for the pair of them."

"You said a couple of days."

"Yes; she's going to a friend until Thursday, and then she's coming here on Thursday morning. They'll pick her up on Saturday afternoon, on their way back from Gatwick." Philip was pleased with his fait accompli and Caroline smiled at his obvious delight, despite her own apprehension.

"He's going to overdo it again isn't he?" she appealed to Angela.

"I think I'd better go, before I'm forced to take sides. I'll pop in before Emily arrives, but I'll leave you in peace this weekend. Give me a ring if you need anything."

Angela's voice was as calm and cheerful as ever, but Caroline was all too aware of the gentle, implied warning and her body felt leaden as she returned to the brightly lit sitting room. Angela obviously knew that the present stable state couldn't last much longer.

Her mother phoned later, after Phillip had gone to bed. She mentioned casually that she'd been surprised to get another phone call from Alex and that he'd asked to be remembered to her.

She slept badly that night. Coded messages were mixed up in her dreams with smiling brown eyes and a deep, reassuring voice. Strong arms were wrapped around her, but when she woke up she wasn't sure whether they'd been Phillip's or Alex's.

CHAPTER 10

The first thing she noticed, as she opened her eyes, was that the sun was streaming through a gap in the curtains. She sighed with relief and she lay there for a moment, watching the sunlight dancing low down on the wall opposite her, as the breeze from the open window gently lifted the curtains. She was impatient at her own stupidity, but she had an illogical and superstitious belief that Phillip's present, improved health would last exactly as long as this wonderfully unexpected spring weather.

Easter weekend arrived and it was the warmest since records began. The tabloids ran headlines along the lines of 'Phew What A Scorcher' and 'Flaming April' which made Caroline think of poor flaming Jane. She still hadn't resolved the dilemma of whether or not to contact her and, so far, it hadn't seemed appropriate to ask Phil for his views. She was absolutely certain that it would upset him and she didn't want anything to spoil the weekend. They had invited Heather and Cliff, Stan and Prue and Mrs Heath – with Dora, of course – to a barbecue lunch on Sunday and she was determined that they were going to relax and not do a thing at all on Saturday.

Phillip's skin was prone to sunburn at best and now that it looked so thin and so delicately drawn across his bones Caroline fussed around him with high factor creams and a giant sun umbrella, before collapsing next to him in a deckchair.

"You've made me look like a baby's bottom," he grumbled later, when he returned from the house with some cold beers clutched precariously in his free hand.

"Better safe than sorry," she muttered, looking up briefly from her book and giggling at his cream-streaked face.

"Isn't that the woman your mother's planning on doing a travel book with?" He peered over Caroline's shoulder.

"Yes. She lent me one of Francesca's books, just out of interest. This one describes Brittany. I just hope they don't attract hordes of tourists to Gascony." She pulled a face. "What are you reading? I haven't seen that before."

"It's Alexander Buck's latest thriller. Heather bought it for Cliff and he said I could have it first, because he's busy marking examination papers at the moment."

"That's nice," Caroline said and carried on ostensibly reading her book, though her mind wasn't in Petts Wood or Brittany.

Sunday's barbecue went well and at five o'clock they were still sitting outside, although the warmth had gone out of the April sun by then and clouds had begun to build up. Suddenly a few drops of rain fell and Caroline shivered. "Someone must have walked over my grave."

"You know we aren't allowed to make terminal comments," Phillip scolded her.

Everyone laughed, but it was uncomfortable laughter and Caroline felt that the magic of the day had been eclipsed. The party broke up soon afterwards and they all rushed for their houses or their cars to escape the thundery downpour. Only Dora braved the storm and nobly vacuumed the leftovers off the lawn.

"How did you think it went?" Phillip asked later as he lay back, delighting in the luxury of being in bed, after an exhausting day.

"It was fun but you must be worn out," she replied, smiling at him sympathetically. "It went really well right up to the last few minutes."

"That was my fault."

"No," she said thoughtfully. "No, I think it was mine. The sudden rain just changed my mood. I don't know why."

"It's only a thunderstorm you know," he reminded her, "and the sunny weather is forecast to last all next week. Shall we take Emily to Richmond Park on Friday, if it's nice? We could put Dora and a couple of deckchairs in the boot and Vicky said that she'd be bringing her bike."

The contrast between the eager, bright eyes and the pallid, wasted face suddenly overcame her reserve and she put her arms around him, rocking him gently against her and kissing the soft tufts of his newly-emerging blonde hair. He held her tightly to him and she leaned back against the headrest, still cradling his head against her breasts. They stayed like that until she sensed from his breathing that he'd gone to sleep. Then she lowered him carefully onto the pillows and wrapped the bedclothes around him. She tiptoed out of the darkened room and dragged herself up the stairs, overcome with apprehension. She lay for a long time, her eyes fixed on the faint glow cast by a solitary distant street light. The turmoil in her mind matched the raucous discord of the storm.

Phillip had been absolutely correct in his weather forecast. She'd been too distracted to draw the curtains before she'd gone to bed and now the sun was shining low and bright across her counterpane. She still felt confused by her mixed emotions of the previous evening, but in broad daylight the practical streak, inherited from her mother, made her smile at her own stupidity. She was deluding herself if she thought she had any decisions to make. The choices were between her husband – ex-husband even – who was shortly going to die, and a man to whom she had spoken for less than ten minutes, found rather attractive and would probably never see again. Two negatives were not going to make a positive however long she gnawed away at them. What's more, the man in question was rich, famous and entirely out of her league.

She definitely wasn't in love with Phillip. She was more certain of that now than ever. She had reacted to him last night as she would have reacted to a wounded puppy – no more and no less – and she'd have to make that clear today, without hurting his pride. She was fairly sure that his feelings for her fell into more or less the same category, with a bit of "Carry on Nurse" thrown in.

Her thoughts returned to Alex. She wondered whether her mother had been entirely truthful about Alex's phone call. Had he really asked about her? If so what had her mother told him? There was a faint possibility that she would meet him down in France and that was all she could hope for at the moment. She got out of bed decisively and headed for the bathroom, feeling that she could face the day better now that she had put her emotional affairs in order.

The sun must have woken her earlier than she'd realised, because when she put her head round the dining room door, Phil was still asleep and when she went into the kitchen she saw that it wasn't even half past seven. She wandered into the garden with a cup of tea. It was chilly, despite the sun, and she pulled her dressing gown more tightly around her as she drifted around, abstractedly dead-heading the camellias. Dora squeezed through the gap in the fence and pressed her great shaggy body conspiratorially against her legs. Caroline shared her last digestive biscuit with the dog and then turned quickly towards the house as she heard the faint sound of the telephone through the closed windows. No, she must have been mistaken. She stopped and listened carefully. The only sound now was Mrs Heath's voice, raised sharply, the other side of the hedge. Fastidiously, Dora wiped the crumbs from her whiskers against Caroline's dressing gown, leaving a slobbery trail, and loped home obediently. "Filthy beast," Caroline muttered after the dog's receding figure and went back into the house. She thought she could hear Phillip's voice; perhaps he'd been calling her for ages. She hurried towards the dining room and was certain that she heard the telephone being replaced.

He was lying back against the pillows, with his eyes closed and his face had that frightening grey pallor, which she had scarcely seen in all the time that he'd been home.

She rushed up to the bed and put her hand on his forehead. "Are you all right? I don't remember your taking your tablets last night. Are you in pain?"

He smiled at the frantic tone of her voice. "Stop fussing, you silly thing." She picked up the uncertainty in his voice. "I'm still half asleep. I'll be bright as a button once you've brought me a cup of tea. Honestly." He made a lop-sided attempt at a rakish grin and looked at his watch. "Good God woman, it's still the middle of the night."

She stood in the kitchen, stirring the teabags in the pot and worrying. The more she thought about it the more certain she became that the telephone had rung and that Phillip must have answered it. The fact that the caller had unsettled him and that he hadn't seen fit to mention anything to Caroline meant that it must have been Jane. "Oh damn!" She peered into the pot. She'd vented her anxiety on the teabags and now there was a cloud of leaves suspended in the murky brown liquid.

"That was quick," Phillip teased her when she returned at last with her second attempt.

"Quick and perfect," she smiled, ignoring his sarcasm. "By the way, did I hear the phone go quarter of an hour ago?"

"Yes. It was a wrong number. Somebody wanting a number in Liverpool. I can understand someone calling the wrong Grant in Petts Wood, or even in Surrey," he reasoned, "but how can they be out by nearly three hundred miles?"

The trouble with Phil was that he was so plausible, she thought later, stopping with the iron poised mid-way over a shirt. If she were less charitable she decided, stabbing dexterously at the collar, she'd say that he was an inveterate liar, but that wasn't fair really. She draped the shirt carefully round a hanger and smoothed out the folds. His lies were never worse than white lies, but he could never resist embellishing them. He referred to it as 'adding a bit of background colour' she thought, smiling. She was still debating whether or not the caller had been Jane when the kitchen door burst open, making her jump.

"Penny for them," Liz Walsh said briskly. "Sorry, I didn't mean to frighten you. Phil's in the shower, so I popped in for a chat."

"Good, I'll make coffee," Caroline offered. "Any excuse to stop ironing. How do you think he's looking today? "

"Well he's still in better shape, physically, than I'd ever have hoped, but he seems dispirited." She gave a short, caustic laugh. "It's hardly surprising in the circumstances. It's more surprising really that he's managed to remain so consistently cheerful. I don't think that I could," she added, "Could you?"

"No, he amazes me and this weekend he's been so normal – he actually insisted on inviting friends round for a barbecue yesterday."

"He's making a big effort for your sake, I'm sure," Liz pointed out gently, "and that alone must be pretty exhausting. We mustn't begrudge him his off days."

"My niece is staying for a couple of days at the end of the week. Do you think it'll be too much for him? He insists he's looking forward to it, but I'm a bit dubious."

Liz smiled as she stood up to go. "It'll do him a lot of good to see a face that isn't expecting the worst."

"Oh dear. Am I such a picture of gloom?"

"No. Give yourself credit for doing a fantastic job, honestly, but don't fret if he's having a bad day. Leave him to it, give him some space and carry on with your own life for a while. Ironing's the most wonderful therapy," she laughed. "You can do mine as well if you like."

Caroline took Liz's advice and spent the next few days catching up on chores around the house, writing letters and tidying up the flowerbeds under Phil's instruction. Heather had left him another few sheets of information to enter onto the computer, but once he'd done that he was happy to sit outside, pottering around in the sunshine, either reading or sleeping. Caroline wasn't sure whether he was exhausted after his exertions of the past ten days, or whether the mystery phone call had made him more introspective, but he seemed happy to be left quietly to his own devices for a while. She sat in his room on a couple of evenings and watched television with him after he'd gone to bed, but he avoided any physical contact with her and she felt illogically slighted by this.

"Poor chap just can't win", she reflected contritely.

CHAPTER 11

She was up early on Thursday morning, but not as early as the postman. There were two postcards on the hall carpet from Vicky and Edward. One was for Emily – a picture of a gondola being propelled past the Bridge of Sighs by a handsome and lavishly – costumed gondolier – with a very neatly written message on the back. *The weather is super and the hotel is awfully grand. We saw a wedding yesterday. The bride looked really pretty and her gondola was decorated all over with ribbons. We miss you, and we'll see you on Saturday. Love from Mummy and Daddy. xx*

The other card was a picture of the newly restored Doges' Palace in St Mark's Square. Last time Caroline had been to Venice the whole building had been swathed in scaffolding and tarpaulins – now it glittered as if it were encrusted with gold leaf. She shook her head in disbelief when she turned the card over. Vicky had filled every available space with a minute and unintelligible scrawl, leaving only the address and the stamp in a cramped little island.

There was a sound from Phil's room so she went in. He had got up and drawn the curtains. Now he was staring out as if to fix the sight of his beloved garden permanently in his mind's eye. Although the back of the house faced west there was already a small splash of thin, spring sunlight spreading over the end of the lawn. Bright spots of light danced through the new leaves of the cherry trees and across the wrought-iron seat which they had bought when they'd first been married.

"You're up early. Why don't you sit by the window, in the sun, and I'll bring you your breakfast? Here's a card from Vicky and Edward. See if you can decipher it." She watched the tall figure limping across the room, leaning on a single stick, the dressing gown hanging in gaping folds on his thin frame.

"Well, have you made any sense of it?" she asked, five minutes later as she skilfully manoeuvred a small table into place with her toe and set a tray loaded with tea and buttered toast next to him.

"That looks nice," he smiled up at her and she was relieved to see that the greyness and strain had been partly dissipated by a good night's sleep. He looked as relaxed as he had at the weekend. "Bugger off dog. Home!"

They both laughed as Dora tore hersef away from the toast and settled on a position halfway between the breakfast tray and the open French windows.

"I don't know how they've managed to do so much in twenty four hours," Phil said finally, after he'd wiped the butter off his hands and returned to inspecting the card. "They only arrived on Saturday and the postmark is nine o'clock on Monday morning. I thought that the idea of the holiday was to spend a week in bed producing an heir."

Caroline giggled and rested her chin on his shoulder. "Go on, read it to me."

"Well they're staying at the Royal Danieli."

She pulled a face. "Very grand."

"They met a couple at the airport, who live near them – Winchester, I think it says – and they all took the vaporetto to Burano on Sunday. Now there's something about the gorgeous colours of the houses. Yes, the houses are painted in gorgeous, soft tones – the whole place is a living Canaletto." He finished in triumph. "They had lunch on the terrace of a waterside restaurant – recommended apparently in the book that we gave them – and bought some cream lace flowers from an old woman who was sitting, weaving, in the main square."

"Is that all?"

"No," he laughed. "This reminds me of Latin A Level – find a word that you recognise and guess the rest of the plot. Right. I've got it. "Nick and Julia are staying with friends on the Lido, so we probably won't see them again. We had a drink in Harry's Bar on Sunday night and then ate at the Acciughetta – a popular local cafe, behind the Danieli. Hope Emily is no trouble. Love V & E. xx" He suddenly looked intently at Caroline. "Do you think this will work for them?"

"Do you mean the baby, or the marriage?"

He shrugged. "Both, I suppose."

Before Caroline could reply they heard Liz Walsh opening the door behind them. "You two look perky. I wish I felt half as energetic. I've had an awful night. My neighbour was rushed off in the small hours with suspected appendicitis and I waited up with his wife. I don't suppose there's any tea left in that pot? Ooh, that's pretty." She looked at the card, while Phillip limped into the kitchen to fetch another teacup.

"I'd love to go to Venice," she said wistfully. "You know,

he's much brighter again this morning," she mouthed, nodding in the direction of Phillip's retreating back."

"Emily's coming today and he's looking forward to that. He's determined to make an effort for her sake."

"We can all achieve a little bit more if we've got a goal and everyone feels more cheerful if the sun's shining. There. End of homily," she announced.

Emily was delivered just before lunch by a large, cheerful young woman, who disgorged child, suitcase and bicycle from an enormous estate car, which still seemed to have more than its fair share of young occupants, strapped into every available seat, even after Emily had been extracted.

"Heavens, is this a school outing?" Caroline asked, after greetings and introductions were over.

"No, they're all mine. We're off to my mother's for her seventieth birthday. Otherwise we'd have loved to keep Ems for the weekend. I must go before they all start killing each other," she rolled her eyes in mock despair.

She was tall and slim, with straight brown hair tied back with a ribbon. She wore sensible, flat deck shoes, well-ironed jeans and a striped shirt, tucked neatly into a narrow leather belt.

"Suffragette material, or the backbone of the Raj, in another existence," Caroline reflected as she stood waving at the seething carload. Small hands were fluttering from the windows and they heard the final receding shriek. "Bye Em, bye." as the car pulled sedately away.

Emily swung from her aunt's hand, as they walked into the house and then hopped around, chattering, while Caroline unpacked her clothes and Phil admired the bike. "We went to Thorpe Park on Sunday; it was really good, but I was a bit frightened on the big dipper," Emily volunteered. "Uncle Phil says we'll take a picnic to Richmond tomorrow. Can I take my bike? I don't ever fall off now."

Big eyes pleaded up at Caroline and she picked the little girl up and hugged her. "Who's my favouritest niece in the world?" she teased, dumping Emily unceremoniously on the kitchen table.

The child giggled. "Silly, I'm your only one, but I think Mummy and Daddy would like more babies. I think babies are a bit boring." She shrugged non-committally and caught the postcard that Caroline dropped into her hands. "Doesn't it look pretty? Why have the boats got curly ends?"

95

Caroline had to admit that she'd never considered the question and sent Emily to fetch Phillip for lunch. She looked up a moment later to see Phillip coming through the kitchen door, leaning on his stick and Emily propelling herself along behind, at high velocity, on his walking frame. "Watch me, Uncle Phil," she shrieked. "I bet you can't go this fast. I can go really fast on my bike too. Can I ride it on the pavement this afternoon?"

"He's good with children," Mrs Heath commented quietly, later that afternoon, as they watched Phil, in his wheelchair, organising Emily and her bike. The two women were leaning over the dividing hedge, chatting and watching the display of cycling skills. Caroline felt an inexplicable pang of guilt. She wasn't sure why she hadn't conceived, but she was certain it had been her fault – she had refused to undergo the battery of humiliating tests. Mrs Heath must have read her thoughts, because she suddenly put her arm round Caroline's shoulders and said gently, "perhaps it was for the best."

Mrs Heath's words kept coming back to her that evening as she watched Phillip with Emily. The child was bathed and sitting on the sofa with Phil, engrossed in a game of Monopoly. Caroline had been playing but, after landing on Emily's Park Lane Hotel, she had been relegated to banker. As she watched them chattering and laughing her mind floated away.

"Auntie Caroline, you're not listening. I've won and you're not to take any notice of Uncle Phil – I didn't cheat. He's just not as good at Monopoly as I am."

"You landed on my Electricity Company and you didn't pay up."

"You weren't watching, so that's fair."

"Children!" Caroline scolded with mock severity, "this will end in tears, mark my words. You are both to get into bed at once and I'll bring hot drinks."

"Can I just tell you something first, something really exciting?" Emily's eyes were sparkling, although her face looked a bit pale after her long day and the change of routine. "Uncle Mark came to supper last Friday and he brought his new girlfriend. She's called Tessa and she's really, really lovely." Emily looked from one to the other in triumph. "I think Uncle Mark wants to marry her. I asked her if I could call her Auntie Tessa, but everyone laughed and she said she liked just Tessa best." Emily looked at Caroline with a small frown on her face. "Mummy said it was an embarrassing thing to ask, but I don't see why." She shrugged dismissively.

"A very sensible thing to ask in my opinion," Phil agreed. "Anyway, I bet you've concentrated their minds a lot."

She looked at him with her head on one side. "Is that good?"

He pondered for a moment, sucking his lower lip. "Definitely – very good!"

Emily looked thoughtful when Caroline went in to tuck her up. "I like it in your house, but it won't be as nice when Uncle Phil isn't here."

"Well, you make him feel much, much better and more cheerful." Caroline said and gave her niece a big hug and a kiss.

She was tired by the time she'd settled Phil as well, but her mind was restless and she didn't fall asleep for a long time. In fact she was sure that she'd only had her eyes closed for five minutes when Emily came burrowing into the bed with her. "Can I read you a bit from the book that Tessa gave me last Friday? I crept down to look at Uncle Phil but he was fast asleep."

Caroline put her arm round the child and leaned back, still feeling as if she could sleep for hours and half listened, half dozed while Emily read her the story of James and the Giant Peach.

"You are listening aren't you?" Emily gave Caroline a rousing prod. "I'll read you the rest later," she promised, closing the book decisively. "Shall I get dressed ready for going to Richmond? Then I'll lay the table for breakfast. Mummy says I'm really good at laying the table."

"I feel as if I've been on a week's hard labour," Caroline confessed to Liz later. "I'd forgotten that children had such boundless energy."

"Get her to help make the packed lunch and then at least you'll know exactly where she is," was Liz's parting advice.

The magnitude of the preparations seemed entirely out of proportion with the modest scale of the excursion, but by eleven thirty they were heading for the car, having loaded the bicycle, the wheelchair, two walking sticks, the picnic basket, a travelling rug, a couple of deckchairs, Dora, Dora's bowl and a plastic bottle of water.

"She hasn't been sick in the car for ages," Mrs Heath assured them as they drove off.

"If she's sick in the car she can get out and walk home," Caroline muttered to Phil as she drove off.

The Park was fairly quiet, despite the glorious weather, and even the pond was nearly deserted. A middle aged man was helping his grandson to operate a radio controlled boat and two young women were pushing babies in prams.

Emily raced off on her bike, circling the pond with difficulty, on the dried-up, bumpy surface.

"It's nearly twelve years since we last stood next to this pond."

"I should have brought a bag of bread."

"That's not all that's missing."

"It's the wrong pond for a start." She didn't mean to sound sharp, but she didn't want his regrets to spoil the day. "Let's stay here for a bit. I'll fetch the deckchairs."

They were just considering unpacking their lunch, when a school minibus stopped and disgorged a dozen or so large teenage botanists.

"Come on. Let's go on, to one of the wilder stretches. We might see the deer if we go further into the park."

They didn't see any deer, but they suddenly recognised the place where they'd stopped, all those years ago, when Caroline was about to go away to France for three months. She pulled into a lay-by and switched the engine off.

"Your aunt and I stopped and sat under that tree the first time we met," Phil turned round to explain to Emily.

"Did you kiss her?"

"Do you know, I'm not sure. I think I might have. Do you remember darling?"

Caroline tried to sound as deadpan as Phil, but her voice trembled a little with supressed laughter. "Once, perhaps…"

Emily soon lost interest in this line of enquiry. Kissing was soppy.

They unloaded the car and set their sights, wistfully, on a clump of trees several hundred yards away. Then they gazed at the heap of paraphernalia that they'd brought.

"I don't suppose even Hannibal had this much stuff."

"No, and he'd got several hundred elephants."

"Well we have a very serviceable conveyance. Come on, let's load everything onto the wheelchair and Ems can take Dora and the dog bowl." He put the bowl solemnly on Emily's head and she wobbled off, across the grass, balancing very carefully, with the dog lead grasped tightly in one fist.

"She'll be all right as long as Dora doesn't do an emergency stop for a pee," Caroline observed, as she loaded up the wheelchair. "Oh, don't be silly. You can't possibly walk that far. It must be nearly half a mile."

"You can always come back for me if I collapse in the middle and I doubt if it's even quarter of a mile."

Apart from the distant murmur of the traffic and the view of Roehampton, sparkling in the bright April sun, it could have been the depth of the country, they decided, as they looked with satisfaction at their final encampment.

Phillip lay back in the shade, once they'd finished their picnic lunch, half dozing and half watching Caroline making a daisy chain for Emily. They were within two hundred yards of the tree that he and she had lain under, oblivious to the rest of the world, on the day they'd met in Kew Gardens. "What do you think went wrong?" he asked, as Emily raced off on her bike with Dora yapping at her heels. "Do you think that there was something wrong right from the beginning?"

Caroline stretched out on the grass next to him and struggled to formulate an answer. "You wanted children."

"So did you."

"Yes, I did, but you've always felt it was my fault that we didn't have a child."

"I didn't blame you, sweetheart, I just thought that if you'd persevered with the tests we'd have known where we stood."

"I did try," Caroline replied, her voice scarcely more than a whisper.

She could still remember the day now. She'd been to her general practitioner and he'd suggested an appointment with a woman consultant at Charing Cross Hospital. It had been a glorious morning in early September and she'd parked in the large multi-storey car park in Hammersmith and then taken a taxi. There'd been a slight breeze which had ruffled her hair as she'd stood on the edge of the kerb, listening to the roar of traffic from the Hammersmith flyover and she'd worried that she'd be dishevelled by the time she saw the gynaecologist. Phillip had offered to come with her, but she'd insisted she'd be fine on her own.

The hospital was modern and the gynaecology department was decorated in attractive, muted colours. Tanks of tropical fish were grouped around the waiting room, shaded by elaborate arrangements of potted plants. Caroline had felt quite relaxed as she'd listened to the splash of the fountains aerating the tanks, and flicked through a fairly elderly Country Life.

"Mrs Grant," a smiling nurse had called her name and led her off to a small dressing room. The hospital gown had a complete complement of velcro fasteners and she could still remember wondering if that was the main advantage to being a private patient.

She had been quite unprepared, however, for her own reaction to the examination. The gynaecologist, a charming woman who looked far too young to be a consultant at a leading London hospital, tried hard to sooth Caroline, but in the end they'd had to give up. The table with the stirrups, the tray of instruments and the stark brightness of the overhead light had brought back all the memories of that terrible teenage party and the subsequent humiliating questions and physical examinations by the police doctor.

One of the nurses grabbed a bowl – just in time – and Caroline spent nearly an hour weeping and being sick. In the end they had telephoned Phillip and he'd fetched her home. He'd sat up all night with her, talking and soothing and then they'd quietly dropped the matter, but she'd always felt that he'd have liked her to try again. The fault could have been his, of course, she occasionally reasoned, but in the end they had just accepted their childless state.

They sat without speaking for a minute or two. "You resented my parents too." His voice was quiet, but she felt the accusing edge.

"Yes, I did in a funny way, despite the fact that I had never met them. They were an immovable and unassailable presence in our lives and I couldn't compete with them. In death they achieved a state of near-perfection which I, living, was unable to match. Or, at least, that's how it often seemed to me. I suppose it's the same feeling that a second wife has, when she marries a widower – always being compared slightly unfavourably. I don't think that we were ever as happy in Petts Wood as we were during that year in Durham." She put her hand on his arm, and smiled consolingly at him, but he seemed not to see her.

"I know that you've never felt it was our own home. At the time it seemed such a waste of money to sell it and buy another one and, besides, the carpets and furniture were practically new." He shook his head in a gesture of defeat. "I was a fool and I'm sorry I was so obstinate."

"We're both equally to blame you know. Why didn't we have the guts to sort this out ten years ago?"

"Because we just didn't and then it slowly became too late

once the resentments built up."

They were still sitting there, silently leaning against each other, when Emily came panting up to them, her face a picture of indignation and fury.

"This stupid dog!" she spluttered. "I keep throwing sticks for her and she just stands there looking at them with her paw in the air! Stupid dog!" She faced the animal, eyes ablaze with frustration.

Dora gazed happily up at the child while this tale of her inadequacy was poured out.

"Oh darling, you do look hot. Have a cold drink of orange."

Phillip tried not to laugh as he explained the problem. "She's a setter."

"So?"

"Setters don't fetch, they sett."

"What's that supposed to mean?"

"They watch where the object lands, usually a dead pheasant, or something like that, and then they lift their paw and point out where it's gone," he explained patiently to his disgruntled little niece. "So she's showing you where the stick is, so that you can rush off and fetch it yourself."

She stomped off crossly and they heard her mutter, "Stupid bloody dog. Can you bloody believe it!!!"

They shook with silent laughter. "She's been listening to Edward on the phone," Caroline observed.

She smiled as she looked across at Phillip and then glanced back at Emily. They had both fallen asleep in the car before they'd even crossed Wimbledon Common. The first sign of life was a small voice from the backseat. "Do you like fish and chips, Auntie Caroline? They're my favourite."

CHAPTER 12

The kitchen still stank of fish and chips next morning. Caroline was first up and she poked her head around Phil's bedroom door. He didn't move and his voice was dry and faint. "I'll take it more slowly today I think. I'm quite tired."

"That's a good idea. Why don't you have a day in bed? You'll feel much brighter tomorrow if you do." Caroline bustled around the room, drawing the curtains.

"It's not so nice today." Phil's voice was without emotion, but there was no mistaking the finality of his tone. For a moment she couldn't bear to look at him and remained, quite stationary, looking out of the window.

"I'll have to put the deckchairs in the shed. It looks like rain. Still we've been very lucky – it's still only April. It might clear up later." She turned round, but he was just staring into space and he only managed a laboured smile when Emily appeared.

She looked at him with her head on one side. "Why are you dying before granny and grandpa and great-granny?"

As Caroline slipped out of the room she heard Phillip say very solemnly, "because God needs a hand with his garden."

"You're silly. I'm surprised that God wants a silly gardener," and she bounced into the kitchen to help her aunt.

To Caroline's relief Emily's direct approach seemed to improve Phillip's spirits and by the time Edward and Vicky arrived to fetch her he was up and dressed.

"Thank you very much for having her. We had a marvellous time." Vicky looked radiantly happy, as she swooped upon Emily and then hugged Phillip and Caroline. She had her father's dark colouring, like Mark and a suntan always suited her.

Edward staggered in with a large carrier bag. He looked as healthy and relaxed as Vicky.

"Hey. Who's this then?" He seized Emily and threw her up in the air.

Emily was considerably more interested in the contents of the carrier bag, than in the adoration of her parents, so Edward put her down and Vicky distributed the presents. "There's a lot of tourist tat," she mouthed as Emily exclaimed delightedly at a doll in national costume and a pencil-box in the shape of a gondola. The cotton tee shirts were very pretty, but didn't have the same instant appeal as the doll. Phil and Caroline had a joint present – Phil had always admired Vicky's commendable practicality – of a very attractive set of framed, sepia line-drawings.

"We really won't stop," Vicky announced, once the unpacking was over. "Just a coffee would be nice," and she followed her sister into the kitchen, closing the door conspiratorially behind her.

"I'm sure I'm pregnant." Her face was radiant, and she followed her sister round the kitchen, hopping just like Emily had.

"Well, if you carry on like that, you'll drop it on my kitchen floor," Caroline observed rather sourly. "Oh, I'm sorry love. Of course I'm pleased. I really didn't mean to sound cross, but Phil's having a bad day and I'm sure he realises that he's just going to get steadily worse now. He's been in remission for more than a month and we knew it couldn't last." She faltered, unable to continue and Vicky cradled her in her arms, making the little comforting noises that she used to make to Emily when she was a baby.

"I'm sorry. That was tactless and selfish." Vicky sounded abject. "I just feel so happy at the moment that I wasn't thinking straight."

Finally Caroline drew away and wiped her eyes. "No. It wasn't your fault but I'm not very good at being brave. Poor Phil is coping much better than I am. Anyway, you idiot," she gave a shaky little laugh. "How can you possibly know you're pregnant? You only went away for a week."

Vicky looked smug. "I knew I was pregnant the minute I conceived with Emily and I'm just as certain now. We're going to call it Venetia."

"He'll get a bit of stick from the rest of the rugby team," Caroline observed with feeling and a minute later Edward walked into the kitchen to discover the cause of the merriment.

"Well what about Cornetto if it's a boy? Or perhaps you could be more specific about its place of conception," Phillip proposed, sucking his lower lip and giving every indication of careful consideration. "What about vaporetto or …"

"You've got no romance in your soul, that's the trouble with you," Vicky interrupted.

Caroline felt a fleeting pang of envy for her sister, as she saw the way that she and Edward looked at each other. She longed to confide in Vicky about Alex, but they were all getting ready to go and there wasn't really anything to confide. She was a bit old for adolescent crushes, she told herself sternly.

It took her by surprise when Vicky turned away from the car and seized her arm. She led her just out of earshot of the men and whispered, "Who's a dark little horse then? Mother says that she's had six phone calls from the divine Alexander Buck in the last ten days."

Caroline blushed furiously. "He's house hunting near Montegut, that's why he's ringing her."

"That's not what she says." Vicky squeezed her arm encouragingly, and climbed into the car.

"Let me know as soon as you get the results," Caroline called after the departing car.

Phil had retired to bed by the time Caroline walked thoughtfully back into the house.

"I'm curbing your social activities after tomorrow," she announced, sitting on the bed and taking his hand.

"What's happening tomorrow?"

"Mark's bringing Tessa to lunch. I can cancel them if you'd prefer," she offered, scrutinizing his drawn face.

Phillip lay back, with his eyes closed, and an angelic smile on his face. "No, I must see this bird of Mark's. Edward says she's got legs up to her armpits."

"Sounds jolly uncomfortable to me," she snapped, but in the event she was just as impressed by Tessa as the men were.

* * *

Phil struggled to the front door to let them in and Tessa kissed them both as if she'd always known them. She gave no impression of being shocked by Phil's appearance, though Mark cornered Caroline in the garden later to question his sudden further deterioration.

"The deterioration is normal, I'm afraid," she explained. "It was the apparent improvement of the last few weeks that's been abnormal." She gave a dismissive shrug. "Anyway, how are things with Tessa? She's absolutely super. I hope you're not going to get rid of this one."

"I'd marry her tomorrow, but she won't commit herself to anything. I'm still hoping she'll come down to France with me in August for a few weeks, but she hasn't organised her holidays yet. She's very independent and I'm not top priority."

"Well, at least one of us is happy at the moment," and she

described Vicky's euphoria of the previous evening as they walked back into the house with a bunch of garden flowers for Tessa.

"She can't possibly be sure, can she?"

"She insists she is and she was certainly right last time. It would be lovely for them all."

She wrapped the flowers in wet newspaper and went back into the living room. Phil was enthusiastically reading the blurb on the back of a set of tapes. "That's marvellous. Thanks very much. I'm a great fan of his."

"Mark said that you were and I just happened to see them when I was browsing in Waterstone's."

His previous girlfriends had always annoyed him by slipping "we" into every conversation and simpering at him, as if they were mystically joined. Now he felt irrationally cheated because Tessa didn't adopt this affectation. Also, she'd stated her intention of going back to Chelsea tonight, alone, because she had some work to do, which might be occupying her until at least Wednesday.

When they left, after tea, Tessa was happily clutching her bunch of freshly-cut flowers and Mark looked quite put out.

"Nice girl," Phil said, sitting down breathlessly. "Old Mark looks like a lovesick spaniel."

"I think she is very fond of him. You can see that from the way she looks at him, but she's just more independent than his previous ditzy floozies."

"Ooh! Catty!" Phillip exclaimed. "That's not like you. What happened to female solidarity?"

"I was never that keen on Julia – a vacuous little gold–digger if you ask me – and you look tired."

Angela appeared half an hour later. "Sorry I've neglected you. How are things?" She raised her eyebrows questioningly when she saw Caroline's grimace. "I'll take a look at him."

Phillip was half sitting, half lying against his pillows and the skin on his face was ashen.

"How do you feel today?"

"Like death."

"Well, that's lucky," she said briskly. "Are you comfortable, or do you need more pillows?"

"I'm all right like this." He attempted a faint lop-sided grin as the two women left.

Angela gave Caroline a squeeze. "Bear up love. I know that this is a shock after the last weeks, but it had to happen. We'll all be here to help you both cope. The doctor will call tomorrow to adjust the morphine."

Phillip had gone to sleep when Caroline returned to check on him, so she switched his light off and went back into the living room. She couldn't focus her mind on watching television, or reading, so she drifted around aimlessly, tidying the room. She turned over the tapes that Tessa had brought – Alexander Buck reading his latest thriller – and put them on the coffee table... She felt too shaky to look at the publicity photo on the back or to read the blurb. There really was nothing more that she could usefully do. She went upstairs, but she still felt too wide awake to sleep so she stripped Emily's sheets. They had a nice soapy smell to them – soap and small girl – and she pressed them to her face for a moment before remaking the bed.

This is ridiculous, really ridiculous, she decided as she finally crawled into bed. She lay for a long time with her eyes wide open, in a sort of limbo of neither thinking nor sleeping, but suddenly she was disturbed by a noise which she couldn't identify at first. She reached out nervously for the light switch and then realised that it was Phillip's voice, coming very feebly over the baby alarm.

She ran downstairs. "What's wrong darling? Can't you sleep?" He shook his head and she saw the trace of tears on his face. She wiped them away and held his hand.

"I'm sorry to wake you up, but I was frightened. I'm all right now. Will you sit with me for a while?"

She nodded and squeezed both his hands between her own. Neither of them spoke again for a long time. She wasn't sure whether he'd gone back to sleep, as his eyes were closed, so she just sat there gently stroking his hands. She shivered suddenly and walked over to fetch his dressing gown from the armchair.

He spoke behind her, "I'm all right again now. I don't know why I suddenly panicked and you're cold. Do you think that I could have those tapes that Tessa brought? A bedtime story might send me to sleep."

She fetched the tapes and the little portable player that the staff at school had given him – in another lifetime, she thought – and plugged it in. There was a faint whirring sound followed by an introduction and then the voice of Alexander Buck.

Phillip leaned over and turned the machine off. "Are you all right darling? You've gone terribly white."

She shivered again and then gave him a reassuring smile.

"I'm fine, honestly. I just got a bit cold. Turn it back on again and I'll listen to the beginning with you."

She didn't hear the words, just the voice.

The mellow sound washed over her. Phillip was looking a bit irritable now and he turned the tape off again. "You're fidgeting. Are you sure that you're all right?"

"Sorry love," she pulled a contrite little face. "Actually I'm a bit cold and tired. I'll leave you to listen in peace, if you're sure you'll be all right."

She kissed him goodnight and then sat on the bottom stair for a long time listening to Alex's low soothing tones drifting through the door. Finally she went up to bed and lay thinking, comforted by the cool darkness. She smiled as she finally drifted into sleep. No-one could stop her dreaming.

CHAPTER 13

The wide glass doors leading from the kitchen were fully open and Harriet sat at the long table, leaning on her elbows, staring out at the view. She loved this house and its surroundings more than any she'd ever known, more even than the childhood home that she'd so adored. She loved the golden tones of the old stonework, which blended into the golden shades of the garden and the farmland beyond.

In the distance was a field of young flax and next month it would be transformed into a shimmering, pale, blue, heat haze. Nearer to the house rape had been planted, for the first time since Harriet could remember, and even on overcast days the golden gleam gave the impression of perpetual sunshine. Just opposite the gateway was an unplanted meadow and this year the red field poppies had taken over – their brilliance interspersed with the more subtle magenta spikiness of the wild gladioli.

She leaned back and closed her eyes, breathing in the scent of the honeysuckle which was wafting into the kitchen from the courtyard. By the time the family arrived – her heart gave a sudden lurch at the thought of Caroline coming on her own – the sunflowers would be fully out. Last year her neighbour had brought her an enormous bunch of the huge blooms, which she had dried over the winter and, in return, she'd given him a tray of geranium cuttings. She enjoyed the informal bartering system that operated in the depth of the French countryside – La France Perdue – as her Parisian friends scornfully referred to it. Well, the longer it remained lost and unchanged the better.

She swept her newspapers together into an untidy heap and walked into the garden. The dog was lying under a palm tree, his eyes closed, trying to ignore the kitten, who was swinging from one of the palms and occasionally landing on him. "Stop it you little cannibal," Harriet suddenly shrieked, lunging forward to grab him before he could sink his claws into a lizard, which was darting across the warm stones around the swimming pool. "You're a monster." Harriet held the small creature in front of her face and he rested a soft paw on her nose, blinking, unabashed by her admonishments. Harriet gave him a cautionary, playful shake and put him back down.

She walked down the steps and gazed into the clear blue water of the pool. There was a faint scattering of bits on the bottom, but maintenance was Mike's department – he found it relaxing – so he'd enjoy vacuuming that up when he came home. The water was still quite cold but she might be able to persuade him to swim with her after dinner. Swimming naked, late at night, was one of their great pleasures. She stood transfixed for a moment recalling the cool silkiness of the water against her skin and Mike's body touching hers. Good heavens, what was a woman of fifty eight doing having erotic thoughts in the middle of the morning? Mike always predicted the coldness of the water would have a shrivelling effect. She laughed as she turned away from the water to inspect her garden. It was surprising how it actually had quite the opposite effect...

This was a good time of year for garden flowers, before the summer heat inflicted its punishing regime. She picked a bunch of bluebells and smelt the delicate fragrance, then snapped off a small spray of early pink roses. The geraniums were beginning to revive, after their winter hibernation in the courtyard, and their colours in the pots around the pool were fresh and jewel bright. Harriet wandered among them, picking off the dead flowers and rearranging the pots. She checked the skimmers at each end of the pool and lifted a large toad out of one. The kitten rushed to have a look, as Harriet placed the rescued animal gently on the lawn, but he backed off again uncertainly. "Coward," Harriet laughed and watched the large toad amble away in peace.

Every morning Harriet made the same tour of inspection and now she turned reluctantly back towards the house, just glancing quickly at the delicate, bright green tree frogs lined up in orderly formation on the vicious yucca leaves. She wondered idly why they all faced the same way, and which frog made the initial decision.

She was a tall fair-skinned woman, still good looking at fifty eight and rather admired by the Gascon men, who referred to her as 'La Grande Blonde'. She hoped that 'grande' referred to her height, but found herself pulling her stomach in defensively, just in case.... She was taller than Caroline, but otherwise they were very alike, though her blonde curls owed more to a bottle than to nature nowadays. She and Caroline were very similar in a lot of ways, she reflected – the other two were definitely Mike's. They were dark and outward going like him; less sensitive than their mother and sister. Perhaps, though, they weren't as tough deep down. Caroline was certainly demonstrating an unexpectedly tough streak at the moment.

Harriet walked back into the kitchen and the sight of the big clean room brought home to her again, with a pang of misery, her present and immediate problem. Madame Lartigue was no more – yesterday had been her last day at Lasserre – and Harriet's tempting advertisements had only resulted in two enquiries. One had been from a young, single mother, with a three year old child, looking for semi-permanent employment. "Just put it right out of your mind," Mike had insisted with uncharacteristic vehemence. "We are not taking on any lame ducks and that is that!", and the other call had come from a jovial, elderly lady, with four Bassett hounds, who did professional house sitting and pool maintenance for absent owners. She had been just as appalled at the thought of helping in a fully inhabited house, as Harriet had been at the thought of having four extra dogs, so they'd parted on good terms, but with Harriet no nearer her goal.

She couldn't believe that there were really no requests for work and she went through her pile of periodicals again, even more thoroughly. Nothing at all and she was just shoving the whole lot unceremoniously into the bin when she heard Mike's car crunching to a halt on the gravel and the slamming of his car door. "How was the journey?" she shrieked, hurtling towards him, her arms outstretched. He looked tired under his suntan, after his – if it's Tuesday it must be Dusseldorf – tour of the Ruhr Valley. "Come and sit by the pool, and I'll bring you a drink. Do you fancy the rosé? It's nice and cold."

He gave her a squeeze before she could rush off and she bent to kiss him. "I've missed you and I'm going to miss Madame Lartigue even more."

He laughed as she headed for the house. "Well, at least I know now where I stand in the pecking order. I assume that you haven't had any more responses to your ad?" He called after her.

"Sod all! Absolutely sod, bloody, all!" she confirmed, setting the wine down in front of him.

"Never mind love. She'll be back again before the family arrives so I don't know why you're fussing."

"That's all very well, but May and June are just the worst two months she could have chosen. I'm not worried about the cleaning as much as the animals. We're both going to be away a lot and I don't know who I can ask to look after things for us. You've got several business trips lined up and I'd like to spend time with Caroline. I spoke to her yesterday and poor Phillip's declining fast now. Oh dear! I feel so desperately sad for them both and I must be available to help her... afterwards. Then there's Vicky being pregnant... "

"Rubbish! I've never heard such rubbish. She can't possibly know she's pregnant. I'll bet you anything you like that she's not."

"A garden hammock?"

"A garden hammock versus a gas-fired barbecue?"

"Gas-fired barbecues are naff and suburban."

"And extremely convenient."

"All right then. Done! She was right with Emily wasn't she?"

"Honestly, darling I can't remember after all this time, but what I do know is that she's been trying for eight years and the chances of suddenly striking lucky now seem slim... at best."

"Well, pregnant or not, there's still Caroline to think of. Then, on top of all the family problems I've got the book to research. By the way it sounds as if Mark has persuaded this new woman of his to come down in the summer so I hope Madame Lartigue will be back by then – I don't want to be a screaming harridan."

"It won't be the first time and it certainly won't be the last time," he teased her, flinching from the threatened blow. "Anyway, have I missed any family news during the last four days?"

"Not really." She reflected for a moment. "Vicky possibly being pregnant... Phillip... Mark and Tessa... Caroline. She phoned, quizzing me about Alex. She obviously found him very attractive when they met at his book launch but now she's persecuting herself because he's famous and can't possibly be interested in a little nobody like her. I don't know what to say to her."

"I thought you said he'd asked about her when he phoned."

She shrugged noncommittally. "Well he has and I must say he has phoned rather often since he met her, but I'm not sure if that means anything. I can understand Caroline's reservations... He must have plenty of sophisticated literary ladies throwing themselves at him and she's very vulnerable at the moment."

"Let's have lunch. I'm too tired to worry about my offspring at the moment. Isn't that the phone?"

"I'll answer it. You have a snooze for five minutes."

She raced into the hall, willing it not to stop ringing before she got there. "Oui, bonjour! Oh, hello Honor... thank you... yes that would be lovely." It was cool in the hall and she flopped onto the chair and kicked her sandals off. "Well he only got in five minutes ago and he's tired, but I'm sure he'll have revived by tonight." She hooked one sandal back onto the end of her toe and threw it in the direction of the kitten, who was busy removing the tail from a lizard in the open doorway.

Suddenly she realised that Honor had asked her a question and she tore her eyes away from the cat's homicidal activities. "Oh, you poor thing – well you can't possibly give a dinner party if you've got toothache." She listened patiently as Honor protested that it wasn't too painful. "Well the best dentist for miles around is that woman in Peyrusse Haute – Bernadette Tibeau – I'll find her number for you." Then Harriet laughed as she recalled her daughters' preference for Pierre Didier. "There's also an extremely dishy dentist at Vic sur Baise and I'll give you his number as well, but I don't think he's nearly as good."

Honor seemed reluctant to terminate the conversation and Harriet's mind became more and more focused on lunch and her domestic problems. Honor was lonely really, Harriet supposed, and once she started talking she could go on for ages. "No, I haven't had any responses." Harriet was jerked back to attention for the second time. "The main problem is that I'll probably be in England quite a bit and Mike will be away more than usual too. Well, if the worst comes to the worst, the animals will have to go into a kennel and I'll find someone to come over to clean the pool and cut the grass." She listened again, smiling into the receiver. "I couldn't possibly allow you to do that – no. It's very kind, but you're much too busy to take on my domestic problems." She laughed and shook her head. "All right, we'll discuss it tonight and I really do appreciate the offer. Yes, of course – see you tonight and good luck with the dentist."

"What's wrong with you?" Mike asked when they were eating lunch in the shade of the linden tree. "You're looking disgruntled."

"I'm quite gruntled actually, it's just that Honor Kershaw does talk non-stop and she's offered to look after things for us while we're away.

"Well that's very kind of her, darling." Mike patted her hand absentmindedly and carried on surreptitiously reading the front page of The Times.

"Yes I know, but I just don't feel we know her well enough to let her do things like that for us. What do you think?" No answer was forthcoming and Harriet sighed.

Honor Kershaw put the phone down and chewed her lip. She hadn't realised how lonely she'd be on her own in rural France. She'd even begun to wonder whether she'd been a bit hasty in divorcing Laurence. It wasn't that she regretted the loss of Laurence – he'd been boring her witless for the last couple of years – but she hadn't anticipated Simon Chandler digging his heels in, at the last moment, and refusing to leave that pathetic little wife of his.

A large grasshopper suddenly landed on the floor next to her and she was surprised at the solid resistance of its body as she ground it under her foot. She wiped her sandal against the edge of the carpet and walked away from the bits of greenish debris with a feeling of distaste. She went into the garden but it was too hot to sit outside and she wandered into the shade of the adjacent barn. She was using this area as a makeshift studio and she looked around it now with open hatred. Everything about her life was makeshift and tawdry at the moment.

Her mind flitted back to her childhood and the day when she and her mother had moved into her new step-father's house. She'd only been four years old, but she could still remember that feeling of rage and jealousy when she'd walked into that other child's bedroom and seen the obscene display of possessions. Felicity had been aptly named – she was a good-natured, amiable six year old when Honor's mother married her widowed father - and she had tried hard to be kind to the younger child, but she'd been no match for Honor and her jealous tantrums.

In the end her mother and her step-father had been no match for Honor either and her constant demands and her destructive rages had driven a wedge between them and ultimately destroyed their marriage. She'd been just ten years old at the time and it had been her first real taste of her own power.

Honor knew how to make the best of herself, but even the most carefully applied make-up was unable to hide the ugliness of her expression as she looked with naked discontent at the stacked canvases and the disorganised array of paints. Four husbands had failed to provide her with the material comfort and security she craved. The only need which they'd all satisfied, and a faint smile lit up her face at the thought, was the need to grab what wasn't hers. She'd wrecked four marriages, seduced the barely – protesting husbands of four devastated women, and now she'd suddenly been out-manoeuvred by Simon Chandler's silly bitch of a wife.

Well, everyone was entitled to make one mistake, but at fifty seven she couldn't afford to repeat the failure. She suddenly thought back to the previous Thursday and her discontented expression gave way to a speculative smile which transformed her face. That had been a good evening and it had certainly sent her thoughts off at an unexpected tangent.

She'd been pushing her trolley around the local supermarket, buying a lone artichoke and a punnet of strawberries when Mike had hurtled round a corner and crashed his trolley into hers. Harriet was away and, like her, he was doing bachelor shopping. They'd laughed and then they'd chatted for a while. Finally she'd suggested that he replace his single state rations and have dinner with her instead.

She picked up her brush and stood in front of the easel. Before she'd phoned Harriet she'd been working on a large water colour of the distant hills with a church spire and a lonely poplar tree on the horizon, but suddenly the light was all wrong and she couldn't take it up where she'd left off. The paint had long since dried on her brush and she realised that she had been staring at the unfinished canvas for the best part of half an hour.

Mike was an attractive man and they'd really got on well. She wondered whether he'd told Harriet that they'd had dinner together. She'd discover this evening when they came round for a meal, because they'd be bound to mention it at some stage if he'd told her. She'd have to work at persuading Harriet to let her feed the pets and keep an eye on the pool.... She could suddenly envisage herself enjoying life by the pool on a more permanent basis – and, apparently, there was a very nice flat in Pimlico too....

CHAPTER 14

Caroline and Angela were sitting opposite each other in the sitting room. It was nine o'clock and the rain was still falling steadily. It had been raining all day and the leaves, which had collected in the gutter outside the sitting room window, were forcing the water to overflow in a maddeningly persistent stream. Angela was coming every evening now and Caroline realised the significance of that.

"What I just don't understand is how it could happen so suddenly. Last Friday he was walking across Richmond Park and eating fish and chips with Emily. Now, a week later, he's barely able to spend more than an hour a day out of bed. Is this how it normally happens?" Her eyes looked red and tired as she searched Angela's face for an explanation.

"I'm afraid that nothing is normal in this game. The disease itself is an abnormality, after all." She gave Caroline an encouraging smile. "He was lucky to have those last few weeks. He rallied to an extent that none of us would ever have predicted. Now he's slipping away fast and he's not in pain so I think that it's better like this. It's the way that I'd want to go," she added.

After Angela had left Caroline went into his room. He was asleep and his breathing was very quiet. At first she'd been frightened that he wasn't breathing at all, but then she'd seen the faint fluttering of the skin at his throat. He'd been listening to his tapes when he'd fallen asleep and she gently disentangled the wires from his hands. He was using headphones nowadays, because he sometimes woke up in the night and didn't want to disturb her.

He didn't realise, she thought guiltily, that he was listening to the only sound that she longed to hear. Sometimes during the day, in his short periods of wakefulness, he listened without the headphones and then she came and sat quietly next to him. Now she turned everything off, except for his small nightlight, and steeled herself to make the phone call that she'd put off for so long.

"Jane? This is Caroline Grant."

The following Saturday, Caroline left Prue to watch over Phillip. "You'll recognise her, because she's got gorgeous auburn hair and she's about your height and build – perhaps a tiny bit more buxom."

Prue glanced down modestly at her own magnificent bust. "But not quite on my scale."

Caroline saw her as soon as she walked into the cafe. She was sitting at a corner table and she had the fragile beauty and wonderfully translucent skin that often goes with auburn hair. She was wearing a pale green tee shirt, which enhanced her colouring and off-white linen trousers. Caroline felt very ordinary as she walked towards her and shook the other woman's hand.

"Jane Osborne," she said quietly, as they sat down facing each other.

They were awkward with each other at first and then started talking at the same time. "Sorry..." they both continued simultaneously and then they laughed selfconsciously. The ice was partly broken and Caroline gestured that Jane should speak first.

"You'd already split up, you know, several months before I met him," her tone was defensive and Caroline smiled and nodded her assent. "We had a marvellously happy three months and then of course he realised that something was wrong. He'd tried to believe, for ages, that it was indigestion and when they finally operated it was already too late. You know all this don't you?"

"Yes, we used to meet occasionally for a drink. I always thought that he seemed more relaxed after he met you." Caroline gave her companion an encouraging smile. She guessed that Jane was younger than her – definitely not thirty yet.

"I stayed with him until he'd recovered from the operation and then, of course, he went back to work, in between his courses of treatment, but as soon as he began to look... you know," she hesitated in her anxiety to find a word that wouldn't sound too harsh, "... different and then to lose his hair... "A single tear rolled down Jane's face and Caroline pressed her paper napkin into her hand. "Well, then he said that it was all over and that he didn't want to see me again."

"He didn't want to be harsh but he just couldn't bear you to see him looking so terribly changed," Caroline said gently. "He's very vain you know and the loss of his looks was the bitterest blow of all."

"I was very depressed when I saw your wedding photos," Jane smiled. "Both of you so good-looking, that I got an awful inferiority complex. And you're still stunning, of course."

Caroline felt embarrassed and muttered something incoherently flattering in return. Jane looked grateful and continued speaking. "When I heard how much better he was after he came out of the hospice I began to wonder if there'd been a mistake in the diagnosis, but I know that he's declining quickly now."

She saw a look of surprise flash across Caroline's face and she blushed. "My mother knows Sally very well – Sally Heath – so I sometimes phone her for news. I hear that Dora's adopted Phil."

"She was asleep under his bed when I left." They both sat for a moment, lost in their own thoughts. Finally Jane broke the silence.

"Did you meet anyone else? Oh, I'm sorry. I had no right to ask you that."

"I don't mind," Caroline assured her. "No, I just left because I didn't think that our marriage was working any longer and I was pleased when Phillip met you. I'm sure that he intended marrying you."

"No." Jane's voice was firm, "No, I don't think that it was ever more than a fling for him. I always felt that he wanted you back." She shrugged as Caroline shook her head vigorously. "Well we'll never know now, so there's nothing to be gained by speculating, I suppose."

"I'll ring you if the situation changes." The euphemism wasn't lost on Jane and she nodded, swallowing hard to maintain her composure. "You're still at the same address are you?" Caroline asked, trying to change the subject.

"Yes, I'm actually in the middle of buying a flat in Chislehurst, but it won't be ready until the first week of September. I'm staying with a friend from the office at the moment and although there's plenty of space at her house, I can't stand her boyfriend, so it's not ideal."

Caroline felt a tremendous sympathy for the younger woman and she hugged her when they parted. "Be brave and I'll be in touch," she promised her. For no discernible reason she went home feeling better able to cope.

Mrs Heath was pottering in the garden when Caroline drove up. "Guess who I've just had coffee with?" She gave Mrs Heath a knowing little smile and was amused by her neighbour's uncomfortable expression.

Prue raised her eyebrows questioningly when Caroline walked in. Phil had fallen asleep, sitting almost bolt upright, dwarfed by the mountain of pillows. They tiptoed out, closing the door slightly and sat down in the kitchen. "He was awake for about an hour. In fact we were discussing the prospect of a single

European currency and he was just as opinionated as ever. He fell asleep about five minutes before you got home," Prue finished her progress report. "Well, how did you get on?"

"You've met her, so you know that she's a very pretty girl – scarcely more than twenty five, I should think – and, I'm sorry to disappoint you," she laughed, "but I liked her a lot and we got on well."

Prue nodded. "I had heard that she's a very nice girl." Her voice was slightly cautious.

"Don't worry. I know there's a spy in the camp. I expect there's a radio receiver in Dora's collar."

"Idiot," Prue giggled. "But they do know each other very well. Is she going to come and see Phil?"

"No. I think that it would upset him and it wouldn't achieve anything now. But I promised that I'd keep in touch. I felt very, very sorry for her actually."

After Prue had gone Caroline liquidised some vegetables for Phil's lunch and put it on a plate, then she reluctantly removed more than half of it. She sighed as she fluffed it up with a fork in an attempt to make it look more appetising.

He was awake again when she took the food in and she sat with him, trying not to look anxious. Angela had brought him a sheepskin under blanket, and a cradle to keep the bedclothes from pressing onto his legs, but he was spending so long in bed now that it was difficult to keep him comfortable.

He took a few spoonsful and then smiled wanly at Caroline. "I don't want any more," he said in a hoarse whisper and she knew that he wasn't talking about the food. She took the plate away and when she came back he was asleep again. She sat next to him, with her eyes closed and must have drifted into a light sleep herself because she suddenly heard Phil's voice again. "Caroline."

"Yes darling," she leaned over to catch the faint words.

"I don't want any bloody vicar choosing my hymns. I want the two we had when we got married." He stopped for a moment. His breathing was laboured and she helped him to sit up. "*Lord Of All Hopefulness* was the first one and the other one was *Love Divine*. I bet you'd forgotten."

She nodded, not trusting herself to speak.

"So had I," he confessed, "but I found the Order of Service in the hall drawer. And your father read that poem – *If* – by Rudyard Kipling. Do you think he'd mind doing it again?"

He lay back again and she let him down gently onto the pillows.

"What are you going to do with the ashes?"

"What would you like me to do?"

"Well, they'd be awfully good for the roses..." He'd gone to sleep again and she felt very alone and frightened.

Angela arrived at about eight o'clock that night and went straight in to see him. She was just as brisk and cheerful as usual and Phillip woke up briefly.

"Well, how are you? I hear you've idled around in bed all day."

"Yes, but I'm getting bored now. I don't think I'll stay much longer." A flicker of a smile passed across his gaunt face.

"You should try to sit outside for an hour tomorrow, the forecast is good."

"I think I fancy a more radical change of scenery." He winked at Angela and then dozed off again.

She pursed her lips thoughtfully as she ushered Caroline out of the room. "Have you eaten anything today?"

"I had a toasted teacake this morning with the other woman." She tried to sound light hearted but it wasn't a success.

"Right, let's go and make supper. I was only going to stop for ten minutes, but you're obviously not looking after yourself."

They rummaged around the kitchen for a few minutes in companionable silence and then Angela asked casually. "So what was she like then?"

"Hmm, poor girl," was her only reaction to Caroline's description of their meeting, but she looked thoughtful.

They went and sat in the living room after they'd eaten, and talked quietly with the doors open, listening for sounds from Phillip. "He's sleeping peacefully," Angela whispered, after she'd just had another quick look.

Suddenly Caroline felt herself blush as Alex's voice came quietly through the open doors. "Mark's girlfriend brought him the tapes of a book and he listens to them when he can't sleep. Sometimes he uses headphones, but they're a bit of a fiddle if he's feeling tired."

She tiptoed into the hall and popped her head round the door. She could see his hand reaching feebly for the volume control, but she didn't disturb him. "He's all right," Caroline announced, sounding brisker than she felt.

Angela gave Caroline a shrewd glance. "This man's got rather a gorgeous voice." She raised her eyebrow enquiringly as Caroline blushed for the second time. "Do you know him?"

"I met him at the launch of his latest book. I went along with my mother...she knows him and he's planning on buying a house near my parents in France."

"Does he look as sexy as he sounds?"

"Yes." There was an edge of sadness to Caroline's voice and Angela didn't pursue the subject.

"My turn." Angela got up and walked softly across the hall. She didn't come back and Caroline suddenly felt that the sound of the tape recorder was increasing and filling her head in a terrifying crescendo. She knew that it was illogical – it was the same quiet background buzz – and nothing had changed at all. But it had, of course, and she suddenly knew the reason with frightening clarity.

Angela met her in the hall. "Yes, it's all over and he looks very peaceful."

Caroline didn't know what she'd been expecting but Phillip didn't look any different now – just more relaxed if anything.

Angela led her to the bedside chair. "Sit with him, while I call the doctor." Then she walked round to the radio. Caroline anticipated that she would switch it off, but instead she turned the volume up slightly.

Phil's hand was still warm. she stroked it gently, as she had on so many evenings during the last two months and listened to Alex's reassuring voice.

Angela returned with a cup of coffee. "Here. I've put a drop of brandy in it." They sat side by side and waited for the doctor. Saturday, May the first, Caroline thought. Exactly three months since he'd gone into the hospice. The consultant had been accurate in his prediction.

She phoned Jane while the doctor was with Phil and the poor girl arrived looking wan and red eyed. Caroline left her alone with him. There was a tapping at the kitchen door and Prue walked in looking anxious. One glance at Caroline's face was enough. By the morning the room was full – Mrs Heath and Heather had arrived as well.

Harriet and Mike arrived at lunchtime, having caught the early morning flight from Toulouse. Everyone else had arrived by ten o'clock. Caroline stayed calm, dry-eyed and almost disconnected, while feverish activities went on around her. Jane moved into the house to keep her company.

"It's weird you know," Edward said to Vicky as they drove home on the second day. "They sit there, side by side on the sofa, like the Indian widow and the concubine, waiting for suttee."

"Jane has been staying at the house since the night Phillip died. There's absolutely no resentment between them and I don't think I've even seen either of them cry yet. I'm sure it's because they're sharing their grief that they're able to cope with it. I know we're all here to do the practical things, but if every single one of us vanished overnight I'm not sure they'd be particularly affected. It's peculiar, but I almost feel as if I'm looking at a stranger at the moment, even though Caroline and I are normally so close. She's completely withdrawn into this other relationship."

"You mustn't resent that she's found a way of dealing with her grief."

"Oh, I don't resent it at all; I'm relieved to see her so composed in the circumstances. I'm just surprised to see this sympathy developing between them when I'd have expected to see wariness, at least, or even open animosity."

"I wonder what Phil would have made of it? Don't you find it strange that we're all here without him? It's almost like a birthday party without the star performer."

They drove on in silence for a while and then Vicky slipped her arm around the back of his neck. "You know I'm seeing the doctor tomorrow?"

"Will he be able to confirm anything so soon?"

"I don't need confirmation," she said smugly. "I know."

The funeral was arranged for a week Thursday and Caroline was too involved with all the preparations to spend much time brooding.

"Have you got anything black to wear? Do you want me to go out and buy you something?" her mother asked with a little worried frown.

"No, I shan't wear black." Caroline thought back to the skimpy blue frock that Phil had always liked and had come so close to removing, twelve years ago on Richmond Common.

In the end Caroline had worn cornflower blue and Jane had worn emerald green. Caroline walked down the aisle, holding her father's arm and looking straight ahead, her face composed into a slight smile. Jane came next, holding Harriet's arm and the rest of the family followed. The crematorium was packed and some extra seats had been squeezed in at the back.

Vicky kept her arm through Edward's and tried to be as strong as her sister, but a few tears broke through and she just left them to roll down her face. It was the sight of the two women wearing what were obviously his favourite colours that was so unbearable to watch. Edward pressed her arm closely against him and she blinked back the rest of her tears. She wished she could share her own happiness with her sister – she'd had the result of her pregnancy test the previous evening.

Tessa held Mark's hand tightly and gave a huge sigh as they walked back to their car. "I couldn't have been so brave... not if it had been you."

Mark's heart lurched. They had known each other for two and a half months and it was the nearest that she'd come to making any sort of commitment. In fact Phillip's death had altered their relationship in more ways than he'd expected – she'd rearranged a couple of very important clients in order to take two days off. Yesterday she'd left the flat before him and he'd found her at Caroline's house, preparing food, doing flowers for the crematorium, and bullying the Red Cross into removing the hospital fittings.

"The flowers made all the difference, you know. The crematorium would have looked so impersonal otherwise."

"Yes," Tessa said simply, "And I'm glad for Caroline that so many people turned up. I hope we made enough food yesterday. Do you think that they'll all come back to the house?"

By the time Caroline had finished speaking to all the members of the congregation and thanked the vicar, she felt exhausted and sat silently in her parents' car as they drove home.

Quite a crowd of people were already at the house when she arrived back, but there were plenty of helpers and she slipped quietly up to her room and lay down. She longed to sleep The doctor had given her sleeping tablets, but she hadn't taken them and now she felt almost deliriously weary. Then she suddenly and illogically remembered Angela's words, weeks and weeks ago, about not letting Phil sleep, because he wouldn't sleep that night. She staggered off the bed and splashed cold water on her face, then gazed critically at the result. She looked terrible, but widows were meant to look terrible, so that was all right. The house was packed and the noise was deafening. Phil had always been incurably sociable, so he'd have been gratified by the turn-out, she decided, as she slipped between the noisy groups, trying to remember all the mourners' names.

By seven o'clock everyone had gone except for family and close friends. "For God's sake woman, sit down," Edward insisted and pressed her down onto the sofa. She offered no resistance as he lifted her legs onto a cushion and removed her shoes. "Don't move. I'm getting you a whisky," and he returned with one for both of them. "There are enough people racing round, clearing up. You have a rest while you can." He squeezed onto the sofa next to her. "Now you can't move."

She capitulated and suddenly found that she was being drawn into a perfectly normal conversation. Edward told her about Vicky's positive pregnancy test and she was thrilled by the delight written all over his face. Her mother joined them next and Caroline felt the strangely disembodied sensation of being a fly in a far distant corner of the room watching three completely unknown people having a conversation. She saw Jane talking to Tessa and Mark in the hall doorway and they smiled across at each other.

Her mother's voice cut into her thoughts. "Well, she insisted and I think she's awfully lonely since her divorce, so in the end I agreed. I was actually very grateful, because poor old Doodle is too ancient to put in the kennels now."

"Sorry mother, I missed the beginning of that. Who's lonely and what's that about Doodle?"

"I think Dad and I told you about her at our anniversary party. She's called Honor Kershaw and she's rented a house in the village for six months. She's an artist and she's come down to get over her divorce and do some serious painting. Anyway, we've got to know her – at least I have more than your father – and when she knew I was looking for someone to feed the dog and so on, while we were away, she volunteered. I was a bit embarrassed about accepting at first but she said she'd enjoy doing it and I think she finds life in Peyrusse Haute awfully dull after London."

Edward laughed. "You want to watch it you know. You'd better keep Mike on a lead if there's a free range divorced lady roaming around – they're notoriously predatory."

"Did I hear my name being mentioned?" Mike came up and sat on the end of the sofa, putting his arm around Caroline.

"Edward thinks you're about to be devoured by Honor Kershaw, darling. What do you think? Will it be safe to let you go back without me next week?"

"I'll try my best to fight off her advances, but she's a big powerful woman. If she's really lusting after my body I may just have to give in."

"Come on." Tessa suddenly appeared with a large tray. "It's time this girl ate some real food."

"I'll stay on for as long as you need me," her mother announced. "Will you be able to manage without the car, darling?" she asked Mike. "Mark will give you a lift back to the flat."

Jane offered to stay too, if she wanted her, just as she had every night since Phillip had died and now, as Caroline watched the rest of her family preparing to leave, she was struck by the most frightening feeling of emptiness that she'd ever experienced in her life. The tension and hard work which had sustained her previously had been swept away and all that was left was a terrible gaping sense of anti-climax. She couldn't remember ever being as grateful for company as she was that night.

CHAPTER 15

Caroline lay in bed next morning, feeling sweaty with panic and terror, confronted as she was by this sudden prospect of endless solitude. Her limbs were leaden and her life was without purpose. "I know we'd parted," she explained to her mother when Harriet appeared with a cup of tea, "but he was still there for me to talk to and discuss things with. We often had dinner together and we were truly good friends; we actually cared about each other. Now that's all gone for good and I'm frightened of facing life without him."

Harriet sat on the edge of the bed and stroked her daughter's hand. "Of course you'll miss him. You mustn't ever try to forget him, but in time you'll learn to enjoy the memories and not be distressed by them."

"Would it have been much worse if we'd still been living together as husband and wife? I suppose it would have been, especially if we'd had children. Phillip wanted children more than anything. I failed him I'm afraid."

"He told me about your panic attack when you went for a fertility test and he sympathised. He felt guilty too, apparently, because he didn't go for tests and he might have been the one with the problem. He told your father this, when we were at Alex's book launch and your father came round to mow the lawn."

Caroline nodded and sipped her tea. "Heather says we must always look forward, never backwards, but sometimes it's hard not to have regrets."

"You shouldn't have any regrets, sweetheart – absolutely none at all. No one could have done more than you did in the last few months and Phillip was terribly grateful. He told me that his greatest regret was that he let you go in the first place."

Caroline rummaged under the pillow for a tissue and hiccoughed great sobs into it. "That's not fair, though, because Jane made him very happy. He was much happier with her than he'd been latterly with me. The saddest thing is that he died before he could marry her."

The phone rang while they were talking and Harriet answered it.

"That's really kind of you to offer. She's just here, have a word with her. It's Tessa," she said handing the phone over. She walked around the bedroom while Caroline was talking and then pulled the curtains back to look outside. The garden had been Phillip's great joy and within the confined suburban space he had created a glorious, mysterious wilderness – a planned profusion of shade and light; flamboyant colour and riotous greenery. She stood and stared until she heard the sound of Caroline replacing the telephone. His presence was everywhere. She wondered whether it would be easier for Caroline to grieve while she remained in this state of total immersion. The more painful thing, perhaps, would be to open a drawer, in the future, and suddenly find a single unexpected memento.

"Tessa offered to cancel her appointments for the day if we needed her. I wouldn't let her, but she's very kind. Mark's really picked a winner this time."

"It's taken him long enough," Harriet sniffed, "although Julia wasn't too bad I suppose."

"She was the best of an undistinguished bunch. That's all you can say for poor old Julia."

"Darling! That's unlike you to be so catty."

"It made me cross to see him manipulated by such a string of vacuous bird-brained trollops. But you're right – she was the best and I felt quite sorry for her at your party. She looked such a sight in that dress and Mark was so obviously irritated by her. I hope she'll find someone else to appreciate her." She lay back against the pillows for a moment and thought about a more specific "someone else" but this morning she found it difficult to bring his face into focus. She heard her mother pouring another cup of tea and she relinquished the blurred image.

"I wonder if this is permanent." Caroline returned to the subject of her brother. "What do you think?"

"Who knows. He's bringing her down to France in August. They're coming for three weeks, so that might settle things, one way or the other. He's almost thirty one and she's twenty nine, so they're hardly children. Have you said anything to him? I wouldn't dare," her mother said, pulling a face.

"No. He poured his heart out to Phil, but that must have been nearly three months ago. I don't think he'd even held her hand then, so I imagine that's a bit out of date now."

"Mmn... yes, but she won't move into his flat because she's based in Chelsea and Docklands is much too inconvenient. It's time he stopped being a yuppie and bought something sensible in... in..."

Nowhere seemed to spring readily to mind.

"Westminster," Caroline announced firmly. "That would be a good compromise."

Her mother disappeared to get dressed but Caroline still couldn't bring herself to get up. For three months her life had revolved solely around Phil's requirements and she couldn't bear the thought of going downstairs to face the empty room. She hadn't had a moment to think about it before the funeral, but now she felt aimless – there was no shape to her life.

She heard the sound of Jane and her mother talking on the landing and finally there was a tap on her bedroom door. Jane was already fully dressed. "I couldn't sleep last night so I decided to get up and go to work." She shook her head as Caroline began to protest. "No, really – I think I will. I must try to return to normal and your mother's going to be here. I've just spoken to her and we've agreed that I'll come back for the weekend while she spends a couple of days with your father. Otherwise she won't see him before he goes back to France. You don't need us both and we're not helping if we're just sitting around moping. I'll be back tomorrow morning. What will you do today?"

Caroline smiled at the subtle hint. "You're right. We must all try to get back to normal and I promise that I'll do something today – I don't know what, but something. Weed the garden perhaps or clear out some kitchen cupboards. Have a good day at work and I'll give you a progress report tomorrow." She heard the front door close twice while she was dressing and there was a note from her mother leaning against the kettle.

> Darling! Gone shopping. See
> you in an hour. I'm expecting a call
> from Dad, so will you listen out
> please? Love M xx

Caroline took a deep breath and looked into the dining room. It was eerily unchanged. There was absolutely no indication that it had ever served as a sickroom. She'd been aware of Tessa giving directions to the Red Cross driver, but she hadn't realised how thorough she'd been. The dining room table was gleaming and smelt of polish. There was a bunch of trailing nasturtiums in a silver rose bowl on the side board and the only tell-tale signs, Caroline noticed, biting her lip, were the four dents where the wheels of the

127

heavy hospital bed had pressed down on the carpet. Each dent was slap in the middle of a fried egg and it was this irrelevant observation that released the tears.

"It's the wheel marks in the middle of the fried eggs," Caroline explained when Harriet came back and then she sat, leaning her head on the dining room table, half weeping and half laughing at her ludicrous answer. "It's this awful carpet. Mark said once that the pattern reminded him of American breakfasts. I've always hated it, but I just felt terribly upset suddenly, seeing the dents from Phillip's bed. Why are the trivial things so upsetting?"

"It's like having a very painful graze on your knee. Everything that brushes against it is just agonising. Come and have a coffee in the kitchen – I've bought a couple of Danish pastries. Did your father phone? Oh! That'll be him now – shall I answer it?"

Caroline heard the distant murmur of her mother's voice coming through the hall door and had a vague feeling that she wasn't talking to her father. There was a distinctly social tone to her mother's conversation, so she was quite prepared when she called her to the phone. She was less prepared for the voice she heard at the other end.

"That was a nice surprise. Your father gave him the number apparently."

Caroline sensed her mother was fishing for information, but there really wasn't any to impart. She remembered people describing what it was like to be introduced to the queen – a glow of pleasure, but absolutely no recollection of the actual words exchanged. His voice had been warm and sympathetic and he'd promised to call her again, but he hadn't suggested a meeting. "He just phoned to sympathise – that's all."

Her mother nodded, obviously not entirely happy with the paucity of the information, but unable, for once, to find a way of extracting any more. "Good. Well I'm sure he'll keep in touch."

Neither of them mentioned Alex's call again, but Caroline felt buoyed up by it all afternoon as she attacked the weeds and the overgrown lawn. In fact the feeling of well-being lasted right through until nine o'clock when her mother suggested watching television. It was the last episode of the serial that Angela had said they might enjoy watching, three months ago. They had never watched it, not even once, so she realised she was being illogical, but the association was enough and she pleaded tiredness. She managed to reassure her mother that she was just exhausted after a day in the garden, but it was late that night before she slept, her head still buried in the pillow to stifle her sobs.

"You look brighter this morning," Harriet remarked when she came in with tea on Saturday morning. Funnily enough, despite the previous night's tears, Caroline actually felt better. Perhaps grief wasn't a bottomless pit. Perhaps it was possible to pump the pit dry of all the tears in the end. "I'm going over to the flat until tomorrow afternoon, to see your father. Jane said she'd be here before lunch. Will you last until then on your own?"

It was ten o'clock when Harriet finally left and Caroline was alone in the house for the first time in nearly three months. There was a time when she would have welcomed the solitude, but today it wasn't solitude it was oppressive loneliness and she didn't know how to deal with it. Her first instinct was to rush across the road to see Prue, or slip through the fence to talk to Mrs Heath and Dora. No, she had to face up to this and sooner rather than later, she decided as she paced up and down the kitchen, fitting her feet carefully into the tiles and avoiding the cracks. The silence echoed around her – she could hear her own breathing and the soft slap of her shoes on the plastic floor. She wondered how long she'd take to go mad if she carried on living alone. Jane would probably arrive in about an hour's time. She should try to achieve something in that hour to prove to herself that she was coping. She suddenly remembered that she'd noticed, that morning, that the linen cupboard was in a mess so she struck off upstairs with the kitchen steps.

Double duvet covers, single duvet covers, valances, sheets, bath towels... she was just ticking off the neatly folded linen to the tune of an old Beatles' song, when she heard Jane opening the front door. "I'm in the airing cupboard," she shrieked, wobbling on the steps in her effort to shout around the door. "I've nearly finished – put the kettle on and I'll be down."

"How are you feeling?" Jane scrutinised her for a moment as they sipped the hot coffee but she didn't wait for an answer. "You look brighter actually. Is there any news?"

"Alex phoned to offer his condolences."

"And... ?"

"And nothing. He said he'd phone again."

"Well I'm sure he will in that case and now I'm going to

make lunch for you. I'm glad I went back to work yesterday, you know. I feel as if I've re-joined the world. How was your mother?"

"It was nice having her here and I still feel terrified on my own. I thought I'd go mad this morning until I remembered the airing cupboard needed sorting out. And I really had to screw myself up to actually do it. What's the plan for this weekend?" She watched Jane pottering about the kitchen and felt immediately comforted by the bustle and companionship.

"Tell me where you met Phillip?" Caroline was taken aback by Jane's non sequitur. "I met him in The Science Museum of all places," Jane continued.

"Kew Gardens and then we went on to Richmond Park. Why do you ask?"

"Would it be silly to spend the weekend revisiting those places? Perhaps it would be silly, but it might just be helpful to go back together. Oh dear! Tell me if you think I'm being a maudlin fool."

Caroline considered the proposal for a moment or two. "Where shall we go first? Let's drive in to The Science Museum this afternoon and go to the parks tomorrow. He used to get cross with me for not being very interested in scientific things."

* * *

It was the first time Caroline had driven for nearly a fortnight and it felt peculiar to be in charge of her own life again – peculiar but reassuring. Central London was congested but they weren't in any rush. In some ways they were dreading actually arriving and it was quite nice to sit in traffic jams – almost in a state of suspended animation.

"I'd forgotten how busy it is at weekends," Jane whispered as they weaved through the crowds of visitors at the museum, conscious of the sharp clattering of their heels as they hurried across the shiny expanses. "We met upstairs – looking at some funny knitting machine." She led the way and then looked around, confused for a moment. "There!" She walked up to the huge showcase and then gave Caroline a stricken look. "He was standing next to this plaque and I was the other side. He walked round and then he started to explain that it was a sort of forerunner of the computer. It seemed perfectly normal to stand there chatting to a total stranger. It was a terribly hot day so he asked me if I'd like to go and have an ice cream. This was the only thing I looked at in the museum and then we walked to South Kensington and sat outside a little cafe with ice creams and mineral water."

"Do you want to wander around on your own for a bit? Would that be better?"

Jane took hold of Caroline's arm and drew her closer. "No, I think it's better with you here, because he talked about you straight away, as soon as we got outside. I don't think then that he believed your marriage had broken down irretrievably."

They walked slowly around the huge display several times, totally immersed in their own recollections until Jane stopped dead and leaned her face against the cool, protective glass. "That's enough I think. Let's go and have the ice cream."

They crossed Cromwell Road and headed for South Kensington, but the small ice cream parlour had vanished and been replaced by a temporary Sue Ryder shop. "Well perhaps that's a good thing," Jane murmured. "We've had enough nostalgia for one day. But I think it's been therapeutic in a way."

They drove home in near silence, both too involved with their own reminiscences to talk, and made supper in the same preoccupied silence. They stood on the landing for a long time after supper, their arms around each other in a comforting embrace and later Caroline lay staring wide eyed into the darkness, unable either to sleep or to cry, listening to the soft, barely discernible sound of Jane crying gently.

Jane looked tired next morning and her freckles stood out harshly against the unnatural pallor of her skin. "I'm afraid I'll be nodding off in the car today – I didn't sleep very well last night."

"We needn't go, you know, if you don't feel like it. Let's just sit in the garden today."

"No. I'd like to go. Let's make a bit of a picnic – although I don't suppose we'll feel all that much like eating."

Caroline's car looked very sensible in the small parking space where Phillip had once parked his totally impractical sports car. She could still envisage it crouching there, at least a foot lower than its neighbours.

It was still fairly early when they walked through the gates and the air smelt damp and fresh as they strolled down the deserted main avenue, past the beds of glorious spring flowers. "Phillip used to come here for ideas and inspiration," Caroline explained. "That's why he was here the day we met – he's always adored gardening. He always used to adore gardening," she corrected herself. "I can't quite think of him in the past tense."

They walked on until they came to the pond. "He was sitting on that bench, pretending to read a book and I was feeding the ducks. Two little boys came up to share my bread – they'd be fifteen or sixteen now I suppose. Phillip and I recognised each other at once, of course, because you know we were both at Durham University. That was such a coincidence, really." They both stared at the water in silence, as if mesmerised by the kaleidoscope of ripples crossing and weaving in the wake of the ducks and then they moved slowly along the bank. By the time they had walked all the way round the water's edge the traditional Sunday strollers had begun to appear, drifting through breaks in the massive, flower-laden bushes.

"It was later than this when I met Phil – the first week in June and the rhododendrons were past their best. Today they're absolutely perfect." Caroline gazed up at the huge blooms and then turned to Jane. "He'd be pleased that we'd seen them looking so magnificent. Shall we take our picnic down to the river?"

* * *

Harriet straightened up and ran her fingers through her hair. Considering how small the flat was it always took her a disproportionate length of time to clean it out. She crouched in front of the fridge for one final inspection and then sat back on her heels, chewing her lip thoughtfully. He'd been cheerful enough when she'd driven him to Victoria to catch the train to the airport, but he'd been rather abstracted during the rest of the weekend. In fact she'd been slightly irritated that he'd forgotten to take the present she'd bought for Honor Kershaw. It had taken her ages to find a suitable silk scarf and now she felt even more guilty about letting her look after the house and the animals. Well, she'd phone and thank her and tell her the present was on its way.

She'd been looking forward to seeing Caroline again, after the weekend, but as she drove south, around Clapham Common, she found her thoughts wandering back constantly to Mike. They hadn't actually rowed, but they'd been a bit scratchy with each other for most of the weekend. She knew he was having problems with his latest contract and he probably wasn't looking forward to spending a fortnight or more at Lasserre on his own. She felt depressed, suddenly, that they'd had an unsatisfactory weekend. Not much to complain about really, she sighed, not after thirty six years. She'd phone from Petts Wood before she went to bed, to make sure he was all right.

Caroline and Jane were sifting through photographs when Harriet arrived. "We've had a nostalgic weekend," Caroline explained, "and now we feel calmer. How was Dad?"

"Oh fine – I'll phone him later if you don't mind."

It was quite late on Sunday evening when Caroline heard her mother's voice on the phone. Jane had already left, to sort herself out for work on Monday, and Caroline came downstairs in her dressing gown. "Give him my love," she called out as she crossed the hall.

Harriet followed Caroline into the kitchen, looking thoughtful." The answer machine was on. He must have forgotten to turn it off I suppose, although it's odd that he needed to put it on in the first place. Never mind. He'll ring back in the morning, I expect."

Caroline was pottering in the garden next morning when she heard the phone and she saw her mother going to answer it. Ten minutes later Harriet appeared through the kitchen door.

"That was your father. He'd turned the answer machine on while he was cleaning the pool and then Monsieur Lartigue turned up and invited him for a drink. I feel so silly now, but I was really worried last night when he wasn't there."

"Did that woman cope with everything?"

"Apparently everything was fine and he's going to thank her today. So let's forget about your father's problems and concentrate on yours. Do you feel strong enough to start replying to your letters? You know people don't expect longwinded replies as long as you just put a little personal message of thanks. I'll help you."

"Well, that's fourteen down and eighty seven to go," Caroline sighed, pushing the piles carefully to one side for her mother to set the lunch things. "I don't even know some of these people, but they all write such wonderful things about Phillip. I suppose people have to say nice things in letters of condolence, but I really get the impression they mean everything they say. He was so popular with everyone. I wonder why our marriage just didn't have that magic ingredient that you and Dad have managed to achieve."

"I think it's luck as much as anything. You thought you'd got something very special when you married him," Harriet reasoned, stirring the salad dressing with an unfocused expression on her face. "People just sometimes grow apart, I suppose."

"Oh damn." Caroline jumped up to answer the phone. "I'll be quick. Do you want to put the quiche back in the oven for a moment?"

Harriet laughed when Caroline finally rushed back into the kitchen. "I'm glad that was a quick call – I can't imagine what a long call would be like…" She suddenly looked hard at Caroline's slightly flushed face. "Ah, I see. Any news?" She tried to look casual.

"He just wondered how I was coping. He's researching his next book and he phoned from Edinburgh. Apparently his next hero is going to be a wild, reckless Scot, but he was a bit secretive about it. Anyway, he promised he'd ring me when he got back to London." She laughed at her mother's expression. "Nothing more at all, so don't sit there looking agog. He's just being nice and sympathetic. Let's eat the quiche before it dries up."

There might be absolutely nothing in it, Harriet thought later that day, but the heap of condolences seemed to be disappearing more cheerfully post phone-call than pre phone-call.

* * *

Caroline lay in bed on Thursday morning, wrapped in her own thoughts, yet distantly aware of the faint patter of rain against the bedroom window. It was now a week since the funeral and just over a fortnight since Phil had died and she hadn't anticipated that the pain would actually get worse rather than better. Even the thought of Alex hadn't been able to shift the weight of misery during the night. Her mother had said that the little things would be the hardest to bear and last night it had been the immersion heater. Phillip had been promising for years to sort it out but he'd never got down to it.

The first "gloop" of the air bubble had woken her up and brought back vivid memories of the early years of their marriage. It had invariably woken them up and they'd always made love as a result, so they'd had a standing joke about the disadvantages of curing what Phillip nicknamed their "call to action". They'd stopped noticing it in recent years, or perhaps they'd pretended not to notice it – she wasn't sure which.

Once she was completely awake her mind started a disjointed trawl of so many problems that even Caroline began to wonder if she was inventing some of them and she decided to go downstairs to make an early cup of tea.

She jumped when she opened the kitchen door. Her mother was already sitting at the table, leaning forward on her elbows and stirring abstractedly at a cup of coffee. Her mouth was set in a thin line and she was gazing intently at the swirling liquid. She looked up when Caroline walked into the room and managed to smile but it was an unconvincing gesture. "I've just phoned your father and the answering machine is on again. I don't understand what's happening. There's a phone by the bed, so I can't think why he's bothered to turn it on."

"Well, it's only quarter to seven, so even in France it's only quarter to eight." Caroline tried to be reasonable, but Harriet looked unconvinced. "I expect he went out last night and forgot to turn it back off when he came home. You know how disorganised he is sometimes if he's preoccupied or busy."

"I've known him go out and forget to plug the thing in, but I've never known him just leave it on like this. If he's there he must be able to hear the first few rings before the machine answers. I just don't think he's there. And if he isn't there, where is he?"

"Did you leave him a message?"

"Yes, and yesterday afternoon and again before I went to bed."

"That'll be him now," Caroline laughed with relief as her mother raced off into the hall.

"I suppose I was being a bit fanciful," Harriet admitted with a grudging smile when she came back into the kitchen. "Apparently he and Monsieur Lartigue took the lawnmower to be repaired in Monsieur Lartigue's trailer and then they both went and had supper in the cafe in the village. Your father just forgot to unplug the answering machine last night and he was in the shower when I rang this morning. I just got myself wound up I suppose, but it was the second night in a row. I think Monsieur Lartigue is probably very lonely – after all Bernadette's been in Australia for nearly two months now – and so he's been pleased to have your father's company for two evenings. I don't know why I started to flap."

"Well it's quite ridiculous. I can't imagine what you think he's going to get up to. He's hardly been a roaming husband in the last thirty six years. I don't think he'll start now."

"No, I'm sorry. Anyway why are you up so early?"

"I just couldn't sleep. The immersion heater woke me up and then all the memories and worries came flooding back so I came down to make a cup of tea."

"Well, at least you can make an early start on the letter writing. Angela and Heather are coming later aren't they? I thought I might stay with Cliff and Heather this weekend. I haven't had a good natter with them for ages and I assume Jane is going to spend

Saturday and Sunday here. I don't really understand why you two get on so well, but since you obviously do, I'll leave you in peace."

Caroline smiled, "I don't know either really. You'd think we'd hate each other, I suppose. But actually, having Phillip in common, has brought us together in a peculiar way. Since neither of us can have him now we might as well help each other to come to terms with our loss. And it's rather reassuring to know he replaced me with such a lovely girl." Caroline stuck her lower lip out thoughtfully. "I'd have hated it if she'd been awful."

Harriet stood up abruptly and thrust her hands deep into her dressing gown pockets. "I'm going upstairs to dress. I'm sorry I was such an idiot this morning. I'm not usually so irrational, but I panicked."

"Dad would be amazed if he knew what you were thinking," Caroline teased and gave her mother a hug. "He might actually be flattered."

"Honestly, Harriet," Heather scolded, when she popped in later. "It must be your age or something. Besides, whoever could he be having an affair with in Peyrusse Haute? The average age of the population is ninety five. The poor man is obviously going to pieces without you and having to cope with the answering machine, on top of everything else, is just the last straw."

Harriet spread her hands out in a gesture of submission and laughed. "Things just get out of proportion in the middle of the night. I feel a real failure. I'm meant to be supporting Caroline and she's ended up talking sense into me."

"Don't be silly," Caroline butted in. "I wouldn't even have the willpower to get out of bed without you. Really, she's been so supportive," Caroline insisted to Heather and Angela. "She's helped me with the replies to all the letters of condolence and she's kept me sane."

"Jane's been more help than I have."

"Jane's help is different because she loved Phillip in the same way that I loved him. Jane's offered to help me go through his clothes this weekend. We thought they should be given to charity. What do you think? Is it too soon?"

Angela looked across at Heather and then at Caroline. "We wanted to talk to you about that actually. Heather and I know several charities that are always desperately short of decent clothing, but only you know whether you can face up to sorting through his things yet. If you can do it," she prompted gently, "it'll be a marvellous relief to get it over and done with."

* * *

"You don't look so pale today," Jane observed, carefully sliding a large, flat cardboard box onto the kitchen table, and licking her greasy fingers. "A four seasons giant pizza. Let's eat it while it's hot."

"Well I'm not exactly sparkling company, but I've achieved a lot this week, so I'm feeling more positive. How about you?"

Jane shrugged, and divided up the pizza with careful precision. "Going back to work has been the best possible distraction I suppose. I'm not sure that I can bear to go through his clothes though." She suddenly looked very young, and Caroline felt that she'd imposed too much on her already.

"Then you mustn't. Mother's gone to stay with Heather for the weekend and they're coming back tomorrow night for Heather to collect the stuff, so I've got nearly two days to do it and, if I haven't finished, they'll help me. I must try to do it this weekend because, as long as I don't do it, it's hanging over me and I can't even think about picking up my life again. Can you understand that? I don't want to forget Phil, but I can remember him without keeping drawers full of socks and Y-fronts. Why don't you go and do something else while I make a start on it?"

Jane placed an olive stone delicately on the side of her plate, and shook her head at Caroline. "We'll do it together. It'll be easier with two of us. I just went wobbly for a moment."

They marched upstairs, armed with luggage labels and giant bin liners, but they were beaten back constantly by memories. "Let's start with easy things, like underwear." Caroline heaved a hiccoughing sigh as she picked a tiny piece of fluff from the sleeve of one of his suits. "I don't think I can face anything too major yet."

"You hold the bag, and I'll tip the things in," Jane suggested, and they began to make better progress.

"Summer casuals next – tee shirts...shorts...swimming trunks." Caroline called them out systematically and Jane tipped them in.

"Shirts?"

They were just dithering over the best way to deal with the shirts when Prue phoned to invite them to supper and they were grateful for the excuse to stop.

"Well, does it seem any easier today than it did yesterday?"

Caroline shook open a plastic bag and stared into the black void. "It's not any easier but it seems less strange than it did yesterday. We were just going to start on the shirts weren't we?"

"Yes, but I can't bear to bundle them all higgledy-piggledy into a bin liner; they are all so beautifully ironed," Jane objected, so they made wobbly piles of neatly folded shirts and tried to slot them, as tidily as possible, into the bags. "Not too bad, I suppose," Jane gave grudging approval.

"We can put suits and shoes straight onto the spare room bed, because Heather will probably bring some boxes with her," Caroline suggested. "Then that's nearly everything done."

"What about cuff-links and things like that?" Jane asked, as she looked round at the empty cupboards.

Caroline carefully tipped the contents of Phillip's dressing-table drawer onto the bedspread. She smoothed her hand across the jewellery to spread everything out and then turned over the bits that had landed upside down. It was just like playing Scrabble.

"Please," she waved at the pieces. "Please choose whatever you'd like to have."

Jane picked a pair of cufflinks made of heavy gold with inset moonstones. Caroline had given them to him for their fifth wedding anniversary. Are you sure you don't mind?" Jane asked hesitantly as Caroline swept everything back into the drawer.

"Don't be silly." Caroline sounded more certain than she felt. Perhaps her father would like Phillip's gold fountain pen. There was no point in hanging on to it all.

"Let's stack the filled bags on the landing, out of the way," Jane suggested sensibly, "and then we've only got the sweaters to sort through.

When Heather and Harriet turned up, about an hour later, both girls were sitting downstairs, too distraught to even cry any more. Jane was cradling a blue cashmere sweater – Phillip's favourite during the time she'd known him. Caroline was clutching the thick old sweater that he'd found in the back of the car all those years ago – 'pongy', he'd called it – and which he'd spread under the tree in Richmond Park…

They didn't move when the two older women arrived, so Harriet and Heather left them there while they got on with loading

Heather's car. Harriet took one last look around the bedroom and finally closed all the empty drawers and cupboards. She pursed her lips when she went back downstairs and Heather made signs that she was going to leave. Neither Caroline nor Jane gave any indication of noticing when she kissed them goodbye. Harriet sighed.

She's had reservations when Angela had encouraged Caroline to get rid of Phillip's things. It just seemed so soon and now she didn't know what to think. The sight of his redundant clothing had induced a more acute sense of loss than even the sight of his body had produced. The empty cupboards symbolised the absolute finality and, faced with the girls' terrible despair, Harriet felt at a complete loss.

"Can I make you something to eat?"
They both shook their heads without glancing up and Harriet looked from one to the other helplessly. She marched into the kitchen, her high heels making a reassuring clatter on the hard tiles, and looked round for inspiration. Some rousing choral music on Radio Three lifted her spirits and five minutes later she walked into the living room with a tray for each of them. "I don't care what you say," she announced, "you are both going to eat something." She handed out the scrambled eggs and gently removed the two precious sweaters. "Would you mind if I turned the television on for half an hour? There's something I'd quite like to watch."

* * *

"It was really quite frightening," she told Mike later, on the telephone. "I really didn't know what to do with the pair of them. I was tempted to call Angela since she'd been the one to advise getting rid of his clothes. Anyway, by the time they'd eaten their scrambled eggs and watched 'Have I got news for you', they were more or less recovered again." She listened, smiling, to Mike's reassuring voice at the other end of the line. She really had been an idiot to suspect him of anything, just because he'd been a bit disorganised about switching the answering machine on and off. "I thought I'd try to book a flight for next Friday, she responded to his query. "Can you manage until then? Do you miss me?" She laughed as he reeled off all the near disasters which he'd failed to cope with in her absence. "Well I'm glad I'm indispensable… I'll speak to you soon – yes, I love you too. Bye darling."

Caroline woke early on the Monday morning. Her eyes felt sore and she rubbed them with her knuckles. Well, that's made matters worse she observed critically as she peered at her blotchy face in the bathroom mirror. She padded across the room and looked into Phil's side of the huge wardrobe. The void was like an open wound. She looked at the compressed mass on her own side and winced at the contrast. She took out some of her own clothes – some of his favourite things, that she hadn't even worn for years – and hung them on the empty expanse of rail. The sweater that she'd saved from Heather's charity collection was lying on the bed and she picked it up again. She hadn't noticed last night that it had a very old, curling dry-cleaning ticket safety-pinned into the label. She smiled softly. It had been past its best twelve years ago, so the old softy must have dry-cleaned it and kept it for sentimental reasons. She hugged it to herself and then put it, neatly folded in the middle of his empty shelf. She was jolted out of her reverie by faint sounds coming from the kitchen. She dressed quickly and went downstairs, feeling as if she'd made appeasement to some god.

"I'm going to make a list after breakfast," she informed Jane as they crunched their toast. "There's still the accountant to see – but he's arranged to come here so that won't take long. The letters of condolence are still arriving, of course, but not in such daunting numbers. If I answer them hot off the doormat they won't start to pile up again."

Jane nodded encouragingly and reloaded the toaster. "I must go now or I'll be late for work, but I'll phone again for a progress report. You look more cheerful today, but don't try to be too brave. Take advantage of having your mother here for another week. Are you relieved that we did the clothes at the weekend? It seems like an enormous hurdle overcome."

Caroline closed her eyes and reflected after Jane left for work. There were going to be good days and there were going to be bad days. She was quite aware of that, but this had started as a good day so she needed to take advantage of it. She took her mother a cup of tea in bed. Her mother was looking more relaxed again and she'd miss her when she went back to France. She was disturbed in her musings by a sound at the door.

"Any toast and coffee going?" Angela poked her head around the kitchen door.

"You're as bad as Dora," Caroline laughed as she set out a clean plate and prepared some fresh coffee.

"I hear that you've had a busy weekend," Angela skirted

around the subject delicately.

"Yes. We've cleared out all Phil's things and it was the hardest thing that Jane and I have had to do. I thought I'd already cried myself empty, but seeing all his clothes brought it all back again – only worse. Heather was a real brick and took everything away last night. Then Mum revived us both with scrambled eggs. I feel so relieved, this morning, that we did it. Thank you for encouraging us. Now that it's all over I can see that it was the right thing to do."

Angela accepted the gratitude with a pleased little shrug. "I'm a wise old bird, you know. Now what are the next goals? And can I be very nosy and ask if you've heard from the man with the sexy voice?"

He rings her regularly," Harriet butted in, walking into the kitchen at that moment and greeting Angela warmly.

"Oh, Mum! He's rung twice, that's all, and just to sympathise," Caroline remonstrated. "And, yes, I have several goals to concentrate on. I must answer the rest of the condolence letters and arrange meetings with the solicitor and the accountant. Then there's the bank manager and…"

* * *

This was the first time that Caroline had been on her own in the house, for longer than an hour, since Phillip had died, and she sat down with the newspaper and a cup of coffee. In the end her mother had flown back to France on Saturday morning and Jane had left last night after a relaxing weekend of doing nothing in particular. It was quite a pleasant sensation to be alone in her own house; free to do whatever she liked – quite a luxury in fact for the moment.

She scanned the paper. On the front page there was the usual misery in the world at large plus an exposé of some politician's scurrilous sex life. She skipped over the next few pages and settled down to study the cultural scene. A couple of new plays opening in the West End…she'd go to the theatre more often in the autumn. A new film had been released to good reviews…'French' she noticed…Something to watch out for next time she was in Peyrusse… She turned over to Veronica Brake's section. She did in-depth interviews and sometimes her subjects were a bit obscure but sometimes they were quite well known…Her throat felt dry and her hand was unsteady as she hastily pushed away her coffee cup.

The photograph was a good one, occupying nearly as much

space as the text. He was smiling and she found herself, unconsciously, smiling back at him. The article was entitled 'Another Mega Buck' and lower down the page was a quote in bold print: 'a 90% male readership but a 90% female fan club'. Caroline scanned through the words quickly for the personal details that were always given greater prominence than the literary achievements. There was a mention of his ex-wife, divorced just over a year ago, and another of his eighteen year old son. There were no revelations of any new relationship. She could have wept with relief. The interview had taken place in his London flat, which was described in complimentary detail and there were recurrent references to his charm, warmth and attractiveness. His latest book was his twelfth and it was receiving an enormous amount of media hype.

There would be two book signing sessions – in Waterstone's and in Foyle's – and then he would be going abroad for most of the summer. She struggled to breathe normally but a large weight was pressing down on her chest. So she probably wouldn't see him during the summer. But he'd said that he'd be down in France and, after all, he had rented the Mannering's house for six months. Reason was on her side, but there it was in black and white – research on his next book would take him to South America for a few weeks, but he refused to give any more details. Then he would be spending two weeks in Australia and Japan, collaborating on the film adaptation of his latest book.

The article talked about his love of France and his disappointment at not being able to spend more time there. Towards the end of the piece she asked him about the heroines of his books. Did these James Bond-style sultry lovelies conform to his own ideal of female beauty? This question had obviously amused him and he's listed several qualities that she'd need to possess. "And looks?"

"Not too tall… slim… pretty… blue eyes… curly blonde hair…"

There were some jolly quips from Veronica Brake about angels and disappointed brunettes and that was that.

* * *

Waterstone's and Foyle's both had large advertisements for the book signings on the same page as the article, and she checked her watch. It was too late for Waterstone's, but she'd go to Foyle's tomorrow. She reread the article several times and felt herself blush as she weighed up the hope engendered by the last few lines against the disappointment of his not spending much time in France this summer. She was probably fantasising but she felt that the scales had come down, marginally, in her favour.

She tore up to the bathroom and gave her face a critical inspection in the mirror. Her eyes still looked dry and slightly pink-rimmed. Her skin was tired and flaky; the famous curls were lank and unkempt; her legs were hairier than Sylvester Stallone's chest. If that weren't enough she only had twenty four hours to repair some of the damage and she didn't have anything suitable to wear.

The hairdresser had had a cancellation so she could have an early appointment tomorrow. The Bromley Beauty Salon could do her legs after lunch today and then she could spend the afternoon shopping for something to wear. She hadn't driven anywhere on her own since Phillip had died and she felt quite a mixture of excitement and apprehension.

* * *

"You look as if you've been shopping," Prue observed when she popped in later that evening and saw all the packages. "Do you fancy supper with Stan and me tonight?"

"Thank you. That's really kind but I can't. I'm going out tomorrow and I've got things to do this evening. But stop a minute and look at my new dress."

Prue returned home feeling strangely anxious. "Well I hope it's not just a flash in the pan," she muttered to Stan. "She's suddenly very cheerful."

Caroline stood in the kitchen, humming happily, and looked at the instructions on the face pack. 'Mix with tepid water, apply smoothly and leave for at least two hours'. Better eat something first, she reasoned. Then there were a couple of good programmes on the radio. What more could a girl want? She applied the filthy brown gunge, popped a witch-hazel pad on each eye and cursed to herself, half an hour later when the phone rang.

"Whatever's wrong with you?" her mother sounded anxious. "Have you been to the dentist?"

Caroline tried to stop the phone banging against the concrete shell. "I've got a face-mask on… yes I'm fine…I'm just trying to improve on nature a bit. Have you got any news?" She listened dreamily while her mother prattled on. She was coping better than she'd imagined without Mme Lartigue and she'd received a nice postcard of Sydney Harbour. Honor Kershaw had been to dinner the night before with a few other neighbours and she'd insisted, apparently, that she'd really enjoyed looking after the animals and the pool while they'd been away. So now Harriet felt less guilty for having allowed her to do it. There wasn't any other news except that Vicky had started to feel very sick in the mornings, which Caroline knew already. Finally her mother rang off, finding this one sided conversation rather unsatisfactory.

Harriet put the phone down and turned back to Mike. "I think Caroline must be going to Alex's book signing tomorrow. I can't think why else she'd be bothering with a face mask."

* * *

Hmm. Caroline wriggled to see her back view in the mirror. She was quite encouraged by the result. The hairdresser had cut her hair nicely and she was pleased with the dress. She wasn't sure she'd derived a great deal of benefit from being cast in concrete for two hours, but her eyes looked slightly less bloodshot after the enforced rest. If she left now she'd be in town in time for lunch, so she'd be able to say that she was in town for the day and just happened to notice… She smiled at her reflection and practiced looing surprised. It wasn't very convincing, but worth a try.

The book signing was starting at half past two and finishing at half past three; she planned on arriving towards the end, in the hope that he might be able to devote a bit more time to her. She watched the queue from a discreet distance, wedged behind a tall bookcase and seemingly engrossed in 'The Reproduction Process Of The Fern'. Heavens, she thought, glancing at the end of the book. They must do it in all sorts of different positions if it takes four hundred and seventy two pages. Her heart was beating frantically now and she glanced at her watch. Ten minutes to go. What if he didn't recognise her? What if he just signed the book and that was that. Well, she told herself firmly, at least then you'll know, one way or the other.

The blue-rinse set were certainly out in force, she noticed, and she could see Alex smiling and exchanging a few words as he signed each book. She couldn't hear what he was saying, of course, but he was certainly making all the old trout smirk.

She slotted the sex life of the ferns back onto the shelf and took a deep breath. The tall woman standing next to him had been with him at his book launch in April and, from the way she was passing books to him and smiling at the customers, Caroline guessed that she was his secretary or personal assistant.

144

The queue was much shorter now and it was nearly half past three. She tried to move forward but she couldn't make her legs function properly. She stepped back and leaned against the bookshelf again, with her eyes closed. When she looked again the queue had gone and he was walking away from her, talking animatedly to two smartly dressed men. Mavis remained at the table, gathering up leaflets and spare books. As she straightened up to leave their eyes met briefly.

* * *

It must have been an hour later when she got back into her car at Bromley Station. She had no idea how she'd got there and her eyes were still slightly blurred with tears. She couldn't face the empty house and had a sudden urge to take refuge in Chiselhurst, with Cliff and Heather. Cliff's car was on the drive and Darren was lovingly wiping it with a chamois leather.

"Hello Miss. How are you?" He grinned with pleasure at seeing her so unexpectedly and put his chamois down. "Boss is out and Sir's round the back, he announced, opening the garden door for her with a flourish.

"Hello," Caroline called waving at Cliff, who was standing next to his lawnmower; a piece of frayed cord in his hand. "The butler let me in."

Cliff smiled with unconcealed delight and strode across the lawn to give her a kiss. How are you sweet heart? You look very pretty. Have you been somewhere nice?"

"Just up to town for a bit of shopping. I wondered if you and Heather would like to come over to supper with me tonight."

"Heather's out for the evening. Am I too boring all on my own?" He pulled a pathetic little face and they both laughed.

Caroline was slightly alarmed when they strolled back to her car, to find that Cliff's car was parked in the garage and her own car, now sparklingly clean, had been driven closer to the hose.

"I let him move the car round on the drive," Cliff mumbled, looking guilty and Darren gave her a conspiratorial wink.

"Well it looks very nice – thank you."

They both rushed to open the door for her and, on a sudden impulse, she gave Darren a kiss as well as Cliff.

The thought of making supper for Cliff gave the rest of her day a new purpose and she decided to invite Prue and Stan, and Mrs Heath, as well. She still couldn't make any sense of her behaviour that afternoon but, if she concentrated on shopping, cooking and laying the table, she might be able to put it out of her mind for a few hours. It was a vain hope however and, despite her domestic occupations, she couldn't erase the memory. For goodness sake, she told herself firmly, he couldn't have been more than five yards away. She'd just been scared of his reaction. Supposing he'd simply rebuffed her. She knew that she was still too vulnerable, after Phillip's death, to risk any further pain; but the missed opportunity was painful in itself.

She put a bunch of flowers in the middle of the table and then sighed as the phone rang. The supper party had seemed a good idea a few hours ago but her heart wasn't in it and she'd never get everything done if her mother wanted a long chat.

Ten minutes after putting the phone down she was still sitting on the hall chair, smiling inanely at a blank wall. She must have produced supper eventually because everyone congratulated her on the food. But, by the time they'd all gone, she couldn't remember anything about the evening except the phone call.

She lay in bed that night with the sheet pulled tight up to her chin, gazing wide eyed into the darkness. He didn't think she was an idiot and he'd been very pleased that Mavis had spotted her. She was going to have dinner with him in ten days' time, as soon as he came back from Scotland.

CHAPTER 16

The pebble skimmed across the grey water, kicking up bursts of white spray as it touched the crests of the incoming waves.

"That bounced five times so I've won," Caroline exclaimed with a laugh, throwing herself down again, to sit cross-legged on the stony water's edge, next to Jane. They carried on, silently tossing pebbles into the grey water, for a long time, both lost in their own thoughts.

The clouds hung low over Beer Beach, heavy with threatening rain and, apart from a distant couple walking an excitable, yapping dog along the narrow border of surf, Caroline and Jane were alone on the shore. There was a cold breeze blowing in from the bay and they were both huddled in sweaters.

"Well, so much for summer in England," Caroline grumbled. You'd never believe it was July the first – it's cold enough to be March."

"It's exactly two months since he died."

Caroline hunched her knees towards her and rested her chin on them, her gaze fixed on the unremitting dullness of the sea. "Sometimes I feel as if he's been dead for ever and sometimes I wake up in the night and see him so clearly that I can't believe he's gone."

Jane shivered and jumped to her feet. "Let's go back to the cottage before we both die of hypothermia."

They walked slowly away from the beach and headed towards a small group of cottages, squeezed haphazardly between the beach and the coast road. They walked in silence, like an old married couple so in tune with each other's thoughts that they don't need to talk any more.

Jane's mother's cottage was lower than its neighbours, set deep into its garden as if it had been dropped from a great height and then allowed to settle. She'd owned the cottage for more than twenty years so Jane had spent holidays here since she'd been a small child. It had been a spur of the moment decision to come down with Caroline to spend time in neutral territory and they both felt more relaxed, even after just one day.

"It's so peaceful not having a phone, Jane announced as she turned the key in the front door. "We don't have to wonder if somebody phones while we were out." She laughed as she saw the stricken expression pass fleetingly across Caroline's face. "Sorry, I forgot that you actually miss your phone calls."

"That's all right. I don't mind really and, anyway, he's gone back to Scotland for a fortnight so even if he could phone me we couldn't meet each other. We're going to have dinner the first Monday we're back."

The poor weather continued for the whole of the first week and every day they walked further and further. Initially the purpose of their walks was to keep warm, but soon they were walking because the exercise and fresh air created an emotional vacuum into which their memories could pour, unhindered. Every evening they returned to the crouching, pink cottage almost too exhausted to eat and even the unseasonal, nightly storms didn't disturb their deep, dreamless sleep.

By the end of that week they had tramped across large tracts of the Marshwood Downs, explored the Blackbourne Hills and walked along miles of the coastal path. The memories had begun to be less painful and often they found themselves laughing quite spontaneously at some of Phillip's traits and habits. Many of which they had both found amusing – occasionally even annoying.

The sun came out in the second week and they carried sunbeds down to the beach. The school holidays hadn't started yet so the shore was still fairly thinly populated. Caroline closed her eyes behind her dark glasses and stretched her arm out to touch Jane's arm. "Thank you very much for inviting me down here. I know it's too soon to hope for a complete cure but I actually feel as if I could restart my life now. I haven't cried once since we arrived."

"No, neither have I. I'm glad it's done you good. This place has had that effect on me for as long as I can remember. Perhaps you'll stop feeling guilty now about Alex." Jane smiled as Caroline began to object. "I don't know why you have been feeling guilty but I know jolly well that you have, so don't deny it."

Caroline didn't answer. She lay there thinking of that first abortive trip to the book signing and their two subsequent meeting. The first time he had invited her to supper and she'd spent all afternoon in a frenzy of anticipation. She was bathed and dressed by half past four and pacing up and down the hall, wondering what to do with herself for the next two and a half hours. By the time she'd forced herself to read the paper and do some chores she'd felt hot and sweaty with anticipation and she'd bathed and changed all over again.

He'd arrived punctually at seven o'clock and presented her with a bunch of roses, before kissing her on both cheeks. The roses were beautifully scented and looked as if they'd come from a real garden, rather than a florist's hothouse. She'd felt herself blush under his direct gaze as she thanked him and she'd turned away, confused by his proximity. She could still smell the fragrance of those roses, nearly two weeks later, and the thought made her feel sick with longing.

The sun felt hot now against her face and she turned over onto her front. That first evening had been enchanted, despite her initial awkwardness. He'd behaved so normally, helping her to put the roses in a vase and then separating the ice cubes for their drinks. She'd suddenly felt so at ease with him and by the time they'd driven off to find a restaurant they were talking as if they'd known each other for ever. She couldn't remember where they'd gone or what they'd eaten. All she could recall was a tremendous feeling of warmth in his company and a sense of being wanted. When he'd taken her home he'd kissed her on the lips – twice – very gently and then he'd left. He'd made no mention of seeing her again but she had known they would see each other as soon as he could manage it.

Caroline sensed a sudden movement next to her and, when she opened her eyes, she saw Jane leaning on her elbow, staring into space. There was a faint smile on her lips. "You're obviously thinking of something nice," Caroline prompted her.

"It's nothing really. A very pleasant, new head of department joined the firm last week and he came and sat next to me at lunchtime on Friday. That's all. We only spoke for a few minutes because he was needed in a meeting. But it was nice to feel a spark of interest in someone – someone other than Phillip. He's probably spoken for, but that's not the point. It just made me think that it is possible to move on. Is that heartless?"

"Of course it's not. I sometimes wonder if Phillip is up there in his heavenly herbaceous border, willing us both to be happy…"

They both lay still again, absorbed in their own thoughts. Caroline's mind drifted to her second meeting with Alex. He'd been very short of time and she'd gone into town to meet him for lunch. He'd kissed her warmly when she'd arrived and held her hand across the table. Their conversation had been more intimate this time and they'd discussed their broken marriages. "It was such a terrible pain that I didn't think I'd ever get over it. Did you feel the same?" Alex stroked the palm of her hand while he spoke.

"It was awful of course and I felt a dreadful failure for not managing to make it work, but he didn't leave me for anyone else – we just drifted apart. Perhaps that's less painful – less of a betrayal."

"It seems a long time ago now," his smile made her heart melt.

He had to leave straight after lunch but he came with her to the station. He took her in his arms in the taxi and they kissed with a ferocity and urgency that she had never experienced before. She suddenly giggled as she remembered the taxi driver's prosaic interruption. "That'll be three pounds fifty Guv."

"What are you laughing about?" Jane interrupted her reverie.

"Nothing really – just something rather silly. Shall we pack up now if we are going to the pub for supper tonight?"

She could still sense the pressure of his mouth on hers and relive the intensity of those kisses. She'd be seeing him again in a week's time. He'd proposed dinner at his flat in Knightsbridge and she hugged the anticipation to herself as they crossed the road behind the beach and walked home.

"You're grinning inanely again," Jane pointed out, "and you've just made that poor driver do an emergency stop. If you're not more careful you won't survive long enough to see him again."

* * *

Harriet put the phone down and ran into the garden to find Mike. He'd been skimming the grasshoppers from the surface of the pool, but he stopped when he saw the expression on her face.

"That was Edward on the phone. Vicky is threatening to miscarry. He sounded absolutely frantic."

"Has she been taken into hospital?"

"Yes, they rushed her in this morning and did some tests. Now she's home again but she has to stay in bed for at least a fortnight. She's ten weeks pregnant and, if she doesn't lose it in the next fortnight, she stands a good chance of keeping it. Unfortunately Edward is in the middle of an important court case and she needs someone in the house with her constantly so that she can rest."

Harriet sat down on the pool steps and sank her head in her hands. "Caroline left yesterday for a fortnight's holiday with Jane, somewhere near Seaton. I know they aren't on the phone so I can't ask her to help.

Mike sat next to her his arm round her shoulders and Harriet leaned back against him gratefully. He'd seemed so preoccupied for several weeks now and less affectionate so she was relieved by this sudden display of warmth.

"I can manage perfectly well you know. You'll just worry if you don't go back. Shall I try to book you on this afternoon's flight?"

She laced her fingers through his and thought for a moment. "Why don't you come back with me? Honor wouldn't mind looking after the animals again. She said that she'd enjoyed it, last time. I hate leaving you here to fend for yourself and, anyway, I miss you." She felt suddenly tearful and pulled his hand down to her breast.

"I can't spare the time immediately but, if I can manage it, I'll try to come over next week. Now shall I phone for a ticket and will you let Edward know that you'll be there tonight?" He kissed the back of her neck and then pulled her to her feet. "Come on darling. Edward will be worrying if you don't phone him straight back."

His tone was gentle and loving but Harriet still had a sense of unease as she walked back towards the house. She heard his voice on the telephone, drifting through his open office window and then he called out to her that he'd managed to get her a seat on the early evening flight. She struggled with an irrational feeling of panic and then walked across the cool tiles to phone Edward.

She packed quickly and threw together a rather scrappy salad for lunch. Mike seemed unusually restless and he took his coffee up to his office, muttering that he'd be back down as soon as he'd solved a problem that was bothering him. Harriet sat at the garden table, hunched over her cup and staring blindly across the valley. She didn't really have a favourite time of year because every month seemed to bring its own particular delights, but normally she looked forward to July for its sheer vulgar abundance. This was the best time of year for the sunflowers. The blooms were newly open and the summer drought hadn't had time to inflict its annual damage on the glorious golden blooms. The big floppy hibiscus flowers were showering the garden with every shade of purple and lilac, and, in the courtyard was Harriet's favourite – a splendid white variety with magenta tipped centres. She sighed. This was the first year, since their move to Lasserre, that she could draw so little pleasure from her surroundings.

Phillip's death had been a tragic blow. Now Vicky was facing a cruel disappointment. But there was something else troubling Harriet as well. It was an indefinable, nagging unease which was weighing down on her constantly. She stood up and paced around the pool but she couldn't shake off this sense of apprehension.

She heard Mike's voice behind her. "Cheer up darling. I expect that Vicky will be all right. She'll certainly feel much better when she sees you. I'm quite sure she will, because I always do." Mike put his arm around her as he spoke and Harriet felt as irrationally cheerful as she'd been irrationally despondent a moment ago. "Have you looked at the figs recently? Walk over with me. They're much better this year than they were last. It must have been the heavy rain we had in June". He smiled as they crossed the garden, hand in hand, to admire the swelling fruit. From this corner they could see the small orchard.

"We'll pick the greengages when I get back, otherwise the birds will have them and it's so nice to have our own fruit in Armagnac at Christmas." Harriet rested her head against his shoulder as she spoke, watching the tiny white and yellow butterflies dipping and swooping in and out of the lavender hedge and, suddenly, she felt all the old magic flood back over Lasserre.

* * *

Edward put the phone down and turned back to face Vicky. She was lying on the bed, looking shrunken and frightened – a small, still effigy against the cream bedspread. "Did you gather what's happening?" he asked, kneeling on the floor next to her to avoid bumping the bed.

She nodded and bit her lip to hold back the tears. "Mum's coming to stay. When is she arriving? I feel so guilty – being such a nuisance."

Edward stroked her forehead, crushed by his love and by his complete helplessness. "Don't be silly. She wanted to come. I'm going to fetch her in an hour and a half's time. Mrs Pratchett will sit with you until we get back and Ems has gone to the Mannering's. There isn't anything for you to worry about. Do you want me to turn the television on? It might help you to relax."

"I don't what I'll do if I lose this baby," Vicky sobbed, ignoring Edward's words completely. "I'll never get pregnant again – I know that. I want this baby so much."

"You haven't had any more symptoms since this morning. If you have complete rest for a fortnight that'll bring you just past

152

three months and Dr Price thinks you'll be over the worst of the risk by then." Edward's voice pleaded with her to take courage from his own optimism but she just shook her head and the tears continued to roll down her pale cheeks.

She lay there silently, with her eyes closed, long after she heard his car drive off. The tears had stopped but she could still feel the tight constrictions on her skin, like snail tracks, where the salty rivulets had dried. The rapid click of her cleaning lady's knitting needles filled the bedroom with a disproportionate noise but she feigned sleep in an attempt to avoid the inevitably distressing anecdotes that Mrs Pratchett would be longing to divulge – friends and relatives who'd miscarried, endured stillbirths or suffered agonies during protracted labours. Normally Vicky would have derived a grim amusement from these exaggerated tales of grief, but not today. So she lay quite still, soothed by the rhythmic clacking and feeling marginally guilty at not indulging Mrs Pratchett's need to maintain a nonstop monologue.

By the time Edward and Harriet got home from Gatwick pretence had turned to reality and she heard them tiptoeing into the room just as woke from an unexpectedly deep sleep.

The sight of her mother induced a fresh flow of tears and, when Edward returned from taking Mrs Pratchett home, he found them sitting weeping together. He felt completely helpless in the face of this terrible female grief and he walked out into the garden. There'd been rain during the night and the air felt fresh against his face as he paced up and down the damp lawn, but all he could see was Vicky's pale, desolate face.

* * *

It was seven o'clock when Mike got home from Toulouse. Harriet had been in better spirits by the time they'd reached the airport, but he'd felt very depressed as he'd driven home – weighed down by a terrible dread. He should have spared the time to go back with her and now he regretted his decision to stay in France. He could still change his mind and catch the lunchtime plane tomorrow. There were usually spare seats in the middle of the week and he suddenly felt a great urge to be with his family and Harriet, away from Lasserre. He needn't even ask Honor to house sit as Mme Lartigue would be back next week and her husband would fill in for a few days.

It was one of those searingly hot evenings which often precede a storm and he paced round and round the paved edge of the pool, revolving his wine glass between his fingers and stepping abstractedly over the recumbent form of the elderly dog every time he completed a circuit. The phone rang and his heart leapt in a nervous panic.

"Hello darling," he sighed with relief as he heard the reassuring tone of Harriet's voice. The line was so clear that she could have been in the next room.

"Vicky's all right at the moment – quite stable – and we are making sure she doesn't do anything at all. Will you manage on you own for a while? I'm sorry for abandoning you constantly. Have you decided whether you can spare the time to come over next week? It would be so lovely and I think Mme Lartigue will be back on Thursday so you needn't bother Honor about the animals."

He smiled at the familiar, breathless rush of information. "I'll try very hard to come over for a few days next week," he confirmed. Why hadn't he just said he'd come tomorrow, as he'd planned in the car? "I'd actually like to come over, but I'm still worried about the deadline for this latest project... Yes, I promise. I'll work non-stop to clear the decks by next week." He listened as she launched into another flurry of instructions. "Well, you needn't have told Honor to be on stand-by. You said yourself that Madame Lartigue would be back." He felt suddenly leaden with apprehension. "No, I'll be really organised about the answerphone this time. You can call me any time. Give my love to them all. – Yes, of course I do. Bye darling." He sat down hard on the nearest kitchen chair and buried his head in his hands.

The phone rang at nine thirty and he considered ignoring it, but what if it was Harriet again? He could have laughed when he heard the cheerful sound of Caroline's voice. "Hello darling. If you're phoning from a callbox I'll phone you back." She sounded happier than she had for a long time and he listened with pleasure as she extolled the virtues of the Dorset coast. He didn't mention Vicky's threatened miscarriage – she sounded so relaxed that he couldn't bear to spoil her mood.

He put on some music and felt calmer as he arranged a few pieces of ham and a sliced tomato on a plate. At quarter past ten Mark phoned and they chatted for nearly half an hour. It was gone half past eleven by the time Mike went to bed and he had just closed his eyes when the phone rang for the final time.

CHAPTER 17

Caroline smiled as she drove down the M3 on Sunday morning. The last couple of weeks had flown since she and Jane had got back from their fortnight on the coast and now she had six weeks at Lasserre to look forward to. She'd been amused by Jane's reaction when she'd packed the car that morning.

"Is that it? I couldn't go away for a night with such a small bag."

She'd explained that she kept masses of summer clothes down there and anyway she'd probably be living in a bikini and T-shirt for the whole summer. Then she'd felt mean for being so tactless. Jane was house-sitting for her and she was worried that she'd be lonely – it certainly wouldn't be much fun and the house would be so full of memories... "Sorry, I'm being very selfish."

"Don't be silly. It'll be a relief to have a bit of peace for six weeks and my flat should be ready by the time you get back," Jane had insisted and Caroline had finally driven off reassured, and more optimistic, than she'd been for a very long time.

Alex was in Peru, researching his next book, but he was joining her for a few days in France in three weeks' time and she had spent the night at his flat after she'd come back from Seaton. She drove automatically, totally unaware of her surroundings, as she thought back to that night.

His flat was in a very smart block in Knightsbridge and she had stood on the pavement for a few moments looking up at it before she'd plucked up the courage to go in. It was a Victorian building, all shining brass and polished wood, and she was just beginning to feel slightly overawed by this heavy opulence when Alex had appeared down the wide stairway that descended gracefully around the glass and mahogany lift. She loved his lack of reserve. He had thrown his arms round her and kissed her, quite undaunted by the public nature of the great patrician hallway, and she'd caught a glimpse of a smile cross the face of the porter. By the time they'd disengaged themselves he was standing behind his desk looking as impassive as ever.

The memories of that evening were still too precious to dwell on and she hugged them to herself with a sigh of pleasure as she turned off the main road and meandered in the direction of the village. As she passed the first signpost – five miles to Stockleigh – she thought again about Vicky. She and Jane had just left for Seaton when she'd threatened to miscarry and the family had maintained a conspiracy of silence. She was grateful to them for not wanting to spoil her holiday, yet she still felt guilty that her mother had come back from France to cope for the second time in two months.

Vicky seemed stronger now, after her fortnight's imposed rest, and the doctor was confident that, at three and a half months, the danger had passed. Caroline was more bothered now by her mother than by Vicky, but she wasn't absolutely sure why. There wasn't a really specific reason for her disquiet, but she'd felt that her mother had been worried by something when she'd come to stay immediately after Phillip's death. Caroline had dismissed Harriet's irrational concern about her father forgetting to turn the answering machine off – that was just a bit of nonsense – but she was sure something else was troubling her. Perhaps Vicky knew what was wrong, or perhaps she was just imagining it; she didn't think so.

Stockleigh looked a bit grey – less attractive than usual – and she found herself feeling childishly excited at the prospect of six weeks in the sun. They were driving down in Edward's car and he was going to stay for the first week and then return for their last week. Mark and Tessa would be overlapping for three weeks too, so that would be fun. She'd had dinner with them the previous Friday and they'd had an enjoyable evening together. She sighed contentedly as she drove round to the back of Court House and parked next to Edward's estate car. This was the first time in a long while she decided, as she yanked at the handbrake, that life was going well for them all. For the moment she forgot her niggling worry about her mother.

Soapy water was dripping from the wheel arches of Edward's car – the great exodus was obviously well under way – and the kitchen door flew open as she started walking across the garden with her small case. Edward and Emily let themselves out and rushed towards her, laughing conspiratorially and rolling their eyes.

"She's puked most of the morning and now she's decidedly tetchy," Edward explained, "but otherwise she's absolutely fine," he reassured Caroline, seeing her anxious expression. "And you look marvellous." Edward stepped back to admire his sister-in-law.

"I feel marvellous thanks. In fact I feel strong enough to face my big sister if you two want to escape for ten minutes."

Vicky was standing in the middle of the large kitchen running her fingers through her hair. She was at that stage of pregnancy where she'd actually lost weight, Caroline observed, as she looked around at the usual organised chaos.

"Don't you dare criticize," Vicky said crossly as she kissed her sister. "You look well." She suddenly stopped grumbling and gazed at Caroline. "We haven't had a real talk for ages. We'll be able to relax by the pool at Lasserre and dissect your love life – I'm dying to hear all about him. Mother was less forthcoming than usual."

Caroline laughed. "Dissect my love life? That sounds very adolescent. But should you be rushing round like this?"

"I'm really only rushing round at half speed – hence the chaos, but Doctor Price says I'm fine. I think it was a bit of a false alarm really and I feel very selfish about dragging Mother away for two weeks. Still, it was fun to have her to myself for the first time for ages. Now I'll get on with the packing while you finish throwing lunch together, if you don't mind. There's cold meat; the hard-boiled eggs are in that saucepan; the salad things are in the sink; and we'll just slum it with ice-cream for pudding."

Vicky waved her hand airily in the direction of the food and disappeared into the hall to juggle with a few more piles of belongings. Caroline noticed, from the corner of her eye, that the piles were getting reassuringly closer to the front door. Edward and Emily could risk coming back into the house soon.

"What about my bike? I must take my bike or Grandpa won't believe I've learnt to ride it." The enormity of the possible omission struck Emily forcibly in the middle of lunch.

"Don't be silly. Have you seen all the stuff piled up in the hall? Daddy's already said there's no room for everything," Vicky set her mouth firmly and Emily's chin wobbled.

Caroline concentrated hard on her plate as Edward waggled an eyebrow meaningfully at Emily. "Absolutely no chance, sweetheart," he echoed his wife solemnly.

"It's my fault for bringing too much luggage," Caroline ventured.

Vicky looked suspiciously at the three innocent faces and then announced in martyred tones that she had to press on, but that if someone would like to bring her a cup of coffee...

"I'll make coffee and sort out the fridge," Caroline volunteered. Vicky's kitchen always seemed more homely than her own antiseptic domain and she liked playing house there. Yuck, some of these things should carry a government health warning she thought, wrinkling her nose with disdain and scooping a heap of aging dross into the bin. As she straightened up she glanced down the garden and saw Emily's bike, heavily disguised under a travelling rug, being manoeuvred into the boot of the car.

Caroline turned away from the window, trying not to smile, just as Vicky flopped down on a kitchen chair, looking less manic. She sat for a few moments with her legs stretched out in front of her, choosing her words. "It won't be the same this year without Phillip will it?"

"He didn't come last year either," Caroline reminded her. "We'd already split up."

"I'd forgotten. Do you miss him?"

"Yes... Oh yes. Perhaps I'd have missed him less if we'd just parted altogether and then he'd died without my seeing him again. But living together – or at least in the same house – for those last couple of months rekindled a lot of old memories... and feelings, I suppose." She shrugged. "I wouldn't have done without that time together – not for anything – but now I do miss him. The strangest little thing will suddenly remind me of him and then I cry... but it's only three months since he died... three months and two days. It gets easier all the time."

"And Alex?"

"I thought we were saving our teenage confessions for sultry days around the pool."

"Can't we just have the teeniest trailer to the main feature?"

"Certainly not. Finish your packing, woman or we'll never catch that ferry."

At half past five Edward squeezed the last bag into the boot and then he and Vicky marched purposefully back into the house.

"Daddy's going to ask Mummy if she's remembered things," Emily confided. "Then Mummy's going to get really cross and tell him he can do his own packing next time."

Sure enough, Caroline thought she could hear a heated discussion wafting through the open window.

"Then we can go," Emily giggled.

****

The ferry was one of those huge new super-tankers and Edward had booked a rather impressive family suite.

158

"Real beds! Smashing!" Vicky said, stretching herself out thankfully on the nearest one. "I really feel as if I'm on holiday suddenly."

"Look Mummy, there's a fridge full of drinks. Can I have a coke? And there's a telly and a bowl of fruit. Can I have an apple?" Emily's enthusiasm was contagious and suddenly they all felt ridiculously festive.

"Gosh, a proper bathroom," Caroline added to the general excitement. "In the ordinary en suite accommodation you can pee, clean your teeth and shower without moving from the spot."

"I've booked a table for dinner while you've all been studying the facilities," Edward announced, leaning on the door frame and contemplating his family. "You've got exactly ten minutes to tart yourselves up. Come on Ems, let's have a look round while we're waiting."

The boat was a far cry from the old ferries he remembered from his childhood which always reeked of beer, petrol and vomit. They wandered among the glittering shop fronts and Emily gazed longingly at a display of glamorous costume jewellery. He was just about to weaken and buy her something when he spotted Vicky and Caroline waving in the distance and he dragged her away from the temptations of Mammon.

Seeing the two sisters so close together he was struck forcibly by how vulnerable they both appeared and, ignoring her vociferous protests, he hauled Emily along even faster in his desire to protect them from the crowds. Caroline looked marvellous really, he reasoned, considering everything she'd been through, but her face still looked transparently thin and her eyes were too large for her small face. The sun would do them both good and Harriet would love fussing over them.

The sight of Vicky made his insides knot up. This baby had been her dearest wish, but pregnancy really didn't suit her. She'd been the same when she'd been expecting Ems – sallow and haggard, he thought disloyally – but she'd start to bloom in about a month's time. The threat of a miscarriage had been the last straw, but that danger was over now, thank God. Harriet had been a wonderful support, although he and Vicky had both felt that she'd been less relaxed and sunny than usual. The strain of Phillip's death had left everyone feeling below par.

"You look worried, darling. Are you all right?" Vicky appeared at his side, smiling up at him, and pressed his hand.

Her face was transformed when she smiled and he felt so moved by this sudden radiance that he bent and kissed her. Caroline walked on ahead of them, swinging Emily's hand in hers, and then gave the child a big hug as they waited for Vicky and Edward to catch up. Emily hopped from foot to foot impatiently and Caroline barely suppressed the urge to follow suit.

Nobody was quite as cheerful the next morning as they sat in the car in the pre-dawn gloom waiting to disembark. Vicky looked as leaden as the sky, but she insisted she'd be all right if she could sleep in the back of the car for a few hours. The early morning grimness had a depressing effect on them all but, as the dawn broke, just north of Angers, their spirits lifted and Vicky was so sound asleep that they dared to talk again.

They made good time once they got onto the motorway and even Edward – not a natural Francophile – conceded that it was a 'fantastic road system'… all things considered. By the time they reached Niort Vicky was awake and they drove into the car park of the service station feeling absolutely famished.

"What I don't understand," Edward grumbled, stabbing at his food with obvious disgust, "is how a nation of such self-professed gourmets can produce such terrible motorway food."

"It's all described in such flowery terms. Either no one bothered to show the menu to the cook, or else he's dyslexic," Caroline agreed.

"The quality of the food improves in inverse proportion to the quantity of irrelevant hyperbole," Edward announced, making a grand gesture with his fork.

"Whoever said that?" Vicky asked in admiration.

"Me – just then."

"No, you idiot. Who said it originally?"

"Still me. It'll go down in the annals of catering as "Maude's Maxim on Inedible Nosh.""

Emily wasn't sure why the adults found this conversation so amusing, but she gave a token giggle, just to be sociable.

"Have you stopped feeling pukey?" Edward asked Vicky as they walked back to the car.

"Yes, I'm fine now. Shall I drive?" She knew he'd refuse.

"You sit in the front," Caroline insisted and I'll get in the back with Ems."

Despite the air conditioning the car seemed to get warmer as they drove further south and by the time they turned off the final section of motorway, Caroline was feeling drowsy. Emily had been asleep ever since they'd left the service station and she was sprawled haphazardly now, with one arm wrapped tightly around a large stuffed dog called George and the other flung across Caroline's lap. Occasionally her mouth would move and her face would twitch, as if she was talking to someone in a dream. She was dark, like both her parents, but with Edward's more pronounced features, not her mother's slim oval face.

Cocooned by the secure warmth of the car Caroline allowed herself the luxury of drifting back into the private pleasures of that night at Alex's flat. They'd walked up the thickly carpeted staircase, hand in hand, and the door of the flat was ajar. Her first, brief impression was of high ceilings and books heaped on every available surface, but neither of them was interested in anything at that moment, except their terrible need for each other. He'd undressed her tenderly, caressing and kissing every inch of her body as he'd removed the hampering clothes. There was no strangeness or reserve between them, just an overwhelming compulsion to respond to each other's desire. He'd led her into the bedroom and continued to caress her as he'd pressed her down onto the bed, his hands and lips bringing her to a frenzy of arousal. Finally she'd arched against him, drawing him deep inside her, unable to wait another moment and waves of pleasure had engulfed them both, leaving them clinging together in an ecstasy of relief.

An unprompted smile crept across her face as she recalled the bliss of that first lovemaking. Vicky glanced back at that moment and Caroline felt herself blush under this sudden scrutiny, but Vicky just raised an eyebrow enquiringly at Emily's sleeping form and turned her attention back to Edward.

She looked out of the window abstractedly. They were crossing the Landes now, the road forging straight across the flat countryside. She was never sure whether this was the most boring part of South West France or the most attractive. The flat scenery, interspersed with large tracts of forest, reminded her in some ways of Suffolk although the architecture of the villages was quite different. It was an area of predominantly second homes – mostly belonging to the French – so in winter it gave the impression of being one big dormitory belt. There were plenty of people around today, however, because it was the first weekend of August – the traditional start of the French holiday season and the busiest weekend of the summer. Shutters were open and lawnmowers were creating dusty tracks through the overgrown grass. She remembered Phillip's amusement as he'd watched the French take enormous pride in lawns which would have been dismissed as hayfields in England.

She stopped focusing on the scenery and returned to her own private thoughts. She and Alex had clung together for a long time in silence, then he'd released her slightly, just cradling her against him with one arm and they'd talked about all sorts of small personal things. She couldn't even remember now what they'd talked about, but it had been easy, as if they'd known each other for ever.

Finally he'd sat up and his eyes had travelled over her naked body, while she'd lain there, unembarrassed, delighting in his open admiration. "I'm not a very good host, darling," he'd apologised, drawing her up to sit against him. "Let's have a shower and then I'll make dinner."

She couldn't remember much about his bathroom except that it was large and lined with white tiles and dark wood panelling. They'd stood in the shower together and made love again under the warm spray. Then he'd dried her, wrapped her in a dressing gown and led her towards the kitchen. This was her first proper look at his flat and she'd pulled back in the hall to take it all in.

The double doors into the drawing room were wide open and she'd had the impression of a room lived in by two different people – there was an elegant backdrop of soft apricot walls, lined with beautifully bound books and a stunning collection of pictures. "My ex-wife was an interior designer," Alex had anticipated her curiosity. Stacked within this elegant shell, on every available surface, were tottering piles of books, magazines, box-files and half-open reams of paper – obviously the busy chaos of the second inhabitant. "It always drove her mad that I couldn't conform to her ordered lifestyle. I did try to at first... Come on, you'll get cold hanging around in the hall. I'm going to make us something to eat."

The kitchen was on the same grand scale as the rest of the flat, but the old fittings had been stripped to the natural wood and laden with Mason china so the effect was surprisingly cosy. Alex had settled her into a Windsor chair while he rummaged in the fridge. "It's all instant I'm afraid – artichokes, smoked salmon and strawberries and there's a bottle of champagne cooling. Will that do?"

In the end they'd abandoned the artichokes, on the grounds that they'd take too long to cook and, after struggling through the salmon and strawberries they'd gone back to bed with two glasses and the rest of the champagne. Finally, even the champagne had remained un-drunk.

She must have fallen asleep at last, because she suddenly heard Vicky's voice very close to her. She opened her eyes and then closed them again, confused. When she looked the next time Vicky was still there, smiling at her.

"Did Emily squash you? She was sprawled all over you. We thought we'd stop for a drink. Do you feel like something cold?"

Caroline shook her head and looked round blankly. "I don't think I'll get out thank you. I'm still half asleep and I'm not thirsty."

"We've only got another hour to go, but Edward was desperate to stop. I don't know why he's so stubborn about driving – I was quite happy to take over for a bit." She shrugged as if the workings of her husband's mind were a complete mystery to her and followed Emily and Edward to the small cafe.

Caroline pressed her eyelids tight closed and then opened them again. She didn't want to tear herself away from her own thoughts for a while. The memories of that night were so blissful that she just wanted to dwell on them, uninterrupted, for as long as possible. He'd be back from South America in two weeks' time and they'd have a glorious few days together in France. She stretched like a cat, contented and lazy from the heat and the anticipation. Then she realised suddenly that she was extremely uncomfortable and very thirsty. She climbed stiffly out of the car and waved to the others. "Sorry to be a nuisance. Can I change my mind and have a small beer?"

"Well this is more like a French summer," Edward sighed, leaning back and tilting his face towards the sun. "It's heated up significantly since we left Niort."

"I must have slept almost all the way across the Landes." Caroline sounded surprised. "I don't remember very much after Bordeaux."

"How much longer?" Emily pestered.

"About an hour. We should be at Lasserre just in time for you to go to bed." Her father nodded with mock severity.

"Granny's not as mean as you are. I want to show her how good I am at swimming. I'm going to do two widths!"

Emily began to hop about on the pavement and finally she persuaded them to climb back into the hot car. This was their favourite stretch of the journey. They drove through attractive, arcaded bastide towns, their covered market squares throwing welcome patches of shade onto the stiflingly hot cobbles. As always they admired the pretty half-timbered houses and the churches with their strangely cantilevered bell towers. The fields were arranged in contrasting patterns – the glorious chaos of the sunflowers next to the military neatness of the vineyards – and the huge watering gantries were swinging back and fore, like prehistoric stick insects, over the occasional expanse of maize. Some of the land had been newly mown and the yellow-ochre stonework of the scattered farmhouses merged into the parched gold of the earth, the ubiquitous scarlet geraniums being their sole adornment.

* * *

"There's Grandpa!" Emily suddenly yelled and Vicky covered her ears in pain.

They could see Mike waving and beckoning and Harriet racing out of the front door just as they pulled up on the gravelled turning circle. There followed an eternity of chaos as everyone kissed everyone else, forgot who they'd done and started all over again. Finally Mike called a halt. "Right let's get your things out of the car and then we'll have a cold drink by the pool." He looked anxiously at his two daughters. "You two go and sit in the sun while Edward and I unload the car."

"I've put you all in your old bedrooms, except that Ems can have Mark's room. Mark and Tessa can have the flat – we aren't letting it this year.

"I just think I'll check that they're putting things in the right place," Vicky dithered for a moment and then disappeared after the men. "Come on Ems. I'll help you find your swimsuit," she called over her shoulder and Emily raced after her, making peculiar whooping noises and dragging a slightly reluctant Caroline in her wake.

Caroline reappeared ten minutes later in a new bikini. "I'm going to have a quick swim, just to cool down and then I'm going to have a good look round the garden. I don't think I've ever seen the hibiscus and the geraniums looking so fantastic."

She gave an involuntary grimace as the cool water touched her hot skin. Vicky emerged from the house and stood with her arm round her mother for a moment as they both watched Edward towing Emily around on an inflatable alligator. Then she slipped into the pool and swam alongside her sister, feeling totally relaxed

164

for the first time since she and Edward had come home from Venice.

It was a perfect evening and they sat talking long after they had finished dinner. The candles had burnt low, but there was a full moon which cast strange patterns of light and shade across the garden, through the branches of the massive old oak.

"We'll certainly sleep well tonight. They woke us at five o'clock this morning on the ferry and Edward must be exhausted after all that driving. Do you know, I'd forgotten quite how gorgeous it is here." Vicky gave a long sigh of pleasure and curled her toes against Edward's foot, which was stretched out towards her under the table.

He leaned forward and squeezed her hand. "Why don't you go to bed? I wouldn't mind another swim if no one minds." He strolled over to the pool house and turned the underwater lights on and Emily stood gazing, enchanted by the brilliance of the illuminated blue water. She watched for a minute or two as her father swam up and down with long clean strokes, but even she didn't have the strength to resist when Harriet finally led her off to bed.

It was late by the time the house was quiet and Harriet wandered back down into the kitchen to turn everything off for the night. She found Mike standing in the doorway looking out into the warm night with Doodle lying at his feet. "He's getting old – he hardly bothered with anyone tonight," she remarked sadly. "He just slept under his palm tree. How did you think Vicky and Caroline were looking?"

"They're both a bit thin, but I expect you'll feed them up. He put his arm around her shoulders and led her away from the doorway. "Stop worrying about everyone and let's go to bed."

She had an odd premonition when she walked past Caroline's door and she tapped gently before letting herself in and closing it behind her. "Are you all right, darling?" She asked as she settled herself on a corner of the bed. Then she saw the tears and drew her daughter towards her. They didn't speak at first, just rocked together wordlessly in a tight embrace.

"I thought things were going well for you now," Harriet said at last, drawing away from Caroline slightly and looking at her appraisingly. "I thought how content you looked when you arrived this evening. Do you want to talk about it?"

"Everything is marvellous with Alex." She gave a convulsive

little sob. "It's better than I'd ever dreamt a relationship could be. Oh dear!" she hiccoughed and a fresh crop of tears ran down her face. "I sound like a sixteen year old."

Harriet smoothed her daughter's hair away from her face with a gentle rhythmic motion, feeling the wetness of her tears beneath her fingers. She didn't speak, just waited for Caroline to continue in her own time. The sobs subsided at last but it was a long time before she felt composed enough to speak again. "I didn't realise how many memories there would be here. I've learnt to cope now at home. I've opened every drawer and every cupboard and I've confronted all the unexpectedly painful reminders but now I'm starting all over again. Added to which is the terrible feeling of life being so unfair..." Caroline shook her head in despair and buried her face in her mother's shoulder again. "We had so much happiness here in the early years and now he's dead, but I'm starting a new life. That is unfair, isn't it? I'm sorry." She sat back and gave her mother a helpless shrug. "It's the middle of the night and we're both too tired to philosophise about the fairness of life."

"If life were fair, darling there'd be no poverty and no pain for anyone. I think that what's happening to you at the moment is totally fair." Harriet smiled at Caroline and wiped the last tear away with her finger. "Your marriage ended, your husband died and now you've found someone else to share your love. I know you feel guilty about Phillip, but you loved him and helped him right up until his death. I think he'd have been pleased if he'd known about Alex. Do you think he might have guessed?"

"I sometimes wonder that myself. By the way," Caroline's face suddenly lit up with pleasure, "Jane has met someone at work and it's so nice to see her looking happy for once."

"Does that mean that you're applying one standard to her and another one to yourself?"

"I suppose it does, but Phillip and I were married for nearly ten years and she only lived with him for nine months."

"So you assume she loved him less?"

"Sorry, that was very judgemental wasn't it? I didn't mean it to be."

"Is there any news of Alex? He's stopped phoning me lately. I suppose that means he doesn't need a go-between anymore." Harriet gave Caroline a quizzical look and smiled to see her daughter blush. "Stop dwelling on the past and irrational feelings of guilt and grab this happiness while you've got the chance." Harriet kissed Caroline goodnight and stood up. "I'm going to bed now, but don't forget I'd like some more grandchildren."

CHAPTER 18

The sun was already quite high in the sky when Caroline awoke and she felt surprisingly refreshed and rational. She'd lain for a long time, after her mother had gone to bed, haunted by a jumble of memories, but finally she'd fallen into a deep sleep and now she felt as if her life was back in perspective.

The kitchen was empty when she went downstairs, but there were a couple of croissants, under a net, on the kitchen table and she could hear voices and laughter coming from the pool. She refilled the coffee machine and walked out into the sunshine.

Her father was standing next to the pool. He was wearing a large sun hat and he was systematically moving the vacuum cleaner up and down the bottom of the pool, with a dreamy expression on his face. Edward was gazing intently at the two small tubes of liquid which analysed the chemical cleanliness of the water. Vicky was lying on a sun lounger doing absolutely nothing. She waved to her sister. "The boys are playing with their swimming pool and Ems is plastering sun tan cream on her dolls. Come and talk to me – this heat is wonderfully soporific." She saw Harriet emerge from the courtyard and called out, "I'll help you with lunch when you're ready. But for goodness' sake come and sit down for an hour."

"Actually, if you don't think I'm being too antisocial I'm going to devote a bit of time to my travel notes. I promised to send Francesca a draft of the first section next week." She turned to Caroline. "I don't suppose you fancy helping with a bit of research do you? You might find it quite interesting." She wrinkled her nose as if she wasn't totally convinced herself.

"What's the problem then" Caroline asked, rubbing a dollop of white cream onto a patch of skin that was turning the colour of Brighton rock. "Isn't it just a case of explaining where places are and slapping down a few dates?"

"Honestly! What a philistine!" Harriet snorted. "We're doing all that, of course, but the new angle is that we're going to interview people in their homes, in the street, sitting around in bars and cafes, etcetera, to give the reader some authentic local colour, backed up with photographs of real domestic interiors. So it would be a fantastic help if I had someone to operate the tape recorder and cameras. Francesca's putting together the purely factual geographical and historical details, because she can do most of that from London, but I'm doing the "Gossip from Gascony" side of the operation."

"What about some line drawings?" Vicky suggested.

"Yes, I thought of that too and I've found someone to do them; a nice young woman called Lisette. She's going to concentrate on the exterior views of typical Gascon buildings, but we thought that real photographs would be useful for the modern life slant because they prove we aren't being fanciful."

"Well, if you really think I'll be some use to you I'll do it. It might be fun I suppose." Caroline sounded dubious.

"I'm touched by your enthusiasm," Harriet pulled a face and rolled her eyes at Vicky. "We'll try two days this week and see how much we get done. Auch should be an interesting place to start and there's a good restaurant there for lunch."

"Right, I'm warming to the idea. Are you reviewing hotels and restaurants as well?"

"Not in any sort of professional way, but we'll mention them if they're in a particularly attractive location and if we've enjoyed eating there. What we're really aiming at is a guide book that someone might actually choose to read for its entertainment value, not just for its dry information."

"Are you really going to call it "Gossip from Gascony? It's a bit Whickeresque," Vicky said, looking doubtful.

"No. Probably not – it sounds too trivial. Francesca's keen on "Gateway to Gascony" but I think that sounds rather like the opening of a supermarket."

Caroline laughed. "Does it have to be alliterative?"

"No, but I suppose it might make it more memorable." Harriet weighed up these imponderables. "Anyway, I'll draw up a plan of action and we'll go on Wednesday and Friday if you're sure you don't mind," she appealed to Caroline.

"You're selling the idea to me and it'll stop me from peeling. We could do Thursday as well if you like." She felt suddenly magnanimous after her initial lack of enthusiasm.

"Something's organised for Thursday, I think." Harriet screwed her face up. "I'm going really gaga you know," she confided to her daughters. "Yes! I've got it! Honor Kershaw's coming to lunch. Her lease has finished on her house in the village and she's decided to go back to England. I think she's been bored witless here for the last six months. Anyway, I said she must come round and meet you all before she goes back. It'll be a relief to have some company, because your father doesn't like her very much and he's so off-hand with her that it's quite embarrassing sometimes. I think she's all right and she's looked after things for us a couple of times when we've been away. Still, Madame Lartigue's back from Australia, so we don't actually need Honor now." Harriet laughed apologetically. "Oh dear, I didn't mean to sound quite so mercenary about her."

They watched their mother walk back into the house and heard the final slap of her flip flops as she disappeared into the courtyard.

"I'd forgotten how peaceful it is here. Although Stockleigh is pretty tranquil, there's still the distant sound of traffic and voices."

"It's not just the quiet, it's the lack of artificial light – Petts Wood is lit up with an awful yellow glow all through the night," Caroline grumbled into her beach towel. "It's impossible to see the stars. Where is everyone by the way?"

"Edward's taken Ems and Doodle on a bike ride round the lake at Peyrusse and Dad's up in his office. I gather he's worried about business. He seems very preoccupied and Mother said on the phone that he's been working very long hours lately. I think she's quite concerned about him."

"I've noticed that they're not as relaxed together as usual. When she came to stay after Phillip died I thought she seemed quite on edge about something."

Their conversation was interrupted suddenly by their father yelling from his office window. "Telephone call, Caroline – quick, it's from Lima."

Vicky was grinning when Caroline returned to the terrace, looking slightly pink. "I think you've fobbed me off for long enough now with this tale that he's mother's friend and that you hardly know him at all. I hear that he's absolutely devastating and that he's besotted with you."

Caroline laughed. "You'll meet him soon so you'll be able to decide for yourself."

"When you were little I'd have pulled your hair for being so annoying."

"And I'd have screamed and screamed and screamed."

"Well you have the happy glow of a woman who's having plenty of satisfactory bonking, so let's take it from there."

"You're very vulgar."

"Well you're not denying it, anyway," Vicky pointed out.

"He phoned regularly after Phil died to ask how I was coping, but I didn't go out with him until a few weeks ago. I've been to dinner twice and to lunch once..." She laughed at her sister's encouraging expression, "and to bed for one whole, glorious night."

Vicky nodded, obviously pleased by this revelation. "So, what does he look like?"

"I think you've missed your vocation – you should be working for the F.B.I. He's medium height, with straight, thick brown hair – starting to go very slightly grey – that he runs his fingers through when he's agitated. His eyes are hazel and when he smiles they seem to light up from inside. He has a wide, sensitive mouth – some people say he has bedroom eyes, but I think he's got a bedroom mouth. He's slim, forty two and very attractive without being traditionally handsome..."

"And you're in love with him."

* * *

Despite her initial lack of enthusiasm Caroline was quite pleased to have something to do while she was waiting for Alex to come back from South America. If she just sat around thinking about seeing him again she suffered from inexplicable light – headedness and an inability to breath. She got up early on Wednesday morning and flicked through her wardrobe for something appropriately pioneering to wear. A vision of Kate Adie sprang to mind but she had to settle for something marginally more frivolous and abandon her hankering for a pith helmet.

"You look pretty, darling," Harriet muttered, putting paid to Caroline's final pioneering aspirations and staggered into the kitchen loaded down like a Texan tourist.

"Whatever have you got there Mum? I thought we were going to Auch, not round the world with Michael Palin."

Your father thought we should take his camera and it's not worth taking it unless we take all the paraphernalia that goes with it – the zooms and wide angle lenses and things. Then there's my camera, some spare films, Edward's polaroid and the tape recorder."

Caroline neatly fielded the spare films before they hit the kitchen floor and then prised her mother's fingers away from the rest of her gadgetry, letting the whole lot slide onto the kitchen table. "Now, can you operate Dad's camera reliably? ... I thought not and neither can I." She pushed it to one side together with its impressive selection of add-ons. "What about your camera?"

"Oh, that's a really marvellous little... "

"Exactly," Caroline interrupted, "so we'll take that. Now, whatever do you want this polaroid thing for? Last time I saw Edward use it was at Emily's christening, and all the photos he took turned yellow within the fortnight, so it's obviously not one of life's more vital bits of equipment." She pushed it onto the reject pile and laughed at her mother's crestfallen expression. "Cheer up. We'll do wonders with your camera and the tape recorder."

"I don't know where you get your bossiness from," Harriet complained as they crunched across the gravel to the garage. "Now, I hear that Alex phoned yesterday, from Peru," she continued without a pause. "Is he coming down here soon, or mustn't I ask?"

"He's flying into Toulouse on the tenth and we're going to spend a few days together before he leaves for Australia and Japan. Will you mind if I just disappear for a while?"

Harriet smiled and patted Caroline's hand, "I'm sure we'll cope without you." Then they drove without speaking for a while, unsure what to say next, until Harriet finally broke the silence. "You're both very lucky," was all she said and Caroline was reminded again fleetingly of her previous, inexplicable unease about her mother.

Suddenly Harriet pulled into a lay-by and pointed ahead. Her face looked so radiant, as she gazed across the countryside at her favourite view, that Caroline immediately dismissed her niggling doubts.

"There, isn't that magnificent? And it's even more spectacular at night with the cathedral and the tower illuminated. It looks just like a performance of son et lumière."

This first stunning glimpse of the old town of Auch on the distant heights was briefly eclipsed, as they drove on, past an urban tail-back of dreary, unappealing shop fronts – the usual mixture of under-subscribed poodle parlours and photocopying bureaux; the notices in their windows peeling and faded almost beyond recognition. Caroline was just wondering what the shopkeepers would do if anyone had the temerity to enter one of these faded establishments, when there was an abrupt change of scene and they emerged, after a suicidal road junction, in a bustling and attractive tree-lined boulevard.

"It looks like a French impressionist painting, with all those cafes spilling out onto the pavement. Do you think it's mandatory to carry two baguettes?"

"Yes, especially on a bicycle," Harriet grimaced as she gave a wide berth to a couple of wobbling, bread-laden cyclists and crossed the River Gers in the direction of the upper town.

"Let's sit here for a moment and have a strategy meeting," Harriet said as she parked the car under the shade of an immense old tree. She put her glasses on to scrutinise her notepad.

While she waited for her instructions Caroline craned up to get a better view of the Cathedral and the Tour d'Armagnac, suspended almost vertically above them, overhanging the River Gers.

"Right." Her mother had gathered her thoughts. "Would you like to start with bars and cafes? I'd like notes on settings, ambience, service and anything else you think is worth commenting on. There are lots of interesting little shops in Auch too, so just jot down anything eye-catching and take lots of photographs. I'm going to try and organise a couple of appointments with local people. I thought it would be useful to talk to a young family living in one of those modern flats on the other side of the river – they must have a stunning view of the old town and of the Escalier Monumental. Then I'd like to talk to someone old, who's lived here from birth – preferably in one of those ancient houses bordering the Pousterles."

"What are they?"

"Narrow alleyways of steep steps that run down from the upper town to the lower town. We'll run up and down a few to work off our lunch."

"And the Escalier Monumental?"

"The monumental staircase. That's two hundred and thirty two steps and we'll do that one twice."

Caroline rolled her eyes in horror. "You know I could have been gossiping by the pool with Vicky?"

"I know, darling. You're a real little martyr."

"So who takes the camera?"

"You do. Please take as many architectural features as you can, because even if we decide that we'd prefer line drawings Lisette can work from the photos."

"Lunch?" Caroline pulled a pathetic little face.

"We'll meet at twelve thirty outside the tourist office which is a really stunning half-timbered building on the corner of Place de la République, near the cathedral. Pick up all the leaflets that you can while you're there. There should be masses of people in the square so try to get some good photographs of local characters – lots of black berets and baguettes. Here you are, you'll need this."

Caroline clutched the proffered notepad like a lifebelt and watched her mother walking away, her high heeled sandals making a brisk clatter on the warm cobbles. She'd always had a weakness for unsuitable shoes, Caroline thought idly, as she tried to remember her instructions. She steeled herself to cross the busy embankment road, away from the river, and wondered what perverse pleasure French drivers gained from accelerating whenever they spotted a pedestrian on a crossing.

The great Escalier was immediately in front of her, but she was reluctant to leave the riverside yet, despite the roar of the traffic, so she strolled on for a few hundred yards. The road suddenly opened up into a large square, revealing a profusion of black berets playing boules under a canopy of pollarded plane trees. A small bar gave a grandstand view of the game and some partisan black berets were giving noisy advice and rude criticism from behind their glasses of pastis. She sat at the one vacant table and ordered a coffee, only to discover that she had knocked the French national pastime from pole position. She blushed at first, under their unselfconscious scrutiny, then she took a deep breath and gave them a dazzling smile, "Bonjour Messieurs."

Ten minutes later she was walking away with copious notes on their view of life in general; the disastrous effects of the presidential elections; and the abysmal standard of their compatriots' skill at boules. She was so pleased with her first foray that she felt like giving a little skip. Two spare films were going to be completely inadequate.

As she returned towards the vicinity of the Escalier she noticed an intriguing little sign pointing towards a narrow back street of tall houses. Pizzeria – hardly very French – one hundred metres, and she made a quick detour.

A tall portly man in a long striped apron was standing, rocking back and fore on his heels, on a small raised terrace under a magnificent Harrods – green awning. A minion was despatched to fetch Caroline's mineral water while the patron engaged her in conversation. Finally, when she'd divulged the purpose of her visit, the whole family was squeezed onto the terrace for a photo-call and she was persuaded to stop and share a bottle of wine. Full marks for ambience, she noted in her book, as she approached the monumental staircase for the third time.

She wished she hadn't drunk the wine when she saw it towering above her, but she forced her legs to move up the interminable steps. The statue of d'Artagnan was at the halfway point so that was a marvellous reason for a rest. Very handsome – he'd got bedroom eyes too she thought irreverently. While she was gazing at him a party of French schoolchildren came milling around, unmistakably continental with their narrow shorts and their little pastel-coloured leather rucksacks and she finished up her first film.

It was worth the slog, she decided, plonking herself down on the parapet wall and staring around her with a sigh of satisfaction and relief. To one side was the breath-taking view over the Gascon countryside and to the other was the sun-streaked golden stonework of the old prison tower and the massive cathedral – Basilique Ste Marie.

Caroline gazed in awe at the massive twin towers of the cathedral, set squarely on top of the magnificent Renaissance facade. This was the main entrance and three gated archways opened into the vast arcaded porch. She and Phillip had never explored Auch – he'd always elected Pau when they'd felt a need for urban distractions – and she was pleased to have this opportunity. Her footsteps echoed in the immense building and she stopped, feeling suddenly very insignificant, to take in the daunting proportions. She helped herself to an information sheet from a display near the main entrance and noted that she was standing under a particularly fine organ by the seventeenth century master, Jean de Joyeuse.

As she stood, craning up at it, she was aware of a woman standing near her, staring into the cavernous space of the ancient cathedral as if her eyes were actually fixed on some quite different scene. She was tall and dark, probably about her parents' age and Caroline's attention was caught because of her slightly inappropriate appearance. She was heavily made up and wearing a beautifully-tailored, silk trouser suit in a glorious shade of emerald. Her black hair was cut in a style which looked slightly too youthful, but it was shown off to perfection by the vibrant colour of the silk; all just a bit too exotic for lunch-time Auch.

Caroline turned away from the woman, and from the organ, and wandered down towards the altar. This cathedral had been the scene of such tremendous hostilities during the Hundred Years War, she reflected, and yet it still induced a comforting feeling of peace and security.

The altar was lit by eighteen stained glass windows, dating from the sixteenth century – the work of someone called Arnaud de Moles, she read from her fact sheet – and famous for the almost caricature – like realism of the subjects' faces. She moved slowly past the windows to the real highlight of the cathedral. Definitely worth stumping up the five francs, she decided, rummaging in her bag and glancing past the attendant to the famous choir stalls.

These one hundred and thirteen richly carved choir stalls were built at the same period as the stained glass windows and they were arranged in two tiers. Above them, around the wall, was a frieze depicting fifteen hundred figures taken from legend, mythology and the Bible. Caroline was fascinated by the clarity of these figures, but however hard she tried she couldn't actually put a name to any of them. One rather splendid aquiline profile bore a disturbing likeness to Alex and she wandered back out into the sunshine, feeling quite wobbly at the thought of seeing him before long.

She had three-quarters of an hour before she was due to meet her mother and she could actually see the tourist office so she had time in hand. After putting a new film in her camera and taking some photographs of the three entrances to the cathedral she headed for a pavement cafe that she'd already earmarked on the opposite side of the square. It didn't have quite the eccentric charm of her previous two watering holes but it's location more than compensated she wrote solemnly in her notebook. She was beginning to sound like an estate agent, she decided, and she drew two neat little smiling faces next to the description of the cafe and a passable replica of the Michelin "good view" logo. The waiter gave her a very engaging smile, when he delivered her coffee, and asked her if she was on holiday, so she decided to add a third, smiling face.

She was just gathering up her possessions, ready to leave, when the woman she had seen in the cathedral came and sat down across from her at a corner table. Almost simultaneously she saw Pierre Didier, the dentist, cross the square in front of her. She was almost certain that he recognised her, but as she started to raise her hand in greeting he turned his head away abruptly and she was surprised to see him join the dark woman. They kissed quite formally, but she noticed that their heads were very close together as they talked and the woman had placed her hand on top of his.

They appeared to be on quite intimate terms.

Caroline didn't know the dentist particularly well, but she knew him well enough to be absolutely certain that the glamorous lady was not his wife. Madame Didier was the nurse at the dental practice and she was much younger than this woman, with long brown curly hair which she knotted up in an elaborate chignon.

The situation was so intriguing that Caroline forgot the time and suddenly she noticed that the baguettes in the large square were now moving at a brisk, single-minded pace – France was about to close down for the customary two hours. Reluctantly she tore herself away from the dental drama and dashed to the tourist office.

Despite the midday heat the old building was cool on the inside, cool and spacious. It had the same feeling of history, seen and survived, as the cathedral and even the racks of gaudy leaflets and posters couldn't detract from the fineness of the architecture. Caroline sifted through the masses of information, balancing her selections carefully on the end of a bookcase, until she became aware that the customary "au revoir" to departing sightseers had been replaced by "bon appetit" and she was coming perilously close to encroaching on serious lunchtime eating. She seized her pile of freebies apologetically and rushed out, while the assistant assured her it was not at all a serious problem; nevertheless locking the door smartly behind her.

Her mother was already waiting when she stepped outside and she felt instantly disorientated by the blinding sunshine after the cool darkness of the tourist office.

"There's an excellent restaurant just down this pedestrian walkway. We'll be a bit extravagant today. There's also a very famous one in the next square and the chef's just been awarded his second Michelin star. It's a marvellous place to go for a really special celebration." Harriet imparted this information with a bland expression and Caroline wasn't sure whether there was more to this than mere academic interest. She didn't pursue the matter and they sat down to a very good meal of regional specialities, mostly duck-based.

Harriet's morning had been just as successful as Caroline's. The mayor's secretary had organised two interviews for the afternoon in exactly the locations Harriet had wanted. "She was absolutely sweet," she explained as she helped herself to a large slice of Pyrenean ewe's milk cheese. "It's much better than cow's cheese," she urged. "Now, do we need more films?"

"We are running low – I was a bit extravagant this morning. By the way I had a quick look around the cathedral just out of interest."

"What did you think of it?" Harriet asked, eyeing Caroline over the top of her wine glass.

"Mostly splendid, a bit shabby in parts, but definitely worth a visit."

"Francesca's doing all that historical documentation."

"I know, but I couldn't resist a quick peep and I've taken masses of photographs. I think those Renaissance facades will look better as pen and ink drawings, but we'll have a better idea when we see the prints."

They'd both been so keen to impart their respective information that they'd almost finished their lunch before Caroline found a moment to tell her mother about the dentist and the mystery woman. "I don't suppose the meeting was significant, but I'm sure Monsieur Didier recognised me and he was looking very shifty."

"I'm afraid it was significant – I hear that Madame Didier has taken the children and gone to stay with her mother in Paris. He's had to find a new dental nurse in a hurry, because his wife more or less ran that practice."

"Who's the woman? She looked much older than him."

"I don't know, but I've heard that he's absolutely infatuated with her. He must be mad to destroy his family like that. I can't understand men who are so weak-willed and I've no time for women who go all out to ensnare married men."

The waiter hovered with the dessert menu. "Croustade de Gascogne," they both chose in unison and they finished their apple tart without mentioning the dentist again, but Harriet's mouth was still set in an angry line when they walked back out into the sunshine.

"Well how did it go?" Vicky asked when they struggled home that evening, just in time for supper.

"We are exhausted," Caroline said with feeling and she and Harriet collapsed on a couple of deckchairs.

"We've coped magnificently without you," Mike pointed out as he handed everyone a glass of chilled rosé wine. "Vicky and I've made supper."

"I helped too, didn't I Mummy?" Emily wailed, glaring at her grandfather.

"Grandpa and I were just going to say that we'd never have managed without Emily." She tweaked the little girl's nose playfully. "So tell us how it went."

"Caroline took masses of photographs and got chatted up in every coffee bar in Auch. We had an excellent and very economical lunch," she grinned sheepishly at Mike, "and altogether it was a very encouraging start. I must phone Francesca and compare notes." She ran up the steps to the house, still as brisk as ever in her high-heeled sandals.

Caroline shook her head as she watched her mother disappearing into the house. "I don't know where she gets her energy from. Anyway, it was a very interesting day. We talked to a couple in their nineties, living in a fascinating old house just behind the cathedral and the wife had actually been born there. They'd only had electricity installed five years ago. They showed us some marvellous photographs – old sepia prints – of their families and then we took photographs of them. They didn't want us to leave. I thought I'd take them a little present – something typically English – and they'd love to meet Emily."

"Would I have to speak French?"

"No, but you'd have to dole out lots of kisses." She teased and Emily pulled a repulsive face. "Then we went and talked to a young mother with a baby, living in a brand new flat with a balcony overlooking the river, on the opposite side from the old town. That was just as interesting in its way, because the French idea of interior decoration is so different from ours for a start. Anyway, Mother's quite encouraged now she's made a start."

"I certainly am," Harriet agreed, coming back into earshot. "I'll sort out all the notes and recordings tomorrow and then, after Friday's trip, we'll get all the films developed so that we can see what's what."

"You haven't forgotten about Honor Kershaw coming to lunch tomorrow have you?"

Harriet stared at Caroline in horror. "It had gone right out of my head. Damn! Well she won't expect anything too elaborate I don't suppose."

"You two can concentrate on the great literary work and I'll make lunch," Vicky insisted. "If we have a barbecue the men will do most of the hard work. Ems and I can buy the food in Peyrusse market in the morning. Don't you dare argue," she looked fierce as she saw her mother open her mouth to object, "or I'll change my

179

mind."

* * *

"I thought she'd never go," Edward grumbled as he and Emily carried trays full of dirty plates and glasses back into the kitchen.

"The trouble with barbecues is that the cooking pans are so greasy and they never fit in the sink or the dishwasher." Harriet stabbed without much effect at the large dirty rack and then she laughed. "We are a couple of old miseries, aren't we?"

"What are you two moaning about?" Vicky walked in from the courtyard balancing an assortment of empty bottles and dirty glasses on a serving dish. Edward grabbed it from her and pushed her onto the nearest chair.

"Stop rushing around. We're coping perfectly well without you, aren't we Harriet? And it wasn't a particularly serious moan – I just thought she'd outstayed her welcome a bit."

"Have I missed the great woman and has the swimming pool turned green yet?" Caroline called to them as she struggled into the kitchen with a large cardboard box. "I'm sorry I've been such an age, but when I got to the supplier he couldn't find the part and he sent someone off to a wholesaler on some industrial estate I'd never heard of. Anyway I went to Marks and Spencer's while I was waiting. Toulouse was swarming with tourists and I'm exhausted." She sank into a chair and fanned her face with her hand.

"You're an absolute angel to go all that way and if your father can fit it this evening we should be able to get the pump working before too much damage is done. Edward threw a bit more chlorine into the skimmers, just to be on the safe side." Harriet shrugged helplessly. "It's the first time we've had to replace such a major part in nearly fourteen years." She looked around the chaos in the kitchen and remembered Caroline's other question. "Yes, you've missed Honor, I'm afraid, although she's only just gone."

"What was she like?" Caroline turned to Vicky.

"Very glamorous, but she tried too hard – you know the type; over dressed and over made-up. Am I being catty?"

"Grandpa didn't like her," Emily confided. "I watched him and he didn't speak to her ever – really not ever. And I didn't like her." She wandered out into the garden after this announcement so there was no opportunity for further elaboration.

Edward raised his eyebrow. "A typically predatory divorcee, if you want my opinion. She's perfected the technique of making you feel you're the only man in the world who's worth talking to. Quite false I'm sure, but after Emily's crushing criticism I almost feel sorry for the woman."

Harriet joined in the laughter, although she looked slightly troubled. "I thought it went very well, but I wish Mike would be a bit more civil to her. I've never known him be that off hand with anyone before. But he's never liked her."

"Are you still planning your trip tomorrow? I'd quite like to come too and have a bit of an Armagnac dégustation." Edward announced, suddenly remembering something that was much closer to his heart than Honor Kershaw.

"Why do you want to do something disgusting and can I come too?"

"It's not disgusting, silly. It's French, and it means having a taste of something – Armagnac usually or wine. You'll have to ask granny if there's room in the car."

Harriet had disappeared into the larder, but she re-emerged at that moment. "Of course there'll be room. It'll be great fun. Do you want to come Vicky? We might even persuade Mike to take some time off."

In the end Vicky declined the invitation because the car made her feel sick in the morning and Mike declined because he was juggling with a deadline.

The peace of the empty garden, after the noisy carload of explorers had left next morning, had an immediately soporific effect on Vicky and it was almost midday when she woke up. The sun umbrella was no longer casting a shadow on her and she woke up, uncomfortably hot and disorientated. The kitchen was cool in contrast, and she pottered around making coffee for them both – the tiles feeling blissfully refreshing under her bare feet. Her father would be feeling quite neglected, she thought, as she walked up his office stairs. Doodle plodded up after her, ever hopeful that a few chocolate digestives might fall off the tray, so they were both surprised to discover that the office was empty.

CHAPTER 19

"I feel like walking out on the whole lot of them," Harriet grumbled, as she and Mike lay in bed on Tuesday night. "Vicky's been grumpy and Emily's whined non-stop ever since Edward left on Sunday," she sighed, as she came to her real moan, "and Caroline's driving me potty. The man's arriving tomorrow morning and she's behaving as if she's going to the electric chair."

"She's probably worried. She doesn't know him very well after all..."

"Don't be so reasonable," Harriet snapped. "She's known him for more than three months and she's been to bed with him so she needn't act like a Vestal Virgin."

"One roll in the hay doesn't make a summer."

"Idiot," Harriet chided him. "But honestly – you know she's planning on bringing him back here for lunch? Why isn't she going straight back to his place for a bit of...."

"Don't interfere!" He interrupted. "If she wants to bring him here first she's probably got her reasons." He lay still for a moment. "Did I hear Mark on the phone tonight?"

"Yes and he didn't sound particularly cheerful either. I think he might have had a bit of a row with Tessa. I get the impression that he's keener on settling down than she is. Anyway, they'll be arriving here in less than two weeks' time, so perhaps the break will do them good." She snuggled up against him. "I've lost interest in my children suddenly. Let's concentrate on us instead."

She started to run her hand down his body but he caught it in his own and pressed it back down onto the bed. "I'm sorry, darling, but I feel a bit sick. Do you mind if we just go to sleep?"

He turned away from her and she lay in the darkness next to him, biting her lip to stop the tears from forming. His back was an insuperable barrier and she edged away slightly, frightened of this sudden constraint between them and certain, with a gnawing black certainty, that it wasn't anything to do with feeling sick.

Caroline set her alarm for half past seven. She'd need to leave the house at eight thirty, she reasoned, if she was to be in good time for his plane. The thought of seeing him again was making her heart beat so hard that she could hear it through her T-shirt, as insistent as the school metronome. She had decided to invite him back to lunch and now she couldn't imagine why she'd made this decision. The only thing she wanted to do was go straight back to his rented house and make love for three days. So why this perverse prevarication? Was she frightened that he didn't feel the same about her after two weeks' separation? That was irrational because he'd phoned her whenever he'd been anywhere civilised enough to boast a phone. She could have wept with frustration at her own stupidity and yet she knew that for some irrational reason she was going to go through with her plan. Perhaps she was afraid of appearing too eager? Surely she didn't have to play schoolgirl games at thirty two.

Despite her apprehensions she fell asleep quickly, but she was awake long before the alarm next morning and went straight into a state of catatonic terror. She showered and sprayed herself with scent. Then she sniffed in panic – she smelt like a Bangkok brothel – and showered a second time. Now she noticed that she was beginning to peel, so she slapped liberal quantities of after-sun all over. If he grabbed her too hard at the airport, she'd shoot straight out of the terminal building, she thought gloomily, and tried to wipe some of the grease off on her bath towel.

She'd already decided to wear her new bikini with a linen halter top and her white shorts. That looked rather seductive, she decided, contorting herself in front of the mirror to catch every angle, but on the other hand it didn't look as if she'd tried too hard. Then she packed enough things to last three nights – the first sensible thing she'd actually done in the last twenty four hours. She raced for the car, clutching her overnight bag and a croissant, but she was much too excited to eat the croissant and she threw it out of the window to a surprised roadside dog.

When she saw him standing next to the luggage carousel she felt quite faint. He looked sunburnt and fit after a fortnight of living rough in Peru and he was wearing a simple pale shirt with equally pale trousers. He could have come from a different planet from the rest of the garishly-dressed holiday crowd. She walked across to the stand and fetched a trolley, reasoning that he might need one, but actually gripping it as a means of steadying herself. He noticed her at once and that wonderful smile lit up his face She held on tightly to the trolley and swallowed hard.

Finally he was walking towards her. He put his arms around her and held her close to him for a long time, brushing her hair and her neck with his lips. Had she expected a more openly passionate welcome? She wasn't sure what she'd expected, but she heard herself prattling inanely, in an attempt to hide her confusion.

Once they were in the car he ran his fingers down the side of her face and kissed her again very gently on the mouth. Then he took both her hands from the steering wheel and pressed her palms to his lips.

He rested his arm on her shoulder as she drove and she knew that she'd made the wrong decision before the words were out of her mouth. His voice had a slight edge to it as he accepted her invitation to lunch. There was a car included with his rented house – an absolute jalopy he explained – but if they could pop in there on the way to Lasserre he could pick it up and unpack his swimming shorts.

He left his arm on her shoulders but it didn't feel as electrically charged anymore and she sensed that the intimacy had gone out of their conversation. He gave her a very entertaining account of his trip to Peru, but she felt that it had the makings of an after-dinner speech, and that he'd glossed over the more serious aspects of the trip. When they'd been in London he'd hinted that the purpose was to research the drug trade, but now he made it sound as if he'd been on a package holiday. A guide had taken him to Macchu Picchu, the "lost city" of the Incas, a place of breath taking beauty, in the shadow of the Andes, and he'd been air lifted by helicopter to explore the slopes of Mount Huascaran – Himalayan proportions and a pretty impressive sight, apparently.

Well, that left another twelve days unaccounted for, and he obviously wasn't going to divulge any more for the moment. He sat back in his seat, still cradling her shoulders with his arm, and looking out thoughtfully at the rolling Gascon scenery. She had the impression that his mind was a long way away, perhaps recalling the Peru that the tourist didn't see.

Suddenly he turned his attention back to Caroline. "Has your mother made a start yet on her Gascony travelogue? She and Francesca Penn are a pretty talented team."

Caroline launched into a description of their research in Auch. It was very small beer compared with the Peruvian jungle, and they both started to relax as they considered possible book titles. "Gerrymandering in the Gers" was Alex's favourite and although they both laughed at this ridiculous suggestion Caroline knew that she'd caused a restraint between them, which the laughter hadn't quite erased.

The house he was renting was prettier than Caroline had

remembered, from her one brief visit to its owners several years ago, and the garden was delightful. The hibiscus and the wild roses had taken over and were growing in colourful contrast to the yellow sun-baked earth. Alex reversed the old Deux Chevaux out of the garage and looked at his watch. "We'd better go, it's nearly half past twelve."

She didn't want to go anywhere, but she got back into her mother's car and followed the little red Citroen. When they were quite close to her parents' house he gave a frantic hand signal and pulled over. She did the same, assuming that he'd broken down and he jumped out and walked back to her. He crouched down next to her open window and spoke urgently. "Why did you decide to hide behind your parents like this? I leave again on Saturday morning and all I wanted was to spend three whole days with you. I thought after our night at the flat that was all you wanted too. Now I feel as if you're running away from me. If you're still not ready for another commitment you must tell me and I'll understand." He stood up and walked back to his car.

She longed to run after him, but she couldn't move. She wasn't even sure how she put the car into gear and followed him back to Lasserre. Once they reached her parents' house he behaved absolutely normally, just as if he'd never delivered his veiled ultimatum, and gave the impression of enjoying every moment of family life. He and her father played piggy-in-the-middle with Emily in the pool. He chatted animatedly to Vicky and had long discussions with Harriet about literary reviews.

Caroline, alone, felt she was being neglected and she slipped quietly into the pool and stretched out on an airbed. Suddenly she felt his presence near her and his warm hand brushed against her thigh. The pleasure of his touch against her cool skin made her shiver, but he mistook her reaction and moved away. "I didn't realise that you found me so repugnant," he snapped and she watched, panic-stricken, as he got out of the water and strode across the terrace to speak to Harriet. The words drifted across the garden – an appointment with an estate agent at four o'clock – and she saw him picking up his towel.

She sank right under the water in her rush to climb off the lilo and she sped after him, across the garden, still shaking the water out of her hair.

"Have I got time to dry my hair?" she smiled up at him breathlessly, resting her hand on his arm. "My bag's packed already

– I put it in my mother's car this morning."

"Did you see the way he looked at her?" Vicky drooled, after they'd lurched off in the Deux Chevaux. "I don't remember Edward ever looking at me quite like that. I don't know how she could stand there so calmly."

"Well he's a bit of a professional smoothie and I suspect they'd just had a little tiff," Harriet said sagely. "I don't suppose he'd anticipated going out to lunch."

"Well it certainly wouldn't have been my choice if I'd been her and I'd just picked him up from the airport."

"Vicky, you're a married woman and you're pregnant," Harriet said reprovingly. "I just hope he doesn't let her down."

* * *

"Why didn't you say you were intending to stay with me?"

"I thought it would be obvious, but I wasn't sure that you wanted me to." She put her hand on his, as it gripped the steering wheel of the wilful old car. His hands were long and slim and she gently stroked her fingers along the smooth dark hairs.

"How could you think that after that night at the flat?" His voice was quiet, hardly more than a whisper.

She shrugged slightly and blushed. "I suppose I was frightened that it didn't mean the same to you as it did to me and then I think I was expecting a ...warmer... welcome at the airport."

He gave a short laugh. "You are a little goose. Did you expect me to screw you on the luggage trolley?"

She slid her arm around his neck. "Nice...but a bit public...and then I definitely wouldn't have taken you back to my parents' for lunch."

Her hand rested on his shoulder and he turned his head to nibble the ends of her fingers. "I'm sorry I snapped at you in the pool."

He turned off the road onto a forestry track and then he kissed her. It seemed to go on for ever and she opened her eyes to see him smiling at her. She drew his face down towards hers again, but he put his finger lightly on her lips. "There's an old Gascon peasant in a black beret waiting to show us his ancestral home and he's already been waiting for ten minutes."

He held her close for some moments longer and then she slid reluctantly back onto her own seat. "I'm not sure that I look respectable enough to go house hunting." She brushed her hair back from her face with her fingers and looked up at him, her eyes

186

radiant.

"You're beautiful," he said simply, and then he grinned. "Anyway I'm planning on making you look much less respectable later on."

"Promise?"

He extracted the estate agent's details from the glove compartment. "Stop trying to seduce me and read the instructions for finding the place."

He drove back over the bumpy track and onto the road. "Well?"

"I'm trembling too much to focus."

"Try holding it the right way up, sweetheart." He turned the paper over gently and put it back into her hands.

"Right." She took a deep breath and concentrated on the dancing words. "Drive straight across the unmarked cross-roads immediately after Montegut village." She looked at the estate agent's description on the attached piece of paper, and a couple of photographs slid onto her lap as well. "It looks nice."

"I've cross-questioned them on the phone and there don't seem to be any obvious disadvantages – no sewage works or high-rise flats."

"I think you'd better slow down. Now fork right at that ruined wattle and daub cottage and then turn left at the sunflowers."

They were in the middle of gently rolling hills, with fields of the huge yellow blossoms on all sides. As the track dipped and wound in front of them they caught the occasional glimpse of a sprawling terra cotta roof line and the familiar golden tone of rambling stonework.

"I think this is actually the drive," Caroline volunteered, looking anxiously for further clues. It *was* the drive and, a few seconds later, they were bumping under a high stone archway into a shaded courtyard.

"You'll have to do the talking," Alex insisted, looking suddenly less confident. "My French is almost non-existent. I can only manage "parfait" and "très joli"."

"That's all you'll need, I think; it really does look quite perfect and exceedingly pretty. Here comes your old Gascon peasant," she whispered as a tall, good-looking woman came out of the front door, extended her hand graciously and introduced herself: "Madame Laffitte".

They walked around the outside first and while they examined the garden and the view she told them that it had been her father's home and that, although he had moved out, he was still in good health.

"That's quite important because of the complicated French inheritance laws," Caroline explained after she'd translated the information.

Apparently the view stretched right down south to the Pyrenees, but in summer the mountains were only visible if bad weather was forecast. Today they were comfortingly hidden in a heat haze. The garden was a wilderness, but Caroline had been well trained by Phillip and she recognised all sorts of flowers and shrubs waiting to be rescued. To one side was a massive old oak, and on the other side, casting shade over a small pond, were a weeping willow and a huge mimosa. Madame Laffitte's father had planted those, but not the centuries old oak, she told them with a smile.

"This is the first house I've seen that I think I like as much as Lasserre," Alex announced. "I knew I was going to like it as soon as I saw the picture."

"And it's got a view of the Pyrenees," Caroline pointed out. "Or it will have in the winter months."

Madame Laffitte smiled at them and then said something to Caroline which she didn't immediately translate.

"What did she say?" Alex looked enquiringly at Caroline's uncertain expression. "Is there death watch beetle or something?"

"There probably is," she flushed slightly, "but she actually said that my husband must learn to speak French."

Alex smiled and nodded his agreement at the owner's daughter and said firmly to Caroline, "Tell her that you're going to teach your husband to speak French as soon as we move in."

The inside was cool and dark in contrast to the sun-baked garden, but Caroline was in too much of a turmoil to absorb very much of it. All she knew for certain was that life was suddenly perfect and so was the house. Madame Lafitte rushed around opening shutters, with Alex's help, but Caroline just stood in a daze and stared.

"Well what do you think?" Alex asked, pressing her hand, as he took in the wealth of detail, lit up in the soft afternoon sunlight. She couldn't bring herself to answer him – she just squeezed his fingers between her own.

They wandered through the cool interior in a trance. Most of the ground floor was quarry-tiled, except for one room, which retained its handsome old flag-stones. Madame Lafitte was obviously proud of the house, although she explained to them, with a cheerful shrug, that she and her husband lived, from choice, in a brand-new, centrally-heated villa with every modern convenience.

"Absolutely nothing's been spoilt," Caroline sighed with satisfaction. "The evier is in perfect condition." She ran her hand over the ornamental old stone sink. "The fireplaces are lovely too, especially the big inglenook, with the bread oven."

"The beams look sound," Alex pointed out, on a more practical note.

Madame Laffitte nodded encouraginly at them both and spoke briefly to Caroline before disappearing in the direction of the courtyard.

"She says that we're to take our time looking around upstairs, because she wants to go and collect some things from the barn."

"How long has she given us exactly?"

She put her arms round his neck and gave him an impulsive kiss. "Not that long," she scolded and steered him towards the wide, carved staircase.

Upstairs were four large rooms, exactly the same as downstairs.

"No bathroom," Alex remarked.

"Lasserre didn't have a bathroom when we bought it, nor that big kitchen, but there's masses of space here for you to install a couple of bathrooms."

He turned her towards him and put his arms around her. "For us to install them."

She looked down uncertainly, but he put his finger under her chin and made her look at him. "I thought Madame Laffitte organised everything this afternoon, perfectly satisfactorily."

She didn't have time to reply, because they heard brisk steps on the stairs and the lady herself walked in, explaining as they looked around the large bedroom that this room had the best view of the Pyrenees.

"Do you want me to ask her anything?" Caroline offered, as they stepped outside again into the blinding sunlight.

"Can we come and have another look tomorrow?"

"She says that she'll instruct the estate agent to give us the keys whenever we need them," Caroline relayed dutifully.

"This courtyard's too attractive for just parking cars," Alex remarked as they walked back to the little Deux Chevaux, after shaking hands with Madame Lafitte. "We could fill it with flowers and eat out here. Where shall we put the pool?"

They stopped the car on the drive and looked back at the house. Madame Lafitte drove past them, waving.

"Well?" Alex asked

"It's perfect."

"I don't mean the house."

"Neither do I."

He held her tightly to him and they watched as the shadow of the huge oak tree lengthened across their newly-discovered paradise.

He shifted to look at his watch. "Let's go and eat in that little restaurant at Saint Magnan. We should get to know our new village."

"I don't feel hungry," she said, clinging to him.

"This may be your last chance to eat before I go." His eyes were teasing her.

"I'm not tidy enough to go to a restaurant."

"You're very tidy." He gently pushed a stray, blonde curl back from her face. "There, tidy and perfectly edible."

They arrived at Saint Magnan before the restaurant was open, so they sat at the nearby bar and had a cool drink while they waited. The tables were spread out across the wide pavement in the warmth of the evening sun and the big covered market, with its massive beams and arcaded side streets, made a dramatic backdrop.

"I don't want you to go."

"I'll be back soon and then we'll be able to start properly – no more uncertainties and separations."

"I'm frightened."

"Whatever for?"

"I'd only loved one man before I met you and, first of all our marriage failed, and… and then he died." She faltered. "I couldn't bear anything to happen to you. Do you think I'm jinxed?"

"I think you're adorable."

She smiled, "That's what you said when we first met."

"It was love at first sight."

"Don't tease me." She looked solemn.

"I'm not. It really was. I pestered your mother almost daily for news. I should have felt ashamed of myself, because I knew that I was waiting for your husband to die – but I was too smitten to feel ashamed."

"And you aren't frightened?"

He leaned across the table and took her hand. "I have every intention of living until I'm at least a hundred and you'll be a seductive young girl of ninety two. Now, let's have something to eat."

The restaurant had spilled into an external courtyard for the summer months and they sat under a vine-decked pergola.

"This is romantic," Caroline smiled at him and the love in her eyes unsteadied him.

He swallowed hard, to regain his composure and then they began to talk. It was just as easy as it had been that night in his flat in London. He'd already told her all about his son, James, nearly nineteen and studying at art college. "Now that he's older I'd like him to have a home where he can bring his friends – a flat in Knightsbridge is all right for parties, but it's very claustrophobic. He'll enjoy France. Will you mind having him around sometimes?"

She shook her head and toyed thoughtfully with her casserole of wild boar. "We'll be a real family – as long as he doesn't resent me. I suppose that my mother told you Phillip and I had wanted to have a baby? It just didn't happen and I couldn't bear to undergo all those awful tests."

"She said you'd have liked a baby, but nothing more."

Caroline explained the bare facts of her teenage trauma – it seemed much less important now than it had when she'd poured it out to Phillip, twelve years ago. "So, when I went to the gynaecologist for tests to see why I couldn't conceive, I just panicked and couldn't go through with it. Phillip sympathised but I think he always blamed me that we didn't have children and in the end it was partly responsible for destroying our marriage."

"Did he go for fertility tests?"

"No, but it's usually the woman's fault isn't it?"

"I think that's probably an old wives' tale. The chances must be equally divided. Perhaps we'll be lucky – if you'd like that."

She laughed softly, "That would be nice. How many did you have in mind?"

"Two would be a reasonable start." He squeezed her hand "Do you want coffee?" She shook her head, not trusting herself to speak suddenly. "Good. We'll go." He dropped a couple of notes on top of the bill and guided her out of the restaurant.

They hardly spoke on the way home and she sat bolt upright, staring ahead. She watched in a daze as he fished her bag off the back seat and then she allowed him to propel her into the house. She turned towards him as soon as the front door had closed behind them and their hands and mouths couldn't wait any longer. They struggled to undo each other's clothes, their fingers made clumsy by the urgency of their desire, until they stood naked in the dark hallway crazed with longing.

"This floor feels cold," Alex took his mouth away from hers for a moment and started kissing her ears and eyes. "Can we wait long enough to go up to bed?"

Caroline drew his hands towards her breasts with a sigh of pleasure and then reluctantly released herself from his grip. "I love you," was all she said and then they began to move towards the stairs. It took an age to get to the top because they clung and kissed on every step but finally they reached the bedroom. Alex drew her down on top of him and they were lost in such an intense pleasure that it seemed as if it would never stop.

They lay locked in each other's arms for a long time afterwards and then he made love to her again, less urgently this time, but slowly and tenderly. Then they slept until the sunlight woke them up.

He leaned on his elbow and looked down at her face, which was streaked with pink where it had been pressed against his chest. "How are you?"

She brushed her fingers against his hair and sighed, "Happy, blissfully happy and madly in love. What about you?"

His hands slid down the soft, smooth skin of her back and he drew her to him again. "Oh darling," he whispered into her damp hair. "Darling...."

The phone rang at eleven o'clock. Caroline was padding round the bedroom, wearing one of Alex's shirts, her hair still wet from the shower and he was shaving. She heard him speaking rather slowly and clearly so she guessed there was someone French on the line.

His face looked slightly grim when he put the phone down. "That was the notaire. Someone else is showing interest in the house and we must sign some sort of legal agreement today, or we'll risk losing it."

"Well, we can easily be at the notaire's office before midday. It's only twenty minutes to Vic sur Baise." She gave him such an appealing smile that he felt his insides melt.

He drew her to him and ran his hands over her body, naked

under the voluminous shirt. "You can't run around the bedroom with next to nothing on like this and expect me to be excited about going to see the notaire."

She rubbed her hand ruefully against her face and pulled away from him. "You've only shaved one half of your face – it's like kissing a hedgehog. Come on, let's go to Vic. We'd be miserable if we lost that house."

Twenty minutes later they were on their way to Vic sur Baise. "I'll miss driving this car," he shouted over the noise of the Deux Chevaux as it bounced along like a giant perambulator. "Shall we buy one once we're living down here?"

Vic sur Baise was a bustling, lively little town, but they were too anxious to reach the office before lunch to spare any time for sightseeing. The notaire was a tall elegant man, younger than they'd expected and to Alex's relief he spoke almost perfect English. Apparently there was another interested party, but the agreement hadn't been drawn up yet, so nothing had been signed.

"But in that case we can't sign anything either," Alex reasoned, "and I'm going away on Saturday morning for three weeks."

The notaire considered for a moment and then announced that all Alex needed to do was organise a banker's draft for the deposit and give power of attorney to Caroline. This was drawn up immediately, with much smiling and nodding, by the notaire's secretary and Alex gave Caroline a triumphant grin as he signed the last page.

"Well we've done it." Alex put his arm round her shoulders, as they walked back towards the car, deafened suddenly by the midday siren "If the estate agent's still open we could pick up the keys and have a picnic in the house to celebrate."

They were lucky – the grocer was chatting to a friend, so he hadn't shut up shop and the estate agent had been delayed by a late phone call.

"That was close," Carrie laughed, as they collapsed back into the car, panting.

"I'm not sure I'll ever get used to everything shutting at twelve o'clock," he sighed, slightly exasperated. "And the champagne won't be cold."

"Never mind. We could stand it in the pond for half an hour," she suggested.

They noticed the name of the house as they turned into the

drive. "La Plaisance," Caroline read out. "I like that. Names are very important."

Alex struggled to open the old door and then they rushed round the house opening the shutters, just like the day before. It seemed familiar to them now, almost homely and if anything they were more enchanted on their second visit than on their first.

They found glasses and a knife in a huge cupboard in the kitchen and Caroline made crunchy ham rolls with the baguette. "Shall we take everything into the garden?" she asked. "I think there's a travelling rug in the car."

The oak was casting a wide pool of shade and they put the rug down near it, behind a thick screening of hibiscus bushes. "That's nice – we've found a secret garden." She smiled down at him as he straightened the edges of the rug. "I'm going to fetch the suntan cream and my sunhat from the car."

He'd opened the champagne by the time she got back and she leaned against him to drink it. "Are you ready for something to eat?" she asked, stretching across him to reach the picnic basket.

He held her arm as it passed in front of him and starting with her fingers he kissed the whole length of it. Then he began to undress her. Once he'd removed all her clothes he kissed her on the mouth, but he made no move to make love to her, beyond that. "There, you look much prettier without your clothes on. Now we'll have something to eat."

"What if somebody comes along? I feel very vulnerable, sitting here like this." She pulled a little face and leaned towards him for another kiss. Then she started to undo his shirt buttons. "That's better." She smiled approvingly when all his clothes were removed. "Now it's fair."

He laughed at her contented expression and then he put his head on one side to look at her again. "You look like that painting by Renoir," he said as he placed her sunhat carefully on her head, and pushed a few wisps of hair under the brim.

"I've never had a picnic before, wearing nothing except a sunhat. Have you?" she asked, twiddling her glass of champagne in one hand and picking baguette crumbs carefully out of the hairs on his chest.

"No, but I could get quite addicted to the concept. What do you think?"

"Mmm," she giggled. "But it's a bit like eating toast in bed – you get crumbs in awkward places."

"I'll lick them all off you."

She leaned into the basket again and pulled out a bag of cherries. "Open your mouth," she instructed and then they both sat, with the bag between them, popping cherries into each other's mouths.

"What a waste," he laughed. "You look so sexy, but the heat and the champagne have made me too sleepy to do anything about it. Let's just lie in the sun for a while."

"We'll have to put suntan cream on or we'll burn the bits that aren't usually exposed," she warned, sitting up and squeezing some cream onto his chest and then spreading it carefully all over his body. "Is that nice?"

"It's making me lose interest in having a siesta suddenly. Let me put some on you." He trickled the cream onto her skin and then began to massage it into her, his fingers probing every curve and hollow, until finally he parted her legs, applying the sensuous lotion with slow, tender precision.

She drew his mouth down to hers and wound her legs tightly around him. "I've lost interest in having a siesta too," she murmured.

That evening they ate at home and suddenly all the domestic chores of shopping and cooking, even washing up, seemed infinitely pleasurable – enhanced by their own delight in each other. Now there were just two nights and one day left of their precious holiday, but she tried not to let the thought of the imminent parting spoil any of the magic..

They went back to La Plaisance the next day, feeling business-like with pencils and paper and they sat on the rickety bench in the courtyard while they planned the renovations they'd like to do.

"I'm sure you'll meet some very glamorous women while you're working with the film company in Australia. Promise you'll come back?" She suddenly looked very woebegone and he put his arm around her, letting the paper slip off his lap.

"I can't stand women with corks around their hats."

"Be serious," she sniffed. "Three weeks is a long time."

"We coped with almost six months."

She was struck again by the mellowness of his voice and she thought back to those weeks of listening to it at Phillip's bedside. "Phillip was a great fan of yours, you know. I don't think I've ever

195

told you that. He used to love your books and when he became too ill to hold a book properly Tessa bought him a set of tapes. They were tapes of you, reading your latest book." She took her hand in his and looked down at his fingers. "I felt so ashamed, because I was sitting watching him die, but all the time I was listening to you and the more I heard your voice the more I realised that I was falling in love with you."

Alex increased the pressure around her shoulder and then he drew her to her feet. "Let's go and see if the Pyrenees are visible today from our bedroom."

An hour later she held his face between her hands and asked innocently, "Were they visible?"

"I think we forgot to look, but we've christened the house."

"That's the garden and the house we've christened now." She lay back and looked around thoughtfully. "I like this room and I especially like this bed. Perhaps they'd be willing to sell it to us."

They got up reluctantly and then had one last wander around the house before strolling through the garden and finally peering into the cobwebby recesses of the outbuildings.

"I'll come here while you're away, because then you'll seem closer," she blurted out miserably as they drove away in the direction of Montegut village.

"Well don't mope. You'll have the documents to sign and you could start planning the renovations. It's not as if I'm going for ever." Alex's down-to-earth approach cheered her up and she almost began to feel excited about all the things she'd be able to do while he was away. It would be fun to clear the garden a bit and she could draw up some proper plans for the renovations.

"Will you phone me?" she asked, as they lay in bed that night.

"I'll phone as often as I can, but you're not to worry if I don't phone every day. The time difference may make it complicated and we'll be looking at some pretty remote locations."

She sighed and clung to him and they were still clinging when the alarm woke them up next morning.

They both made an effort to be cheerful as they drove to the airport, but after Alex had disappeared through his departure gate she felt hollow inside and she sat in the car for a long time before she could face the solitary drive home.

The house seemed strange now and she was reluctant to destroy any of the memories of their idyllic three nights, but in the end she stripped the crumpled sheets from the bed and pushed them in the washing machine and cleaned up the remains of supper from the kitchen. Then she dozed in the sun until the washing was done. It was mid-afternoon before she phoned through to Lasserre to ask if someone would fetch her. She put the dear little Deux Chevaux back in the garage, closed the shutters and strolled down the drive to wait for Vicky.

"Don't look so desperate," her sister said sympathetically. "He'll be back in three weeks. How did it go anyway? Did you have fun?"

Caroline told her about the house at Saint Magnan and suddenly the whole wonderful significance of the two days hit her forcibly, flooding her heart with wild happiness. She was longing to tell Vicky – and the whole world – that he loved her, wanted to marry her; that they'd have children. But she couldn't quite bring herself to divulge such precious secrets for the moment. She needed to hug it to herself, very privately, for just a bit longer.

"Well, he was looking at you very adoringly," Vicky remarked, but if she was hoping to drag any more information from her sister she was disappointed.

Harriet and Mike asked her if she'd had a good break but they didn't pry. Alex phoned her from London that evening and then she made her excuses fairly early and went to bed.

"She obviously hasn't had much sleep," Vicky commented drily to her mother as they cleared up in the kitchen later. "Still, it'll do her good."

For some reason both women found this little homily very funny and when Mike came into the room they were still giggling helplessly.

"Whatever's going on?" he asked.

"I don't know really." Harriet shook her head and spluttered a bit more. "I don't know why we were laughing – it wasn't funny at all – Vicky was just being patronising."

Mike shook his head and looked mystified. Thank God Mark was arriving on Saturday. He was suffering from a glut of women at the moment.

CHAPTER 20

Despite her exhaustion of the previous night Caroline woke up early the next morning and lay quietly – taking stock. There were things to be organised back in England and they hadn't discussed any of them yet. What about her job? She couldn't imagine her nine-to-five existence fitting in with Alex's lifestyle. And then there was her house and his flat in Knightsbridge. Perhaps they could sell his flat and her house and buy something that they both liked. This time round she definitely wasn't going to have someone else's taste imposed on her and he'd obviously need a base in England, even if they spent most of their time at La Plaisance. A little smile broke through her worries as she thought of that. Well, it was no use speculating on things at the moment and hurried international phone calls were not very conducive to making long-term domestic plans. On the other hand she didn't want to let Cliff down, especially as he'd battled very hard on her behalf to organise one and a half terms' sabbatical. She'd ask his advice about giving notice, but she wouldn't do anything else until Alex came home.

She felt relieved now that she'd actually confronted the problems and was about to get up, when Emily slid around the door.

"Are you awake?" she whispered. "No one else is, except Mummy, and she's being sick. I'm never going to have babies. Yuk." She pulled a foul face and Caroline laughed.

The little girl climbed into bed with her and snuggled down. "Do you miss Uncle Phillip?" she asked. "Mummy said that I wasn't to say anything about him – she'll be cross." She looked at her aunt with her head on one side and Caroline smiled at the old-fashioned expression on the child's face.

"Yes, I do. What about you?"

"Yes, I do too. Was he scared of dying?"

"I don't think so." She smoothed the little wisps of hair out of Emily's eyes. "And we had fun in Richmond Park, didn't we?"

Emily nodded enthusiastically. "Are you going to marry Alex?"

"I'm not sure. Would you like to be a bridesmaid?"

"Yes, as long as I don't have to wear a pink dress like my friend Amelia wore. It was really disgusting. Her brother said she looked like a stick of candyfloss."

Caroline agreed that it sounded ghastly and that they'd choose a colour together.

"I heard Mummy telling Granny that he's sexy. What does that mean?"

"Sort of cuddly....with nice eyes," Caroline replied cautiously and, to her relief, Emily remembered she'd brought her new book to show her so the subject was dropped.

Emily's reading had improved dramatically in the last few months and she entertained her aunt until they could hear definite sounds of activity clattering up from the kitchen. Then she raced off to find new distractions.

Caroline got out of bed slowly and trailed into the shower. The warm pressure of the water reminded her of Alex's body against hers and she stood leaning her forehead against the cool tiles while she recaptured all the pleasures of those three days. She stayed like this for some moments, with her eyes closed, until she felt composed enough to dress and then she scrutinised herself in the mirror carefully. She ran her fingers lightly around her eyes. There were faint lines there now. She wasn't a child in love... not this time. This was a mature passion between two adults and she should savour every moment, she scolded herself, not go mooning around like a love-sick teenager, just because he was away for a few weeks. There was plenty to occupy her, she decided, and she went downstairs in a more positive frame of mind.

Her mother was sitting in the kitchen, wrapped in a beach towel, and chewing the end of a biro, her eyebrows drawn together with the effort of thinking. Vicky was sitting opposite her and she seemed to be involved in the contemplative process.

"Anchovies," Harriet said, giving Caroline an absent minded wave with her biro.

"Fish fingers."

"Cod steaks," Vicky giggled.

Harriet looked up crossly. "Are you two trying to confuse me?"

"I thought we were playing that word association game." Caroline gave her mother an innocent look.

"Mark and Tessa are arriving tomorrow and your father's taking a list to Peyrusse to do some serious shopping. Think what we need. I don't need red herrings..." Harriet giggled now, as well, then she sighed. "This mass catering is crushing my creative urges."

Caroline grabbed the biro cheerfully. "I'll go shopping. You and Dad can have the day off. Do you fancy a shopping expedition?" she asked and, in the end, the two sisters went off towing a fairly reluctant Emily with them.

It was hot in the car and they stopped for a drink at the small auberge on the outskirts of Peyrusse. They were the only customers and, while they sat under a large sunshade sipping their cold drinks, Emily disappeared to play on a garden swing. Caroline felt ridiculously happy, but she sensed a certain restraint in Vicky. "Are you all right?" she asked. "Is the heat too much for you?"

Vicky hesitated for a moment. "Remember what we were talking about the other day? Well I'm getting more and more worried about Mum and Dad. She's being as bright as ever – but too bright really – and he seems very preoccupied. It's peculiar but they don't seem to gravitate naturally towards each other anymore. Haven't you noticed? If you watch them you never see them being openly affectionate and they used to be such a touchy-feely couple."

The half-forgotten apprehension swept over Caroline again, as it had several times before in the last few months – ever since Phillip had died, actually. She felt guilty that she'd been so preoccupied with her own emotions that she'd stopped thinking about this worry which had been nagging away in the background.

"It's been worrying me for months, off and on, but I've kept persuading myself I'm imagining it, and I've been a bit busy with Alex lately." She blushed and spread out her hands in a gesture of helplessness. "What do you think's wrong? Are we both being over sensitive?"

Emily returned at this point, grizzling because a small French child had pushed her off the swing and they walked back to the car without being any closer to an explanation.

They pushed their trolleys across the supermarket forecourt – both deep in thought – but they didn't have an opportunity to discuss the subject again.

When they arrived home they found their parents in an apparently normal and cheerful mood, in anticipation of Mark's arrival.

"It'll be fun with Uncle Mark here," Emily announced. "When's he going to marry Tessa?"

"You are not to ask him that. Do you hear me?" Vicky waggled her finger and Caroline smiled – Emily certainly had weddings on her mind today.

"I don't know why you're all going to so much trouble," Mike grumbled, retreating nimbly from the kitchen, before he was trapped by the advancing mop. "Mark's not the sort to notice whether the kitchen floor's been done with Brand X or not."

"Tessa might," Vicky retorted and backed out after him with the bucket.

Harriet looked about her, taking in the huge kitchen and the sunny courtyard, visible through the tall windows. No house would ever compare with this one for her, but she had begun to question her priorities lately.

* * *

"Can I ride my bike to the corner?" Emily begged her mother on the Saturday afternoon when Tessa and Mark were due to arrive.

Vicky stuck her lip out dubiously, but Caroline jumped up and grabbed the child. "You're a real little pest," she laughed, tickling her until she giggled and squirmed out of reach. "I'll walk up to the corner with you and Doodle can come too."

Harriet smiled after the little retreating group. "I thought Caroline seemed a bit miserable before Alex arrived, but she's certainly blooming now."

"I think she was nervous. She must have been mad," Vicky added. "Although I can understand it after all she's been through this year – and last year too, for that matter."

Five minutes later they heard the sound of an engine and Mark's car swept up the drive. They all rushed to meet him, but he was already out of the car and with exaggerated politeness he held the passenger door open. Emily hopped out, very pink and pleased with herself.

Two minutes later Tessa and Caroline appeared, wheeling the abandoned bicycle and encouraging one pathetically flagging dog.

"She threw me out of the car," Tessa explained, when all the greetings were over. Then she turned round slowly, taking everything in. "It's absolutely superb. Better even than I'd imagined, despite all the photos Mark's shown me."

"You take her inside and show her the house," his mother suggested. "I'll make tea in the garden and you're in the flat," she called after them and smiled as they walked away. In two weeks' time Edward would be back... and then Alex. This was the closest they'd come for a long time to having the whole family together. If only Mike were more relaxed, but it would only be a temporary

201

problem. As soon as he'd finished this project he'd be his old loving self again. Professional and financial worries were bound to cause a bit of strain. She felt quite emotional suddenly and bustled off to put the kettle on.

Mike came up behind her and put his arms round her. "There, all your babies are home now. Are you pleased?"

She nodded and leaned her head back against him. Then she turned and looked at him thoughtfully. "But I like it when it's just you and me as well."

"So do I," he said and kissed the top of her head.

Vicky was by the pool with Caroline and she called Emily. "I wonder if Granny needs any help. Would you like to go and ask her darling?"

"No; I don't think she does," Emily replied airily, after she'd carried out her inspection. "She's busy kissing Grandpa in the kitchen."

Emily dashed off again and Vicky turned to Caroline. "Do you think we were wrong? They seem perfectly normal at the moment."

Caroline shrugged, "Mum says he's worried about his latest project and I gather he's a bit anxious about money as well – what with the exchange rate and the recession. That's enough to put a strain on any relationship, I suppose. I certainly hope we were wrong."

The charmed atmosphere carried on into the next week. Early on Monday morning Caroline was called into the notaire's office to sign the initial contract and Alex's draft had already arrived so the purchase was assured. Everyone had been pestering her to show them the house, so now she bought some champagne and took them on a guided tour. "It's a pity that Alex isn't here as well." She pulled a forlorn little face. "But I can't wait another fortnight to show you."

"It's really pretty," Harriet exclaimed, her eyes sparkling as the cars drove through the massive archway and stopped in the courtyard. "It's the same wonderful mellow stone as Lasserre."

"Oh Caroline!" Vicky exclaimed. "It's absolutely great. Edward will be green with envy. Oh look, your first lizard!" She pointed at the creature, which was basking on a dressed stone lintel. "That means good luck."

"It's going to be superb when it's tidied up a bit – the view is even better than ours," her father agreed. "The garden's really well stocked. There's been a keen gardener living here at some time." He didn't see the momentary look of pain flit across Caroline's face, but Harriet did and she squeezed her hand sympathetically. "I'll borrow Monsieur Lartigue's trailer and bring the ride-on mower over if you like. With all the long grass cut down you'll both have a better idea of what's growing here."

Her father's casual acceptance of them as a couple made her feel so deliriously happy that she was afraid she might cry. She turned and busied herself with the champagne, but when he proposed a toast she couldn't stop a solitary tear from rolling down her face.

Emily wrinkled her forehead anxiously and wiped it away with a rather grubby finger which left a streak of dirt on Caroline's face and made everyone laugh.

"It's all happened so quickly." She gave an apologetic sniff as she smiled at them, "I'm a bit overwhelmed."

"Let's have another look at the courtyard," Tessa said firmly, putting her arm through Caroline's. "It'll make a gorgeous secret garden."

"I wondered if it would be big enough for a pool, but Alex thought it might be too shady." It comforted her to bring his name into conversations, because it made him seem nearer.

Vicky called to her from the other side of the garden. "What do you think these are?"

She weaved her way through the luxuriant hibiscus bushes, suppressing a smile as she walked past their picnic spot. She'd known the house was gorgeous, of course but, nevertheless, it was reassuring to receive such universal enthusiasm from the family. She peered down at the clump of purple flowers which had caught Vicky's eye, "I think that it's a type of orchid – what a heavenly colour."

Vicky suddenly put her arms round her and the two sisters stood holding each other tightly. "It's so marvellous that we're both happy now. When Alex and Edward come home we'll have a big celebration." They smiled their approval at each other and wandered over to the big oak tree, their arms still entwined.

"I can just imagine little Maudes and little Forbes-Buckinghams – that's a bit of a mouthful – having a tree house in this oak."

"I'd like to have little Forbes-Buckinghams. I wonder if it'll happen. Perhaps there'll be little Hamiltons by then too." Caroline tilted her head discreetly in the direction of Tessa and Mark.

"I'm not sure that things are going so smoothly with them," Vicky whispered. "I just have a feeling," she sighed noncommittally.

They had a barbecue that night and then they swam until quite late. Even Emily was allowed to stay up and Mark spent a long time patiently teaching her to dive.

They crouched, side by side, on the edge of the pool, Emily safely fastened into her armbands and Mike standing in the water as official.

"That's right," Mark encouraged her. "Tuck your head in, tuck your bottom in, and roll forward with your hands like this." He demonstrated the technique. "Grandpa'll catch you if you're scared."

She gave him a withering look, "I'm not scared," and she fell into the pool with a lot of splashing, to tumultuous applause.

"He's awfully good with children," Vicky confided to Tessa. "Oh dear, I'm sorry. That wasn't meant as an unsubtle hint. But he is infinitely patient. She adores him."

Tessa laughed softly. "I adore him too, but I'm just not ready yet to stay at home in a frilly apron, waiting to ask him if he's had a good day at the office."

"I don't think life's necessarily like that anymore. The modern professional woman's meant to have it all – job, husband, children, nanny and a sex-life. That's according to Jackie Collins."

Tessa laughed. "I know that's the theory but, from what I've seen, it doesn't happen like that. Nappies, sleepless nights and enough bags under your eyes to carry the Sainsbury's shopping home. That's the reality."

It was gone midnight when Tessa and Mark wandered through the creeper – hung courtyard into the small kitchen of the flat. A huge toad sat next to the fridge, blinking at them, startled by the sudden light.

"I can't bear the things," Mark shuddered.

"Oh, you darling little chap," Tessa cooed, bending over.

"Thank you, sweetheart, but that's enough about me. Can you just get rid of that foul, slimy amphibian?"

"Idiot," Tessa grinned and carefully scooped the toad through the door.

"What did you think of the house that Caroline and Alex are

buying?" he asked casually.

"It's absolutely heavenly. By the way, have you met him yet?"

"No. Actually she met him while Phil was still alive and, I gather, they were very attracted to each other from the word go, but they didn't really get involved until quite recently. He was very understanding about Caroline's need to grieve. The parents knew him already and now Vicky's met him. I have a feeling Edward may have bumped into him too, on a wine buying trip last year."

"How did he know your parents? I'm a bit confused."

"Mum knew him through their literary connections and he'd been down here to stay a few times, on house-hunting forays. Then she introduced him to my sister and a couple of flashes of lightening and a thunderbolt later..." He threw his hands up in mock incomprehension.

She laughed. "How romantic."

"Yes," he said shortly, "I'm going to bed."

She sat at the kitchen table after he'd gone. He'd seemed happier this evening than he'd been for some time, but now the atmosphere had been spoilt again – her fault for bringing up the subject of Caroline and Alex. They'd been rowing now for four days and she felt helpless. The only thing that would satisfy Mark was a total commitment on her part – marriage, children, everything. She didn't want to give this commitment yet, but she didn't want to back out altogether either. He'd accused her of stringing him along until she found someone better and this had stung her terribly. Now she wasn't sure what either of them wanted. Perhaps they were both bad losers and were afraid of backing down. She went to bed feeling miserable and found him lying with his back to her, feigning sleep.

"I love you," she whispered into his ear. "Don't go to sleep without kissing me goodnight."

"You think that I'll always come running after you, but one day I'll just give up," he said, turning over towards her. "Seeing Caroline so happy today made me realise that you don't love me enough to make it work. If you did you'd want to be with me always, but you have other priorities. I don't have any priorities except you." His voice had a finality to it that frightened her.

"I don't want to end up like my mother, with six children and looking like a washed out old crone before I'm thirty five."

"Your father was a battering drunkard," he pointed out

wearily. "I hope you have a higher opinion of me."

"I've worked hard to build up the business and I don't want to throw it all away yet. My mother..."

"Bugger your mother, for Christ's sake," he interrupted harshly. "I can't help it if the stupid cow fell arse over tits for a psychopathic sod. Now I'm going to sleep."

He pecked her on the cheek and turned over again. Tessa snuggled up cautiously against his back, but didn't dare put her arm around him.

He was awake before her in the morning and went into the kitchen to make the tea. When he came back with the tray she was sitting up in bed, with the sheets pulled over her naked breasts. She looked more desirable than ever under this makeshift covering. "I'm sorry I got angry last night." He kissed her on the top of her head and she pulled him down next to her.

"I'm sorry I made you angry." They looked at each other for a long time, but neither of them could find the words to break the deadlock.

"We'd better hurry," she said at last. "Your mother wants to leave for Marciac at nine."

Mark had been keen to go on this particular trip, because it was the fortnight of the annual Jazz Festival and the town would be buzzing with frenetic activity. The huge square would be full of market stalls and café tables, and there'd be round-the-clock jazz, performed by players ranging from the merely enthusiastic to the internationally famous.

"I think I'll stay to help Dad with Caroline's garden and keep an eye on Emily," he said quietly. "You go." He kissed her very hard and then he walked away, leaving her feeling breathless and confused.

"Are you sure you won't come?" His mother asked as she ushered Vicky and Tessa towards the car. "Marciac's always fun."

But he declined firmly and stood waving towards the departing car – Harriet was driving and Vicky was next to her. Tessa sat in the back and he thought, as he watched them pulling away that she looked less self-possessed than usual.

He was actually pleased that he'd stayed behind because his father seemed to welcome his company and they had a very satisfying morning working on Caroline's garden. They managed to get the ride-on mower onto the trailer and they felt like a party of intrepid settlers when they'd mown their first stripe through the long, dry grass.

"Hooray," Emily shouted. "I like this house," and she clapped her hands enthusiastically.

"We've only paid the deposit," Caroline said nervously. "I hope the owners don't make us glue the grass back on."

They stayed until after lunch, which was a picnic under the oak tree, and then they lay for an hour, dozing in the sun and thinking their own thoughts. Mike had been taken aback at the prospect of having Caroline as an unexpected next door neighbour. It was an extra dimension to add to the maelstrom of confused and incoherent thoughts which were already swirling around in his head. Caroline's mind was clearer. La Plaisance was the only place where she could tangibly feel Alex's presence and she delighted in being there. A morning's manual labour had cleared Mark's irritation with Tessa and made him more optimistic. Emily was cheerful because she nearly always was.

* * *

"I don't know where they find their energy," her father said to her as they sat having a drink by the pool in the early evening. He and Caroline had sunk down in a heap but Mark had resumed his diving lessons with Emily.

"You dive in," she shrieked. "Go on. See if you can dive right to the other end. Daddy can only go half way."

They watched Mark effortlessly dive through the blue water, until he reappeared with his hand on the paving stones at the far end. Caroline looked at her watch and walked reluctantly into the house to make supper for everyone. It was half past six and they'd be back by eight at the latest. Her father offered, half-heartedly, to help but, when she refused, he wandered off to make some phone calls. Doodle was asleep under the big table and gave two semi-comatose thumps with his tail before subsiding again into oblivion. She hummed softly as she rummaged through the fridge to find something to go with the baked potatoes and green salad that she'd already settled on.

She heard Emily's voice in the distance and then she lost track of time. Had she been listening to it, without reacting, for hours, or was that the child's first hysterical scream? She realised that she was running before she'd thought of the answer, but her father was there before her. They both jumped in and grabbed him, but he was heavy and they were out of their depth. They struggled to get him to the side and it seemed to take for ever to pull him out. Caroline could hardly bear to look as her father desperately turned him over and pumped at his chest with his fist. She could feel Emily's body shaking as she clung to her and realised that it was the first time she'd been aware of the child's presence.

Mark groaned and moved his head slightly and tears of relief poured down Caroline's face. Her father stopped pummelling and sat down hard on the ground next to Mark, looking ashen. She could see a large lump on the back of Mark's head. "Keep still," she said softly and she covered him carefully with the nearest beach towels to stop him shivering.

He struggled to sit up, looking grey, despite his suntan, and blinked at them. "I must have knocked myself out for a second. How did you manage to pull me out?"

"Determination mostly and, thank god, Emily yelled loudly," Caroline gasped, still breathless from the effort and the fear.

"Sorry." He said penitently. "And thank you."

"Right we need to take you to out-patients," his father insisted, standing up shakily. "You'll need to be checked after losing consciousness and that bang to your head has to be treated. How do you feel?"

"Sick and shaky, but I think I'm all right."

It took a long time to dress him and he was sick twice. Finally they were able to get him to his feet and into the car. He was still shivering so Caroline tucked a couple of blankets around him and then they drove off, leaving a cryptic note attached to the kettle.

It took them an hour to reach Tarbes hospital and nearly another hour to check him in. By the time he'd been wheeled down to the radiology department and then back up to the examination room they were all exhausted and very relieved to see Harriet and Tessa racing along the corridor towards them.

"He's all right," Caroline told them quickly, Trying to sound more reassuring than she felt. "They're just looking at him now. They've done the x-rays and I think they'll want to keep him overnight for observation."

"Are you sure he's all right?" Tessa clutched at Caroline's arm anxiously.

"Yes. At least I think so. Honestly. The doctor will be able to tell us more as soon as they've finished the examination."

"However did he do it?" Harriet asked.

"He was showing me how to dive in backwards," Emily piped

up, "and he hit his head. It was an awfully loud bang."

Caroline and her father didn't elaborate on the story, but Emily didn't want to deprive anyone of the gory bits. "He sank right down to the bottom and it took ages for Grandpa and Auntie Caroline to pull him out. I thought he was dead."

"He was only under for a moment really," Mike said quickly, in a vain attempt at damage limitation and Caroline squeezed the child's hand warningly as she felt her draw breath to contradict.

"Listen, Caroline and I are fit to drop and Emily's up far too late. Why don't you drive us home darling and Tessa can stay here with Mark?" Mike looked enquiringly from one to the other.

This was agreed and half an hour later Tessa was allowed into the small casualty room, where Mark was lying, his head swathed in an impressively large bandage. He groaned softly as she walked through the door and she rushed over to him. "Oh darling, you might have been killed if they hadn't been so quick to pull you out."

"Sorry." He said despondently. "Today's been a bit of a disaster altogether."

She suddenly looked horrified. "You didn't do this on purpose did you?"

"He shook his head and then winced at the unexpected pain. "I don't think I'd try that, not even for unrequited love."

She bit her lip and looked straight into his eyes. "It's not unrequited and you've no right to say that."

"I think they must have given me something because I feel very dozy suddenly."

She panicked as his eyes closed. "Darling, I love you. Don't die."

His hands looked ridiculously healthy and sunburnt against the white hospital sheets and he opened one eye to give her a lopsided grin. "I don't think I'm terminal yet."

The young doctor came in then and smiled at them both. "Bon soir, Madame, Monsieur; I look in 'is eyes." He demonstrated his narrow torch and peered carefully, several times into Mark's pupils. "I need come each hour." He nodded and started to push through the big swing doors, but something occurred to him and he came back. "You want to sleep wiz 'im?"

Mark looked scandalised and pointed enquiringly at his own bed. The doctor's expression was uncomprehending for a moment and then he gave a delighted laugh and shook his head. "We 'ave beds for ze muzzers wiz ze leetle childs. The infirmière bring one

209

for 'er." And sure enough, a smiling little nurse wheeled a folding bed into the room and handed Tessa a crisp white cotton sleeping bag.

"This is cosy. You look as if you're going in for the school sack race," he smiled, as she slipped off her shoes and wriggled into the voluminous bag.

Her bed was about two feet lower than Mark's but she perched on the edge and reached up for his hand. He'd closed his eyes to try and ease the throbbing in his head, but he sensed the movement of her hand against the sheets and reached out for it. It was warm and soft and he squeezed it reassuringly. It was probably the shock, but he suddenly felt engulfed by misery and absolutely frozen. He began to shiver and she was immediately wide awake.

"What's the matter? Is your head hurting?" She slid back out of her sack and fetched a blanket from the end of his bed. She tucked it around him and leaned over him tenderly. "Shall I call the doctor?"

He was about to shake his head, but he remembered that it hurt so he pulled a miserable face instead. "No thanks. I think it was just a delayed reaction. I'm a bit warmer now."

She stayed there, with her arms round him, until he'd stopped shivering and then she looked hard at his face, tracing the slightly stubbly line of his jaw with her fingers. He closed his eyes again, but she stayed there gazing at him, her face softened by love and worry. Her fingers moved gently across his lips, but he didn't make any move to kiss them and she swallowed back her tears.

The young doctor returned with his torch and she moved from the bed while he bustled around with professional briskness. He shone his torch into each of Mark's eyes once more and then nodded at Tessa in a kindly fashion. "No problem. In morning 'e is going 'ome."

He vanished as silently as he'd arrived. Mark appeared to have gone to sleep again and she crept into her own bed. In the distance she could hear all the discordant clatterings of the big hospital, but this little side ward was a peaceful oasis. She lay there thoughtfully for a long time, listening to his breathing, not sure whether he was awake or asleep. She stretched up to touch his hand again and his fingers moved against hers.

She smiled as she lay there in the dim glow of the single night-light. "I've been thinking lately, that flat of mine is ridiculously small and inconvenient. I'm not sure I even like the area anymore." She felt him rub his finger slowly over the palm of her hand.

"The river can look very depressing sometimes too. Docklands is a bit over rated really," he replied.

"A little house would be nice."

"With a garden?"

"Oh, yes. We'd need a garden."

"We?"

"I may have just proposed to you."

"How long do I have to make up my mind?"

She knelt up, and leaned on the edge of the high hospital bed. "I'm not planning on proposing to anyone else, so I suppose you've got for ever."

"I believe there's a very good Montessori School in Strawberry Hill…"

"Where's that?" she sounded horrified.

"If you'll agree to never find out, I'll agree to marry you." He lay back with a euphoric grin on his face.

* * *

"What I don't understand is this." Mike confided to Harriet the next evening, as he set out a tray of champagne glasses. "She turned him down when he was just being normally idiotic, but now that he's been a real prize prat, she's decided to marry him."

"I expect she feels he needs her to look after him," Harriet said comfortably. "Anyway he's a very attractive prat, even if I am a bit biased."

"She's not exactly lacking in the looks department herself," Mike commented tartly.

"No, they make a rather lovely couple. We should have some more gorgeous grandchildren. Perhaps things aren't that bad after all." She placed her hand on his arm and her eyes were questioning, but he seemed not to have heard her. She turned back to where she'd been setting the table. "Shall we move it a bit further under the shade?"

"No, the sun will be lower by the time we eat – it's perfect where it is." He watched Harriet walk back towards the house, her skirt emphasising the slimness of her figure as she moved. Emily was chasing round the oak tree, trying to catch the kitten and Mark was lying in the shade, being protected lovingly by Tessa. There was laughter coming through the kitchen door. He turned away abruptly and went upstairs to his office. He sat at the desk, looking

211

at the view and then he buried his face in his hands; pressing back the threatening tears.

"Can I help?" Harriet asked, glancing around at the impressive array of food in the kitchen. "I've finished laying the table."

"No thanks." Vicky dismissed her with an imperious wave. "You go and sit down; it's all under control."

"We thought we'd open one of your jars of greengages in Armagnac as it's a special occasion," Caroline suggested.

"I hope they're not a disaster," Harriet said modestly.

"They're always gorgeous," and Caroline put her arm around her mother.

"Edward will be back in one and a half weeks," Vicky counted out the days slowly on her fingers, "and Alex in two weeks and one day. There!" she concluded on a note of triumph. "We should have a big party before we all go home – at least one engagement, a house warming and a puke-free pregnancy."

"I think I'd prefer you pukey," Caroline teased, patting her sister's expanding stomach. "I'm not sure I can take all this hyperactivity when you're in good form."

"Everything will be different next summer," Harriet suddenly reflected, leaning on the back of a chair, her head on one side. "There'll be a choice of two houses to stay in for a start. Probably you'll all be married and there'll be a new baby. I wonder if there'll be any other changes."

Caroline looked startled for a moment and then dismissed the niggling little thought.

"Right!" Vicky announced a few minutes later. "Bring on the happy couple. Dinner's ready."

"Here you are. You must keep the first champagne cork." Mike solemnly kissed his future daughter-in-law, and then passed the glasses round.

It was a wonderful evening and in the end there were four corks to be shared .

"Can I have one?" Emily's eyes shone eagerly and her grandfather handed it over ceremonially.

"Mum should have one for the new book," Vicky suggested.

"And Caroline must have one for her new house," Mark insisted, his arm tightly round Tessa's waist.

"I expect we'll have plenty more corks once Alex comes

back," Harriet nodded knowingly and Caroline blushed as she accepted the final champagne cork.

It was late by the time the last clearing up had been done and Doodle was still vacuuming the lawn optimistically at midnight, while they sat drinking coffee and vintage Armagnac under the whispering leaves of the palm trees.

"Come on, baby brother," Vicky suddenly tapped on the table. "Let's have a speech on this momentous occasion."

"Yes, come on. Unaccustomed as I am...." Harriet prompted him to start.

Mark laughed and struggled to find the words. "Thank you very much for a wonderful evening, for fishing me out of the pool yesterday and for proposing to me at Tarbes Hospital." He addressed each of them in turn. "And if Emily hadn't gone to bed I'd be able to thank her again for having a good carrying voice – just like her mother."

They all laughed and cheered and Vicky flicked an olive stone at him.

"Well the young can stay up as long as they like, but this wrinkly is going to bed," Harriet announced, pushing back her deckchair decisively.

There was a general murmuring of approval and everyone gathered up glasses and coffee cups on their way into the house. Before Tessa followed Mark up to bed she threw her arms round Harriet's neck, "Thank you very, very much. That was marvellous." Then she kissed Mike as well and disappeared through the courtyard into the tiny flat.

Six weeks had seemed to stretch ahead into infinity when Caroline had been on the point of leaving England, but now it was racing by. Jane had sent her a small packet with seven letters of condolence that had arrived after she'd left and as she'd looked at them, the morning after the celebration, she'd felt as though they'd arrived from another existence – another planet even. There was a cheerful little note from Jane, with snippets of local news – the weather had been foul – and a progress report on the purchase date for her flat. Caroline had smiled at the veiled enquiry, 'How are things?'

The letter had been posted before Caroline had spoken to her on the phone, so now she knew exactly how 'things' were. While her mind was focused on England she remembered that she hadn't discussed giving notice with Cliff yet. She'd definitely phone him that night, before it just became too embarrassing – not that he'd be anything except overjoyed, she mused, with a warm little smile.

She'd write to Prue and Angela too. She knew they'd be delighted. She was still sitting on the terrace, faraway, and clasping her packet of letters when Vicky bounced out of the kitchen. She'd definitely progressed from the bilious to the blooming stage, Caroline observed approvingly.

"Have you noticed that holidays are just like petrol gauges? It takes ages to reach the half-way mark and then – whoosh." Vicky threw her hands up in the air expressively. "Still I'm looking forward to Edward coming back."

The next ten days just seemed to evaporate. Mike went back to England on business, but he was due to return for Vicky's proposed welcome-back party and Harriet spent three days locked in top level discussions with Francesca, who'd flown down to compare notes and monitor progress on the book. Caroline couldn't honestly say what she'd done with the time. Alex phoned nearly every day at about lunchtime and otherwise she just seemed to drift in a delirious limbo of anticipation. Occasionally she'd spend the afternoon mooning around the garden at La Plaisance, often returning to sit at the spot where they'd had their picnic. Her niggling suspicion was becoming more of a possibility, but she hadn't said anything to Alex yet. She needed to be certain first and, anyway, the phone wasn't suitable for imparting such exciting news.

Mark and Tessa were dismissed grumpily by Emily. "It's silly, being soppy all the time like that. I don't see the fun."

Vicky was applying her boundless energy to organising a party of ambitious proportions. "I think she's easier to cope with when she's pathetic and pukey. I think I'm still a bit weak for all this excitement," Mark told Tessa with a languid little sigh.

"Try being less active at night and then you might be more use during the day," she hissed back. He pulled her closer and whispered something in her ear which made her giggle and blush. Emily watched crossly from the other side of the pool.

On the day that her father was due back Emily insisted on walking up the road to see if he was coming so many times that she exhausted the patience of Doodle and even her infinitely tolerant aunt refused to make any more trips. Emily was just trying to persuade Mark to accompany her when the car rounded the corner into the drive. She raced madly to meet him and Vicky followed nearly as fast.

The phone rang at that moment and Caroline ran to answer it. She knew it would be Alex. "Hello, sweetheart," she heard his familiar voice and clutched the phone tightly in her hands as she spoke to him, almost as if she were hugging him. "Yes...he's just arrived this minute...Oh that's marvellous. Good. Oh yes." He was going to be back in France on Wednesday morning. He'd phone to give her the time of his flight once he was back in London. "I'm longing to see you darling. I've missed you terribly." She listened for a few moments again. The trip was going well and he had flown to Japan the day before, to spend two days inspecting a possible location for filming the final scenes. "That's exciting...All right, I'll see you on Wednesday....yes, I'll expect a call on Tuesday evening. Bye...yes. I love you too."

She put the phone down and tried to work out when he'd actually be catching his plane home. He was almost half a day ahead, so he'd be leaving Tokyo on Tuesday at midday and arriving in London on Tuesday evening. She thought that was right, but she'd written the flight details down a few days ago, so she'd check them out properly later.

Edward rose to greet her when she walked back into the garden. "Wow! Another gorgeous sunburnt nymph," he laughed, hugging her affectionately. "I wouldn't have recognised either of you," he grinned at Caroline and Vicky.

"What about me?" Emily demanded, slightly petulant from her long vigil.

Edward dangled her above his head and looked up at her very solemnly. "I don't know who you are. I don't recognise you at all."

"Yes you do," she shrieked happily, "It's me; it's Emily."

"Good heavens! So it is. Do you want to help me unpack? There might be something interesting in one of the bags."

"Was that Alex?" Harriet asked. "When's he getting back?" She nodded when Caroline explained the proposed arrival time. "He may be back on the same plane as your father. I couldn't get Dad on the phone last night, so I hope he hasn't forgotten about the party." Her mother laughed cheerfully, but after she'd gone Caroline felt the old uneasiness gnawing at her again. He'd been away for more than ten days now. She couldn't remember his ever being away for that long before and her mother had that fixed, bright expression which she and Vicky had already observed with increasing alarm.

* * *

215

Vicky had persuaded her mother to invite more than forty people, including the mayor of Peyrusse and his wife.

"It's going to be an awful strain talking French all night," Mark grumbled. "There's a limit to the number of times I can say "oui", and still make it sound interesting."

"Well, I shouldn't say it too often to the mayor's wife," Edward gave a conspiratorial wink, "She's a bit of a nymphomaniac."

Caroline welcomed the distraction of all the party preparations, yet she felt frustrated that she hadn't found a single quiet moment to talk to Vicky about her fresh worries. Perhaps she was worrying about nothing, she decided and her mother had certainly seemed perfectly cheerful since Mike had phoned to say he'd be home on the lunchtime flight on Tuesday.

Tuesday was earmarked for setting out tables, mowing the lawn and buying booze. Edward went off to the wine co-operative and filled the boot of his estate car with crates of wine. Caroline counted out sets of cutlery and wrapped paper napkins round them, but by lunchtime she was in such a state of anticipation that she slipped off to her room and lay down to wait for the phone call. She must have dozed off, because she heard her mother calling to say that she'd made tea.

"Oh, isn't that pretty?" They'd arranged half a dozen tables in the garden since she'd disappeared upstairs and Tessa had put flowers in the middle of each one. Caroline was suddenly reminded of the big marquee that she and Phillip had put in the garden for her parents' wedding anniversary – such a long time ago now.

It was really insufferably hot after tea and they all went in the pool, but Caroline found herself being irritated by the noise, as she strained to hear the telephone, so she climbed out again and sat in the shade.

He still hadn't phoned by supper time and at eleven o'clock she crept into the peace of her father's office, armed with her scrap of paper and checked with British Airways in London. "Yes," the calmly efficient lady informed her; the flight from Tokyo had arrived at exactly eighteen forty five. "No," Mr Forbes-Buckingham had not checked onto the flight. Caroline leaned back in the big swivel chair and went cold all over. If he'd missed it why hadn't he phoned her? She tried to think rationally. Supposing he'd been delayed... a car might have broken down... anything quite ordinary might have gone wrong... he'd have been in too much of a rush arranging an alternative flight to get to a phone. The most likely thing of all was that he was on another plane at this very moment and he'd ring from London in the morning. He probably wouldn't arrive for the party, but that was the least important consideration. She had talked herself into a more rational frame of mind and she went downstairs to explain what must have happened. Her father extended their bedroom phone and it sat on the landing outside Caroline's bedroom door all night – silently.

On Wednesday she tried all the airlines with flights into London, but Mr Forbes-Buckingham had not caught any plane out of Tokyo. Mavis was with him on the trip, so she'd have phoned if he'd been taken ill, or been hurt. There was only one explanation that Caroline could imagine – he'd changed his mind and he didn't have the courage to face her with the truth.

She tried to look cheerful in front of everyone else. Vicky had put such a lot of energy into the party and they'd all been so excited, that Caroline kept up the pretence almost all day of insisting there must be a rational explanation, but when the first car drove up she pleaded a headache and slipped away.

Harriet came up to her room later and sat silently on the bed holding her hand, while Caroline lay there, staring blankly at the ceiling. "I'm all right," she said finally, squeezing her mother's hand and attempting a smile. "You go back to the party – I'm going to sleep now."

Harriet left reluctantly, but Caroline didn't sleep and she didn't cry. She was still lying there when the first thin streak of light filtered through the shutters – and she was not the only person to have a sleepless night.

Honor Kershaw had been lying in the darkness for hours – not that London was ever really dark – and finally she decided she might as well put her bedside lamp back on. Laurence had chosen this flat in Brondesbury Park and she'd never liked it. She'd always hated North London in fact, and this was an exceptionally gloomy flat.

When they'd divorced he had kept the cottage in Wales, which was even more depressing than the flat, in her opinion, and she had settled for Brondesbury Park. She looked around at the walls, which were mostly adorned with her own pictures. Selling pictures wasn't easy so they might as well go on her own walls as anywhere else. One wall had been covered with pictures she'd done during the last six months at Peyrusse Haute and Montegut, but she'd removed them before Mike had come to stay for this last ten days. She knew that it upset him to be reminded of what he was giving up for her. She'd replaced them with a series of pictures she'd painted in Tuscany, but they weren't the same size, of course, so there were a few dirty patches on the wall where they hadn't quite covered the spaces.

He'd promised to tell Harriet a month ago, after they'd spent those last few blissful days together, but he hadn't had the courage in the end. This time he'd been adamant that he'd tell her as soon as the children had gone home. Honor didn't have children so she couldn't really understand his worries about upsetting them. They were all over thirty, after all, so their parents' lives were hardly their concern any more.

She turned the light off again and tried to go to sleep, but her mind kept flicking back over scenes from the last six months. As soon as she'd met Mike she'd known that she'd wanted him, although she'd kept Pierre in reserve, as well, just in case... She was impatient with herself for this sudden lack of self-confidence, but she was still recovering from the shock of Simon Chandler's rejection and she'd craved the extra security.

It hadn't been easy, at first, convincing Mike that he needed her as much as she needed him. He'd agonised about the wholesale hurt he was going to inflict on his family, of course, especially on Harriet, and she'd put on a good show of feeling equally guilty and reluctant. Her face softened into a small triumphant smile as she recalled her heart-rending performance. Finally she'd managed to persuade him that they had to consider their own happiness before anyone else's. After all they weren't children and they might never have this opportunity again.

Pierre had been fun and marvellous in bed, but with rather provincial morals – hardly surprising for a small-time Gascon dentist – and she had to think of her own future now. She'd considered keeping Pierre as a lover, but she didn't want to jeopardise her relationship with Mike, so she'd been forced to make a decision. That last night with Pierre had really been worthy of a standing ovation, she decided. He'd gone home convinced that she'd sacrificed their eternal happiness for the well-being of his family. As if she cared a stuff about his whey-faced wife and his two over-indulged brats.

She and Mike hadn't made love very much this time, because

218

he'd been too weighed down by the prospect of talking to Harriet, but everything would be all right again once he'd made the break. He'd promised to come straight back to London and then they'd make a new start. She stared contentedly into the darkness as she considered her future with Mike. Her marriage to Laurence had lasted for six years – the longest yet. If she did that well with Mike she'd be sixty three and the thought of starting again at that age was distinctly depressing. Perhaps this would be the great, permanent love of her life. She gave a cynical laugh as she stared into the darkness and couldn't decide which of the two options was more painful.

Mike had been absolutely adamant that he wouldn't take anything from the family home and that he'd leave Harriet with the flat in Pimlico as well. Well, she could have laughed out loud as she considered the ease with which she'd procured the man. If she could achieve that much in less than six months she should be able to get her hands on an equitable share of the property – or what she considered to be an equitable share of the property, as the second Mrs Hamilton – in a relatively short time. She really felt she deserved a pat on the back for sheer determination and shrewdness and warmed by this self-congratulation she fell into a deep, untroubled sleep.

Mike lay very still because he didn't want to wake Harriet. Her hand was tucked under his leg and he could feel the softness of her breasts against his back. As soon as this party was over he was going to tell her everything. He'd prevaricated for too long already and it wasn't fair on anyone. He was in love with Honor and he wanted to live with her; he just wished it could be achieved without tearing his family apart.

He still loved Harriet and in many ways he wished that Honor had never arrived to complicate his life, but it was too late to go back. A single sob wracked his chest as he thought about everything he was about to walk away from…

Apart from this temporary worry of Caroline's he couldn't remember when he'd last seen all three children so contented. Perhaps they hadn't been so happy since they'd left school and he was going to deal them a crushing blow; all the more crushing for being so totally unexpected. He wondered how unexpected it would be for Harriet. He hadn't made love to her for weeks and the excuses were wearing thin. He'd seen a hurt, puzzled look on her face quite frequently lately, although they were still outwardly affectionate towards each other. He continued to weep silently and he turned his head into the pillow. He felt her hand move slightly as she stirred in her sleep.

* * *

It was broad daylight in the chic coastal resort of Sujima, north-west of Tokyo, but Alex was lying in darkness for the second day. He wasn't absolutely sure of the elapsed time, because he'd drifted in and out of consciousness so many times. The first moments were still sharply printed in his memory. His alarm has gone off at five thirty and he could still recall his sense of anticipation as he'd jumped out of bed.

The trip had gone better than he'd hoped and he'd worked well with the Australian team. He'd expected to have the usual disputes and differences of opinion, but they'd been in agreement over all the main locations and their idea for filming the final scenes on board a yacht off the Japanese coast had been a brainwave. His only reservations, now, were with the casting of the hero's sidekick, but they were going to get back to him in London with a couple of alternative suggestions. Really he had no right to interfere, but he was pleased that his views were being considered. Now he was exhausted and he just wanted to get back to Caroline.

It was a large room by Japanese standards, in an elegant old hotel with an uninterrupted view of the sea. The sea seemed infinitely mysterious, but probably it was only the psychological mystery of knowing that the great, secret land mass of China lay beyond. This was a popular holiday area for rich Japanese and the shoreline had been tastefully developed in both directions with large modern hotels set in enchanting, flower-filled gardens.

Alex turned back from the window and started systematically filling the three large, well-worn suitcases, which were lying around him, open, on the floor. He'd bought Caroline a silk kimono and he smiled as he sandwiched the delicate, brilliantly coloured material, in its tissue paper wrappings, between two of his sweaters.

He had just closed the final suitcase when there was a knock on his door. Mavis was checking that he hadn't overslept and, as he turned to speak to her, the whole room started to rock. At first it was like being on a very rough channel crossing – a rhythmic swing from side to side – and then, in an endless slow motion, the room seemed to turn right over.

His mouth and lungs were full of a thick, cloying dust and he gasped frantically for air. He tried to get up, but he realised that he

220

was pinned under an enormous, jagged beam, which had been interrupted in its downward path by some unseen, miraculous structure, approximately two inches from his chest. He shifted his weight cautiously within the confined space and a pain of such intensity shot through his left arm, that he felt violently sick. He didn't investigate any further, for fear of doing more damage to his obviously broken arm, or of disturbing the precarious masonry, suspended around him like deadly pick-up-sticks.

In the stillness he became aware of distant noises. People were shouting and he could sense a movement and a low moaning sound from somewhere nearby. There was a woman's hand projecting through the rubble and he took it in his. It was warm and he squeezed it gently, relieved to feel a faint response and then his fingers felt the well-known shape of Mavis's ring. Her husband had bought her the ring when they'd been on holiday in Gibraltar and the massive emerald had always been referred to as "The Rock of Gibraltar". Now he could have wept with joy to feel the familiar gem. He called her name and he felt an increased pressure from her fingers but no answering sound. He tried to call her again but his throat was too full of choking dust and the resultant cough caused another blast of pain to shoot through his arm.

He must have passed out for a long time because, when he next strained to listen, the noises seemed closer. They'd be sure to find him soon. He looked apprehensively at the beam, pressing down so near to him and prayed that they wouldn't dislodge it. Well, he comforted himself, at least Japan was used to earthquakes – they'd be well prepared with rescue teams. He began to feel very thirsty now and however still he remained his arm throbbed unbearably. He clenched his teeth, but the waves of pain must have made him pass out again. When he next opened his eyes he realised that the darkness was even more intense than before and that the world had gone totally silent.

It must be night and the rescue teams had disappeared. He panicked; surely they worked through the night with arc lights and heat sensing equipment. He was no longer holding Mavis's hand and he scrabbled in the cruel rubble, as far as he could reach, for this familiar reassurance, but the hand had gone. Tears of despair rolled through the thick dust covering his face as he contemplated the horror of this solitary tomb.

It was a long time before he heard the renewed efforts of the rescue teams and by then he was beginning to lose consciousness more often. He was sitting in a sunny courtyard with Caroline and then he was bouncing along with his arm around her shoulders in an elderly open-topped Deux Chevaux. As he drifted in and out of oblivion he had a recurring nightmare that he was late for something…

CHAPTER 21

"I'm sorry that I didn't come down last night," Caroline gave her mother a forced smile. "I really had an awful migraine."

Harriet nodded sympathetically, noticing that Caroline must have been lying on her bed, fully dressed, all night.

"How did it go? Did everyone turn up?"

"It was a great success." Harriet sounded more enthusiastic than she felt." Why don't you come downstairs and doze by the pool for a bit in the sun?"

"I'd rather stay here, if you don't mind. I'll just lie still until my head's better."

Harriet looked as if she was about to say something, but then she thought better of it. "Do you fancy some breakfast?" she asked instead.

"No thanks."

Everyone crept upstairs, in turn, but she turned down all offers and lay there, staring blankly at the ceiling.

"Look, for Christ's sake," Mike snapped as they sat having coffee, in a companionable gloom, "the man wasn't catching the bus from Peyrusse Haute, he was flying half way round the world. Not so long ago that was a six month voyage. Now you've all got him dead and buried because he's forty eight hours late. I'm going into the village to fetch the paper." He seized Emily by the hand and bundled the startled child into the back of his car.

"He's right," Vicky agreed. "We'll probably have a frantic phone call at any moment."

"Well, he missed a good party and I think we were lucky with the weather last night," Tessa remarked, as the wind suddenly caught the edge of the sun umbrella and tipped it into the swimming pool. "Perhaps we'd better have lunch under cover," she shouted as she dragged the umbrella back onto dry land.

Mike and Emily arrived back, clutching two newspapers and a bag of luridly coloured mixed sweets and Mike sat down with a contented sigh at the poolside table.

"Lunch!" Harriet called, before he'd even had time to focus on the headlines.

"Bugger," he said in annoyance and slapped the pile of papers, unread, back down on the table.

Caroline had refused to come down to lunch and she'd turned down the offer of something on a tray as well. The cheering effect of Mike's rousing little speech had long-since evaporated and everyone was at a low ebb.

"Right, we want to take some crates of 1985 Madiran home with us. Anyone else fancy a trip to the cave?" Mark surveyed the glum faces questioningly. "Come on Ems. Have you ever seen a really big wine cave? It's fun. We'll go for ice creams afterwards."

Tessa and Mark shepherded the child into the car and Mike slunk back to his papers, which were now covering most of the surface of the pool.

"Oh dear," Harriet shrieked. "I hope the newsprint doesn't come off and ruin our ph levels."

Mike looked at her icily. "I haven't seen a bloody paper for two days and all you can think of is bloody ph levels." He strode off, slamming his office door behind him, leaving Harriet looking crestfallen.

Vicky made consoling noises while Edward fished the sodden mass out of the pool. "Anyone fancy a hobby in papier maché, or shall I just throw them out?"

"I'd like to pop into Eauze," Vicky announced suddenly. "I can't bear to sit here moping any longer. Come on Mum; they had some very pretty material in that shop near the bull ring, last time I looked, and I'd like something new for the baby's room."

Harriet informed Mike, rather stiffly, that he was in sole charge of Caroline and they went off feeling that they were, at least, doing something positive.

"Will you re-line the crib as well?" Harriet asked and Edward smiled as his wife and his mother-in-law became entirely preoccupied with baby talk. But he couldn't tear his thoughts away from Alex. Something must have gone wrong; something pretty serious. Surely he hadn't just walked out on Caroline. And, although he didn't dispute the logic of Mike's comments, modern communications made it difficult for someone to disappear without trace. Another Lord Lucan? No, he certainly didn't believe that.

The phone rang with nerve-racking frequency that evening as seemingly endless people called to thank them for the party; Caroline lay on her bed, in an agony of hope, as she heard footsteps rushing to answer, but there was no joyful summons.

She was first up next day and sat at the kitchen table looking pale but composed. "I'm going over to La Plaisance to make sure it's all locked up and then I'll take the key back to the agent," she informed her mother and she refused all offers of company.

The sunflowers no longer had the brilliance they'd had on that first magical visit. The summer heat and lack of rain had blackened the heavy blooms and they hung limply from their massive stems. As she took the now familiar left turn she wondered whether she'd ever see them again in that perfect, golden freshness.

She roamed through the garden, which really looked quite promising after Mark's and her father's efforts with the mower. She struggled with the front door and then walked into the cool, dark kitchen. She didn't open the shutters, but there was enough light coming through the cracks to cast a dim glow. The two champagne bottles were still on the table and so were the glasses, which she'd washed, but not put away. She was just going to open the cupboard, but she hesitated. It looked more as if someone might come back one day if she left those few things lying around. She smiled at her own superstition.

She walked carefully up the dark staircase and into their bedroom. She opened the shutters in here and looked out across the garden. Then she looked straight across to the horizon and saw her first faint glimpse of the Pyrenees – tall and slightly menacing – a sign, in summer, of approaching bad weather. She smoothed her hand across the bedspread, before closing the shutters, and went quickly back downstairs.

The courtyard was sheltered and she sat down on the bench where she'd told Alex about Phillip's tapes. He surely wouldn't want to buy the house now, she reasoned. It would be too embarrassing for him to risk bumping into her, or her family. Perhaps she should buy it and live here on her own. She rested her hand on her stomach for a moment... or not on her own. She swallowed hard and went slowly back to the car. She returned the keys to the estate agent and had a business-like discussion with him about possible dates for finalising the purchase.

"Mr Forbes-Buckingham will be in contact with you himself, as soon as he's back in the country," she confirmed and they'd shaken hand solemnly. Then she went to the fishmonger and bought four kilos of mussels.

* * *

"Hello," Caroline called up the hall when she arrived back. "Is anyone there? I've bought masses of mussels. I thought I'd make moules marinières, as it's Mark and Tessa's last night."

"I bought a crate of a very good, local aperitif," Mark volunteered." Let's try one now."

"The cave was enormous, with huge steel vats going right up to the ceiling," Tessa enthused, happy to see Caroline looking more cheerful. "Mark's bought six crates and I've bought a crate of rosé as a present for the office. I hope it'll all fit in the car."

Vicky was hesitant about bringing up the subject, but the problem was solved by Caroline herself. "Would you have room to take me back with you on Sunday?" Her voice was cheerful – normal. "It seems the most sensible, if there's space, since I've left my car at your house."

"No problem," Edward agreed. "We'll try to stop somewhere nicer for lunch on the way back."

"It's going to be awfully lonely when you've all gone," Harriet wailed. "Isn't it darling?"

"I don't want to go back," Emily announced.

"I expect Pickwick's missing you," Vicky pointed out. "He'll be fatter than ever after not being ridden all summer."

"I'll gallop round and round the field until he's lovely and slim again," Emily replied airily and they all laughed.

After everyone else had gone to bed that night, Harriet sat in the quiet kitchen listening to the croaking of the frogs and the threatening gusts of the wind. Vicky slipped back into the room in her dressing gown and sat opposite her mother. Harriet shrugged. "It's more worrying when she's pretending to be cheerful than when she's just plain unhappy."

"Yes, I know. Can't you persuade her to stay on here for a while? Cliff wouldn't mind, even if she missed the beginning of term."

"She's already hinted to him that she might be giving notice, so that wouldn't be a problem, but I think she wants to go back."

"Edward and I talked about it in bed for hours last night," Vicky sighed. "However you look at it there doesn't seem to be a logical answer."

"No. He's not a boy so you'd hardly think he'd just walk out on her. But he wasn't alone in Australia and Japan. If something's gone wrong, why hasn't someone let us know? You look tired darling. Come on; let's go to bed." Harriet ushered Vicky out of the kitchen and they tiptoed upstairs. Mike was already asleep when Harriet got into bed. She whispered his name, but he didn't wake up.

The sky was not as crystal clear the next day and the wind had really begun to blow seriously. They had put the sun umbrellas away the previous day, but a single, forgotten deckchair had been hurled into the laurel hedge. Harriet hadn't heard Mike get out of bed, but when she crossed to the window she saw him leaning on the gate at the end of the garden. His arms were folded on the top bar and he was staring across their field as if he wanted to fix every detail in his mind, for ever.

There was a breeze blowing through the half-open window and she turned away with a slight shiver. It was half past seven when she opened the kitchen door. The kitten was pleased to see her and arched his tail around her legs, until she fed him. She tickled Doodle with her toe while she waited for the kettle to boil, but he was determined to have another half hour's lie in and gave her a baleful look. "Misery," she muttered, as she put two cups and saucers on the tray with the milk and teapot – Caroline didn't take sugar. Then, balancing it carefully, she pulled the door closed behind her.

Caroline was sitting in her little armchair, looking out of the window and she was already dressed. She seemed to be pleased to see her mother, but there was a frightening emptiness in her eyes.

"How lovely. Why am I so honoured?" she smiled.

"I was up early and I guessed you might be too. Did the wind wake you? It's really been blowing and there's a deckchair half way down the field."

"I didn't notice the wind. I've been sitting here thinking about La Plaisance. I don't think that Alex will want to go ahead with the purchase now. It'll be too awkward for him – having me for an occasional neighbour..." She hesitated and seemed to forget the thread of her thoughts until she noticed her mother was obviously waiting for her to continue. "I thought I'd buy it instead and come down to live permanently. There's nothing particular to keep me in England and I'd find plenty to do down here. Could you bear to have me as a neighbour?"

"It would be a lovely place to bring up a baby," Harriet said quietly…

Caroline swallowed and stared at her mother. "How did you guess?"

"I saw your look when I said something about there being a new baby next year. I could see what you were thinking, but I think

I'd have guessed anyway. Your skin has a sort of bloom."

"I'm not absolutely certain and I'd thought that Alex would be the first one to know... but obviously not."

"I won't say anything. Here. Drink this tea while it's hot."

Caroline sighed and smiled at Harriet and this time it was a real smile. "I'm glad you came in this morning. I think you've restored quite a lot of my sanity."

Her mother leaned forward impulsively and hugged Caroline. "Having you all down here has restored mine too, so that's fair."

Tessa and Mark were the first to leave that morning and, by the time everyone had appeared for breakfast, the car was packed.

Harriet pulled a face. "Oh dear this is very final."

"I thought you were going to be in London next Thursday," Mark pointed out. "So we'll see you on Thursday."

"Come and have dinner in my flat, before I sell it," Tessa added.

Vicky stuck her lip out dismally. "It's an awful anti-climax now that they've gone and it'll be our turn on Sunday."

"I'm going to pick up the papers during the intermission," Mike announced. "I'm into serious news deprivation syndrome now."

"Poor love," Harriet said absentmindedly. "Will you pick up the Saturday Figaro as well please?"

"I don't know why he fusses." Vicky rolled her eyes at her mother. "It's always the same bad news."

"I heard the tail end on the radio this morning and it's all about a ferry capsizing in China, with thousands of people on board and an earthquake somewhere unpronounceable."

"These Chinese ferries must be absolutely enormous," Caroline mused, "or else they pack them in like sardines."

Ten minutes later Mike was back with a face like thunder. "The woman's closed to go to her nephew's wedding. Can you imagine this happening in a civilised country like England? Can you imagine old W.H. shutting up shop because a minor Smith was getting married?"

"Oh darling, you have had a week. We'll fetch the whole lot tomorrow, and you can have a real news binge."

"It'll be history by the time I get to read it."

Edward turned to his father-in-law. "What about that tree

that's leaning over the garage? Shall we look at it after lunch since we haven't got the papers to read? It would be easier to take it down with two of us."

"I hope Edward persuades him to do it," Harriet confided to her daughters, "because there's a real storm forecast tonight and we don't want it to go through the garage roof."

* * *

Edward rolled his eyes upwards in despair as he looked around the gloomy lunch table, a couple of hours later. "Women!" he mouthed at Mike.

"What are you two muttering about?" Harriet stared from one to the other suspiciously.

Edward grinned and put his arm round his mother-in-law. "Mike and I are feeling so emotionally drained," he paused with a dramatic sigh, "at the thought of no one seeing each other until next Thursday, that we thought we'd take you all out for the rest of the day." He winked at Mike.

Harriet aimed a playful blow at his stomach. "You're making fun of us. But that would be nice wouldn't it?" She glanced enquiringly at Vicky and Caroline.

"Where Daddy? Where? Where?" Emily jumped up and down, clinging to her father's tee shirt and he pressed his hand firmly onto the top of her head.

"Down!" He laughed. "Down boy!" and Emily giggled and squirmed out of his grasp.

Edward looked at his watch. "You girls can pack, while we sort out the tree. Maude's Magical Mystery Tour will start at four sharp."

"You're very silly," Emily announced. "No you're not! No you're not!" she shrieked and clung to him, as he picked her up and galloped down the pool steps, holding her at arms' length over the water. "I'm sorry. Don't throw me in. Help! Mummy!" She shrieked hysterically and raced back to her mother, pink and dishevelled, when he finally released her.

Vicky grasped her firmly by the hand and pursed her lips disapprovingly at Edward. "If we're going out in an hour and a half, madam, you can help me to pack and then you can have a bath."

Emily gave her father a conspiratorial grin and allowed herself to be marched off.

"I'm all packed already," Caroline told her mother, when everyone else had disappeared. "Shall we weed the roses? I feel like doing something useful."

Despite the wind it was pleasant in the garden. Caroline and her mother chatted as they worked and they could hear the men's voices coming from the back of the garage. "I hope they can do something with that tree." Harriet straightened up and looked anxiously at the dead branches, projecting above the roofline. "It's definitely leaning more now than it was at Christmas."

"The wood will be useful too," Caroline observed. "It'll save you buying so much next year."

Harriet tugged at a resistant rose sucker. "Yes, and it's been dead for such an age that it'll be dry enough to burn straight away."

The men strolled back, deep in conversation. "We just can't risk doing it, darling." Mike called out to Harriet.

"No, it needs a good push in the right direction with a tractor. Otherwise there's a risk of it falling on the telephone wires."

Harriet looked from one to the other. "What'll we do then?"

"I'll phone Monsieur Lartigue on Monday morning. It'll only take five minutes with a tractor and then we'll be certain that it won't hit the roof or the wires."

Vicky waved out of the bedroom window and laughed at Emily who was waving out of the next window, wrapped in a towel. "We're ready to be whisked off. Do we need to wear something smart?"

"Why won't you tell us where we're going?" Emily persisted, as they all squeezed into the car, quarter of an hour later.

"Cos then it wouldn't be a mystery."

Emily stuck her lower lip out, unconvinced by this answer, and then allowed herself to be distracted with a game of I-Spy. She was just wailing, "Grandpa's cheating. Wristwatch begins with "R", not "W" so it's my turn again..." when Edward turned off the road and parked next to a huge lake, dotted with rowing boats and pedaloes.

Emily's face lit up. "Ooh! Are we going on a boat? Can I go with you Grandpa?"

* * *

"I feel like Ophelia." Vicky said dreamily, trailing her fingers in the water, when the party had finally been divided up, more or less to everyone's satisfaction.

Edward and Caroline pedalled furiously while Vicky and Harriet watched admiringly from the stern.

We're winning," Emily cheered as the smaller boat slowly

overtook its ungainly sister vessel. "Pedal faster Grandpa."

Edward and Caroline sat back, laughing and lifted their feet off the pedals.

"I'm knackered!" Edward complained. "This wind is making it very hard going. We'll go over to the island and back and then we'll find somewhere to eat."

CHAPTER 22

The wind was really blowing hard, straight off the Pyrenees, when they woke up next day.

"It's been trying to do this for days," Harriet said philosophically, pulling pieces off her croissant and dunking them in her coffee. "It'll be all over again by tomorrow morning."

"Not a very nice day for travelling, but you'll probably leave it behind once you get to the motorway; it's probably fairly local." Mike observed.

"When are you coming to see us? I want to show you how high I can jump on Pickwick."

"I might come to see you next weekend." Harriet swung the child round and then hugged her. "You take care of your mummy for me until then."

"I'll ring you if I have any news," she said quietly to Caroline. "Don't give up hope."

She and Mike walked arm in arm to the end of the drive and watched the car until it was a small speck in the distance. "I suppose two out of three isn't a bad success rate," she said dolefully. "But we failed with the most crucial one I'm afraid."

"I still think everyone's jumping to too many conclusions too soon," he ventured. "Let's give the poor chap the benefit of the doubt for a bit longer."

"It'll do her good to get on with her normal life again, but I'm worried about her going back to that house. It'll be very depressing for her, on top of everything else, to face up to all those memories of Phil again."

"Look darling," Mike gave an exasperated sigh. "I know they're still your babies, but you must learn to let go. You can't worry about them for ever. Vicky's happy and she's expecting another baby – so that's marvellous. Mark and Tessa are, apparently, going to get married – and that's marvellous too. Caroline is extremely unhappy at the moment, although I still think that we've all blown it out of proportion. And if he really has dumped her... well that sort of thing happens unfortunately and I think she'll probably pick up the pieces again, given time. Now, let's stop thinking about the children, and let's get on with our own lives. Please, Harriet."

She was about to reply when there was a very loud splintering noise, followed by a crash from behind the garage.

"I know, I know. You needn't say it." Mike stared at the wreckage. "I should have asked Monsieur Lartigue to come weeks ago."

"It's missed the garage," Harriet tried to find something positive to say. "But now we won't know whether the children have got home safely."

"I'll saw the tree up today and we'll go into Nogaro first thing in the morning to let France Telecom know the line's down. We'll phone the children from there at the same time. Now, let's make a start on this tree."

"Right. You saw it up, and I'll cart it away in the wheel barrow."

They worked until well into the afternoon and by the time it was all stacked in the woodshed the storm had blown itself out and the perfect weather had returned.

They sat in the garden that evening, exhausted by their efforts, and surrounded by the remains of supper, too tired either to speak or to clear away the dregs until Harriet finally broke the silence. "Poor Caroline. I wish things would work out for her. She seems to attract disasters. I suppose if Alex has had a change of heart it was better to stop now before it went any further – but I can't understand why he hasn't had the guts to tell her to her face."

"Let's give up speculating, darling," Mike sighed. "We're just going round in circles."

She leaned her face against his shoulder and looked out over the garden. She'd switched the outside lamps on and the garden glowed, golden, in the subdued light. "It is nice having it just to ourselves," she agreed softly, "and it's quite relaxing knowing that the phone can't ring. Shall we have an early night?"

"You go on up. I've got a few urgent things to do in the office. Don't wait for me…"

The house seemed strangely quiet next morning and, when Mike opened the shutters, he saw a thick littering of twigs on the lawn. But that was the only sign of the previous morning's gale. "I expect they had a calm crossing last night. There's not a breath of wind." He turned back to Harriet as he spoke and smiled as she blinked sleepily at him. "You have a lie in and I'll fetch the tea."

But she climbed resolutely out of bed. "Let's have breakfast

233

by the pool and go to Nogaro early. I won't feel happy until I know they've all arrived back safely."

He shook his head in despair, but he knew it wasn't worth arguing. The air had lost its stormy sultriness and the temperature had fallen slightly, he noticed, as he looked at the thermometer in the courtyard. He could hear Harriet pottering around with the breakfast things as he strolled around the corner of the house to join her. She'd set the table under the drooping branches of the linden tree and now she was standing thoughtfully, with one hand resting lightly on the corner of the blue and white checked cloth, as she considered whether she'd forgotten anything. The sun was touching her shoulders as she moved and her skin was tanned after the long, warm summer.

She nudged the dog away gently with her foot and pulled a chair out. She called out to him as she saw him walking towards her, across the lawn. "Isn't this perfect? Come and sit down." And she lifted her face for him to kiss her.

His heart was so constricted that he could hardly breath; he couldn't delay telling her much longer. Suddenly he was aware of her voice, sounding cruelly normal. "We should be at France Telecom by ten. They'll probably have it all working by the time we're back."

It wasn't far to Nogaro and, as they drove along, Harriet suddenly noticed the turning to Saint Magnan, through the fields of blackened sunflowers and she sighed very quietly. Mike patted her hand. "She'll perk up once she's home and everything's back to normal," he said, ashamed of his own platitudes.

Harriet didn't say anything but she didn't imagine that going back to the house where Phillip had so recently died would be a very 'perking' sort of experience.

They walked into the cool corridors of the telephone company and detected a slight curl to the lip and the raising of a perfectly formed Gallic eyebrow, as the assistant repeated, "A tree? Dead for some years you say?"

It would be sorted out immediately, she informed them, as they slunk out rather humbly. "There you are," Harriet announced, "She thinks you should have done something about it sooner too."

"Don't nag. Let's go and buy some phone cards."

Mark wasn't at home, but Tessa answered her phone at once. "Yes, we had a very easy journey and we spent Saturday night on the Vendée Coast... Thank you for a marvellous holiday... We'll phone tonight if you're reconnected... Yes, bye... Love to Mike too."

"Happier now?" he asked. He felt suddenly as if he was somewhere on the outside of this charade, forced to participate but completely disconnected.

"Mmm. Yes. I'll just try Vicky. Caroline may still be there."

Mike looked at his watch. "It's not half past nine yet in England. They won't have been home for long."

Vicky answered after half a dozen rings, but they were still busy unpacking so Harriet didn't keep her talking. "I'll ring you tonight darling. Is Caroline still with you? Oh, yes. Yes it would be nice. Speak to you later. Yes, bye."

"She's trying to persuade Caroline to stay on for a few days. She's worried about her going back to that house so soon." She looked up at Mike with big anxious eyes.

"Come on, let's sit in the sun with a beer and then we'll go back to Peyrusse Haute." He ushered her in the direction of the colourful main square and an empty table at the busy little cafe. "By the time we've picked up the papers the phone lines will probably have been repaired. You've got to hand it to the French you know – their nationalised industries are very efficient."

And he was absolutely right. They noticed the glossy new wire suspended between the perimeter post and their garage roof as soon as they turned into the drive.

"Now I feel more secure," Harriet beamed cheerfully. "I'll make some coffee shall I?"

When she came back with the two cups he was frowning with concentration and slotting sections of paper in and out of each other like a manic cardsharp.

"Right. They're all in order now. Don't mix them up."

"Don't be bossy."

"They go back to Thursday. Where do you want to start?" He glanced at the headlines – Japan shocked by devastation that couldn't happen – and then at the picture covering half of the page. He whistled softly as he stared at the photograph of twisted wreckage. He flicked through the paper quickly, seeing more and more horrific scenes and stark headlines. The particular significance didn't hit him until he turned to say something to Harriet.

But she was staring at another paper without speaking. He looked over her shoulder and read, half way down the page: "Hopes fade for safety of British Crime Writer." Her hand felt cold and it was trembling so much that he had to hold it still, so that he could carry on reading: "Alexander Buck, the internationally acclaimed British writer, together with his PA and three members of the Australian National Film Company, were still unaccounted for last night. Units of foreign experts struggled alongside the dazed Japanese rescue teams, in a frantic attempt to find the remaining survivors."

Harriet felt herself fighting for breath, and Mike held her close, as he tried to work out the chronology. She was looking at Friday's paper, which meant Thursday's news – possibly, at that distance it could even be Wednesday's news. He started working systematically through all the papers for more information, but there was less about the catastrophe in the subsequent issues.

The Sunday papers had a condensed version of the disaster, with more lurid photographs and interviews with survivors, but no more mention of Alex. One grim little piece caught his eye. "Two women and a dog were found alive last night – but rescue workers have begun to give up hope of finding any other survivors in the twisted ruins of this devastated coastal paradise."

"Caroline probably hasn't heard anything about it yet," Harriet muttered, too stunned even to cry. Mike was still scouring the papers. The headlines painted a terrible picture of inefficiency and chaos. The shock-proof buildings, the pride of Japanese technology, had been unable to withstand the magnitude of the tremor, and specialised teams with tracker dogs and heat-sensing equipment had taken more than twenty four hours to fly in.

They heard the telephone ring inside the house and he squeezed her shoulder reassuringly as he stood up to answer it. "That'll be the engineers testing the line."

She sat staring blankly as he walked away from her. The colour had gone from the garden suddenly and the scene was running past her like old Pathé News footage. He was gone for a very long time and when she saw his face as he walked back towards her she knew that it hadn't been the engineers on the phone.

CHAPTER 23

Vicky put the phone down and turned back to Caroline who was standing at the stove with the coffee pot.

"That was Mum. She was phoning from a box. That tree came down across the lines just after we left.... She sent her love."

"Did it damage the roof?"

"No. Apparently not." Vicky stopped throwing shorts and tee shirts into the laundry basket and smiled coaxingly at her sister. "Stay here for a few days. Don't go back to that house yet. Just give yourself a bit more of a break."

Caroline shook her head helplessly. "I think that I must go back today. Jane will be there for the rest of this week, so I won't be on my own – yet." She laughed at Vicky's stubborn expression. "But I'll stay for lunch if you don't mind."

She helped with the heaps of laundry and then she telephoned Jane at her office. Vicky was absolutely right, of course, about the house. She didn't want to be there on her own, but if she stayed for lunch and then pottered around in Bromley for a while, Jane might be home before her.

It was two o'clock by the time Caroline drove out of Stockleigh village and she took a deep breath as she settled her hands firmly on the steering wheel. The green was deserted and she suddenly felt an awful sense of panic at leaving the security and comfort of her sister's house. She forced herself to stare ahead and she didn't see the frantic figure run, waving, into the middle of the road behind her.

It was a typically overcast English day and occasional drops hit the windscreen – just frequently enough to cloud her visibility, but too infrequently for the wipers to function without squeaking annoyingly. Her mind kept drifting hopelessly back to that shady house surrounded by the fields of sunflowers. She felt herself crushed again by loving arms and she swallowed hard to shake herself back into the present.

Jane had said she'd be home by half past five, so if she stopped and did some shopping – she looked at the car clock and calculated swiftly – she should be home well after Jane. She headed for Bromley, taking a short cut through streets of inter-war villas, their gardens uniform in their suburban neatness and she thought of massed hibiscus and wild, tumbling honeysuckles.

She shivered as she parked the car and for several minutes she wasn't sure whether she could get out and face the crowds, but finally she forced herself to join the afternoon shoppers swarming around the food counters at Marks and Spencer's. She wanted something special for dinner tonight and Jane had said she'd be home early.

She was dreading seeing Jane in some ways, because she'd be expecting to hear all about Alex and it was all too painful still. She saw a man at the check-out and from the back he reminded her of him. It was just the angle of the head and the corner of his mouth, as he smiled at the woman who was with him. She gulped and rushed over to the fish display. She leaned hard on the edge of the cold glass and breathed hard. She still had to pay for her shopping and then face the drive home. This was not the place to break down.

She gazed blindly at the packet of Finnish gravalax in her hand. There was a woman, with a small child in a baby buggy, looking at the fish counter as well. She had a list in her hand and Caroline noticed that she was pregnant – about six months pregnant, perhaps – and she wondered what it must be like to be going home to a loving husband, putting a child to bed and then making supper together. Perhaps he'd be protective and insist she put her feet up and rest. The woman smiled at Caroline and she realised she must have been staring. She smiled back, embarrassed, and rushed to the till with her basket of shopping.

Her mouth was dry as she drove up The Avenue and she was tempted for an irrational moment to turn round and just drive away – goodness knows where – back to the ferry perhaps. Then she noticed that the garage doors weren't completely closed and she could see the bumper of Jane's red Fiat. She parked on the drive and opened the front door. Jane was on the telephone when Caroline walked in and, wordlessly, she passed the instrument over and disappeared into the kitchen.

* * *

Harriet got up from her chair once more and paced around the pool. She was at the furthest point from the house when she heard the phone ringing and she raced up the steps and across the garden. Mike followed her inside and leaned on the door frame, trying to piece the information together from the single-sided conversation. When Harriet finally put the phone down she leaned back and closed her eyes, unable to speak for a moment.

"Well?" he prompted at last.

She opened her eyes and gave a great sigh of relief. "That was Jane. He's going to be fine and he was pulled out two days ago. Caroline has raced off to Heathrow to try and get a stand-by flight." She was laughing and crying at the same time. "She's willing to go by any route available, obviously. The embassy people were completely out-of-date when they phoned this morning. Alex has a broken arm and he's generally battered and very weak, but he's going to be fine. Mavis is more seriously injured – both her legs are broken and she has internal injuries, but she's off the danger list. Alex tried to catch Caroline at Vicky's but, apparently, he missed her by minutes. They're all planning on flying back towards the end of next week if Mavis can be moved. I can't believe it." Her eyes were shining with tears as she looked up at him.

"So all your babies are sorted out now," he smiled. "Come and sit down before you collapse. Shall I fetch you an Armagnac?"

"I feel so knotted up after today that I don't think I could face drinking or eating at the moment. How about you? I feel so thrilled for Caroline and Alex that I think I need to work off steam. What about a swim?"

He shook his head. "Let's walk down to the lake and try to unwind."

Harriet took Mike's hand as they walked across the coarse stubble that covered their field. She felt so relieved and overjoyed for Caroline that she could have done hand-stands across the valley. She squeezed his hand, but it remained slack in hers. "Damn," he muttered, "I've got a bit of straw in my shoe," and he stooped to investigate the irritant. He straightened up and walked on, several paces ahead of her and she followed him, feeling a renewal of the strangeness between them, which had been partly eclipsed by the recent dramas.

A pair of buzzards swooped quite close above them and a stoat, red as a fox, wriggled through the dried vegetation just to their right. The blue haze of the sloes was visible on the perimeter hedge and she'd be making this autumn's sloe gin soon. Beyond the hawthorn bushes was a distant, glimpse of water, where the growth was sparse. The path to the lake crossed a stream at this point and Harriet hurried to catch up with Mike, but he seemed unaware of her presence and he didn't wait for her. She called to him and he stopped momentarily to help her through the undergrowth which flanked the stream, but when she tried to hang on to his hand he said that it was too difficult to walk along the narrow path like that and he walked ahead again.

The lake looked grey in the early evening light and they stood still at the edge of the cool water for a long time, watching two muskrats swimming quite close to them. One of the animals climbed onto the bank and started washing itself, just like a cat, and Harriet put her hand on Mike's shoulder. He put his arm around her suddenly and she glanced up at his face, but his eyes had a distant, unfocused look in them, which made her shiver and move away from him.

They walked on quietly, trying not to startle the muskrats, until they came to a raised bank at the end of the lake. They often sat here in the evening, watching the sun set behind a pair of distant barns. Someone had bought the barns now and they were being converted into a holiday home, but their silhouette from the end of the lake remained unchanged. A pigeon tower dominated the group of buildings and the blood-red setting sun made bold horizontal streaks between the sharp lines of the buildings.

Harriet sat with her legs bunched up in front of her, resting her chin on her knees and gazing over the smooth surface. The ripples of the muskrats were no longer visible.

She heard Mike's voice as if through a long tunnel and she felt as if she'd been listening for an eternity without grasping the meaning of what he was saying. It was far away, yet clear at the same time, and she sat, twisting her wedding ring round and round between her fingers in stunned silence, as his words impinged on her brain. She wanted him to stop talking but she didn't have the means to stop the flow. She could hear him saying, "I'm sorry, darling," over and over again but she couldn't find the words to reply. Her ring had been heavily faceted when they'd first been married and, as she turned it now, she noticed that it had worn perfectly smooth over the years. Perhaps she should take it off and give it back to him, or just throw it into the leaden water. Her fingers worked away at the gold band as if driven by some inner compulsion.

She hadn't even liked Honor Kershaw very much. The children hadn't liked her. Mike had always claimed that he couldn't stand her, so that had been a lie, just a deceitful pretence. The deception was as hard to bear as the infidelity. How could he turn his back on all those years of happiness, and hurt so many people, for the sake of someone whom he'd only known for such a short time? She heard herself snapping suddenly, "Don't call me 'darling'," and then felt frustrated with herself for having picked on such a trivial issue.

Mike said very quietly, "I don't call *her* 'darling' and I still love you and the children. It's just that I'm in love with her and that's a different emotion. I didn't want it to happen."

She gradually became aware of his weeping next to her and she turned instinctively to comfort him. They sat for a long time, until the tower on the hill opposite was just a dark shape and the red glow had sunk below the horizon. Harriet rocked him in her arms, feeling his tears soaking through her blouse, but her own grief was too great to release and she sat staring over his head into the darkness. Then she pressed her eyes closed and the black void was filled with the dancing paper hearts of thirty six St Valentine's Days.